MANCHESTER MOLL

Emma Hornby

CORGI BOOKS

TRANSWORLD PUBLISHERS
61–63 Uxbridge Road, London W5 5SA
www.penguin.co.uk

Transworld is part of the Penguin Random House group of companies
whose addresses can be found at global.penguinrandomhouse.com

Penguin
Random House
UK

First published in Great Britain in 2017 by Bantam Press
an imprint of Transworld Publishers
Corgi edition published 2017

A CIP catalogue record for this book
is available from the British Library.

ISBN 9780552173247

Typeset in 11/13.25pt ITC New Baskerville by Jouve (UK), Milton Keynes.
Printed and bound by Clays Ltd, St Ives plc.

Penguin Random House is committed to a sustainable
future for our business, our readers and our planet. This book
is made from Forest Stewardship Council® certified paper.

MANCHESTER MOLL

000002149386

Emma Hornby is the author of *A Shilling for a Wife*. Before pursuing a writing career, she had a variety of jobs, from care assistant for the elderly, to working in a Blackpool rock factory.

She was inspired to write because of her lifelong love of sagas and after researching her family history; like the characters in her books, many generations of her family eked out life amidst the squalor and poverty of Lancashire's slums.

Emma lives on a tight-knit working-class estate in Bolton with her family. You can follow her on Twitter @Emma-HornbyBooks, find her on Facebook at www.facebook.com/emmahornbyauthor or visit her website www.emmahornby.com

Also by Emma Hornby

A SHILLING FOR A WIFE

For my own family who once lived cheek by jowl with the fearsome Manchester scuttlers. Thank you for your strength and for the inspiration – this book is for you. And my ABC, always x

Many a good tussle have I had with other classes of criminals, but I would rather face the worst of these than a scuttler . . .

Jerome Caminada, Manchester detective

Chapter 1

DRAGGING HER SCRAP of the itchy blanket from
beneath her sister Sissy's skinny frame, Moll Chambers
frowned curiously. She had that feeling again, low in
her tummy. Why, she wasn't sure; she could never put
her finger on it.

She wasn't afraid, no, no. Of her mam? Well, sometimes. A little. But she never showed it, and Mam knew
if she lifted her fist to her, Moll wouldn't stand for it like
the others.

No, it wasn't exactly fear. The only sensation she
could liken it to was when, as a child, she, Sissy and their
brother, Bo, got drunk on their mother's gin and stole
Mr Crocket's horse from his yard. They had ridden it,
much to the amusement of following urchins, through
the cobbled streets, singing and shouting greetings to
passers-by. Turning into Jersey Street's broad thoroughfare, the horse shied suddenly when a dog ran across its
path, and Moll, sat nearest its rump, had fallen backwards. Those moments, suspended mid-air, seemed to
last minutes rather than seconds and she'd never forgotten that tumbling feeling in the pit of her stomach
before she hit the hard flagstones.

That's what she felt now – always felt when the first,

bawdy notes drifted down the street. Like her insides had dropped to meet her toes.

A noise like iron striking iron punctured the stuffy room – her father's cough. With a quiet growl of irritation, Moll kicked back the blanket and, standing in her cotton shift, shook the creases from her navy-blue skirts, dressed quickly and stomped to the window. She could just make out a dark figure weaving its way down Blossom Street and was in no doubt who it was when, again, their singing rang out to pierce every corner of her world.

She shook her head. Davy Preston's handiwork, no doubt. Bastard. Surely he must know how Father was?

'Is that your mam come home, our Moll?'

'Aye. I'd best collect her afore she wakens the soddin' street.'

'Good lass,' her father murmured as she slipped past, and her anger mounted.

Snatching a shawl from a nail in the wall, she threw it over her shoulders and hurried for the front door. Sickly light from street lamps spewed across the tumbledown road, illuminating the filth, and in her barefoot state she chose her step carefully. The balmy night still carried the stink that the night soil men had left in their wake but the noise, louder now she was but feet away, poisoned the air more.

'*And young Willy West did whisper to me, "Meet me at noon 'neath the old apple tree."*'

'Mam,' Moll hissed, quickening her step. 'Christ sake—'

'*And meet him, did I, just like I'd been told. But five minutes in, he grew ever so bold.*'

'Quiet, Mam.' Taking her arm, Moll made to steer her to their door but her mother, hat askew over one eye, hooted with laughter, grabbed Moll's wrists and dragged her in a stumbling dance across the pavement.

'*"Willy, you bugger, release me!" I brayed, yet secretly liking where his hand had strayed . . .*'

'Right, that's it. Get in the bloody house, Mam, or so help me—'

''Ere, shut tha rotten trap and let honest folk catch some kip! Knocker bleedin' upper will be doing his rounds shortly.'

Moll whipped around and squinted at the bedroom window of number ten, where a woman in her middle years was leaning out. 'All right, Mrs Coombes. I'm getting her in.'

'Hurry up about it. Disgraceful doxy; she wants carting to the asylum, she does!'

Despite her embarrassment, love and loyalty lifted Moll's chin. 'Say that again to my face, if you dare,' she growled up. 'So help me, I'll tear the hair from your scalp.'

'Why, you bold young bitch!'

Having reached their door, Moll shoved her mother through and turned back to glare at the woman opposite. She was about to yell that Mrs Coombes had room to talk about doxies, and her with a daughter whose back barely saw the light of day, when two youths turning the corner caught her attention. One stood head and shoulders above the other, though the latter was by no means short. 'That you, Bo?' she called.

'Who wants to know?'

She heard her brother laugh at his companion's quip.

'I want to know, Uriah Croft, and less of your tongue.'

Tut-tutting her annoyance, Mrs Coombes withdrew from her window, shutting it with a resounding slam, and Moll sighed inwardly. Bloody neighbours. Bloody Mam. Bloody *life*.

'I asked at the gin palaces. She weren't there.'

Moll shot Bo a lopsided smile. 'Nay, I know.' She jerked her head to where their mother lay sprawled on the stairs, snoring. 'Came home not a minute since, singing her head off.'

He leaned over her shoulder to glance inside. 'Bloody Preston.'

'Aye, more likely than not.' She stepped aside to let the lads in. 'Help me get her into bed, Bo.'

'It's all right, Moll, I've got her.' As though lifting an infant, he picked up their mother in his thick arms and carried her through.

'All right, Moll?'

She peered at her brother's friend across the gloomy passage. He had his hands in his trouser pockets, flat cap pulled low, obscuring his face. The difference in him when Bo wasn't around never failed to surprise her. When had this change towards her started? She couldn't recall. A month ago; maybe two? She hadn't mentioned it and neither had he. But it was there. Her heartbeat quickened.

'You look tired.'

She couldn't contain a bitter laugh. 'I'm tired, all right. *Sick* and tired, of it all.'

He reached her in one stride and rested an arm on the wall above her head. He wore no jacket, shirtsleeves rolled to the elbow against the summer night, and heat from his bare arm flushed her cheeks further. He smelt faintly of rough soap and tobacco and when she lifted her head to look at him, she caught a hint of ale on his breath. Combined with his own lad's scent, it was enough to set her pulse racing.

4

'Davy Preston . . . We're working on it, me and Bo,' he told her.

'Aye, I know. Ta for going with the lad the night to search for Mam. I fret about him out on his own, what with them sods breathing down his neck every chance they get. Why won't they leave him be?' she asked, voice hardening. 'They'll not half think so if I ever catch them at it.'

'Don't, Moll. Just don't.'

'He's my brother. I'll not see—'

'And I'll not see you hurt. Bo's big enough to see to hisself. They'll grow bored soon enough.'

She arched an eyebrow. 'Aye? Well, they're taking their time about it. It's every bloody day, Uriah. On his way to work, on his way home – any chance they get, they're on at him. Almost every lad from these streets hereabouts are in the Bengal Tigers. Not Bo. They'll not drag him into it while I'm around.'

'It's his size the gang want him for. He's bigger than any lad the Prussia Street lot can boast.' He drew a hand across the fine stubble on his chin. 'Let's just see, eh? They grew bored with pestering me, eventually, didn't they?'

Moll heaved a sigh. Uriah and lads like him, who refused to join the gangs terrorising their streets, stuck to the shadows when venturing out for fear of confrontation. At best, they would be subjected to an interrogation, with members wanting to know who they were, with the usual cry: 'Who's this lad?', where they were from, what they were doing on their stomping ground and above all to what gang, if any, they belonged. At worst, they'd be coerced into joining their ranks, often by force. Otherwise they would be set upon and beaten terribly before being chased off their patch.

'I'll be with him when I can,' Uriah continued. 'These scuttlers are beyond vicious when the mood strikes, and the Bengal Tigers are the most feared in Manchester. I've heard even Salford's scuttlers are wary of venturing across here. Don't involve yourself, Moll.'

Bo's tread sounded and they jumped apart.

'Mam's snoring loud enough to stir the dead. Father won't settle with that racket.'

Moll rolled her eyes. 'I'd best go in, case he needs me. You'll be all right getting home, won't you?' she added to Uriah – realising too late her error when he grinned and raised his eyebrows at Bo. 'What I mean is—'

'Careful, Moll. You sounded near human for a minute, there!'

Just as Uriah had quickly reverted to his usual manner with her in front of Bo, Moll followed suit, as though by some unspoken agreement.

She tossed her head. 'I couldn't give two hoots either way. I were only asking, what with your injured leg, an' all . . .'

He exchanged a bemused look with Bo. 'My leg's not— Jesus, Moll!' he yelped when she landed a swift kick to his shin. Grinning again, he bent to rub it. 'Very ladylike, I'm sure.'

'Serves you right,' she shot back over Bo's chuckles. 'Go on, get gone, we want our beds.' To her brother, she added, 'You, in.'

'I'll meet you at the corner in t' morning, Bo.'

'All right, lad.'

Uriah turned at the door and Moll caught the briefest of winks, meant just for her. The corners of her mouth twitched in response.

'Night, sourpuss.'

'Sod off, Uriah,' she trilled back before slamming the door.

A determined sun, casting diamond-shaped shafts of light through the numerous holes in the curtain, coupled with the smell of burnt toast, pulled Moll from sleep the following morning. Soft humming wrapped around her like a cloak and she smiled wryly. How Mam managed it after a gin-soaked night, she didn't know.

An empty mug on the floor by her parents' bed told her that her father had had breakfast – if you could call it that, Moll thought bleakly; he barely ate enough to keep a sparrow nourished nowadays – and he was sleeping peacefully. Otherwise, the room was empty.

'Toast, lass?' Wiping her hands on her apron, Ruth Chambers glanced across the sparse kitchen with a sorry smile when Moll entered, then lowered her gaze. 'Sit and have yourself a bite afore our laddo there has it away.'

Bo laughed, and Moll cast him an accusing look. 'You've soon forgot about last night.'

'She's trying,' he mouthed back. 'Leave it, eh?'

Moll waited until their mother crossed to the fire for the kettle before saying out of the side of her mouth, 'And what's she trying, like? To ruin us? If Father discovers that sod's sniffing about—'

'He'll not. Besides, I asked her. She weren't with Preston. Not seen him in days, she said. Happen he's gone for good?' Bo suggested hopefully, then sighed when Moll shook her head. 'Aye, well. I'd best be away.' He tossed the last piece of charred bread into his mouth, crossed the room and kissed their mother's cheek.

'You off, lad?'

'Aye.' He put on his cap and as he shrugged on his rough jacket, added quietly, 'See you later, Mam.'

7

It was more a question than a general farewell, and sadness fluttered in Moll's chest. Their Bo, big as any man, looking down on their mother with the expression of an infant fearful of being abandoned – not a sixteen-year-old ready to enter the world, marry, have children and live independently in a few short years. He was as needy of her as a child. He wanted what he'd never really had.

And would they see her later? Would she be here upon their return from work, like other mams, busy at the fire with the evening meal, her only concern feeding her children after a day's toil, and her husband lying ill in his bed? Moll very much doubted it. They would see her, all right, but not until the gin shops were shut and the inns and taverns kicking out.

'Bo kiss Sissy! Moll, Bo kiss Sissy!'

Moll nodded to the pouting child beside her and smiled at her loud giggles when Bo kissed Sissy soundly on the brow.

'Bye, Moll.'

'Aye, lad. And Bo?'

He turned at the door with a knowing nod, but she said it anyway:

'If you and Uriah see other foundry lads on t' way, catch up with 'em, eh? Them scuttler swines are less likely to—'

'Keep your voice down,' he whispered, frowning, motioning to their mother.

'They're less likely to accost you if you're with company,' she continued, albeit quieter. 'Anyroad, Mam should know about this.'

'Nay. She'll only fret. They'll grow bored soon enough.'

'That's what Uriah said. Me? I'm not so sure.'

Weariness dulled his brown eyes.

'Just stay away from them. They're no good, Bo.'

He nodded once and was gone.

Moll pushed her worries to the back of her mind and lifted the teapot. After filling her mother's mug then her own, she plucked down the tattered towel used for everything from drying pots to their own bodies and passed it to Sissy. 'We've to be off ourselfs in a minute. Wipe your hands and face, there's a good lass.'

Sipping her tea, she watched her mother flit around the room, clearly looking for jobs to do as an excuse not to sit and face Moll's questions about last night. After wiping a surface that was already clean, Ruth began rearranging the cheap ornaments on the mantel, and Moll rolled her eyes. 'Sup your tea, Mam, afore we leave.'

Her mother blew at dust Moll knew wasn't there from the tin clock then, with obvious reluctance, slipped into a chair.

Mam was a beauty, plain and simple. How, the way she was, was anyone's guess, but there was no denying it – though Mam herself did, always had. Her neat figure belied the fact that she'd borne seven children and her smooth brow showed none of the hardship she suffered from burying all but three, and from life in general. Now, her hair was parted down the middle and bound in a tight bun but when loose, it swayed about her shoulders like liquid. Every night, as a child, Moll would brush it until it crackled, swish-swishing the wood handle in soft flicks, and the candlelight picked out shades of copper and orange-gold and melted butter, which she likened to the autumn leaves shed each year in neighbouring Salford's Peel Park, which pranced dizzyingly on the wind.

Moll reached up to finger her own hair. It was all

right, she supposed: shiny black with a slight wave to it, but nothing like Mam's. Nature had blessed Sissy with their mother's delicate appearance, whereas Moll and Bo had their father's striking dark looks and strong features. She was taller than her mother, fuller of breast and hip, larger, louder, in every way. It made her feel like a clomping great dray horse in the company of a graceful deer.

Then there was the other mam with the gin bottle in her hand. The one who sang lewd songs, cackled like a crone at their concerns, held them in crushing embraces and swore how much she loved them until it felt you were drowning on spirit-fumed fog. Who yelled and struck out with small bunched fists for reasons only she knew. Who stroked their cheeks, glassy eyes deep with real tenderness. The one who shamed them in front of their neighbours, or wailed like a beast in pain with self-loathing. The ugly mam. The mam they loved every bit as the sober one. Bloody Preston . . .

'Sorry, lass.'

Moll stared at Ruth for a long moment then reached across the table and covered her hand with hers. 'Aye, I know.'

'I weren't with Davy, honest.'

She didn't believe a word but nodded. 'Bo said.'

Silence hung between them.

'I'll . . . stop. I will, our Moll.'

'Aye.'

'I promise.'

'Aye, Mam.'

Ruth curled her slender fingers through hers. 'You're a good lass.'

'Sissy good? Sissy good, Moll?' her sister demanded, patting her shoulder.

'Course you are. You cleaned your hands and face well, an' all.'

She beamed. 'Did I?'

'You did. Go and fetch your shawl, now, eh? Owd Evans will have kittens if we're late.'

'Will he?'

'Aye. Go on.'

Their mother watched her youngest child as she went. 'You're like a mam to that poor lass,' she murmured, her tone tinged with guilt, 'and it's not on. I should . . .' She sighed. 'I will, I'll stop, Moll.' She glanced at the clock and rose. 'I'd best give Jilly a knock. She should've been here by now.'

The two-up, two-down terrace, which they shared with two other families, was identical to every other flanking the street in both layout and condition: rotten with age and damp and choking with people.

Cockroaches and rats paraded through every home as though part of the family, and Moll didn't know of one household that didn't house a hedgehog to keep the bug numbers down. Sissy had named theirs Bertie and it was a nightly trial coaxing her to leave the prickly beast in its box beneath the kitchen table each night rather than take it through to bed.

Most kept a cat for the same purpose, though their blue-grey tom had met his end the previous week under the wheels of a passing coal cart and, as though sensing it, the rats were growing bolder.

They always kept food from vermin's reach in a cupboard on the wall by the window, but only yesterday Moll had entered their kitchen to find a huge black rat, as big as their feline had been, hanging mid-air by its long teeth from the cupboard handle, after the heel of stale loaf inside, bold as you like. The sight turned her stomach.

11

Mrs Coombes across the road had promised them a pick of the litter her cat was carrying but, after last night's performance, Moll doubted the offer still stood.

The Luchettis, Italian ice-cream sellers in their twenties, and their three lads, inhabited the upstairs rooms. Moll and her family occupied the downstairs two, and Jilly Sax and her husband were holed in the cellar, where they had dwelled longer than all of them. Lack of peace and privacy went hand-in-hand, but so too did help and companionship. There was always someone to call on for a chat or in times of need, and Moll wouldn't have wished it any other way.

The stick-thin woman who followed her mother into the kitchen, now, hobbled across the flagged floor leaving sighs and apologies in her wake.

'Eeh, so late . . . My Alf . . . Bloody knees playing him up again. Aye, lass, aye,' she added, flapping her hand to the door when she caught Moll glancing at the clock, 'youse go. I'll tend to your father, see he has a bite of summat, God willing. I've half a jar of beef tea warming by my fire that Alf couldn't finish. I'll fetch it in a minute. Go on, afore you're late.'

'Ta, Jilly.'

'No thanks needed amongst friends, my lass. 'Ere, Sissy love,' she told the girl, who had dragged her shawl over her face and was feeling her way to the door, 'what you like, eh? Pull your ruddy shawl up, else you'll have a mishap. Eeh, I don't know, silly girl.'

'Jilly silly!'

'Nay, Sissy's silly.'

'Nay, Jilly! Jilly silly! Silly smelly Jilly!'

This was a running joke each day, and Moll and her mother exchanged smiles for this big-hearted woman they were fortunate to call a friend. Many folk were either afraid of this twelve-year-old with the mind of a toddler, or openly scathing. Not Jilly. The moment she'd helped deliver her in this very room, she developed a bond that was almost as strong as the Chambers' own with the girl who now stood head and shoulders above her. Woe betide anyone with a mind to wag a vicious tongue towards Sissy in Jilly's earshot.

With Sissy skipping between, Moll and her mother left the house and turned right, for Sid Evans' butcher's on Union Street, where Ruth had scrubbed floors some twenty years; Moll had followed suit as soon as she could hold a brush.

The barbed-tempered widower, well aware he wouldn't find another pair of hands to clean his premises as well as they did on the pittance he paid, tolerated them fetching Sissy along with a tangible air of irritation. They strove to ensure he had as little reason to snap at the weak-minded girl as possible, but keeping her occupied whilst they worked was a constant battle. She grew restless easily and soon abandoned what little tasks they set her to keep her busy, and would wander off if they turned their backs for a second.

However, they had little choice in the circumstances. Sissy fretted when not in their presence even for short lengths of time and, if she was honest, Moll fretted over her, too. The girl could be difficult and no one could handle her as she could – a fact that, Moll knew, both saddened and filled her mother with guilt in equal measures. Ruth wasn't around enough, they all knew it, and so Sissy clung to the one person who was a constant in her life.

Besides occasional knots of women gossiping by front doors, the streets were mostly empty. The multitude of canal wharves, works, cotton mills and factories, some

13

as tall as six or seven storeys, which loomed over the town like giants surveying their busy ant workforce, had swallowed Ancoats' residents for the day and already the air was thick with sulphurous smoke spewing from tall chimneys invading the morning sky. Even in the height of summer, the sun's rays struggled to penetrate the pall, to which domestic hearths added, and every street, lane and court lay in relentless gloom.

Situated on Manchester's eastern fringe, the densely populated area of Ancoats was its industrial heart and one of its poorest. Crime, disease and death rates were amongst the highest in the country. Large portions of the city housed Irish who had come over during the famine; now, living cheek by jowl with their English counterparts, a new generation of Manchester-born Irish struggled every bit as much as their parents had to eke out a life in this hell on earth.

Given the colossal population, open spaces and recreation grounds were few and far between, depriving residents of much-needed respite on their one day off a week from the relentless toil that was their lives. It was little wonder most escaped their miserable reality at the bottom of a bottle.

With as many alehouses as homes packed into each street, retreating from cold dwellings and griping children with hungry bellies was too strong a pull, which, for most, ensured that their lot would always remain their lot. You did what you must to get by, to survive in whatever way you knew how and if you happened to wake of a morning, you thanked the Lord for another day and got through it the best you could. Such was life.

Moll had never questioned the way of things. This was how folk existed. God's hand alone determined your station in life. Questioning His will, the Church taught them, was a sin. His design wasn't theirs to wonder at, and she didn't bother. Things were as they were. Was it fair? Of course not. Could and would things ever change? She highly doubted it, so what was the point in over-thinking, over-dreaming?

Now, as they turned out of German Street and the butcher's came into sight, they involuntarily quickened their pace. Pressing Sissy closer, Moll kept a watchful gaze on a hungry-eyed pack of dogs rummaging in the stinking refuse that filled the streets. Desperation would see them break into savage fights if a scrap of food was found, and they viewed passers-by who ventured too close as competition.

Her sister whimpered and Moll shushed her softly.

'Bite Sissy, Moll!'

'Nay, lass. They'd not get near you with me around.'

'Will they not?'

'I'd kill the buggers with my bare hands first.'

Her eyes were like saucers. 'Would you?'

'Aye.'

'Sissy loves Moll. Moll? Love you, Moll.'

'And I you, lass.' She could feel their mother's eyes on them and knew, if she'd turned, she'd have seen the pain that would have shone in the hazel depths. Part of Moll was sorry but another wanted to ask Ruth what did she expect? Was Davy bloody Preston worth it? Lord, how she loathed him . . .

'Get through there and begin your work, you're late,' snapped the butcher before they were through the door.

'And you're a sod,' muttered Moll, leading the way to the tiny back room beyond the counter to fetch the pails and brushes. Her mother touched her arm, frowning, and she suppressed a sigh. Without a word, they hung up their shawls, rolled up their sleeves and got to work.

An hour and a half later, Moll had finished scrubbing, cleaning and dusting Mr Evans' living quarters and with Sissy trailing behind, singing quietly, she descended the stairs to empty her pail. After tipping its contents into the back lane, she leaned against the door frame, closed her eyes and pressed her fingers into the small of her back.

The morning had warmed and distant birdsong soothed her tired mind. If not for the stink from the privy, she could have almost imagined she was in the gardens of her dreams instead of here. She smiled, as she always did, at the thought.

Some Saturdays, after work, she took Sissy to the public library on King Street, the site of the old town hall near the city centre.

Her literary abilities left a lot to be desired. The 1870 Education Act, passed in the year of Moll's birth, saw numerous board schools erected in Manchester throughout the following years. She, and later Bo, attended sporadically and the smattering of the three Rs – Reading, Writing and Arithmetic – they were taught had left little impression. A second Act in 1880 made school attendance compulsory but by then Moll had reached the maximum age required to attend, thus rendering her education over before it had really begun.

Nevertheless, the peace, the feel and smell of the books was the main pull and many an enjoyable hour was had poring over exciting tales, from pirates on the high seas and cavalry in bloody war battles, to her favourite: the lives of the genteel ladies of country estates, who had nothing better to do to while away the hours than sit in breathtaking drawing rooms, crocheting or pressing flowers into pretty scrapbooks.

Their milky-skinned hands were forever hovering by

the bell pull to summon their maids, who would fetch them dainty sandwiches on sparkling silver trays and pour them delicious drinking chocolate into bone china cups decorated with sprigs of blue flowers, or pink, or green – always flowers, though, for flowers were beautiful, weren't they, and sweet-smelling, like the fine ladies themselves?

Moll smiled again, this time wryly. A chipped mug with stinging nettles painted on would likely befit herself!

She yawned, stretched, and with Sissy following, went in search of their mother. She found her on her knees in the Red Room, as her sister called it, a wide-benched area to the back of the shop used for preparing the meat. The metallic smell of death hit the back of her throat and she grimaced.

''Ere, Mam, hand me that brush. I'll finish up in here.'

'Nay, lass, I'm nearly done,' Ruth replied through puffs, giving the torn oilcloth an extra robust scrub and smiling when the stubborn black bloodstain faded. 'There. Now, just let me wash myself at the pump and—'

'Get your filthy hands away from there, you young simpleton!'

At the butcher's bellow, Moll glanced down and around, then exchanged a horrified look with her mother. *Sissy* . . . As one, they rushed towards the shop.

Fear and dread that allowing her to wander might cost them their jobs gave way to fury at the sight that met Moll. Mr Evans stood in the middle of the shop floor with his arm raised whilst at his feet, bleating like an injured lamb, lay Sissy, one side of her face livid red.

'Come in here thinking you can touch my produce, do you, you hard-faced article? God alone knows where you've had them hands of yourn with the way you are – picking around in your own shit, no doubt—' The last word wobbled in his throat when Moll, having rushed forward, grabbed his thick wrist.

'Don't you even dare! Lass or no, I'll fight you right here and now if you lay another finger on her.' Fists bunched, eyes blazing, she stood her ground as he took a step towards her. 'I'm warning you, Evans. I'll do for you and gladly dance the hangman's tune if I must. You leave her be.'

Shock slackened his mouth. Then he struck out suddenly, catching Moll off guard.

The slap, its sound rebounding off the whitewashed walls like the crack of a whip and mingling with her mother's cry, sent Moll sprawling across the sawdust floor. She rose to her knees, gasping, and glared up at him but before she could speak, Ruth silenced her with a flap of her hand.

'She's short of a darn good thrashing, that's her trouble – and that along with her,' the butcher added, jerking a thumb at a snivelling, terrified Sissy. 'I've warned you till I'm blue in the face to keep that thing you call a daughter from under my feet. And what do I find today? Stroking the ruddy pig carcasses in t' window, she were, asking 'em what their names were! Many a long year I've kept you in employment and that raggedy arse of yourn from the workhouse doors. Aye, what thanks do I get? Bloody none, that's what.'

Ruth's face had paled to the colour of tripe. 'I . . . Thank you, sir.'

He blew out air slowly and tugged on his drooping moustache in contemplation. 'I'll have no more carryings on like today, d'you hear, missis?' he asked finally, and Ruth visibly sagged in relief. 'One more instance like this 'un, and youse are out on your ear.'

Her reply was barely audible. 'Aye, sir. Terrible sorry, sir.'

'But Mam—!'

'That's enough, Moll.'

'But . . . ! How can you bow and scrape to the brute after he's just struck your children? Listen 'ere, Mam, I'll not—'

'Nay, *you* listen, my lass, and listen good. I've had just about enough of your tongue. Apologise to Mr Evans.'

'Never!'

Her mother crossed the floor and hauled her to her feet. She stared at Moll with empty eyes and a weary but desperate quaver sounded behind the word: 'Apologise.'

Pain of betrayal scorched through Moll like liquid fire and tears stung at the butcher's smug sniff. 'Mam . . .'

'Now, Moll.'

Clinging to what little pride she could muster up, Moll brushed the wood shavings from her skirts. Then she lifted her chin and, going against every screaming fibre of her being, said, 'I'm sorry.'

'Sorry what, girl?'

A soft sigh left her mother but Moll didn't look at her. 'Sorry . . . sir.'

He nodded, satisfied. 'Collect your shawls from out back and be gone, the pair of you; and get that dim-witted animal out of my sight.'

Swallowing humiliation and injustice, and a burning rage that shook her very bones, Moll took Sissy's hand, turned on her heel and strode from the shop.

'Lass, wait.'

Gulping at the lump threatening to choke her, Moll quickened her pace.

'I had no choice.'

'You had every choice, Mam!' she cried over her shoulder. 'How could you allow him to treat us like that, your own flesh and blood? Lord, I allus knew you were weak-spined, but this—' As soon as the words were out, she wished she could bite them back. She halted with a sigh.

'Aye, you're right. I'm weak, allus were. We can't all be like you, Moll.'

'Mam, I didn't—'

'That temper of yourn is going to get you into trouble one of these days.'

'It's that which gets me through life, that stops sods like him back there taking advantage.' All anger had left her and it was in a voice thick with tears that she added, 'He called the lass an *animal*, Mam.'

Her mother reached for her hand and squeezed it. Then she stooped and pressed a lingering kiss to Sissy's head.

They continued on to Blossom Street in silence.

Chapter 2

JILLY GESTURED TO the jar of rich, red-brown liquid on the table and raised her shoulders helplessly. 'I tried but he'd not touch a drop, poor love.'

'I'll see to him,' said Ruth as Moll made for the room next door. 'You get your barrow ready, lass.'

Her tired body cried out at the thought of hawking the streets with the heavy load of potatoes warming in the fire's embers. Then at the prospect of a chat with Polly and the opportunity to vent her anger at the morning's occurrence, she brightened a little. She could always count on her friend to cheer her up, whatever life threw her way. What she'd do without her, lately more than ever, Moll didn't know.

After thanking their neighbour and seeing her out, Moll crossed to the makeshift handcart that sagged in the corner like a sleeping drunk in a doorway, which Bo had knocked together from scavenged wood and rust-riddled perambulator wheels. It was hell itself to manoeuvre but she tolerated it; he'd been proud as punch with his efforts and she hadn't the heart to replace it. Not that they could afford to. It did its job well enough, depending on its mood.

'Drank it all, Moll. Drank it.' Sissy tipped her empty mug upside down to prove her point, sending drops of weak tea to form small puddles on the scrubbed table.

'Good lass. Go and try at the privy while I get the tatties out the fire.' Moll was placing the last hot jacket potatoes on to the scattering of embers in the large tin bowls on the barrow when her mother entered. She turned and lifted her eyebrows expectantly. 'How's Father?'

'Sleeping. Listen, Moll, can you take Sissy with you? I've some errands to see to.'

'Errands?' Silence greeted her. Her mother was staring at the rag rug, plucking at her bottom lip, and Moll's stomach dropped. 'Mam . . .'

'You'd like that, eh, Sissy? Go with our Moll? I'll nip downstairs, ask Jilly to sit back in with your father an hour more. See you later,' Ruth finished before Moll could protest, and slipped from the room.

But for Sissy, she'd have followed and tackled her; the poor lass had had enough upset for one day. The front door signalled her mother's departure and Moll took a deep breath, almost not daring to check.

When she glanced to the mantel, her worst fears were confirmed: the jam jar behind the clock, where they kept their money, was empty.

Jersey Street's mills and factories were spewing out their workforce as they turned the corner. Cursing the wonky barrow to all hell's horrors, Moll hurried across the cobbles, Sissy meandering behind with one foot in the gutter.

Across the road, a voice called her name over the thunder of clogged footsteps and hum of chatter and, catching a flash of Polly Wainwright's wide grin and flame-coloured hair, which stood out starkly against her red shawl, she raised a hand in greeting.

Murray Street Mill, Rodney Street Mill and the smaller Jersey Street Mills' hungry workers descended on Moll like an army of beetles and within ten minutes, the barrow was all but empty. However, each day was different. Some, she'd sell up in the blink of an eye; others, she'd barely sell a one. Everything depended on what the poor had to spare and there was nothing Moll, Polly and others of a similar trade could do but cross their fingers that they would have a successful afternoon. Smiling at the happy sound of coins jingling in the pouch tied to her waist beneath her long skirts, she motioned to Sissy to follow and pushed the barrow across the street.

'How you getting on?'

Polly nodded to the tray suspended on rope around her neck and the half-dozen pies remaining. 'Nearly finished up, lass. You?'

'Aye, same. It's a good thing, an' all,' she added without thinking.

Polly swept back a wave of curls from her face and sighed. 'Oh, Moll . . .'

'Aye.' There was nothing else to say; no further words were needed and none would change the way of things.

'But what'll you do about brass for the market? You'll need your supply of tatties for next week. Look, I can help you out with a few coppers if you'd only ask.'

'I know. Ta ever so, Polly. I'm hoping Scotch Tess will allow me my next batch on t' slate till I get straight. She's done it often enough in t' past, God knows. Ay, we'll manage somehow. We allus do.'

'That rotten mam of yourn should be ashamed,' Polly blurted, green eyes flashing, then shook her head. 'I'm sorry, it's not my place to pass judgement. It just pains me, lass, seeing you working every hour God sends for her to line the gin-sellers' pockets.' She paused to serve a customer then asked, 'That fella still sniffing around her?'

'Course he bloody is. I don't know what this Preston's game is; I just pray he soon slithers back beneath whatever stone he's crawled from in yon Bolton. I mean aye, Mam's allus had a weakness for the drink, as you know, but since he turned up, she's worse than ever. And what with Father . . . I'm at the end of my tether, I am really.'

'Eeh, lass. How is Robert?'

'Bad, Polly. I can't remember the last time he ate, says it makes him sick. He's just sleeping, or coughing, day and night. He'll not allow us to send for the doctor no more – not that we've the brass for it, mind. It's like . . . It's like he's given up.'

'Don't say that. He'll rally, you wait and see.'

But Moll caught the note of uncertainty in her friend's tone and though she too had already begun preparing herself for the worst, hearing it from another's tongue caused her chest to tighten in panic. Tears blinded her for a moment and she blinked furiously.

'Here's your Bo coming with the Croft lad.'

Despite her troubles, Moll couldn't help smiling at the wicked twinkle in Polly's eye. 'Give over, will you. There's nowt between me and Uriah and never shall be.'

'Huh! If you say so, lass.'

'I do,' she said mildly, then pulled a face at Uriah across the street when he stuck his tongue out at her.

'All right, sourpuss?'

'I were till I saw you.'

His face spread in a slow grin and, feeling Polly's amused gaze, Moll turned her attention to her brother before her blush surfaced.

'Tatty, lad?'

'Aye. Ta, Moll.'

She passed him one then held out another to his friend, who hesitated. 'D'you want it or not?'

'I, er . . .' His smile had vanished and a pink hue crept up his neck. He patted his pockets and shook his head, and her heart contracted at his embarrassment.

She thrust the potato into his hand and at Bo's surprised expression, hastened to say, 'Don't make a habit of it, Uriah Croft.'

'Ta, Moll.'

'I don't know what you're thanking me for. You're paying double the morrow.'

A smile hovered about his generous mouth and something behind his slate-grey eyes made her heart bang.

Bo shot him a wry 'Aye, that's the real Moll!' look, and she forced herself not to speak out. *Nay, it's not,* she wanted to tell her brother. *It's the game we've begun playing, for God alone knows what reason, around folk. I think he's sweet on me and, to be honest, I like him too, but it's as though we're infants pretending to dislike each other to mask the truth of it.*

Was Uriah ashamed to have folk know he'd taken a liking to her? she mused as she watched him eat. She wasn't the prettiest lass hereabouts, true, but surely what she saw in the cracked mirror propped on the window ledge back home wasn't wishful thinking?

One or two lads had been known to set their cap at her but what with Mam . . . and Sissy to look after, she'd not had the time nor inclination to encourage their attentions. Or perhaps her being older than Uriah was the problem? It was only by a year but still, some lads could be funny about things like that. Or was he unwilling to chain himself to a family such as hers? Did he look at Mam and see a vision of what his future wife might become?

Wife . . . ! Lord, me and my daft imaginings – all this could very well be just fanciful thinking, she reminded herself, yet knew full well it wasn't. She shook her head and turned her attention to Sissy.

'Come on, lass, let's get home to Father, eh? I've my baking to do afore preparing the evening meal.'

'I don't know how you manage, love,' murmured Polly and to Moll's embarrassment, fresh tears sprang to her eyes. *Because I must, Polly. Because if I don't, who will?*

'We'd best get back.' Bo inclined his head to Uriah, who nodded. Their place of work was some distance from Jersey Street but for Bo, the trek was necessary for the free midday meal. 'Tell Mam I'll not be late home, Moll,' he added brightly, and her guts lurched. *Oh, Bo . . . Damn it, Mam . . .*

She swallowed a sigh. 'Aye, lad.'

He gave her a dazzling smile then stooped to tickle Sissy. 'Be good for our Moll. I'll see you tonight.'

'Will you, Bo?'

'Aye, lass . . .' His words died and a deep frown slowly creased his brow. He settled on his haunches, lifted Sissy's chin with his forefinger and tilted her head. 'Moll?' He glanced up questioningly. 'She's bruised.'

All eyes were on her. Her own tender cheek and eye gave a twinge in response and she pulled her tattered shawl closer. 'She took a tumble, Bo. We'll speak later,' she continued when he looked to say more. Now wasn't the time. He'd only spend the day fretting. 'Go on, you'll be late.'

Bo's wasn't the only lingering look as they made their way back towards Mill Street and the Wire Works; Uriah's curious stare strayed over Moll, too. When they disappeared, she sent up a silent thank-you that Sissy hadn't mentioned, in her innocent way, the truth of the morning's events.

'What really happened? Come on,' Polly ordered, tucking her arm through the crook of hers, 'out with it.'

By now, the streets were all but empty and as they passed up Poland Street, Moll gave her friend an account of Mr Evans' behaviour. With gentle sighs and supportive arm squeezes, she did what Moll could rely upon her to: listened without interruption. And when she'd finished, Polly, as always, was ready with sage advice.

'Lass, you need to sit your mam down and have it out with her, proper, like. Keep your calm, no shouting, and have a reet good talk, unburden them poor shoulders of yourn. You can't carry on like this and, more to the point, neither can Ruth. You need each other, now more than ever. Do it, love. Tell her how you feel. Summat's got to give.'

Moll didn't see what slightest bit of difference it would make. Mam would likely get defensive or upset – either would lead to the same outcome: running from her troubles to find solace at the bottom of a bottle. But Moll knew she must try, and told Polly so. Her friend was right. Her tolerance was all but burned out; on top of everything else, she couldn't take much more of this.

'I'll do it, Polly, I promise. I just wish I knew at times how her mind works. Her disloyalty – taking that sod's side over ours, earlier – hurt more than the blow he delivered, it did really. I could understand her reasoning, that she were frickened we'd lose our places and the much-needed brass it fetches, were she not how she is. But she weren't, I'm certain, thinking of the good of the family. For what brass we scrape together, she

27

throws down her neck without a thought for rent, coal or grub.

'It's left to me and Bo to fret and find the shillings needed for when the rent man comes knocking, to scratch together enough for a meal of sorts of an evening. It pains me to say it . . . she's my mam and I love her . . . She's selfish, Polly, through and through. And our Bo will come rushing in, later, expecting her welcome and . . .' She heaved a long sigh. 'It cuts me to the bone that we're not enough.'

'Cut, Moll? Sissy see? Bleeding, Moll?'

She forced a smile as her sister studied her face then reached for one hand then the other, turning them this way and that in search of injury. 'Nay, lass, I'm fine.'

'Cut, Moll?'

She put a reassuring arm across Sissy's thin shoulders. 'Nay. I'm all right.'

'Are you, Moll?'

'Aye, Sissy.'

Her sister's fine eyebrows knotted in confusion. She turned her attention to her own hands. 'Bleeding, Sissy?'

Polly watched, expression soft with pity, and when Sissy's searching grew frantic and her voice rose in confusion, she plucked a pie from her tray and waved it under her nose. ''Ere, Sissy love. Go on, take it, good lass.'

Moll smiled, grateful for her friend's thoughtfulness in averting the girl's attention. The last thing she needed today was Sissy having one of her moments here in the street. Ignorance bred fear, resulting in lack of empathy and understanding. Some folk could be cruel beyond belief in the face of mental infirmity. 'At times, I wonder what I'd do without you, Polly Wainwright.'

A smile warmer than a summer sun lit the older

woman's freckled face. 'Soft ha'porth. Well, this is me.'
She motioned to a few doors down then took the last
penny pies from her tray. 'One for yourself and be sure
to give t' other to your father, with my love. Go on with
you and your ruddy pride,' she added on a laugh, rolling her eyes, when Moll hesitated. 'I'll see you the
morrow, love.'

'Ta, Polly.'

On a flash of bright teeth and carroty curls, she swept
away indoors.

The golden pastry winked in the sunlight and the
aroma of spiced meats made her mouth water. Sissy
grinned up at her before taking a bite of her own. The
rich juices ran down her chin and she scooped them up
with her finger and popped it into her mouth. Moll
glanced down, tempted by the feast sitting warm in her
hand but shook her head. She hadn't had anything
since waking bar a cup of tea and a few morsels of Mam's
burnt offering, but her own wants could wait until evening. She'd give her pie to Jilly, she decided, as thank-you
for sitting with Father. And she'd do her damnedest to
see he at least took a few nibbles from his own.

As they walked the short distance home, her thoughts
switched to Mam, and that odd churning sensation
gripped her stomach. Bo would be trawling the streets
again later – why he bothered, Moll didn't know. He
rarely managed to locate her at her usual haunts these
days; clearly, Davy was taking her further afield. And
what mood would she be in upon her return?

Moll shook her head with a range of emotions: anger,
sadness and frustration; but mostly helplessness. Father
didn't need the stress of this. Lord, *they* didn't need it.
She might have promised Polly she'd talk to her but
what was the point? Mam vowed almost daily to change

her ways and never did. It would be, as always, an utter waste of breath.

Lost in thought, she failed at first to notice Mr Luchetti from upstairs waiting by her door, until he stepped towards her through the passage. Seeing his expression, her smile died before it had chance to surface.

'Moll . . .'

'What's wrong? Mr Luchetti, what is it?'

The tall, kindly-faced man ran a hand through his lank hair. He cleared his throat twice then wetted his lips. 'Moll, I . . . do not . . . *Povera bambina* – you poor child.'

The strangest sensation overcame her. All sound melted and silence, like a living thing, seemed to clasp her in a firm embrace. A heat rose from her toes, up, up, towards her chest, neck, face, then as though an invisible force sucked it back, it left her at a dizzying speed and an icy blanket engulfed her, inside and out. She staggered and the Italian caught her arm.

'Jilly sent for me. I said I would watch for your return to . . . prepare you . . .'

'Ta . . . Mr Luchetti. I . . . the barrow, could you fetch it inside . . . please, and, and . . . Sissy . . .' Moll heard the calm words but not in a dozen lifetimes would she have believed they came from her. At any rate, her mouth wasn't moving, or at least she couldn't feel it moving, and all thought had deserted her. 'I must see to matters . . . A coffin, fresh candles, too, and . . .'

'Not now, not now,' he murmured in his melodic accent, taking her arm as she made to return to the street. 'Not now,' he said again, and tears glistened on his dark lashes. He reached for the barrow, which she'd abandoned by the front step, dragged it inside and

30

closed the door. Then he squeezed her fingers. 'Jilly's waiting inside.'

'Aye, of course, I . . . Jilly. Aye. Aye.'

'You must face it, Moll. *Dio vi benedica e vi dia forza.*'

'Aye.'

'I'm with you. Worry not, I've got you.' Supporting her by the shoulders, he guided her through into the kitchen.

Jilly rose slowly from the fireside chair. Her red and puffy face crumpled. She crossed the space and on a loud sob, said, 'Robert, your father, lass—'

'I know.'

'I'm sorry, so sorry. Eeh, poor lass . . .'

'Ta for . . . sitting with him. Go on down to Mr Sax, he'll be needing you . . . bad knees . . . and . . . Oh.' Moll glanced at the pies she'd forgotten she held. 'I've . . . For you, to say thanks.'

Jilly's lined face creased further. She turned confused eyes to Mr Luchetti, who mouthed something about shock and going to fetch a dram of brandy. Then he slipped out and Moll felt herself pressed into a chair.

Jilly knelt before her and stroked gnarled fingers down her cheek. 'Moll, lass. Oh, I'm so sorry . . .'

Words had stopped meaning things. They didn't sound right to her ears, like they were being spoken back to front. She nodded, smiled. She looked down at the pie in her lap. 'For Father, with Polly's love. Just . . . a few nibbles and . . . He'd have felt better, wouldn't he, Jilly? Not . . . eaten for . . .' She frowned, couldn't recall. 'Days? Days, Jilly? Beef tea – no, he'd not touch . . . Aye. Aye.' She felt her frown deepen. 'Did he . . . say . . . ? Was he able . . . ?'

'Lass . . . Oh, lass.'

Moll caught in Jilly's tone that he had. She smiled. 'That's good.'

'Oh, Moll. Poor Moll, come 'ere.'

She saw the arms wrap around her but felt nothing. A whooshing noise, like water hitting its mark from a heady height, filled her ears and from far away, sharp ringing grew louder. Tightness gripped her chest. She gasped. She gasped again, short spurts of air that almost choked her. When the scream tore from her, the arms around her tightened and she clung, drowning, drowning, in a pain she'd never before known and doubted she would again.

'Cut, Moll? Bleeding? Moll? Hurt, Moll?'

Sissy's confused wails slowly penetrated the fog. Moll reached behind her unseeing and pulled the girl into the embrace.

'He's free from pain, my lasses. Think on that. He'll need you to be strong – and you will, aye, you will. You'll bear it, Lord willing, somehow. That's it, you let them tears out. That's it,' Jilly murmured through her own, rocking them both. 'Let it all out.'

'What were his final words?'

Jilly pulled back to look at her. 'He . . . He . . . Oh, lass.'

Moll knew the answer without having to hear it. She closed her eyes. Then she wrapped her arms around herself and sobbed her broken heart out.

Chapter 3

LONG AFTER SHE'D settled Sissy on the thin mattress before the near-dead fire, Moll sat cross-legged, stroking the girl's hair.

Her parents had always slept in the kitchen for the space and privacy it afforded but since the lung disease – all too common around these parts – struck her father, Moll and Bo had moved him into the bedroom with them to secure him a modicum of peace from their mother's drunken antics.

Tonight, for the first time, he'd sleep there alone.

Earlier, when Moll went to collect their mattress to take to the kitchen, she'd knelt by the bed opposite for an age, not saying much, simply needing to be near her father.

In the flickering candlelight, clutching his cold, limp hands, she'd wept and told him how she loved him, how she would miss him, how thankful she would always be for having been blessed with a fair and affectionate father. His position as blacksmith at the local iron foundry, where he'd toiled daily in sweltering heat striking the anvil, was thirsty work, but she'd never known him to touch a drop of ale. Seeing the evil it did his own parents, then later his wife, it was little wonder.

She'd recounted incidents, memories from her

childhood, asking if he recalled this and that, had smiled at the cherished moments, laughed softly in remembrance. And kissing the sunken, purple-tinged cheek in goodbye, the plain and terrible reality of how life was to be from this day forth hit her anew. As had the equally stark, unjust truth: few around these parts made old bones.

Now, rain, sounding like a thousand crows pecking at the panes, lulled her frozen mind. Behind her, Bo sat at the table with his head in his hands. And like her mother's mocking conspirator, the clock's dull tick-ticking ran on, reminding them of another second, minute, hour of her absence, holding them vice-like in its clogging truth.

Moll had searched every gin and alehouse she could find. She'd walked Ancoats' miserable streets for hours, mouth set in a thin line, fists bunched at her sides, mind as cold and empty as her heart had become. Not a soul had seen hide nor hair of Ruth Chambers.

Bo had arrived home from work whistling a popular tune, and entered the kitchen smilingly, brown eyes bright with expectancy. They had settled on Moll, Sissy on her lap, moved to Jilly, then swept around the space. 'Where's Mam?'

'Eeh, lad . . .'

At Jilly's weary murmur, he'd dragged off his cap and glanced at them in turn. It was his sister he'd addressed: 'Moll?'

The effort it took to raise her leaden eyes from the table had sapped the last of her energy and her tone was barely a whisper. 'Come and sit down.'

'What is it? Where's Mam? What's—?'

'Sit down, Bo.'

His eyes never left hers as he slipped into a chair.

Holding his cap in both hands on the table in front of him, he'd waited for her to speak again.

'Father's gone.'

'Gone where?'

Moll had closed her eyes and shaken her head slowly and seconds later, her brother's soft moan clutched her heart. His large hand momentarily covered hers then he scraped back his chair and went next door. Gruff sobs reached them through the wall. Half a minute later, he was back. He fell into his chair with a thud.

'Where's Mam?' he asked again.

At the choked question, Moll had opened her eyes and the rage consuming her from the inside out must have glinted silver in their depths, for he jerked back. 'Out.'

'Well . . . have you been to look for her, our Moll?'

She'd exploded then. ''Course I've bloody looked!' She threw the words at him like knives. 'I tramped them cobbles for hours afore you returned. She's nowhere to be found.'

'Davy—'

'Oh, Bo, Preston's not at fault, here. She's a grown bloody woman with her own mind. It's her fault, her doing. She should have been here. She should be here now.'

He'd fallen silent, chin dipping to his chest. Noiselessly, Jilly moved around the room, boiling water for tea, collecting the half-loaf and cutting it into thin slices. When a tap had sounded at the door she was the only one who reacted. She'd answered, returning with an earthenware dish that had seen better days: it contained some mode of stew, which smelt of olive oil and macaroni, with cabbage leaves floating on top, from Mrs Luchetti upstairs.

'Reet thoughtful of the lass,' Jilly had stated, dishing

out the watery meal. 'Aye, you find out who your friends are at times like these; look after our own, we do.'

Of course, no one felt like eating besides Sissy. She hadn't the faintest idea what was afoot and Moll hadn't the strength to explain. Jilly had left soon afterwards, promising to return once she'd seen to Alf, but Moll had followed her to the door and in hushed tones, told her to call in the morning.

'But lass, there's . . . matters need seeing to,' she'd said, her ditch-water-coloured eyes flicking to the bedroom door. 'The church and . . . suchlike . . .'

'There'll be time aplenty the morrow for that,' Moll had answered quietly. 'Mam could come back any minute . . .' *And by God, wait when she does!* She'd left the words to hover in the air and at the set look of her mouth, Jilly nodded. She'd made to pat Moll's head affectionately, but Moll had thrown her arms around her neighbour's bony shoulders and hugged her tightly, wishing with all her heart and not for the first time that this woman was her mam instead. 'Thank you.'

'I'll call up at first light. Try and snatch some sleep the night, won't you, lass?'

After assuring Jilly she would, yet knowing it was a lie – how, in the name of *God* would she ever sleep, eat, *live* now her father had gone? – she returned to the kitchen.

She'd had to crush her fist to her mouth at what met her, to stop herself crying out. Bo had crossed to the fireside in her absence and now sat, long legs tucked under him, with Sissy in his lap. They were wrapped in each other's arms, dark head against light, perfectly still and silent, and in that moment, Moll had never felt so utterly alone.

Dropping to her knees before them, she'd encom-

36

passed both, these two she loved more than any other single thing in the world. Bo clutched Moll closer to them and like this they remained; for how long, she didn't know. When they drew apart, Sissy was asleep, the room dark and chilly.

Now, Moll rose stiffly. A glance at the clock showed the hour just shy of ten-thirty and the new, frightening darkness towards her mother wrapped tighter around her heart.

Bo raised his head as she was knotting the ends of her shawl beneath her breasts. 'Where you going at this hour?'

'Where d'you think?'

He rose slowly. 'Nay. I'll not let you. Them streets . . . It's like the end of the world out there at this time of night. They're no place for decent lasses.'

'Keep an eye to Sissy.'

He crossed the room in a few strides and put his hand up, blocking her from opening the door. 'Nay,' he said again. 'You stay. I'll search for her.'

She looked up at him, and a soft smile touched her mouth at his concern, then the anger returned and her eyes narrowed. 'Shift yourself, lad.'

'Moll—'

'The way I am at this moment . . . God help anyone fool enough to try owt with me. I'll never forgive her for this,' she added quietly.

'D'you know, Moll? Nor will I, not this time.'

The look she gave him whispered of every ounce of the unquestionable love she held for him. *I'll look after you, Bo. Always.*

She brushed aside his arm and set out into the clear, black night.

*

Mostly, the inner streets were empty bar the occasional drunk stumbling home. Having searched Great Ancoats Street's watering holes earlier, Moll skirted the main thoroughfare this time, heading out towards Oldham Road. Here, it was much busier. Shouts and music intermingled with bursts of laughter poured from brightly lit bars, and people passed in all directions; some alone, some in twos and threes, some singing, others arguing, their threats and curses ringing off the smoke-blackened houses.

Conversation, women's screeches, even the occasional baby's cry mixed with the rumble of cartwheels and thud of horses' hooves, dogs' barks and, once, a policeman's distant whistle for assistance – a brawl got out of hand, Moll surmised.

Beggars young and old hovered by doors, hoping to arouse the drunks' sympathy or take advantage of their inebriated stupidity. At one den, the door burst wide and the innkeeper, a huge mountain of a man, neck as thick as a toddler's torso, tossed a man on to the wet flags by Moll's feet; his cap followed and the door slammed shut, cutting off the customers' guffaws. The drunk hauled himself up and, mumbling curses, ambled off into the night.

She peered through the windows when she could but if her view was obscured, she was forced to enter. This she did quickly, quietly, avoiding making eye contact. She'd scan the faces then retreat just as fast.

In one beerhouse, a small band of females little older than herself sat straddling a group of young men in the corner, in full view of other customers. One, hard face heavily painted, even had her breasts exposed. Had Bo and Uriah seen this carry-on during their near-nightly searches? Sickened, Moll hurried out.

After a while, her energy began flagging and with a resigned sigh she turned her tired legs for home.

Where was Mam? The question, all day wrapped in fierce fury, was now tinged with worry. She needed her, now like never before. 'I need you, Mam,' she echoed the thought out loud, as though saying it would make her appear. Of course, it didn't. And as she'd done as far back as she could remember, Moll lifted her chin and coped, as she always must.

Passing back the way she'd come, she quickened her step. Gradually, as she left the main roads for narrow lanes and streets, the air became empty of noise. Spittal Street further up was almost deserted and she hurried on. Street lights cast murky, yellow-gold light across the cobbles and in a particular pool ahead, which stroked Primrose Street's shadowy dwellings, she spotted a man urinating against the wall. Drawing her shawl over her face, she crossed the road. Her eyes flicked in his direction as she drew opposite but to her relief saw that the spot where he'd stood was empty, bar the steaming puddle he'd left behind.

A cat yowled, another answered, then all was still. The silence grew. Eerie shapes and shadows sliced the mugginess as clouds scudded through the moon's silver light. Suddenly, the very air seemed to thicken, raising gooseflesh along her spine. She couldn't fathom it – then a garbled voice uttered a lewd comment close to her ear. She sprang back but hands caught her waist and she was sent stumbling against the wall of a corner house. The smell of strong ale and sweat, as the figure crushed her to him, brought bile to her throat and ice to her veins and all she could muster in protest was a strangled croak.

'I've brass to pay.'

Reality smashed through her: he took her for a street-walker. Shaking her head wildly, she tried to yank free but his hold tightened, his fingers digging painfully into her hips.

'I'm no whore; leave go of me!'

Moll was renowned for her temper. She'd an iron will and was proud to a fault. More than one had met with her left hook over the years and many others had experienced a lashing from her blade-sharp tongue. Yet at this moment, it was as though she'd forgotten who she was. Moll Chambers was, to Moll Chambers, a stranger. Her complete panic was too dense for any other emotion to penetrate.

'Please!'

'Stop it. Hold still,' he shouted, sounding almost hurt. 'My brass is as good as anyone's!'

'But I'm not— 'Ere, no!' she cried as he fumbled with her skirts and his hot hand squeezed the inside of her thigh. 'My father's dead!' Why these words left her, she didn't know, said them without thought.

He clicked his tongue and pressed his swollen crotch against her. 'Aye, and *my* owd man will follow suit in a minute. Now come on, stop playing silly beggars and let me in.'

Before she knew what was happening, his thick fingers slipped inside her underwear to stroke the silky down sheltering her innocence, and a scream rose in her.

Then something queer happened. Moll watched, transfixed, as the man rose inches into the air. His eyes widened and he jerked back on his tiptoes. It was then she understood: a tall figure had him by the scruff of the neck. Without a word, it hauled the man aside, sending him whizzing in a one-man waltz across the cobbles.

40

With a grunt, her tormentor shrugged, thrust his hands in his pockets and stumbled away.

Reaching up to press her thumping heart, Moll peered at her saviour through the twilight. His upper face was in shadow; to his mouth and smooth jaw, she said, 'Thank you.'

'You all right?'

He spoke calmly. She nodded.

'You can't blame the fella for wondering,' he said bluntly, though not unkindly. 'What's a lass like yourself doing out alone at this hour?'

'I were looking . . . I'm on my way home.'

'And where might that be?'

'Blossom Street.'

His Adam's apple bobbed above his white muffler. 'Not far.'

'Not far,' she echoed. It was all she could lay her tongue to.

When his hand moved towards her through the gloom, despite her recent ordeal with that varmint, she knew not a shred of fear. His touch, gentler than a butterfly's wing, swept loose hair from her face and tucked it behind her ear. His thumb brushed her cheek in the briefest caress then he turned and walked away.

She watched him, hoping he'd look back, yet not knowing why. He didn't. Even after he'd disappeared around the corner, she stood for a full minute, unblinking and slightly breathless.

She picked up her skirts and ran for home.

Of all the things Moll had planned to say to her mother throughout the torturous hours, when she returned and found Ruth standing in the kitchen in Bo's arms, thought and feeling melted away. She slipped past them and lay, shawl, boots and all, beside Sissy. Within seconds, she'd slipped into a heavy sleep and before it claimed her completely, heard her mother's muffled voice:

'You're the man of the house, now, Bo.'

And his reply: 'I'll look after you, Mam. Always . . .'

Chapter 4

OF ALL THE things a body could think to squander money on – drink, gambling, loose women, whether children were starving, the fire long dead and the whole family without a boot between them – one was rarely shirked: the burial club. The overwhelming humiliation of oneself or a loved one finishing this life with a pauper's funeral was too horrendous to contemplate. Many would sooner skip the rent, risking destitution, than the insurance man's payments.

And so, Robert Chambers was given a decent, albeit poor, send-off and within a week their two little rooms were as though he'd never existed. His presence no longer lingered and only that morning, Bo had confided in Moll that though his love for their father would never leave his heart, the kind, rugged face was already fading from his memory. However hard he tried to conjure it, the features appeared distorted, and Bo was afraid that, one day, he might forget altogether.

Moll could do nothing but hold this lad whose boyhood days, already numbered before tragedy struck, were well and truly over. Overnight, his role had changed and he seemed to be struggling to adjust to this new responsibility. She'd done her utmost to keep things as they were, continued to oversee the running of the household, determined to ease his worry, but the burden weighed heavily on him. He had a family to keep. And Mam, in her subtle way, made sure he knew it.

For Sissy, life was little changed. In the initial days of their father's passing, she'd wandered into the bedroom several times and emerged, frowning, to ask Moll where he was. When told he'd gone to live as an angel with the Lord in heaven, she'd point to the sky through the window and, at Moll's nod, continue with whatever she'd been about, seemingly unfazed.

As for Mam . . .

Moll straightened the ornaments on the mantel, adjusted the angle of the only picture adorning their walls – a faded depiction of Moses in the Bulrushes – and after throwing a last glance around the clean and tidy room, nodded, satisfied.

After collecting potatoes and a knife, she crossed to the cupboard, took out a shrivelled and browning half of a cabbage and eased into a chair.

Waking beside Sissy in the early hours of that awful night to see her mother slumped at the table, watching her in the dim firelight, Moll hadn't moved for what seemed an age. They had simply stared at one another, guilt and blame filling the air around them, so thick you could have sewn a button on it.

'You weren't here and should have been. He died earlier with Jilly by his side instead of you because your need for gin came first. Your own needs allus do, don't they, Mam? Your children needed you, were forced to spend the entire day and night without the strength and comfort of their mother, whilst their father lay cold in the next room.

'I trawled the streets for more hours than I can count

searching for you, saw and heard things I shouldn't, was almost raped by a man who took me for a prostitute, and where were you? Nowhere, as always. Your promises are lies, your apologies empty words I've heard once too often and from this day, things between us will never be the same.'

Moll had delivered this in her mind; not with anger but dull acceptance. What she did utter aloud, she'd said calmly, emotionless: 'Father's final word was your name.' Then she'd turned over, pulling the blanket over her head.

She'd heard Mam crumple; sharp, wrenching sobs seemed to come from her soul. And Moll felt nothing. She'd closed her eyes and slipped back into empty sleep.

'Bread, Moll?' asked Sissy, now, dragging her back to the present.

'Can't you wait, lass? We'll be having our evening meal soon. I've nearly done here.'

'Have you, Moll?'

'Aye. And there's currant cake for afters.'

'Is there, Moll?'

'Aye.'

'With currants in?'

'Aye, lass,' she affirmed with a chuckle.

Sissy returned her attention to the chipped marbles that once belonged to Bo and, after throwing the vegetables into a large pan bubbling on the fire, Moll rinsed her hands in the scullery sink and wandered to the front door. She leaned, arms folded, against the rotten frame, closed her eyes and lifted her face to the sun's rays beating on the grey street.

Although it was Sunday, the street was filled with children and in almost every doorway sat women, bowls perched in long, grubby aprons, peeling vegetables or drinking tea with neighbours, putting the world to rights. Men, some less than sober, lounged against the warm brick walls chatting quietly, or squatted by the roadside playing pitch and toss with coppers they could ill afford to squander.

Were a priest to venture along, Moll knew, there would have been merry hell to pay – the ribald language if nothing else, from both sexes including the children, would have earned them a tongue lashing of the highest order. Gambling and drinking on the Sabbath, lounging idly outdoors instead of giving thanks to the Almighty at church – bare-headed, too, no less! – would have seen them blasted to all damnation. And these people, some hardened criminals, most living hand to mouth daily, and all clawing, constantly clawing at this life which often seemed barely worth the effort, would take it on the chin, either in surly silence or mild amusement.

As far as they were concerned, the Church did little for them and they reciprocated in kind. Even those who did attend were forced to do so sporadically; there was little choice when their Sunday best clothes saw more of the pawnshop than their own backs.

Looking to the end house and the street sign attached, Moll almost laughed at the irony. The only thing to blossom here was wretchedness.

'All right, lass?'

Moll glanced to her right and smiled at Jilly coming up the steep cellar steps, holding on to the low iron railing that bordered them at street level. 'Aye, just catching some air while the veg's cooking.'

The old woman motioned, grinning, to her door below and flapped her apron in an attempt to generate a breeze. 'Aye! It's hotter than Satan's armpit inside.'

They stood, backs against the wall, in companionable silence until Jilly asked, 'Youse all right, then, for grub, like?'

'Aye, ta.'

'You know you've only to ask . . .'

'I know.' Moll squinted into the craggy face, smiled, then closed her eyes once more.

'I've to call in Mary York's cottage shortly for more ointment for Alf's legs.'

'Oh?'

'Aye.' Jilly paused before continuing casually, 'Happen I could cut through Hood Street on t' journey back and stop by St Peter's, walk home with your mam, like.'

Knowing her neighbour meant well, Moll hid a sigh and merely shrugged. 'If you fancy.'

Since Robert's death, her mother had taken to going to church at all hours, sometimes more than once a day. Bo reckoned it must bring her comfort but Moll was sure this new routine held a different purpose: to salve her guilt and seek forgiveness for letting her dying husband down. Either way, it mattered not. She was still drinking, coming home all hours singing her daft songs. Bo continued to trawl the beerhouses of a night in search of her but Moll had given up caring.

'Leave her to it, lad,' she'd tell him, but it fell on deaf ears and when the front door closed behind him, she'd simply shrug and retire to the bed they shared with Sissy. Whether he had any luck or Mam eventually returned of her own accord, Moll neither knew nor asked, but the pair were always back the next morning.

She'd become detached from the whole business. Mam wouldn't change so what was the use in hoping, caring? Even if Jilly walked back with her today, Mam would only slip out tonight instead. Nevertheless, it was kind of the old woman to offer. Sometimes, it scared Moll to dwell on what they would do without her.

And Uriah.

Moll smiled, despite everything. He'd helped not only Bo but herself through these recent dark days and with each that passed, her feelings for him had grown. Still, they kept up the pretence in front of others but she'd sensed their closeness deepen further. He'd even stroked her cheek the other night when he called on Bo. Her brother left the room to fetch his jacket and cap and Uriah had bent by her chair and asked how she was bearing up. His eyes were as soft as his voice and when she'd assured him she was managing, he'd slowly brushed his fingers along her jawline, smiled, then, hearing Bo returning, turned away, leaving her fizzing with shame-tinged desire and confusion.

Where was it leading? she wondered, as she did daily. Where did she want it to?

A burst of laughter jolted her from thoughts of another, who had similarly stroked her cheek last week in the moonlight. She glanced across the street, where a band of seven or eight youths stood lounging on the corner. One, a buxom girl around her own age wearing a large hat adorned with tatty red and green ostrich feathers, locked gazes with her. The smile slipped from her face, and Moll frowned at the steely look that had appeared in her eyes. Glancing at her companions, who had fallen silent and were also staring at her, Moll's curiosity got the better of her.

She lifted her chin questioningly. 'What are youse lot gawping at? Have I sprouted a second head without noticing, or summat?'

A murmur trickled through the group then, as one, they crossed the cobbles towards her and Jilly.

48

It was as they neared that realisation of who this lot were hit her like a gale force wind and she almost staggered, so strong was the rush of anger. What with recent troubles, this particular worry had completely slipped her mind; she hadn't asked Bo how matters stood since before their father passed, she realised, ashamed.

She sent up thanks he was visiting Uriah then glanced to the corner, willing him not to return, for if he did and this shower rounded on him, she wouldn't be responsible for her actions and it would make matters ten times worse for him.

'Keep an eye to our Sissy a minute, would you, Jilly?'

The older woman, eyeing the newcomers, made to protest but Moll shook her head.

'Don't fret. I'll be but a few minutes,' she assured her quietly and, giving backward glances, Jilly disappeared inside.

These motley gangs of youths, who called themselves scuttlers, had been terrorising Manchester and Salford's streets for decades.

They fashioned their gang names on the districts where they sprang. How many individual gangs there were, no one really knew – thirty or forty, maybe more? Some had as many as fifty to a hundred members and more could be relied upon should the need arise.

They expected any lad living in the tangle of streets and courts surrounding their patch to join – and by carrot or stick, usually got their way. They regularly trawled their stamping ground searching for new recruits. As they were doing with Bo, the scuttlers, in their mission for fresh meat to swell their number and reputation, used every tactic in the book, from cajoling to intimidation and molestation. They stalked and harassed potential members relentlessly until, as was often the

49

case, they wore them down, victims submitting just for an easy life.

But not Bo, Moll swore to herself now, as she had countless times. Never her Bo, she'd make sure.

In some small way, she almost understood the practice's lure. For folk who were born, bred and died in these streets, whom higher classes viewed as the dregs of society, with no future or prospects, these grey cobbles were their world. Their patch of earth, meaningless to the more privileged, was all they had, something solid they could lay claim to in a world where they had nothing else. They were fiercely territorial. These mean streets were theirs and they would protect them to the death if necessary.

Feuds were infamous. Opposing gangs met regularly to fight and were widely feared and avoided in every quarter. They battled anywhere, from open spaces to the streets; woe betide anyone caught in the crossfire. Bottles and stones rained on all who trod and afterwards, the flags and cobbles were littered with remnants of their fights.

They were merciless in their dealings with rival gangs – and those who voiced their disagreement with the practice. And it was this mindless, animalistic violence they doled out without hesitation on anyone who dared stand against them that, like other decent residents, Moll found sickening. Man, woman, children or the elderly, it mattered not; scuttlers discriminated against no one. Only last month, word circulated that one gang had viciously attacked and blinded a God-fearing, hard-working father of twelve, stabbing him in the eye for confronting them over causing a ruckus outside his home.

Scuttling was viewed in their inner circles, regardless

of rank or gang, as a youth's sport, and by around the age of twenty most had outgrown the violent pastime. Leaders or 'best lads', upon stepping down, usually handed their revered role to younger brothers, and so it continued with seemingly no end in sight.

However, this one now – clearly the leader of the Bengal Tigers, so named after adjoining Bengal Street where most members lived – Moll saw was at least in his mid-twenties. Around her height, with dark eyes and darker hair cut short at the back and sides, his face was a patchwork of battle scars, proof of years of active service. His billycock – a style of bowler hat – sat jauntily at the back of his head, as did his male companions', displaying a soaped-down fringe over the left eye. White, bell-bottomed trousers and black jackets completed the uniform.

Gangs sported individually distinct attire, identifying them instantly as scuttlers to rival crews and others. Their girls wore striped and patterned skirts and shawls, and bright stockings, to match. Specifically coloured mufflers, as well as narrow-toed, brass-tipped clogs, were universally worn by males both for fashion and as a tool, as were the thick buckled, elaborately designed leather belts around their waists. And Moll knew there was at least one clasp knife secreted on each person . . .

The leader halted, the rest forming a half-circle around him. 'Is he home, then?'

She raised herself to her full height and stared him straight in the eye. 'Nay, he ain't, so why don't youse lot bugger off back up your own end. He wants no truck with you.'

A ripple of surprise then anger passed through the group and as one, they loomed closer.

'We'll soon remedy that, whore.'

Moll tried her best to contain her building fury. Mostly, these street fighters, despite their limited years, were powerfully built from years of manual labour. Yet even the stunted few, though pathetic in appearance, were not to be underestimated. Like their thicker-muscled counterparts, they were battle hardened, *life* hardened, and what they lacked in height and brawn, they made up for in sheer tenacity and utter fearlessness. Nevertheless, she refused to be cowed.

'You'll leave my brother be. He ain't like youse and I'll do my damnedest to see it stays that way.'

'Hark at her, uppity cow,' piped the female with the ostrich feathers, and on closer inspection, Moll recognised her as the bare-breasted customer in the Oldham Road beerhouse the night she searched for her mother. The girl had been laughing raucously, head thrown back and a bottle in her hand, breasts in the face of the lad in whose lap she'd been sat – this lad, Moll realised, glancing back at their leader.

'I'll give you the milling of your life in a minute,' the girl added with a snarl, leaning in. 'Now tell us where Big Bo's at.'

Instinctively, Moll's fists bunched. She folded her arms to stop herself lunging at the hard-faced mare. 'You favour an infant's been at your face with the paints.' She cocked her head as though in thought then nodded, smiling. 'Nay, I know who you remind me of. Them clowns I saw that time when the circus came to town.'

A lad at the back with thick eyebrows and lips to match sniggered, shattering the charged silence, and the furious girl rounded on him, delivering an ear-splitting slap to his face. She made to strike him again but the leader gripped her wrist.

'That's enough, Vick.'

'Enough? *Enough?* Whose side is he on?' she screeched, 'and as for *her*!' She made a grab for Moll's hair but he blocked her path.

'I said enough!' His eyes flashed threateningly, as though daring her to disobey him again.

After a moment's hesitation, she dropped her gaze then glanced once more at Moll with murder in her eyes. 'You'll rue your words, that's a promise,' she hissed before falling silent.

The leader stared at Moll and though a smile played around his mouth, there wasn't a trace of amusement in his steely glare, nor his voice, when he said, 'Let's go.'

'But boss, what about the morrow's meeting?' blurted a gangly lad at his shoulder. 'We need Big Bo—'

'Shut it, Winters.'

'But Rat Green and his lot—'

'I'll not tell thee a second time,' he growled to his friend, who in Moll's opinion suited the name Rat, never mind the one he was referring to; his teeth poked out so far that his lips didn't meet in the middle and his nose was as pointy as a pencil.

As had the girl, Winters lowered his eyes and with a satisfied nod, the leader repeated, 'Let's go.'

Without further protest, the group walked away. Apart from the girl with the feathers, who shot a hate-filled glance over her shoulder, none looked back.

Moll frowned in surprised distrust. Sickly dread rolled through her guts; they hadn't seen the last of them, she'd stake her life on that.

Jilly, who'd returned unheard and had clearly witnessed at least part of the exchange, stood ashen-faced and it was then Moll realised that not a single neighbour had intervened. The street was almost empty.

Individually, a scuttler was an intimidating presence. In groups, they became a frightening force. Most believed only the foolhardy chose not to avoid confrontation. Most, aye, but not all. Not she.

As though reading her thoughts, a man across the road raised his hand. 'You all right, lass? Don't fret, I'd have stepped in had you the need of it but from what I saw, you managed them just fine on your own.' He chuckled and several others, wide-eyed with admiration, murmured agreement.

Then Mrs Coombes skittered over, all yellow-toothed smiles. 'Eeh, good on you, love. It's about time someone told them troublesome buggers,' she simpered, seemingly having forgotten the heated words she and Moll had exchanged the other week. ''Ere, come with me and choose yourself a kitten. They were born only yesterday but it's yours once the time's right to separate them from the mother. You can have the pick of the litter, aye, you can.'

Jilly's soft snort broke the tension and Moll pushed the scuttlers from her thoughts. Hiding a smile, she followed Mrs Coombes across the cobbles.

Chapter 5

IT WAS AS she dished out the evening meal that Moll casually brought up the afternoon's incident with Bo. He sat staring into the orange-blue flames of the fire, feet on the hearth, and he raised his head slowly.

'Who did you say?'

She spooned out the last of the cabbage before repeating, 'Are you familiar with the name Rat Green?'

'I don't . . . Nay, I don't think so.' He shifted in his chair. 'Why, our Moll?'

Inclining her head to the table, she waited until he'd seated himself beside Sissy. 'Because,' she said, keeping her tone light, 'it seems he's the reason the Tigers want you on their side.' She glanced up from her plate when silence greeted her. Her brother was staring at his food, frowning. 'Bo?'

'Aye?'

'D'you know about a meeting betwixt the scuttlers the morrow?'

'Aye,' he admitted after a long pause, and her heart sank to her boots. 'Lad, name of Winters, cornered me in work, said as how the Tigers need me and won't take no for an answer.' He breathed a weary sigh. 'He said to meet them on Maria Street at seven.'

'Oh?'

'Aye, in the ginnel to the Royal Oak Inn on Jersey Street.'

'And what did you say?'

'Same as always: I want no truck with it.' He lowered his spoon to run a hand over his eyes. 'They came here the day, didn't they?'

'Aye,' it was her turn to admit, wondering if she'd made matters worse for him, and was heartsore when he muttered, 'You shouldn't have spoken to them as you did, Moll.'

'Someone needed to. D'you know, Bo, I've seen grown men cross the road at scuttlers approaching. What's the world coming to when kiddies not long out of short trousers are ruling the streets? They'll not get you,' she finished with quiet determination.

'Oh, Moll . . .'

Raw acceptance in his hollow laugh scared, saddened and infuriated her in equal measures. She shook her head emphatically. 'They'll not, and that's a promise.'

She motioned to his bowl and they continued the meal in silence.

An hour later, having just washed the last dish and replaced it on the rack, she was deliberating whether to throw away her mother's meal, still warming by the fire but now shrivelled to ruin, when light knocking sounded at the door.

Upon entering, Jilly flicked her eyes around but didn't ask whether Ruth was home. She didn't have to. It was the same almost every night, now.

'All well, Jilly?'

'Aye, lass. I've called up to see if you fancied a game of cards. My Alf's having a good day the day thanks be to that ointment; it'll be a treat for him to see a fresh face. Bo don't mind keeping an eye to young Sissy; d'you, lad?'

He smothered a yawn with the back of his hand, smiled and shook his head.

'Aye, Jilly, I'd like that.'

'Well come on then, lass. There's a pot not long brewed.' The old woman cast an affectionate smile towards Sissy, dozing on Bo's knee, bade Bo goodnight then ambled out.

'I'll not be long, lad.'

'There's no rush, Moll. You deserve an hour to yourself for once.'

His thoughtfulness brought a smile to her and as she passed his chair she stroked his hair as a mother would her child's. He caught her hand and kissed it, they grinned at each other, and with a lighter heart, she followed Jilly downstairs.

The dim, dank cellar always made Moll shudder; tonight was no different. Though Jilly kept it scrupulously clean and did her utmost to make it homely, it was what it was: a joyless, airless hole in the ground.

Rivulets of condensation ran down the damp-stained walls and a fetid odour choked all it touched. Whatever the hour, a gloomy blanket covered everything; daylight hours, no matter the season, did little to brighten the space. Even in the height of summer, a candle had to be lit as the sun's rays failed to reach the corners through the narrow strip of high window on a level with the street outside.

How they and countless others had borne these dwellings, Moll didn't know. They were as close to hell as a body could reach and sometimes even Jilly joked she was sure she heard Lucifer himself banging on his ceiling if they made too much noise.

57

When the Industrial Revolution first stretched its giant legs, people swarmed the northern towns, in search of work, in colossal numbers. Despite the jerry-built homes erupting like boils to swallow the land, overcrowding increased and cellars were subdivided to house more families.

The middle of the century had seen the Manchester Corporation introduce the New Streets Act to improve living conditions of the underclass, and sanitary inspectors sallied forth into the slums. Their findings were damning. The shut-down of almost five thousand cellars used as dwellings quickly passed. However, in the following years, closure rates were poor.

Landlords, up in arms at the prospect of losing money, campaigned against the move and the Property Owners' Association stepped in, delaying progress. More than a decade later, fewer than a thousand had closed. Those that had merely exacerbated overcrowding problems. Cellars were at least preferable to the streets, and more desperate souls simply tore down the boards and turned the savage caves back into abodes. Nevertheless, the Sanitary Committee persevered and inhabited cellars slowly dwindled.

The odd pockets still existed, either overlooked or undiscovered, though their days were severely numbered. The Saxes and folk of their ilk awaited the summons to depart with quiet dread. Despite everything, this was home. Cellar rents were around half that of the houses above – which was all some could scrape together. Any roof was preferable to none. What would become of them? At their time of life, an uncertain future was a fearful notion.

'Sit yourself down, lass.' Alf now flashed Moll a gummy grin across the room.

'How you fettling, Mr Sax?'

'Ay, you know, you know.' He plucked at the tartan blanket covering his knees. 'Not so bad the day, anyroad.'

'That's good then.'

Jilly gave her husband an affectionate smile then motioned to Moll to do as he bid.

Alfred Sax had been employed at the nearby Flint Glass Works for many years but since his legs had begun playing him up, their earnings now rested on Jilly's many and varied skills. These ranged from cooking daily meals for recently widowed beer-seller Mr Locke and his two sons in adjoining Gun Street who, by their own admission, couldn't find their way around a kitchen between them with a map apiece; to tending as midwife to local women; even reading tea leaves if anyone required guidance from the soggy black dregs. She'd turn her hand to anything to put a crust on their plates.

A garishly bright orange teapot stood in the centre of the battered table and Moll shook her head as her neighbour, tongue peeking out in concentration, poured tea carefully into three empty jam jars, their glass misty white from countless washes.

'I don't know how you've skin left on your hand, Jilly. That teapot's older than me.'

Jilly returned it to the table and smiled wryly at its broken handle, of which only a quarter remained. 'There's life in the bugger yet.' After blowing on her knuckles, red from contact with the hot ceramic, she sat back in the hardwood chair. 'What d'you fancy first, lass? Whist?'

'Aye, owt. I'm just glad to be away from home a while.'

The old woman nodded understandingly, reached

behind her to a shelf and brought down a tin box, tinged green with age. 'Whist it is, then.'

By the third game, Moll felt more relaxed than she had in a long time. The weak tea and Jilly's home-made ginger scones, coupled with the crackling fire, soft candlelight and easy company, soothed her like a warm embrace and she sighed contentedly. But for Sissy and Bo, she could have stayed here for ever, cellar or no.

'It's nice seeing that bonny smile of yourn,' said Jilly, as though reading her thoughts. 'Times have been harsh of late, lass, I know, but they'll ease, you'll see. That business this afternoon didn't help, I'll bet.' She smacked her gums together angrily. 'Bloody young divils, eh? They're short of a sound flogging. Wipe the wickedness from them in a heartbeat, that would. Aye, aye.'

Weary dread dampened a little of Moll's happiness. As she'd done earlier, she murmured, 'They'll not get him.'

'I should think not! He's a good lad, is Bo, a good lad, like your father afore him.' *And a credit to none more than thee,* spoke her eyes. 'Aye, they'll grow bored soon enough.'

'That's what Uriah says, but . . . What?' Moll asked, smiling, when Jilly grinned.

The old woman studied her cards before remarking innocently, 'Nice lad, yon Bo's friend. Handsome to boot, an' all, wouldn't you say, lass?'

Moll was glad of the dim light as her cheeks grew hot. 'Don't you start. I've enough of that from Polly.' Husband and wife shared a knowing look and laughing, she added, ''Ere, give over! He's Bo's friend, is all, and nowt to do with me.'

'We'll see,' was Jilly's sage reply, and she chuckled when Moll threw her hands in the air in exasperation.

'Oh, all right, you touchy young beggar, yer. There's time aplenty for thoughts like that, anyroad, and you not long turned eighteen.'

Their eyes met across the table. Sharing a smile, they continued the game in comfortable silence.

Surprise lifted Moll's eyebrows later when muffled voices and laughter from the street floated through: drink-sodden revellers homeward bound. She stretched and blinked at the star-studded sky visible through the window. 'Kicking out time? It's soon got that.'

'Aye. We calling it a night?'

She nodded. 'I'd best get in. Ta for having me. Goodnight, God bless. Goodnight, God bless, Mr Sax.'

''Night, God bless, Moll lass,' they chimed in unison, Alf making for his fireside chair, Jilly pouring the array of coloured buttons and pack of cards back into the tin.

The drum of clogged and booted feet had passed the window as they spoke and when more neared, neither paid notice. Then a voice sounded, thick with drink, and Moll stiffened. Glancing up, she squinted in the half-light at the pair of feet that had stopped beyond the pane. Clad in lilac boots with a slight heel and black laces, there was no mistaking to whom they belonged.

The swindler on Smithfield Market had assured Mam they came from a governess in Salford. Good quality leather, she'd insisted, no doubt pocketing the ridiculous price she'd asked with a jubilant grin. That the heels were badly downtrodden and the toes scuffed almost white seemingly escaped Mam's attention, as had that the jar was already several shillings short of the rent money. Despite Moll raging at her frivolity and the next few days when their stomachs knew nothing but bread and tea, not to mention hiding whenever a knock came, Mam had done as she did best: tossed her pretty head and promised to buy her daughter a pair next time, as if that was the source of Moll's griping.

'There's Ruth home, lass.'

As though confirming Jilly's observation, giggles sounded outside. Without a word, Moll slipped from her seat. Yet as she reached for her shawl, her hand froze and though her eyes widened, her lips did the opposite, bunching in shock, unable to believe . . . Surely to God not . . .

''Ere, who . . . ?' Jilly murmured, nodding up to the heavy boots now standing by Ruth's, but Moll was already mumbling goodbye and opening the door.

They had their backs to her as she mounted the steps and neither turned when she scraped to a halt midway, gripping the rail, nor did they seem to hear her angry gasp.

Heads pressed on each other's shoulders to stifle their laughter, they headed into the house. Moll followed.

When they stumbled into the kitchen, Bo rose slowly, wide-eyed. Still, standing stiffly in the doorway now, Moll didn't speak. Even had she words at hand, the lead-hard ball in her throat would have choked them. How could she? How *could* she? was all her mind could grope at, and Moll hadn't the answer in speech nor thought.

It was when Davy Preston moved towards her father's fireside chair that her senses returned like a thunderbolt. With one sharp flick of her wrist, she sent the door slamming.

Her mother whipped around, the movement sending her staggering, and her bleary eyes widened but Davy, crossing his feet at his ankles, glanced up at a more leisurely pace, his gaze holding . . . was that amusement in the dark depths? Moll wondered fleetingly before turning back to her mother.

Ruth twirled hair around her finger in a nervous motion and flashed a half-smile. She was silent for a full minute, as though waiting for Moll to speak, but when Moll merely stared at her, face stiff as the father barely cold in his grave, the father who if Mam thought she could replace with the beast sprawled there she had another think coming, Ruth came towards her, hands outstretched. She made to take Moll's own but her daughter snatched back her arms.

'Now, Moll. Don't let's start nowt the night, eh? Lass?'

'What's he doing here?'

Her mother's tongue flicked out to wet her lips. 'He walked me home.'

Moll swivelled her eyes and it was to Davy she responded quietly, 'Well, he can just walk back the way he came, can't he?'

'Aw, lass! Ay, now, Moll! Sit down a while and let's—'

'Not seen him in weeks, you said.'

At this from Bo, Ruth turned, crying, 'Aye! Aye! But I did the night and . . .' Her voice petered off. She stared pathetically from one to the other. 'He's a friend. An owd friend.'

'Aye.'

It was the first Davy had spoken and the smug tone sickened Moll, as did the sight of his feet on the hearth and cap on the armrest, as though he was at home.

'He's nowhere to lay his head the night, Moll love,' Ruth wheedled. 'One night, is all, just one. He's away back to Bolton town the morrow; ain't that right, Davy?'

He just grinned and Moll stared at her mother, growing hot all over with burning rage. From the corner of her eye, she saw Bo shake his head but couldn't lift her eyes to him; it was as though they were glued to Ruth's face.

'Aye, a night and—'

'Nay.'

'Ay, lass—'

'Get yourself the bloody well out!' Moll spat at Davy, yanking the door wide. 'I mean it, Preston—'

The slap rattled the teeth in her head. She was unsure who was more shocked: herself or her mother. They simply gazed at one another, mouths agape. Moll didn't notice Bo cross the room until his arm went around her shoulders. He turned her about and without a word, she let him guide her to the bedroom next door.

As her brother helped her into bed beside a sleeping Sissy, Moll's teeth chattered uncontrollably. Not from the room – the August night was humid – but the coldness inside her, the stark shock and hurt and ... *abandonment* that, in all her years, she'd never known this strongly at her mother's hand.

She wanted to curl into a ball and sob like a baby. She wanted her father. *Father* ... *!* And *he* was still here, in Father's chair, Father's house, with her father's wife ...

'One night, and that's the God's 'onest.'

At Ruth's words from the doorway, Moll felt Bo raise himself on his elbow at the opposite end of the bed. She, however, felt cast in stone; she couldn't move had she wanted. And she didn't.

'Lass, I'm so sorry, so sorry.'

The door closed again with a soft click.

How sleep managed to claim her, Moll wondered, blinking in the darkness, she didn't know. But sleep some she had, almost the moment her mother retreated to the kitchen. To him.

Moll was wide awake, now, and reaching for her shawl. Of their own accord, her legs swung out of bed.

Hearing Sissy and Bo's harmonised breathing at her back, she padded to the door.

It was the feet she saw first. Then the widely parted legs, ramrod straight in the air, the left one level with the high mantel.

The ruby-rose glow from the fire's embers cast the slim limbs in a silver sheen, lending them the appearance of fine alabaster. Long, slender fingers of the same hue were entwined in the dark hair of the head between her thighs.

A wave of something she couldn't describe whipped through Moll's innards like burning blades. Thought sat misty but she knew for a fleeting moment a stirring of hope, that the female wasn't her mother; the long skirts, flung over her head in the chair, were obscuring her face. But the material, bottle-brown and patched in places . . . The kneeling figure by the hearth shifted closer, hands pulling the legs it held further apart – and as it did, it glanced up.

Davy Preston stilled, the only movement about him the flickering firelight illuminating his glistening mouth and chin. Then, holding Moll's gaze in his intense stare over her mother's stomach, he continued, like a thirsty dog, with what he'd been about . . .

The muffled moans floated from beneath the skirts to snap at Moll's heels as she stumbled, mind and heart empty, back to bed.

Chapter 6

HE NEVER LEFT.

Days into October, the first frosts came and with them swept a far icier undertone to the Chambers' little rooms.

Dawn was on the cusp of breaking when Moll finally nodded off and it seemed she'd merely blinked when a rough hand shook her awake. Utter exhaustion stung her eyes but the face, inches from hers, soon scattered away the sleep fog. How she loathed mornings, now, for they brought *him* to her room and his nasty hands on her, his harsh voice telling her to get up.

'Move it.'

She drew the coarse blanket to her chin and glared at Davy silently. Of late, she'd discovered this an effective weapon. Whereas once, she'd vent her anger in shouts, curses, even threats, she'd realised it hadn't the slightest impression upon him. He'd simply stare, piercing eyes creased in amusement. Then Mam would be flying at her, yelling that she should keep a civil tongue in her head – *and Davy the best thing to happen to this family for many a long month, too!* – and Moll had the devil's own temper, for wasn't Davy kind enough to give Ruth brass to buy the egg and bacon awaiting Moll in the kitchen? And hadn't he only offered to waken her so it didn't grow cold, for she'd not enjoy it as much, would she? And he wanted Moll to be happy, aye, he did; he wanted that for them all because he'd taken to them as though they were his very own . . . And on, and on . . .

Or Ruth would cry; great shuddering sobs that had Sissy whimpering in distress and Bo sidling to Mam to comfort her. And all the while, *he'd* look on with that sickening half-smile which Moll would have liked to remove with her two fists . . .

'I said up,' Davy growled now, and Moll smiled inwardly at the angry hue creeping under the stubble of his neck.

He didn't know where he stood when she was silent; she saw it in his eyes. He drew pleasure from goading her into reacting and realising this, she'd gained a power over him he couldn't take back, and he knew it.

In two strides, he returned to the bed and, leaning across until his broad bare chest with its thatch of coal-black hair was inches from hers, cocked his head. Eyes holding barely suppressed fury bore into hers. 'Or is it me tha wants to get you up? That right, then?' He ran his tongue over his lips and his tone dropped. 'Any excuse to feel my hands on you, eh? That it?'

Holding her breath, heartbeat banging in her ears, Moll willed herself to remain calm and hold his gaze, for if she slipped an inch in this constantly raging power struggle and showed a flicker of fear, it would be over, he'd have won, and life wouldn't be worth the living.

Yes. Days were unbearable, now. The nights more so. *Lord, the nights . . .*

Neither Mam nor Preston had made mention of their true relationship and Moll, crippled with rage and shame at the idea, at what she knew and had seen, followed suit. Bo said he took Mam's word as truth but Moll knew he lied. If what she heard reached her ears so clearly . . . Her brother would have to be deaf of a night not to. Thoughts of them together sickened her.

Mam's heartfelt promise the morning following that first night Davy stayed was carved for ever in Moll's memory. Ruth's insistence that they were just friends, old friends since kiddies, sounded so absolute, so genuine coupled with the soft openness in gaze and tone, Moll had wondered whether she'd dreamed . . . *it*. But her mind could never think up something so utterly vulgar about Mam . . . and him – about anyone, surely? she'd agonised, wanting so much to believe it true yet knowing it wasn't. And he'd seen her standing there. He'd seen her and continued. He was disgusting, they both were. *Oh, Father* . . . She was just glad it was she who had walked in and not her brother or sister.

'Happen on second thoughts you should stay abed. I'll get shot of Ruth for an hour and . . . aye. Aye,' Davy whispered again, now, grazing his prickly chin across Moll's jawline.

Bile, hot and bitter, rushed to her throat at his touch and the stale breath on her, and her flesh crawled as though home to a thousand insects. However, her tone was even as she said, 'Leave me be to dress, then, and I'll get up.'

'I thought you might.'

That smug smile! She swallowed furious tears as he sauntered out whistling and dragged herself from bed.

After gulping down piping hot tea and donning her shawl without a word or look to anyone, Moll slipped from the house. The sky, like milky skin peppered with bruises, hung low on the grey rooftops. Heading for the butcher's, she was thankful – something she'd never have believed. Even Evans' presence was preferable to *his*.

So lost was she in thought when reaching Union Street, it wasn't until she was through the dark wood door that she noticed the butcher, red-faced and panting angrily, by the high counter. Moll simply stared at him and he indicated beside her with a flick of his balding head.

Turning, her eyes widened at the shattered glass around her feet. 'Sir? What's happened?'

'Well might you ask, girl. Bloody property-wrecking young scoundrels! 'Ere, leave that,' he snapped as she automatically headed for the back room to fetch the sweeping brush. 'Never mind that a while. I'll see to it.'

'You're sure?'

'Aye, aye.'

She closed the door and folded her arms across her breasts. 'When did it occur, Mr Evans? Did you see who was responsible?'

'Not half-hour since and aye, I know, all right. Young swines!' he burst out, thumping his thigh.

Moll had a sudden urge to laugh. Served the old sod right after his treatment of their Sissy. He was glaring at her again and she asked, for want of something to say, 'Have you informed a constable?'

He sniffed twice and looked away. 'No need for that bother.'

'No need?' She frowned in surprise. 'Surely you'll not let 'em get away with this?'

'Oh, quieten your tongue, girl! I know what I'm about, and get off with it they'll not.'

With a brief shrug, she reached to undo her shawl. 'I'd best get on with my duties—' But his hand on her wrist stopped her.

'I've an errand I want you to run first. Take yourself to Prussia Street and tell that divil's father what's occurred. Tell him I want reimbursing for the window and to curb the antics of that son of his, else I'll be round myself with the police in tow. He'd best steer clear of my shop, his bloody cronies along with him, for it's the judge they'll answer to next time. Aye, you warn his ale-soaked father that!'

Well, of all the . . . ! They sounded a right bunch. What if she delivered the message and the family turned their anger on to her? And Mr Evans the big man, free with his fists where defenceless, weak-minded lasses were concerned! She suppressed a disgusted snort. 'So I'll go and confront this man whilst you . . . clean up?' she asked as innocently as she could, and was gratified when the butcher turned several shades redder.

'Aye, well, I've other matters to, to see to and . . . Anyroad, your young legs'll carry you there and back quicker than mine.'

'What number house?'

'How the bleedin' hell should I know? Use your head, girl, ask about.'

'Well what's the name?'

'Simcox. Now get gone, go on. You've your work to see to yet – twice as long that'll take now your mam's took it into her head to become a lady of leisure.'

Moll paused with her hand on the doorknob and turned slowly to face him. She expected a smug expression at the jibe but his face was blank.

'Summat had to be done, lass,' Mam said when Davy announced weeks ago to Moll that she'd now be working at the butcher's alone. 'After that carry-on with Sissy, we can't risk taking her no more and likely losing the position altogether. You're strong; you'll manage well enough, I'm sure.'

And Preston had nodded agreement across the room, that sickening smile of his playing . . .

Just what was his game? Moll still knew barely anything about him, why he was here – when he would sling his hook. An old friend from being kiddies, Mam said – she'd been raised in Bolton before moving to Manchester in her teens. Davy happened to be in Ancoats months ago and Ruth bumped into him. He'd had some troubles, needed a place to lay his head until he got back on his feet; soon, it'll be, her mother had insisted. He'll be away shortly.

'The neighbours? Never mind what they'll say; I never have, as well you know.' And Moll did. 'I've told, when asked, the truth of it: it's a fearful struggle since your father went, and Davy's lodging a while is aiding with the rent.'

There was no denying it: their money worries had eased considerably. The rent was now paid promptly and they ate better than they could ever remember. He'd even given Mam brass last week to buy Sissy new clogs. And Mam's gin and his strong porter were never in short supply; not a night passed they were not out supping Ancoats dry. Yet how he managed all this when he barely left their rooms plagued Moll with burning curiosity; also worry. She'd bet both eyes it wasn't from legal means; how did that bode for her family?

She was at her tether's end with the whole business, she was. The only shining lights in an otherwise bleak world were Jilly and Polly. Both had been, as always, towers of support. What she'd do without them, she didn't know.

Pushing all thought from her mind, Moll now opened the shop door and turned right, towards Prussia Street.

Even at this early hour, clumps of dishevelled women gossiped on their filthy steps and, as one, watched her pass, hooded eyes flicking over her with a mixture of expressions. Barefoot children swarmed but there wasn't a man in sight. Those fortunate to be employed were toiling in the many works and factories choking the city. The rest were either tramping the lanes searching for a day's graft or, worn down by hopelessness and rejection – or sheer idleness – still abed.

Midway down the pewter-coloured street, she paused by a group of four women and lowered her shawl to her shoulders. Their conversation ended abruptly but none spoke, simply stared at her with empty eyes.

'Where might I find Mr Simcox?' Moll asked one, who was limply holding a sickly-looking baby.

The woman glanced at her companions. Bobbing her greasy head, she then motioned to a house.

'Ta.'

'What you wanting with him, then?' asked a stout woman in her middle years when Moll made to turn.

'Not me. I've a message for him, is all.'

The woman's teeth flashed grey-green in her grubby face as she grinned. 'Then pray you understand liquid language, for you'll get no sense from that skenning drunk divil, lass, otherwise.'

Murmurs and laughter followed Moll across the cobbles but when she reached the house, a glance back showed they had grown bored with the moment's entertainment and resumed their conversation.

A child's miserable cries, intermingled with an adult's hacking cough, filtered through the bunched balls of yellowing newspaper stuffed in the holes of the broken

72

window, but it wasn't until her third knock that heavy footsteps sounded.

Acrid smells of cats, bodily odours and general filth from within smacked her fully around the face and stepping back, she struggled not to openly grimace.

'Aye?'

'I've been sent with a mess—' Moll's speech melted as, taking in the bullet-headed, sallow-faced youth who had answered, understanding slammed home.

She'd thanked God the Bengal Tigers hadn't brought further trouble to her door; whether it came to Bo away from home, he wouldn't say. They had visited twice more but on each occasion, her brother saw to them himself. Both times, the gang had left without a raised voice or resistance.

From the angle of this one's 'pigeon-board' peaked cap displaying the familiar donkey fringe, his dark trousers and jacket, its buttoned-down pocket flaps cut into points, to the flashy muffler at his throat and pointed-toed clogs . . . and of course, the leather belt – a great heavy-looking thing adorned with filed-down nails, depicting stars and serpents – he was clearly a member of the Tigers' rivals: the Prussia Street gang. Mr Evans had somehow got on the wrong side of the scuttlers. And he'd sent her to do his dirty work. Of all the . . .

'A message, eh? For who?'

Glancing under his arm, as he held open the door, at the stinking room beyond, Moll was shocked. Even by Ancoats' slum standards, conditions were dire. On piles of straw, beneath ragged coverings, over a dozen sleeping bodies littered the flagged floor. Bar a plain-topped table propped against the far wall, there wasn't a single stick of furniture. As well as in the pockets of space between occupants, ale bottles littered the table and, at the back, stacks of teetering dishes encrusted with old food.

'You deaf or summat?' The youth thrust his face close. 'Who's the sodding message for?'

'Your father,' Moll answered stonily, standing her ground, 'and if you don't shift yourself out of my face, lad, I'll spit in your eye.'

Surprise saw him do as she bid. 'Temper of an alley cat, you, ain't yer?'

'Aye, and you stink like one. Now, will you fetch your father or not?'

His lips tightened. He folded his arms. 'Who's it from, this message?'

'Evans.'

'Who?'

'Butcher on Union Street.'

A slow and twisted smile creased his face. 'Oh aye? Well, Father's not here so you've had a wasted journey, ain't you?'

She didn't care two figs for Mr Evans, his broken window or whatever was afoot between the two, nor whether his message reached Mr Simcox's ears. It was the infuriating cocksureness of this one that had her leaning over his shoulder. 'Mr Simcox?' she called into the dim room. 'Mr Simcox, you there?'

The scuttler's attitude changed instantly. Shoving Moll back on to the pavement, he spat a stream of curses and reached for his belt. Whipping it off, he wound it around his arm and as the heavy brass buckle swung, she screamed, more in surprised anger than fear, and ducked out of reach. She glanced up in time to see it swing towards her again before a hand shot from behind her attacker and snatched it away.

74

As she knelt, panting, she watched the scuttler turn furiously on the newcomer. However, his words choked him when her rescuer grabbed his throat, pinning him against the passageway wall.

Moll rose slowly. Her right knee throbbed painfully from its contact with the flags and when she scraped a loosened tendril of hair from her face, her hand shook. 'You . . . you . . . ! I'll have you locked up for that, you see if I don't—!'

'Tha all right?' The bare-chested young man still holding the youth spoke quietly, cutting her rant. 'Did it catch you, the belt?' When she just glared at him, he turned back to the lad. 'Get in there. I'll deal with you in a minute.' He thrust him into the squalid room where, to her amazement, no one had roused, and slammed the door. His shoulder muscles rippled as he folded his arms. He stared down at her calmly. 'Tha all right?' he repeated.

His eyes, which contrasted sharply with his jet hair, brows and lashes, were the palest blue she'd ever seen. She nodded.

'Good. Now, what's this all about?'

'My employer, Mr Evans, sent me with a message for Mr Simcox. That scuttler scum brother of yourn in there broke his butcher shop window.'

He stared at her for a long moment then nodded. 'I'll sort it.'

'You'll inform Mr Simcox?'

Another silence. 'I'll inform him.'

'Right, well. Ta.' This was her cue to depart but she didn't. She simply stared at him. He in turn, as though in no hurry to leave, stared back.

'You'll be all right?' Eyes never leaving hers, he motioned to the corner she'd come by.

'Aye.'

'Union Street, is it?'

'Aye.'

'Not far.'

The stirring of a smile touched his full mouth and a jerk deep in Moll's breast stole her breath. 'Not far,' she found herself echoing him, as she had once before, not too long ago.

She turned and headed back to work.

Several hours later, having cleaned the butcher's from top to bottom then stood in biting rain with her barrow of potatoes, Moll made her weary way to Blossom Street. However, despite her tiredness and now-familiar dread of returning home, a small smile played at her mouth. Dear Polly. After selling their wares, she'd insisted on treating Moll to an iced bun to cheer her up. Her warm smiles and kindness were just what Moll's flagging spirits had needed.

When she entered the kitchen the fire was blazing merrily, bathing everything in a comfortable glow, and after dumping the barrow in its usual spot, she held her hands to the flames gratefully.

Bustling around the small space, draping Moll's damp shawl over the back of a chair and mashing the tea, Ruth nodded, smiling. 'Nice eh, lass, a big fire burning for once? See, Davy being here's all for the good; we'd not afford a supply of coal such as that.'

Moll didn't answer. If she spoke her mind, that she'd rather be frozen to her very marrow if it meant him not being here, it would only bring a row and she hadn't strength for it.

'Here, drink this.'

'Ta.'

They sat in silence for several minutes sipping their brews until, glancing around and frowning, Moll asked, 'Where's Sissy?'

With a nonchalant air, her mother flapped her hand. 'Davy's taken her out from under my feet for an hour. An angel, he is. Don't get me wrong, I love the bones of the lass but she ain't half taxing.' Her smile slipped at Moll's expression. 'What?'

'Where've they gone, like? And in this weather? Just letting him go off with her like that; Christ's sake, Mam, we barely know a thing about him!'

'What? *I* know him, have for years!'

Moll had risen and was heading for the kitchen door. 'She'll be fretting for us summat awful—'

'Listen there, now!' Ruth jerked her head at the sound of the front door opening and Sissy's laughter filling the tiny passage. 'Does that sound like a fretting child to thee? I think you forget at times, lass, I'm her mam, not you. I know what's best for her.'

The words stung. Moll had been more of a mother to Sissy – and Bo, aye – than Mam ever had. Mam knew what was best? Three sheets to the wind most of the time and during the odd moments of sobriety, she found caring for the girl taxing? Dear God, dear God . . .

'Moll! Moll!'

The smile she forced as Sissy skipped into the room – and the struggle to keep it there when she saw her holding Davy's hand – physically pained her. 'Hello, lass. Where have you been, then?' She felt *his* eyes on her but didn't look his way, nor when he brushed past her as he crossed to the table did she react, at least not outwardly, though her skin prickled in disgust at his touch.

77

'Outside, Moll. Been outside.'

'Where?'

'Walking, Moll, outside. Look, Moll.' Grinning widely, the girl held out her hand, revealing a soggy paper poke of sugared almonds.

'Ain't you a lucky lass? Davy buy you them, did he?'

'Eeh, kind to a fault, he is,' exclaimed Ruth, shooting the man now lounging in the fireside chair a dazzling smile. 'Fair kindness itself!'

'Nay, Moll. The man, Moll. The bad man.'

At Sissy's words, they turned as one towards her. 'What's that, lass? A bad man bought you them? What bad man?' Moll added, swinging around to Davy. 'What's she on about?'

'Oh, stuff and nonsense.' Running a hand through his hair, he flashed an over-contrite smile. 'I chastised her – she were playing up and I told her to behave, like. Happen I were a bit harsh and I says, I says to her, "I'm a bad man, lass, for that." That's all. Stuff and nonsense.'

Moll's voice came in a growled whisper. 'How dare you! You'd no right.'

'By gum, Moll, there's no harm done! She's taxing at times; didn't I say so myself not a minute past? There, now, see what you've caused?' Ruth cried, pointing to the urine trickling down Sissy's skinny legs to form a puddle at her feet. 'Upset her, you have, with your questions. Take her next door and clean her up. It's your doing, you can sort it.' She patted Sissy's head. 'Go on with Moll, lass, stop that snivelling. You're all right.'

Ruth shot Moll a stern look then crossed to the chair facing Preston's. And Moll, with a terrible feeling she couldn't identify in the pit of her stomach, could do nothing but lead her sister from the room.

*

'Summat needs to be done. I don't know how much more I can take, and that's the truth.'

Bo glanced over the top of his mug but said nothing.

The time was approaching eleven and, as usual, just the two of them sat by the small fire. Though both must be up early for work, they knew without saying that midnight would have long since come and gone before they saw their bed. Moll had decided tonight was the night to make a dent in the growing pile of clothing that needed mending and Bo, as usual, wouldn't retire until their mother was safely back.

'I can't bear how home's become,' Moll continued, her tone bone-weary. 'I'm frickened for Sissy. Summat about Preston's explanation . . . it just didn't ring true, Bo. And Mam can't, or refuses to, see.' Sighing, she dropped into her lap the pinafore she was darning. 'The poor lass wet herself. I'd have pressed her but couldn't, nay, without distressing her further. If I discover he's touched a single hair on her head, I'll run a knife through his gizzard. I swear on all that's holy, I will.'

'Happen . . . ? Well . . . Mam said—'

'Oh, for the love of God, stop defending her.' Moll's interjection held no anger. It was delivered dully, as was, 'One day, and soon aye, them blinkers of yourn will fall and you'll see her for what she is. And Lord help you, for what you'll meet with shan't be pretty.'

'He's banned Uriah from the house,' Bo blurted.

'He's what?'

'Says he don't show him respect, that he's a young upstart.'

'And?' Moll ground out when Bo shifted uncomfortably.

'And that he's sick of him sniffing around here, that

79

it's for your benefit. That you're attracting him like a bitch on heat.' Her brother looked her fully in the face, now. 'Crudely put, granted, but as much as I hate admitting . . . There *ain't* a grain of truth in that, somewhere, is there?'

She was wholly thankful the flickering flames from stubs of candles dotted about barely impacted on the dim room; her cheeks were flaming. *How dare Preston! Dear God, had he said all this to Uriah? Oh, the shame . . . Damn him to hell's flames!*

'Do you harbour feelings for my friend, Moll?'

'What? Of course not! Uriah Croft? Huh!' She cursed inwardly as the flush spread to her neck.

'And Uriah?'

'Nay, nay. It's nowt but Preston's ugly mind. That poisonous fiend's rotten to the marrow.' She blinked, surprised, when Bo sat forward quickly, so close to her now, his knees touched hers, his brown stare wide with intensity.

'I want rid of him. I *mean* to be rid of that bastard, Moll.'

'What can we do?'

'I'll find a way. If he reckons them feet of his are safe in Father's spot under yon table' – he jerked his head behind him – 'he's in for a surprise, for they'll not be there much longer.'

For all his size and strength, Bo possessed a gentle soul and nature to boot. The lad she saw before her, however, showed no resemblance to her brother. Never, in all his years, had she seen him as she did now; his very pores oozed loathing. Sheer rage contorted his every feature and it scared her. She gripped his arm and for a full minute, they simply stared at one another.

'First Mam, now Sissy . . . And you. You've allus looked

after me. Now it's my turn to look out for you. I'll see no one tarnish your reputation, Moll.'

Finally, finally, she had an ally. As she'd predicted not five minutes since, his blinkers regarding goings-on beneath this roof were slipping away. For the first time, she didn't feel alone. So why were prickles of guilt turning her skin to gooseflesh? His anger and the fear of what he might do was, she knew, only part of it. In her mind came the question again – and her instinctive response:

'There ain't a grain of truth in that, somewhere, is there?'

'Nay, nay . . .'

Stifling a sigh, she closed her eyes.

Chapter 7

DAVY LIFTED HIS leg, like a dog preparing to urinate, and broke wind loudly. Grinning, he wafted the offensive odour towards Moll and Bo sitting eating.

'Ay, give over.' Chuckling, Ruth slapped his buttock.

'I'm only having a bit of kidment. 'Ere, look at the faces on them! Anyone would think I'd took a shit in their porridge.' His blast of laughter grew with Ruth and Sissy's giggles.

As one, Moll and Bo pushed back their chairs and made for the nails in the wall by the door. She plucked down her shawl, he his jacket and cap, which they donned in silence.

'You two off out?' asked their mother, smiling at them in turn. 'Aye, go on, enjoy yourselfs. You deserve it, loves.'

'Being Sunday, they're probably away to church to pray for my hole. Soul! I meant soul!' Davy's guffaws drove them from the room, and their mother's, 'Eeh, you! What you like, eh?' gave them a final shove into the street.

Moll shut the front door, pressed her forehead against the house's cool bricks and released a long sigh. Bo gave her shoulder a supportive squeeze and they set off.

The cobbles were slippery underfoot and they chose

their steps carefully. The street had had a fair dusting of white during the night and people either passed mumbling prayers that they would see no more, or shook their heads with the cursory bemoan, 'In for a harsh winter, we are that.'

At the corner of Elizabeth Street, Moll and Bo gave each other a slight nod and briefer smile. Then they turned in opposite directions; Bo for Uriah's, Moll towards Poland Street.

Mam had forgotten.

Gritting her teeth against the painful truth, Moll walked blindly, vision blurred by tears. Thirty-eight was no age, really, and Mam had forgotten . . .

Despite instructing Bo to call on Uriah today, saying that a cheery face would ease his grief, as she planned to do with Polly, when she neared her friend's house she didn't slow her pace. By instinct alone, her feet took her towards Bradford Street and on along Bradford Road to Philips Park Cemetery.

The church and surrounding grounds held a soothing air and, as when her father was laid to rest, she was thankful he'd spend eternity here. In her opinion, he could have found no nicer end than this particular garden of the Lord.

Making for his plot, she traced her fingertips over lichen-spotted headstones of differing shapes and sizes, and tall, faded monuments bearing bygone names of Manchester's affluent residents. *Alfred Butterworth, returned to our Lord in His year 1867 . . . Simon Foster, passed away 14th April . . . Margaret Malloy, also her daughter, Sally Malloy aged 11 years* . . . read Moll, glancing at various inscriptions. So many loved ones gone and many more left behind; lost, lonely, hearts broken beyond repair . . . Drawing an arm across her wet cheeks, she walked on.

'Hello, Father.' She dropped to her knees on the November frost-hardened earth – and her mouth fell open at what she saw.

The cheap posy of blush-coloured rosebuds, the strip of card attached and what was written, stunned her into joyous speechlessness.

'Sorry.' Just that one word, scrawled by what appeared to be a female hand. *Sorry.* Oh, Mam . . .

She fingered the unborn petals' silky tips and for the first time in months, knew a genuine smile.

'Mam didn't forget. Me and Bo thought she had. Oh, Father!'

Moll talked and cried at length. She told her father she, Bo and Sissy – Mam, too – were well as could be, that they missed him and always would. Humming softly, she tidied the plot, pulling weeds and removing fallen leaves with a tender smile. When some time later she departed, she did so with a lighter step and heart.

For despite everything, despite the worsening situation at home, Davy, the drink, the bleakness, she knew it didn't matter, now. Because Mam remembered. She was sorry. And that meant but one thing: there was hope. Aye, there was hope yet.

When she arrived home, Bo was already back and seated with Sissy. They – and even Davy, who stood leaning against the table puffing on his clay pipe – watched in confused silence as, like she'd done at her other parent's feet earlier, Moll dropped to her knees. Her mother gazed at her with a surprised frown and a small gasp escaped her when Moll enfolded her in her arms.

'Oh, Mam.'

'Lass? What's all this? Eeh, now,' murmured Ruth, softly tapping her back.

Moll buried her face in the warm neck. *I miss you,* she

said in her mind, then checked herself and shook her head. *Not miss; as they say, you can't miss what you've not known. Nay, I feel the loss of what I should have had, what all three of us have been deprived of: a proper mother. But we'll remedy this. We'll work through it from today, for you remembered. You care, you must. So we'll try, eh, Mam? Start afresh?*

'I don't believe you, our Moll.'

She twisted around and smiled. 'Nay, lad, all's well. Mam remembered.'

'Nay, she didn't.'

'She did, Bo. I visited Father. I saw the flowers.'

Her brother rose slowly. Placing both hands on the table, he thrust out his neck. 'If there were flowers, they weren't from her. She's forgotten Father's birthday, as we suspected. She admitted it to me not five minutes gone.'

Davy pointed the stem of his pipe at Bo. ''Ere, I'll have him mentioned no more in these rooms, you hear?'

Such a statement any other time would have had Moll flying at Davy with nails and fists. But her mind was taken up with one thing: the expression in her mother's eyes. It screamed contrition. Slowly, Moll got to her feet, hands out in front of her as though warding off a demon.

'Moll . . . Lass . . .'

'You leave her be, Mam,' snapped Bo, adding bitterly to Moll, 'She cares naught for Father. She never did.'

The smashing of Davy's pipe as he threw it against the wall made them all start. He leapt forward, grabbed Bo by the front of his jacket and slammed him against the mantel. 'What did I warn, upstart? Don't mention that corpse beneath this roof!'

'Leave go of him!' Before Moll could, her mother

85

scrambled to the men. Ruth pulled at the forearm pressing against Bo's neck but Davy, as though swatting a fly, sent her staggering. Nonetheless, she rushed at him again. 'You leave my boy be, d'you hear? You leave my boy be!'

Standing head and shoulders above Davy, almost twice his width, with youth on his side to boot, Bo could have felled him with a single blow. But he didn't. He simply stood, eyes calm.

'Ain't I fed you, supplied the coal that's chased the frost from your bones? Ain't I kept this rotten roof over your head? Bloody ingrates, the lot of youse!'

'The workhouse master does likewise for his inmates – and no different we've become since you dragged your carcass across yon threshold.' This came from somewhere deep in Bo's throat. 'My father was ten times the man you could only dream to be.'

'Bombastic young swine!'

When Davy's fist found Bo's cheek, the kitchen erupted. Over Sissy and Ruth's wails and the men's jumbled yells, Moll had to scream to be heard: 'Leave go of him and get from this house afore—' She looked about wildly and snatched up the poker. 'Afore I ram this through your skull! Get out! Get out!' She jabbed the space between them and to her surprised relief, Davy backed off.

Panting, teeth bared, he turned to Ruth. 'You gonna let 'em talk to me like that, woman?'

'Aye, I am.' She shook her head slowly. 'Touch my lad? Nay. I want you out, Davy Preston.'

In the ensuing silence, a range of emotions flitted across his stubbled face. He laughed. 'You'll be sorry for this, Ruth. When you and your brats are destitute in t' gutter, aye it's sorry you'll be. You need me.'

Mam said nothing and when the slamming door

86

rattled through the room, a panicked gasp left her and she jerked, as though to run after him. 'Mother of God, how will we manage?'

'It's all right, Mam, we don't need him. Give me a hand, Bo,' Moll added when Ruth's legs buckled and she sagged against her. 'Help me get her into the chair.'

For an age, they stood around her as she sat slumped, hands dangling over her knees, all three of them like a human shield: Moll and Bo on either side, Sissy clinging to her skirts by her feet.

'Gin.'

Bo glanced at Moll and after a moment's hesitation, she nodded consent to their mother's request. He crossed the room and drew on his cap.

'Go by Oldham Road way, lad,' Moll murmured. 'They'll not recognise you there, will serve you at the counter proper, like. Hereabouts, the drink shops' serving hatches will be teeming with kiddies at this time wanting their parents' jugs filled.'

'Gone, Moll? Mam, Davy gone?'

'Aye,' they answered in unison and their eyes met over Sissy's head.

'Aye,' their mother repeated. 'He's gone, my lasses.'

Euphoric relief burst through Moll and, like Ruth earlier, she sagged. Dropping beside Sissy, she rested her head in her mother's lap.

'Fetch a tallow, lad. A fresh one from the dresser drawer, that's it. You, Sissy lass, bring a saucer from the rack. Clear a space, Moll. Aye, shift the loaf, we'll place the candle there.'

When they were seated, Ruth lit one of Davy's pipe spills and held it to the wick. It flared then dipped, casting its steady yellow light across their faces.

Mam's words, slightly slurred, covered the room like a warm blanket. 'Let this 'ere night mark a fresh start. Your father's gone. Davy, too. Now we've only each other. We've to make the best of it, together. Aye?'

They nodded.

'I'm changed the day.' Ruth prodded the bottle clutched to her breast. 'After this, another drop won't pass my lips, I swear it. I've neglected my kiddies too long and I'm heartsore sorry, but no more. I'm your mam and it's time I acted like it. You've kept our dwellings, worked your fingers to the bone . . .' She paused, drew a shuddering breath. 'You'll know the burden no more. I'll ask Mr Evans for my position back. We'll make do, somehow. God willing.' After taking a gulp of gin, she clasped her hands together. 'Let's pray for your father . . . my husband.'

As one, they followed her action.

Their mother prayed on long after her children. When eventually she opened her beautiful eyes, they were cut-glass bright with tears. Bo squeezed her shoulder and she nodded, smiling.

A calmness settled over the rooms for the remainder of the day.

It was only later, in bed, that Moll recalled the flowers on her father's grave. Who *had* put them there? And for what were they sorry?

Chapter 8

MAM WAS STILL sleeping when they woke for work the following morning; in whispers, Moll and Bo agreed to leave her be.

The kitchen on this day, knowing *he* wasn't here, felt . . . Moll had searched for a word to put to the sensation and came up only with empty. Aye, empty, in a good way. Void of tension, of that sickly undertone they had grown accustomed to. And it felt wonderful. He was gone!

After easing the bottle from her slumbering mother's limp grasp and pouring away the last of the gin, Moll had breezed around, building the fire and making breakfast. She and her siblings had eaten in easy silence and after seeing Bo off, she'd prepared the potatoes to sell later, wrapping and placing them on the embers near the bars of the fire. She'd then helped Sissy with her ablutions, secured their shawls around them tightly against the cutting weather and headed for the door.

Mr Evans wouldn't be best pleased she'd fetched Sissy but he'd just have to lump it. Better Mam slept long today, restore her energy for the new beginning she was to embark upon. The prospect left a warm glow in Moll that even the chill breeze couldn't dampen.

Following the incident with the shop window and her

encounter with that Prussia Street one, her employer had thawed towards her somewhat. He'd discovered, it was clear, a grudging respect for her spirit in confronting what he'd evidently been reluctant to.

And the young man who had come to her aid twice, now, had been true to his word, Moll realised when reaching the shop and seeing the pane had been replaced.

In spite of herself, that tousle-haired, blue-eyed stranger wasn't far from her thoughts all morning. As promised, she kept Sissy close and to her relief, the hours rolled by incident free. She was finishing her chores in the Red Room, Sissy swirling around a square of floor the clean rag Moll gave her to keep her occupied, when the butcher appeared in the doorway.

'I'm almost done, here, Mr Evans.'

He nodded. 'I'll be out back if you need me.'

'Gone out back, Moll?' Sissy asked when he disappeared.

'Aye. Using the privy, I suspect.' Holding her nose, she pulled a face and Sissy fell about laughing. 'Quiet, you,' Moll whispered through her own chuckles, 'else he'll hear and—What in God's name?' she added when heavy banging sounded at the front door. She dropped her scrubbing brush into the pail and went to investigate, calling, 'Mr Evans, I think you're needed. Someone's knocking loud enough to waken the dead!'

She was halfway across the shop floor when the noise was suddenly replaced by another: clogged footsteps thundering past outside.

Happen there's been an accident and they're rounding up helping hands, she thought, hurrying forward. *I'll bet someone's gone under a cart, or a horse has got loose, or . . .* When she opened the door and saw it, just inches from

90

her face, it took her a moment to realise the scream filling her ears was hers. Slamming the door shut, she heaved a stream of bile on to the floor she'd not long cleaned.

'What in the name of God's wrong? Answer me, girl!'

Moll groped for the butcher's hand shaking her shoulder. 'Oh, sir!' She could only point to the door as sickness swooped again.

'Lord in Heaven!'

'Why, sir? Who would *do* such a thing?'

Mr Evans' fleshy face greyed, lending it the appearance of bread dough. He shook his head as Moll made towards him. 'Stay back. There's maggots everywhere.'

'I don't under— What make of man would nail a dead dog to someone's door?'

'It'll be youngsters playing silly beggars, is all . . . Listen, collect yon lass and go on home. Leave by the rear. I'll see to this.'

'My duties . . . ?'

'No bother, just go.'

Moll didn't need another telling; seconds later, she and Sissy were making for the back lane and home.

When they arrived to find their rooms empty, Moll froze between the doorways. *Fool,* her mind chanted until she thought her heart would break. Her eyes flicked to the mantel and within her breast the stir of unwavering love told her it mightn't be true. *Check it, check it.* Half a dozen steps later confirmed her worst nightmare.

She gripped the empty jar with shaking hands. Despair overwhelmed her; she slumped into a chair. *You promised, Mam. Why, just when things were looking up, must you spoil everything?* Could this morning get any worse . . . ?

'Look, Moll. Spider, Moll.'

Sissy's voice hacked through the tumultuous fog. Moll glanced down – and recoiled to see a fat white maggot wriggling up her arm. With a scream, she yanked off her shawl and threw it across the room. Then she put her face in her hands and burst into tears.

The front door opening and footsteps in the passage had Moll blinking in confusion – she must have fallen asleep. She glanced at Sissy playing with her marbles, rubbed her eyes and, looking to the clock, was surprised barely half an hour had passed since . . . Her gaze caught the jar and her face hardened. As she rose, the kitchen door opened.

'Oh no you don't. Don't be coming it with your drunken . . .' Moll frowned. 'Songs . . . I . . . ?'

'Thought I'd supped the brass?' Her mother smiled softly. 'I told thee. Not another drop shall pass my lips. I'm done with that.'

'But the money—'

'I loaned Jilly a few bob for Alf's leg medicine. She's dropping it in later. She's away up London Road, gone aiding a lass struck down with the milk fever.' Ruth held up a wicker basket laden with foodstuff. 'In an awful rush, Jilly were, so I offered to collect the ointment whilst buying in the evening meal. Look.' She motioned inside.

'I'm sorry.'

'It's all right, lass,' her mother said easily. ''Ere and later, Jilly's asked us in to play cards. That'll be nice, eh? We ain't had a game for many a long year, have we?'

That she regularly slipped downstairs for a break from the drudgery of duties she shouldn't have the burden of, when Mam was out supping, Moll didn't mention. She nodded, smiling.

'Now, I'll call downstairs, make owd Alf a sup of tea and apply this stuff to his poor knees. You away with the tatties, soon?'

'Aye, Mam. I'll take Sissy along, eh?'

'Nay, I'll have the lass with me. 'Tain't fair; you've had her all morning. She can help me with the baking.'

A happy smile lifted the corners of Moll's mouth. 'Aye, all right.'

Heading for Jersey Street, that pleasant feeling inside remained. Mam really was trying this time. God willing, she'd continue to. She'd just needed to be away from that swine Preston, they'd known it all along.

Polly noticed her lightness of heart right away and when Moll explained about Davy leaving and the change in Mam already, her friend squeezed her hand.

'Eeh, I'm that pleased for you. You reckon he'll not be back?'

'D'you know summat, Polly, I don't think he will? It's like Mam finally saw him for the divil he is, bashing our Bo like that.'

'He's all right, yon Bo? Sissy?'

'Oh aye, aye. It's as though a storm cloud's passed and the sun's come out.' Moll pulled a wry face. 'Does that sound daft?'

'It sounds lovely. You've a way with words, lass. Robert would be proud of the lovely woman you're becoming.'

'Ay, give over,' Moll scoffed but tears had thickened her throat. 'Speaking of Father, I noticed yesterday someone's left flowers on his grave.'

'Happen it were a friend.'

'There were a note, an' all. It said "sorry", written by a woman's hand.'

'Sorry? For what?'

Moll shrugged, and the older woman's yellow-white brows knitted curiously.

'What d'you think it means? Who could have left it?'

It was Polly's turn to shrug. 'A rum do, that is. Ay well, it'll come out in t' end. Things allus do. Look, here's your Bo and his friend.'

'All right, Moll? By, it's cowd.' Bo blew into his cupped hands and stamped his clogged feet. 'Owt left for me?' he asked, motioning to the handcart.

'That'll warm your insides; get it down thee.' She handed another potato to Uriah and cursed inwardly when a blush crept up her neck at his smiling gaze.

'Smells good. Ta, Moll.' He held out a coin but when she tried taking it, didn't release it, and when she raised her other hand in mock threat, he let go, laughing.

She struggled to hide her smile. 'Swine. I hope that tatty chokes you.'

'I'll bet. Any excuse to give me mouth-to-mouth, eh?'

'Huh! You wish, Uriah Croft,' Moll shot and was flustered when he raised an eyebrow ever so slightly, as though agreeing.

'Mam all right?'

'Eh? Oh, aye. She's spending the day with our Sissy, baking.'

A warm smile creased Bo's eyes. 'Aye?'

Moll had to resist grabbing his hands and jumping up and down like an excited child, for Mam was trying and it felt great. And he felt it, too; it shone from him. And when he pressed her shoulder, having read her thoughts, she grinned.

'Best be getting back to work.'

'Aye, lad. 'Ere, me and Mam's away down Jilly's playing cards, later, if you fancy it?'

'You're all right. I've asked Uriah around. Now that sod's scarpered . . .'

She nodded angrily when his words trailed. That Preston had the gall to think he decided who crossed their threshold; just who the hell had he thought he was, anyway? 'Aye. Now that sod's scarpered,' she echoed, and again, they grinned.

'Happen you'll see me later, then, Moll,' Uriah announced. 'By, twice in one day? You lucky lass, yer!' He nudged Bo and they walked away.

She watched them go and when Uriah turned and grinned, couldn't help chuckling.

'By gum, lass. That lad grows softer on you daily.'

For once, Moll didn't try denying it. 'D'you really think?'

'Not think, I know it. Anyone with half an eye would agree, I'm bound.'

She was silent for a long moment. 'What about you, Polly? Has there ever been anyone . . . ?'

Her friend's eyes softened to the hue of a sun-bleached meadow. 'Once. Many moons ago.' Staring into the distance, she shrugged. 'But it weren't to be.'

'Oh?' Moll probed. However, when Polly busied herself arranging pies on her tray to avoid explaining, she asked instead, 'Will there be anyone else, d'you think? You reckon you'll marry one day?'

Polly's full mouth took on a crooked smile. 'And who'd want me at twenty-seven? It's a bit late for that, now, lass. Nay, it's a spinster I am and a spinster I'll stay. I've Mam and our Katie for company, anyroad. There'll be no fella telling me what I can and can't do and the like; sod that. I'm stopping as I am, ta very much.'

I couldn't do it, thought Moll. *I don't want to be alone the*

95

rest of my days. I want a good man to love and be loved by. I want my own dwelling and kiddies; aye, a swarm of them, and I'll cherish them each day of their lives. They'll never know want with me as their mam. And she'd be good to her husband, too. She'd learned from her mother's mistakes, wouldn't neglect hers as Mam did with Father, with her nights and nights of drink-driven abandonment. Aye, she'd wed, one day. She would.

As Moll made the silent vow, a face flashed in her mind, jerking her heart with cold shock. For it wasn't who should have appeared. Whom she'd believed . . . in time . . .

No. It wasn't Uriah's face at all.

'I'll tell you summat! This lass, eeh!' Alf's hearty chuckles rang through the cellar. Sissy, squealing with delight, scooped up the marbles and, ruffling her hair, he grinned to the women.

'You won again, Sissy love?'

'Aye, Mam. Won.'

'Clever lass.'

'Aye. Cheating, Mam.'

Throwing back his head, Alf roared with laughter and the women fell about giggling.

'A tonic, she is,' Jilly spluttered, wiping her cheeks on her apron. 'A genuine ray of sunshine.' Catching Ruth's eye, her smile slipped. She rose quickly. 'I'll brew another pot.'

Her mother's chin dropped to her chest and Moll suppressed a sigh of pity. An awkwardness had hung over them like smoke all evening. That Mam hankered for a drink was evident; her hands shook when holding her playing cards or lifting her tea to her lips, and Moll was surprised the curl she'd been nervously twirling around her finger since they arrived hadn't withered from her scalp.

Jilly, bless her, was doing her best to distract Ruth from the urge, hadn't stopped nattering. Mam really was trying, they could see it, and so they must, too.

Now, on impulse, Moll slid her hand across the table and covered one of her mother's. She smiled encouragingly and Ruth returned it with a determined nod.

With fresh tea brewed and a plate of Mam's oatcakes set out, the three of them sat in companionable silence, feet outstretched towards the fire, idly watching the old man and young girl with their game. Now and then, Moll glanced sideward and with each look, ill feeling that had built for months melted a little more.

Mam was like an angel sitting there, she thought with warm pride. Truly beautiful, despite what inner torture her gin-starved body must be putting her through. Dear God, that she'd wasted even the short months she did on that devil. Mam could have any man she chose, Moll was certain.

The sudden thought startled her and she cringed with stabbing guilt. What was she thinking? Her poor father barely cold and she . . . But what was Mam meant to do? Not yet, but in the future . . . ? What when she and Bo eventually left to wed and raise families of their own?

Mam would always have Sissy, the girl could never pass a normal life, but . . . Mam wasn't built to be alone. She'd married Father at seventeen and when he went . . . Well, they knew what happened then well enough. Mam was used to being cared for. She'd never had to fend for herself, just wasn't up to it. Yet what make of man would take her on the way she was? But she was trying, determined to change, Moll reminded herself, the fluttering of hope returning.

Moll just prayed she'd stick with it this time. She'd draw only the dregs if she continued with the bottle. Davy Preston and men of his ilk would have her, whichever way but no decent man would look twice; who could blame them? Living day in, day out, with someone like that and all that came with it; the frustration, anger, sorrow, your guts knotted in constant anxiety. The sheer exhaustion from coping with it was crippling.

Moll had seen what it did to her father, wouldn't wish that on anyone else, no, no; though she doubted there was another alive as good as he'd been. But one day . . . Mam needed a man by her side, craved the security, attention. Moll understood this. And when the time came, she'd see Ruth found a good one. She deserved it. Moll knew what bad was, she'd encountered plenty of wrong 'uns in the past, and Mam wasn't one. Weak, selfish, aye, but not bad. Not really.

A slight smile caressed Moll's lips at these thoughts. Her dizzying emotions over the months almost consumed her. Resentment, rage and hopelessness had dimmed to a detached and dead-cold stillness – her body's way of shielding itself from further pain, to stop her going out of her mind entirely, she realised.

Though she doubted Mam would have slung Preston out had it been *her* he pinned against that wall, that she did it for Bo – did it at all – had been like hot rays on frozen ground. A thaw set in and with each minute that Mam tried, another ice shard chipped away. And Moll felt better for it, oh she did. She suddenly felt for their mother what Bo did, wanted to be close to her.

She'd spent so long telling herself she didn't need Mam, that she was strong enough to manage without her, she'd convinced herself it was true. But she did need her. And she wanted her. She was bone-weary of going it alone.

'Moll, lass?'

Dragged from her musings, she blinked, confused, at the four grinning faces. 'Oh. Sorry, I . . .'

'Eeh, you were miles away.' Jilly flicked her eyes upwards. 'I were just saying to Ruth, will the lad not join us for an hour? There's tea yet in the pot. It don't seem right him up there by his own whilst we're here enjoying ourselfs.'

'Go on, lass, you ask him,' her mother urged.

Moll averted her eyes. What she didn't do was tell them Bo wasn't alone. If she did, she'd not have the excuse to nip up there and see Uriah, would she . . . ? And she wanted to, she told herself, yet wondered why that bare chest and those palest of blue eyes, which crept to mind often, had suddenly appeared again.

Filled with an odd mixture of a yearning she couldn't identify low in her stomach and prickles of shame, she put on her shawl and mounted the steps for home.

Besides a cat's call in the distance, the dark street was empty of life and sound. The air struck sharp in her lungs yet despite the cold, she didn't hurry for her door. She stood a moment, eyes trained on the empty corner, and released a soft sigh, as though waiting for . . . something . . . ? She frowned, shook her head, frowned again. Then with a last, lingering look in the direction of Prussia Street, she lifted the latch and slipped inside.

Young male voices, raised in animation, greeted Moll as she passed through the hall. Realising their topic of conversation – lasses – she rolled her eyes, smiling. But making to open the kitchen door, her hand stilled to hear her name. Curiosity getting the better of her, she remained, head tilted.

'Moll ain't said nowt?'

'Nay,' she heard Bo answer.

'But it were definitely Evans' they set about?'

'Oh aye. I heard lads speaking of it at work. The owd man's made an enemy of hisself there and no mistake. I'd not be in his boots for a gold watch, I tell you.'

They fell silent and Moll's hands itched to open the door but she told herself to wait, see what else was said. That Bo knew about the trouble at the butcher's flummoxed her; why hadn't he brought it up with her? Mind you, why, as with the incident with that Prussia Street swine who wielded his belt, hadn't she mentioned anything to her brother, nor anyone else? She didn't have an answer.

Bo's next words didn't quite reach her – then Uriah's harsh, 'And who told you that? They been hounding you again?' sliced the silence, making her jump.

'No more than usual. It were Winters what whispered it in my ear when passing my work bench today. He said as how the Prussia Street lot are getting bolder, that they're growing a name for themselves, and the Tigers'll not put up with it.' Bo's tone dropped and Moll had to press her ear to the wood. 'Rat drew a knife through a Tiger's back a while ago during a skirmish outside the Cass, the concert hall. He's still in the Infirmary, in a reet bad way, like, according to Winters. The Tigers want revenge. Winters said they need me with them, now, more than ever.'

Uriah muttered a curse. 'Bloody wastrels, the whole shower of 'em.' He was silent for a moment before uttering, 'Bo? For Christ's sake, I hope you're not considering what I think you are?'

'Our Moll scrubs at that butcher's; if what Winters says is true, that Prussia lot ain't for letting matters slide

100

with Evans. Supposing she's caught up in it? Happen if I joined the Tigers, I could help—?'

'Have you turned stark, staring mad? Bo, nay! They're just spewing you this to get you onside, can't you see? Steer clear. They're bad news, lad.'

Moll had had to bite down on her hand to contain a horrified protest at Bo's admission; at his next words, she screwed up her eyes and shook her head:

'I'll not see her caught up in owt, Uriah. A body, *any* body, will harm her over my dead one.'

This is why I've kept occurrences to myself, she realised. To protect those she loved, protect *him*, prevent him from doing something foolish. But Lord above, things were worse than she'd thought. That Bo was actually considering . . . What had that lot filled his head with? And what would follow? He'd said he wasn't familiar with the name Rat Green when she'd asked – that was clearly a lie. What else was he hiding from her? Damn and blast those scuttlers to hell's flames, every last one!

'She'll be caught up in nowt. I'll see to that.'

This, from Uriah, brought Moll's shoulders up in a cringe. He was in love with her. Despite his act, it was true. She just *knew* it was all along. He'd spoken with such sincerity, such passion, you'd have to be deaf, dumb and blind not to catch its meaning.

Bo obviously thought so, too: 'Preston reckoned you're soft on our Moll.'

Silence, thick as stew, descended, then, 'Oh?'

Moll's cheeks burned: Holding her breath, she pinched her lips tightly.

'And what says you? He decided your mind for you, did he?' Uriah added.

'Nay, not him. Our Moll when I put it to her.'

That silence once more, and again, 'Oh?'

A laugh, easy with trust and friendship, left her brother. 'Don't look so worried, man! I know Preston's light up top to think it. And as I said, if I had any doubt, Moll's answer put me straight, all right!' He laughed again and there followed a noise, like the jocular slapping of a knee. 'What? Uriah Croft? Huh!' he mimicked her from weeks ago, and dipping her chin, she squeezed her eyes shut.

Oh Bo, Bo. No . . .

'Hm. There we are, then.'

Moll's head drooped further at Uriah's flat response. She returned to the cellar with a feeling akin to a boulder atop her chest.

Chapter 9

IF SOMEONE HAD told her before this day that a body could so rapidly change in so short a time, Moll would have openly scoffed. Yet if ever there was proof, this was it. Mother of God, the state of him . . .

Rubbing days-old stubble, Mr Evans ambled back and forth between the windows, sleep-starved eyes scrutinising every angle of the street.

In spite of herself, despite everything, pity tugged at her. She touched his shoulder then apologised quickly when he jumped several inches, as though she'd scorched him with a branding iron.

'What? What?'

'I'm done for the day, now, Mr Evans.'

He gave a single nod, and glancing back halfway to the door she hesitated.

'Have I to brew you a sup afore I leave? Sir?'

'Eh?'

She retraced her steps upstairs to his living quarters. Returning minutes later with a cup of tea and some arrowroot biscuits – he looked like he hadn't eaten in days – she found him in the exact spot she'd left him, squat nose almost touching the pane.

'Sit down, Mr Evans, and drink this.' To her surprise,

like an obedient child he lumbered to the wooden chair behind the counter. 'Mind yourself, now, it's hot.'

He sipped at it then leaned back and closed his eyes. 'You need rest. You'll finish up making yourself ill.'

'Aye.'

She lowered her tone. 'Has owt else occurred?'

'Nay.' Slowly, he opened eyes dim with weariness. 'But it will. Oh aye, it will.'

Barely a week went by when a scuttle wasn't raging somewhere in Manchester and Salford, so Alf had informed Moll and his wife, solemn face buried in the *Manchester Guardian* which Mr Locke, once he'd done with them, passed on to Jilly when she delivered his meals. Not that they needed newspapers to know. Anyone with ears and eyes in their head knew the way of things.

People and property caught in the frays were commonplace. But this with the butcher was something else entirely. It wasn't the result of being in the wrong place at the wrong time. These were targeted attacks. The scuttlers had waged war on him and it didn't seem they were for stopping.

'That bleedin' dog.'

Moll nodded. Reporting the incident to the police in hope of putting an end to the torment had only seen the gang's antics increase tenfold.

'I should've left the bobbies out of it.'

'But why should you?' she asked, suddenly angry. 'Them swines shouldn't get away with behaving like this! What are decent folk meant to do, like? Sit back with a smile and let them wreak havoc as they please? Nay, sir. Tha did right.'

'Since when does doing right get you anywhere with gutter snakes like them? Badness, it's bred in 'em. Aye, and developed, like a cancer, as they grow.' He

104

grimaced. 'That so-called mother of his what tried wheedling into my good books so I'd drop the complaint – God in heaven, when I told her to sling her hook . . . Never in all my days have I heard such language come from a wench's tongue. Foul, foul.'

'Mrs Simcox?'

His head wobbled in confirmation. His face had turned cherry-red with the passion of his speech, his breathing heavy. Moll nodded to his cup. 'Sup your tea, sir.'

'Defending the buggers is tantamount to accepting what they're about. It's only the lash of the cat o' nine what'll cure them, I'll be bound, for their wastrel parents won't. They're every bit as bad. It's from them the young sods learned this behaviour!'

Moll's opinion of the man who'd come to her aid again had swiftly changed this past week. He hadn't, as promised, spoken to Mr Simcox at all. The butcher told how instead, her rescuer came here following her visit and threatened him into dropping the matter, for his own sake. Mr Evans finished up paying for the repairs himself. That family, the lot, were bad news.

'Happen they'll get bored soon enough.'

The butcher stared at her witheringly and she looked away. The lie had tasted bitter on her tongue.

'Grow up, girl. Get bored my granny's eye! They'll not, for they enjoy it. I've seen it on their faces of a night through the bedroom window when they're out there, the worse for drink, shouting and chucking stones at my premises and kicking merry hell out of my door. Why there's never a bobby about when it's occurring, I don't know. I reckon half the time they turn a bloody blind eye, save themselfs the aggravation, useless dogs.'

'They're after drawing our Bo into it.'

'Aye?'

'Not this lot giving you grief; another shower what call themselfs the Bengal Tigers.'

'Scuttlers is scuttlers. They're all the same to me.'

'And me. I'm at my wits' end with it. Mind, they'll not get my lad.'

They were silent for a long moment.

'You should go. Go on. I'll see thee the morrow.'

'Aye, all right.'

'Ta . . . for t' tea,' he said gruffly.

Moll nodded, drew her shawl over her head and headed for the door. Her hand paused on the knob. 'Where will it end?' she asked without turning.

The butcher's words were as void of emotion as hers. 'I don't know, girl. I just do not know and that's the truth.'

'All because he refused Mrs Simcox a bit of meat on t' tick! Mr Evans said she kicked up a stink so he slat her out and the next thing, her son puts his window through.' Moll paused to serve a tired-looking mill worker before continuing, 'And well, after reporting them over the dog . . . Day and night they're at it, now. How many more the length and breadth of Manchester – Salford, too – suffer this way whenever these scuttlers get it into their heads they've been wronged, Polly? How many more who say nowt for fear of matters worsening? These hooligans want rounding up and flogging to within an inch of their lives, every last one.'

'Ah, don't worry yourself over that one. Let the owd bugger stew. The swine weren't thinking on nowt when he were thumping you and Sissy about, were he?'

'Aye, I know,' Moll agreed with a sigh, 'but Polly, I understand to a degree what he's going through. That lot are not for giving up once they get their teeth into summat. Still they're causing Bo grief, and me – all of us; even Uriah. He's worried about him, an all.'

As she spoke, Moll was thankful Polly was busy with her pies so didn't catch the pain she knew had surely appeared in her eyes. The memory of the conversation she'd overheard, what Uriah must have felt hearing she'd poured scorn on the idea of him, still made her ache with regret.

He still treated her the same, was ready with his banter when they were together, but something had changed. Though subtle, she sensed a cooling in him, and a look she'd never seen before appeared behind his eyes if they strayed about her face too long.

Or was she imagining it – the whole thing even, had all along? she wondered again. Perhaps Uriah hadn't harboured feelings for her to begin with and it was her daft dreamings? Maybe, maybe . . . ? Oh, it was such a mess. Life was one worry following another. Why wasn't anything simple?

She swallowed a sigh. Then she pressed back her shoulders, her fighting spirit to push through rather than sink resurfacing, and she welcomed it like a friend. Fixing a smile, she returned her attention to her hungry customers.

'If you ask me,' said Polly, picking up the conversation when the scurrying townsfolk slowed to a trickle, 'Evans is big enough, ugly to boot, to see to his own affairs. Don't involve yourself.'

Moll nodded. 'Mind, it must have come as a heavy blow, all this. He prides hisself on his bravery, forever harks back to how he survived the Peterloo Massacre of 1819. He managed to give the crazed yeomanry cavalry the slip without receiving a scratch.' She bit her lip as

107

laughter bubbled. 'He reckons fighter's blood feeds his veins.'

'Peterloo of eighteen what?'

'The cotton workers' demonstration – peaceful, might I add – held on St Peter's Field, down the way? So named the Peterloo Massacre for the unjust treatment they received and the blood of the innocent souls shed by the sabres that day? Well, shame on you, Polly Wainwright! Lord above, child, don't you know anything about the history of your people?' Moll admonished in perfect imitation of her old schoolmistress, whose acid tongue could whip the very flesh from your bones – or so it felt when she'd delivered that speech to Moll as a child upon discovering her ignorance of bygone local events.

'Aye,' Moll had wanted to respond, 'I know nowt, for Father's too tired of an evening for tales, works himself to collapse to put a meal in our bellies, and Mam's usually too drunk to string a sentence, can barely recall occurrences an hour since, never mind years.'

'Bold divil!'

Moll ducked, chuckling, as her friend swiped at her.

'Evans were grown enough to take part in this protest, aye? Hold on, 1819?' Lips working noiselessly, Polly counted on her fingers then burst out laughing. 'That would make him now . . . about ninety year old? Lying owd swine!'

'Nay, he *were* there, with his mam.' Playing her role, Moll tossed her head haughtily. 'Well, *in* his mam, if you insist on picking at the facts. Her pains started on the walk home from all the excitement and she'd have borne him in the street but for a butcher taking pity on her. His wife helped deliver Mr Evans on the shop floor.'

'You've brightened up a dull noon no end, lass, with that one! I've heard nowt like it in all my days.'

'That's why Mr Evans became a butcher,' Moll continued solemnly but her chin shook with suppressed giggles. 'Folk told him he was talking *tripe* but he knew one day, his business would *slaughter* the rest. And now you've had the *meat* of the story, what d'you say to that?'

This was too much; Polly doubled over, helpless with laughter, setting her pies wobbling dangerously. 'You and your way with words! Now give over afore I wet my bloomers – clean on this morning, they were!'

Moll wiped tears of mirth from her eyes with the back of her hand. 'Nay. Aw, we shouldn't poke fun. He's at his wits' end with them scuttlers. They're hounding the owd bugger.'

'Well, I'm sure that there warrior blood of his will see him through.'

Moll grinned but her attempt at lightening the mood wasn't to last; the smile slipped when the familiar figures rounded the corner. 'Don't mention Mr Evans to our Bo, eh?' she just had time to warn before her brother's long strides closed the distance. 'All right, lad?'

'Aye. Ta, Moll, I'm fair clemmed.'

She hesitated to select another potato for Uriah. The past few days, he'd bought a pie from Polly rather than his usual from her. Though she told herself he must just fancy a change, that she was being daft, it felt like a personal snub and it hurt. She shot him a sidelong look. 'All right?'

'Aye, you?'

'Aye.'

'You'd never tell by your miserable face.' A slow smile spread across his but before Moll could shoot a usual

109

retort, which she knew he enjoyed as much as she, he turned away. 'Them pies smell good, Polly, as always.'

'Want one, lad?'

'I do, ta.'

Moll's stomach twisted at the dazzling smile he bestowed on her friend.

'Mam all right?'

She nodded at Bo distractedly. 'She were seeing to the washing with Jilly when I set out.'

'That'll keep her occupied a while, eh?'

Moll nodded again. Staying busy helped Mam. It was when inactivity crept along and boredom set in that she craved the bottle most. Nonetheless, she was still trying, and doing it well.

'We'd best eat walking back, lad, time's running on,' Bo announced.

'Summat afoot betwixt you and that Croft one?' asked Polly immediately when the lads had gone. 'You could have knitted a pair of socks from the tension, so thick was it.'

Moll held her hands palms upwards. 'I thought I were imagining it . . . The other week, I overheard—'

'Well, if it ain't the gobby piece herself.'

Both turned at the scathing statement. Polly's face creased in mild confusion but Moll's, when surveying the three girls heading towards them, dropped in weary recognition. *See, now,* she told herself. *What did I say not long since? Life was one worry following another? And I was right.* She really was in no mood for this . . .

'Look at the state of them tatties she's after palming off on folk, girls. Riddled with the blight, they favour.'

Vick made to pluck one from the barrow and Moll grabbed her wrist. 'Keep your stinking hands from where they don't belong.'

'Or what?' asked the girl to her left. She rubbed her sleeve across her nose, scrutinised it, then wiped it on her shawl. 'You were right about her, Vick. Reet uppity bitch and no mistake.'

'Aye,' chimed her other companion, a painfully thin twelve- or thirteen-year-old. She scrutinised Moll through narrowed eyes. 'No one talks to us like that, slut. You'd do well to mind that tongue of yourn.'

Before Moll had chance, Polly rounded on them, aghast. 'Why, you young bitches! Who the divil do youse think you are talking to my *friend* like that? Get on your way, you hard-faced lot, afore I skelp every one of you!'

Given their expressions, it was clear they were indeed not used to being spoken to in this fashion; just what in hell was wrong with Manchester's youths to think this was the normal way of things? wondered Moll, both stunned and disgusted. Then swelling rage smothered all else when the youngest sprang forward and snatched Polly's shawl from her body.

Hallooing with glee, the girls tossed it between them. After several unsuccessful attempts at grabbing it, Moll charged at Vick. Gripping fistfuls of her bodice, she forced the gaping girl backwards in a tottering trot and slammed her against a fishmonger's door.

'Tell them to hand that shawl over or so help me, you'll pay the price!'

'Get your bloody hands *off* me!' Growling like a rabid dog, Vick tried twisting from the grasp but Moll had the advantage of height as well as strength and with a frustrated roar, Vick sagged, panting. To her now-bewildered-looking accomplices, she flicked her chin.

'Vick?'

'Give it to her.'

'Aye?'

Moll's stirring of distrust at Vick's, 'Aye – *give* it to her!' was confirmed; the two girls leapt on Polly and rained blows on her, knocking her to the ground. Moll threw Vick aside, meaning to rush to her friend's aid, but barely got two steps when her hair was grabbed from behind. The hands twisted the tendrils, yanking her head back at a painful angle. Then Vick's face was in hers, eyes spitting pure murder, and a flash of silver glinted at Moll's cheek.

'I warned you, bitch, *warned* you'd rue your words.' Vick pressed the knife's point to her skin. 'Come on, then, bold 'un. Nay, didn't think so,' she murmured when Moll closed her eyes. 'Even the pluckiest soon bend when the chill of the blade's upon them.'

The air was heavy with silence, now. Though she couldn't see the others, Moll felt them near, watching. Despite her fear, a swollen tide of fury gushed through her veins. She met her attacker's gaze. 'So help me, you'll regret this day. *Vick.*'

Some small flicker of – was that begrudged admiration? – touched the girl's features.

'Let her have it, Vick!'

'Aye, give the bitch a dose! She'll think twice next time—'

It began as a low rumble; then the distant noise that cut off the thin girl's words grew and reverberated, bouncing from beyond, then off the rooftops. Brass-tipped clogs pounding the cobbles – the sound was unmistakable.

Vick released Moll but kept the knife aimed in warning and like a bloodhound sniffing for clues, lifted her head. Frowning, she glanced to her conspirators, who nodded.

'A scuttle?'

'Our lot, you reckon? The Tigers ain't planned nowt, mind . . .'

'Happen it's the Prussia mob, or the Allum Street lot . . .'

'We'll keep at a distance and slip away if it's not our lads . . . 'Ere, hold on. Listen.'

A series of high-pitched calls polluted the sky. As though summoned for reinforcements by the battle cries, the girls, throwing Moll and Polly a hate-filled look, picked up their skirts and pelted towards Prussia Street and the war evidently raging.

'Polly? Take my arm. That's it.' After helping her dazed friend up, Moll rescued Polly's shawl from the gutter, shook it out and wrapped it around her. She surveyed Polly's face for injury but apart from a small cut above her eye, could see no real damage. 'You all right?'

'Aye, aye. I can't believe . . . Never have I *ever* . . .'

'They'll not get away with today. Oh ay, look, your pies.' Moll gazed sadly at the produce knocked from the tray during the onslaught. Some had rolled into the gutter to settle in the filth, others lay scattered across the flagstones, but all were damaged beyond rescue. 'Them bitches!'

'Nay, they're only pies. 'Ere, you're bleeding!'

Frowning, Moll reached to touch the tender spot where the knife had pierced her. A trickle of blood came away on her finger. 'It's only a prick,' she assured her, wetting her sleeve and wiping the cut. 'Eeh, will you listen to that din!'

Shouts and curses studded with wild laughter quickly grew in pitch. At the road's end, those responsible – both lads and girls, a dozen or more – appeared before vanishing into the adjoining street.

'Listen to me. Travel home by the back lanes; stay clear of their path. D'you hear, lass?'

'Aye, Polly.'

'Right, come on, get your barrow. Nay, you'll not walk with me today; you've to get straight home. I'm all right, love,' her friend added, dropping a quick kiss to her brow. 'Watch yourself, now. I'll see thee the morrow.'

Moll remained until Polly disappeared from view. Then she turned for home, keeping to the back lanes as promised.

Less than an hour later, after helping her mother and Jilly with the rest of the washing, Moll had just sat down gratefully with a hunk of dry bread and cup of tea when a knock sounded.

She'd have to get it. Mam and Sissy were across the road at Mrs Coombes' collecting their kitten. Knowing her sister, who would scream blue murder when discovering she couldn't take them all and would no doubt have to be prised from the house, they would be a while yet. Moll half rose then sat down again and shrugged. Bugger them. Whoever it was, they would be back if it was that important.

However, another rap came, this time more insistent. Groaning in defeat, Moll crossed to the door.

'Polly?' She blinked in surprise then stood aside. 'What are you doing here?'

'Oh Moll . . .'

Taking in the older woman's flushed cheeks and wide eyes, her stomach flipped in dread. 'What is it? Tell me.'

'Your Mr Evans is dead.'

'He can't be!'

'Lass, he is.'

'But how? When? What . . . ?'

Polly took Moll's elbow and shepherded her to the kitchen. Closing the door, she leaned against it and, voice low, said, 'That racket we heard? Turns out it were that lot you said's been giving the butcher trouble.'

'The Prussia Street gang?'

'Aye. They were outside his premises again. When they left, the butcher, he must have had a bellyful, for he stormed to one of their dwellings to confront the parents.'

'The Simcoxes?'

'I'm not certain but it's likely, from what you've said. Anyroad, Mr Evans finished up giving that swine of a son a sound clouting and all hell broke loose. The lad went for him with his belt, the owd man scarpered, and him and his cronies gave chase. The butcher, being how he was . . .' Polly extended her arms, demonstrating his rotund shape. 'His heart packed in, lass. Neighbours say he keeled over outside his shop and that were that.'

For a good minute, Moll was too shocked to speak. 'And we were mocking him about Peterloo, when all the time . . . It's murder, this is. The scuttlers have committed murder as sure as if they'd stuck a knife betwixt his ribs.'

'Aye and that's why I'm here.'

Moll understood without Polly having to say it. 'Then I'm sorry but you've had a wasted journey. I'm going.'

'Lass, think what this means—'

'That's exactly what I am doing, Polly, can't you see?' She reached for her friend's hand. 'If more folk would only do as I'm about to, if *they* would speak to the police, stand up to these fiends, scuttling would soon die the death it deserves. Why should they get away with what they do? They're worse than savages, Polly, and where will it end?' She gripped the fingers she held tighter. 'This ain't just about Mr Evans. And they're wearing our Bo down, too, slowly, slowly, I can see it. I'll not stand by and see him muck up his future, and he will if he caves. I want the best for that lad and I'll do anything, anything to see he gets it. If that means I've to bear the stigma of informer . . . so be it.'

'Oh, Moll. You are young, after all. You think it'll end there, d'you?'

'The others, them what witnessed it, the neighbours?' At Polly's *What do you think?* look, Moll bowed her head. 'They've already been threatened into keeping their silence. They're afraid to speak out, ain't they?'

'All but one or two,' her friend admitted. 'But no doubt they'll fold soon enough. Let it go, eh, Moll? For all your sakes.'

After seeing Polly out, she sat staring into the fire, consumed in thought.

When she arrived at the entrance of Goulden Street God alone knew how long later, she glanced about and frowned. She couldn't even recall leaving the house, so lost in her troubles was she. Heart banging, she peered at the fortress-like building through the gathering gloom. Then, drawing her shawl up, she hurried on for the police station.

116

Chapter 10

'I'VE BEEN LOOKING for you.'

A warm hand covering Moll's on the metal-studded gate accompanied the quiet words. She turned with a start, her mouth running dry at the sight of him, those pale blue eyes . . . Then her lip curled defiantly. 'Oh, I bet you have.'

'Hear me out. Two minutes I ask.'

'Why should I?' They stared at one another. For reasons she couldn't fathom, she heard herself say, '*One* minute.'

He led her some distance from the station. Then he halted and, leaning his back against a wall, stared down at her from beneath his cap pulled low.

'Well? What is it you want to—?' she asked.

'I don't even know your name.'

'What?'

He inclined his head with the whisper of a smile. 'I said—'

'I heard you. Why on earth d'you want to know my name? What difference would that make? Just say what you've got to say so I can be on my way.'

'Horatio.'

Moll glanced at the hand he'd proffered. When she looked back, he was smiling openly; an even, unassuming smile without cunning or arrogance.

With an irritated sigh, she shook it roughly. 'Right, now, what is it you—?'

'And yours?'

'Look, just tell me what—'

'Not until you tell me. Come on, Christ Almighty. It don't take that much deciding,' he added in mild amusement when she rolled her eyes. 'It's your name I'm asking over, not your hand in marriage!'

At this, she reddened to the roots of her hair without knowing why.

'Well?'

'Moll. My bloody name's Moll, all right? Satisfied?'

'Hm.' He pulled a face. 'I don't much care for that: Moll.'

As her eyebrows rose, her mouth did the opposite, dropping in an indignant O. 'Why, what's wrong with it?' she demanded, sounding, she realised to her chagrin, hurt.

'Moll was my mam's name,' he said.

'Was? You talk as though she's dead.'

'She is. She died when I were three. Bloody upped and left me, she did, and that were that.'

Moll shook her head in confusion. 'What are you talking about? Mrs Simcox—'

'Is my aunt.'

'But . . . the swine about to give me the belt that day; you said he was your brother.'

'Nay, *you* said he was my brother. I just didn't correct you.'

Something like relief passed through her. Then perhaps she'd been wrong to assume they were all of the same ilk? she wondered, yet didn't know why she should care either way. Mind, he mightn't be of their immediate brood but he was still family, her next thought whispered. The selfsame blood runs through him. And it was rotten to the core, must be, for hadn't she seen and heard enough proof? The drunken father, feckless mother, dangerous son – and God knew how many more there were, *how* they were, if the stinking mound of humans she'd witnessed in their home was anything to go by.

'They're a bad lot,' said Horatio now, as though seeing into her mind. 'When my father died, his sister took me in. I'd have finished up in the workhouse otherwise. I often think I'd have fared better, an' all.'

'Why are you telling me all this?'

'Because I need you to know . . .' He paused to sigh. 'I'm not like them.'

'Oh really!'

'Aye.' A hard edge entered his tone at her scathing reply. He stepped towards her. 'D'you know how much cajoling it took persuading my aunt and uncle to let *me* talk you into seeing sense?'

'Seeing sense?' Her anger was building; now, she stepped towards him. 'And talk – like youse already have with Mr Evans' neighbours? Aye, yeah, I'm sure talking were all that passed! Threatened them, you have, into keeping their gobs shut. But I'll tell you summat, you'll not bend me as easy. Youse lot don't frighten me.'

'For your own good . . . Let it go.'

'Tripe! Now, if you don't mind . . .' She made to brush past and gasped when he took her arms and pulled her against him. 'Leave go!'

'Listen to me.' Horatio shook her none too gently, his tone as harsh as his grip. But his eyes didn't seem to match the situation. No anger lay in their depths; they shone with what she could only describe as worry. Worry for her. 'There's no low they'll not stoop to to protect their

119

little Sammy.' The words dripped with scorn for the cousin he clearly loathed. 'As for that divil hisself . . .' His hold on her slipped into one that was almost tender. 'Please, Moll.'

Had she moved her head a mere few inches, their lips would have touched, so close was he. Something warm, safe, burst through her and tears welled up.

'But I must. I must, for my brother's about to go the same way with the Tigers, I know it.' She nodded when Horatio cursed under his breath. 'Now d'you see? They'll not leave my Bo be and it terrifies me. I've done nothing but eat, breathe and sleep gangs, lately, we all have, and I'm bone-weary of it. As Mr Evans said, scut-tlers is scuttlers – happen if I do this, make a stand, others will. Others *should*, they *should*.' Moll was sob-bing, now, something she'd never done in public, yet oddly, knew no embarrassment – and in front of him, too. '*Someone* must do *something*.'

Horatio's eyes traced every part of her face, lingering over her mouth, and moving up, up, to lock with her own. Neither spoke; they simply stared at one another a while. When his arms went around her and drew her to him, it was like the thousandth time. That this – he – felt familiar, she didn't question at this moment. She laid her head against his broad chest.

'I'm not like them,' he repeated and now, without hesitation, she nodded. 'I'll help you. You have my word. But you must trust me.' His heart beat faster beneath her cheek. 'D'you trust me, Moll?'

And her response, again without a second's thought. 'I trust you.'

'She did *what*?' Bo's spoon clanged loudly against his tin bowl.

'Now d'you understand my fears, lad? They're lunatics, the lot.' Moll fingered her cut cheek which Bo, at her reluctance to say how it happened, had demanded to know about.

'What occurred? Tell me.'

Remembering his conversation with Uriah, dread that this might prod him into joining the Tigers' ranks, to protect her, had her shaking her head. 'Lad, it were nowt, really. Anyroad, I gave as good as I got. I'll have no further bother from that quarter.'

His face relaxed a fraction. 'You sure? Badgering me is one thing: I'll not have them troubling you. You've only to say the word and I'll—'

'Nay. Leave it, lad. I can take care of myself, don't you fret about that,' she added with, she hoped, a convincing laugh. 'Come on, you'd best get a shift on afore you're late.'

Throughout this, their mother had looked on from her seat by the fire, saying nothing. When Bo left, she joined Moll at the table. Steepling her fingers, she stared at her elder daughter.

'Sissy, lass, you be gentle with him.' Avoiding Ruth's gaze, Moll nodded to the girl sitting cross-legged by the hearth rocking the kitten, a bonny black and ginger-speckled thing. 'He's just a babby, remember?'

'Is he, Moll?'

'Aye. You promised Mrs Coombes you'd look after him.'

'I'll look after him. Moll? Moll?'

'Aye?'

'I'll look after him, Moll.'

'Sissy's all right.' Ruth folded her arms. 'So, what's—?'

'Oh aye, I know she'd not harm him,' Moll said quickly before the conversation swung in the direction

121

she knew it was taking. 'I'm just saying, it were reet kind of Mrs Coombes to give us the pick—'

'Stuff Edna Coombes a minute.'

Moll glanced away, sighed, then took a sip of her tea. 'What's afoot? Who created that there mark?'

'A girl. We had a set-to; it's daft, really.'

'Is Bo in some manner of trouble?'

She felt a tinge of hurt, realising Mam's concern was for her brother. Mind, what was new there? It had always been that way, hadn't it?

'Lass?'

'Bo didn't want you fretting. Some lads have been pestering him, scuttler lads, but he's told them he wants no truck with them.' She gestured to her cheek. 'I gave the main lad's girl a tongue whipping and . . .'

'What, the alley cat clawed your face?'

Playing it down, Moll nodded.

'Eeh, I don't know. You're allus getting yourself in some scrape or t' other, you are. Happen you'll calm down some day, eh?' Ruth lifted the pot to check its contents then replaced it with a sigh. 'There's the last of the tea, then.'

Moll watched her cross to the window overlooking the tiny paved yard. She was restless again, Moll saw with a dull stirring of dread; Ruth was plucking at her lips agitatedly and her nails were bitten to the quick. 'Mam?'

'Hm?'

'We'll manage, Mam.'

She didn't respond and Moll's foreboding intensified. Her mother wanted a drink. It was how she'd always dealt with times of worry, a false shield of sorts. Without it, now particularly, she was struggling.

But you're doing so well. Don't cave, she silently beseeched Ruth's stiff back. *Summat will turn up. It allus does.*

122

They were feeling Davy's absence, that was the truth of it. However much admitting it stuck in Moll's gall, his provisions were missed. Damn him, they were.

Bo's low wage and her earnings from her potatoes, now her sole income, barely covered the rent. Feeding, clothing and keeping warm four people besides was a near impossible task. The realisation was tempting Mam to ways of old. How they would cope if she returned to wasting their precious little brass on the bottle, Moll dreaded to imagine.

'Fancy the butcher going snuffing it like that,' Ruth said now through the chewing of her thumbnail. 'I were all set to ask for my position back, an' all. Just our luck, eh? What am I good for, now, I'd like to know? I'm fit for nowt but scrubbing, know nowt else, and ain't strong enough at present to take in washing. It's the workhouse we'll finish up,' she added, tone thin with fear. 'Holy Mother, that it's come to this!'

'The mills are allus taking on— I know, I know,' Moll said quickly when Ruth spun around to face her, 'but times are desperate, Mam—'

'Never! I've told you aplenty, no child of mine will ever see the inside of a mill. Them places of death cut down my dear mam. Ruined her poor lungs them cotton spores did. They're the divil's own structures. I'll not have it.'

'Then what—?'

'Anyroad, you'd not last a day the way you are.' Ruth's voice had hardened, and Moll had to bite her lip to stop herself retaliating.

Letting her vent made for a peaceful life. Mam couldn't take her frustrations out on Sissy, her being feeble-minded, and Bo . . . well, Bo was her lad, wasn't he? That left Moll, and afterwards, Ruth showed her

123

remorse in small gestures: a tender stroke of her hair while passing her chair, or that gentle smile beneath sorry eyes. She needed the outlet, to release the pressure. So long as Moll remained silent during the melancholy tirades, all was soon well again. A small price to keep her gin-free was how Moll saw it.

'Moods as black as a pitman's boots. Allus been the same, you have. A fella,' Ruth said suddenly, nodding, 'that's what you're short of, my lass. Someone strong-willed to quell that hot temper of yourn.'

Indignant colour raced to Moll's face.

'Ah! I reckon I've hit on summat.'

'Don't talk daft, Mam.'

'It's not that scrawny piece what's shadowed our lad since they were knee high, is it? Davy used to say—'

'That wastrel said plenty but none true.' That Mam had spoken disparagingly of Uriah was low enough. That she'd brought *his* name up was more than Moll could stand. She put down her mug none too gently and scraped back her chair.

'Where you going?'

'Out.'

'Out where?'

'To secure another position. Mr Evans is dead, remember; that means we're six shillings a week down. Summat must be done.' Someone has to support this family, she added to herself.

'Eeh, lass, come on. I were only teasing about a fella.'

Moll paused in the doorway. 'Good, for you're wrong,' she said without turning. 'I don't need a man. We're not all like you.' She strode out, slamming the door.

She'd barely gone several steps, however, when contrition had her covering her face with her hands. She shouldn't have said that. It was a spiteful shot. Why couldn't she control this tongue?

The answer, in this instance at least, made her bite her lip. Mam *had* hit on something – or had she? Moll wasn't sure, herself. One thing, however, she was now certain of: it didn't involve Uriah Croft.

She'd laid her head against his chest. Dear God, what had she been thinking? she asked herself, as she had a hundred times since. She'd cried in front of him, poured out her fears, told him she trusted him, wondered what it would be like to kiss him; aye, she had. She'd wanted to press her lips to his – right there in the street!

Had Horatio bewitched her? Moll seriously suspected it. After all, she hadn't sought a constable; instead, she did as he asked. She'd watched him disappear into the night then retraced her steps back to Blossom Street without giving the police station a backward glance.

Along with those who witnessed Mr Evans' death, she'd kept her silence and within days, some different soul or other was on folks' gossiping lips. The butcher's only relative, a distant cousin, had wasted no time putting the business up for sale and now it was as if he'd never existed.

'A tragic incident, but if it was his turn to go . . . Aye, you never know when your time's up. He was no spring chicken, was he . . . ? In any event, it was bound to occur some time . . .'

Moll had turned deaf ears to the wagging tongues. And she'd done so for Horatio. *All* she'd done since seemed for him. Every action, thought, every breath. He'd consumed her and she hated herself for allowing him.

Now, as always when passing his street, she settled her

gaze on number nine's sad-coloured door. As usual, he wasn't to be seen.

He said he'd help her. How? Did she even want it? She could answer neither question, and happen she didn't need to. Perhaps he'd just used her to protect his family. It was a possibility, she knew, and the prospect had her guts twisting in sadness. She'd no right to these emotions, this she knew also, but here they were anyway. And she had the strongest suspicion they were here to stay. The very idea was madness.

With a small sigh, Moll pushed all thoughts of Horatio from her mind and looked about. Cotton mills and factories dominated the city. Everywhere, their chimneys choked the sky, like black fingers reaching to throttle the angels in heaven with their sulphurous breath. Enquiring was pointless; Mam would have a blue fit were Moll fortunate to gain employment at one. Thoughts of the strife it would cause set her feet moving again and she headed towards Oldham Road where it was busiest.

In the distance slouched a pewter expanse: Manchester's, if not Britain's, worst slum. It boasted the ridiculously unfitting name Angel Meadow – imprisonment in its deadly jaws was as close to hell as a body could get. Many residents, a large fraction Irish poor, toiled at Smithfield Market. Others worked similarly honest trades, but mostly thieves, bullies, prostitutes and worse clogged every inch. The Meadow folk were rough, tough and not to be crossed.

A sea of narrow courts and alleys ran off into dark pockets at every turn and Moll was careful to keep to the main street. Unless a body knew these labyrinths like the back of their hand, they would be swallowed in a heartbeat. God help any stranger who wandered in.

126

Rag-covered shadows, barefoot and savage-eyed, would be on you in seconds. You'd leave without a scrap to your back and count yourself fortunate.

Horse-drawn vehicles of every size and description, from small carts piled with produce to hansoms, and heaving omnibuses, their crammed-in passengers clinging on for dear life, filled the streets and she chose her steps wisely. A lapse in concentration amidst the chaos of thundering hooves and cast-iron-rimmed wheels meant taking your life in your hands. A constant stream of yells warning folk to make way rang above the general noise; the disordered air was deafening.

Moll enquired at every small business she passed: haberdasheries and drapers, cobblers, confectioners and bakers, druggists, even a solicitor's office, to be told each time, with varying degrees of politeness, that they already employed a scrubbing woman. The few decrepit cellar and garret workshops, which hid behind the respectable veneer of fine linen shirt, corset and shawl makers yet were but glorified sweatshops, she bypassed. Both Jilly and Polly had toiled in such places as lasses and even now, when recalling the appalling conditions and treatment, the pain of their remembrance was tangible.

As she'd passed one where the door was ajar, what Moll glimpsed of the evil-smelling hole had brought tears to her eyes. She'd truly understood, then, her friends' meaning. A dozen or more stunted beings of indeterminate age squatted before a long, low bench. Their raw fingers and squinting eyes, ruined from toiling in bad light – sometimes up to eighteen hours a day – had been fixed in dead trances on piles of snowy material. Heart aching, she'd shaken her head and hurried on.

She walked for what seemed hours. Eyes flitting sky-ward to a cluster of jutting mill chimneys, she was contemplating going behind her mother's back when a screech made her peer down a side street.

A very small and very fat woman, shiny black curls hugging a red face, stood on the back step of an inn, a battered stew pot in each hand. 'Aye, go on! Slatternous swine, you're nowt else! Frickened of work, that's your trouble.'

'Oh, give that fat gob of yourn a rest. Morning, noon and night I've had it these past months; aye, no more!' an unseen female retorted. 'Good bloody riddance!'

Moll smothered a chuckle with her shawl as the fat woman leapt from the step with surprising agility and took off in pursuit in a wobbling run, squawking curses and shaking the pots in her beefy fists. Within seconds, however, she'd bent double and between coughs and angry mutters, sucked huge gulps of air.

The meaning of what she'd witnessed hit Moll. She pinched her lips in contemplation. This woman had just let her employee go; a position had opened. Wasn't it just the opportunity she'd been seeking? But a serving girl . . . ? Her shoulders drooped at the prospect. She could think of nothing worse than working amongst drunkards – and folk around here were as low and bad as they came. She'd suffered enough of that her whole life beneath her own roof, thank you very much. *But think of the brass,* her inner voice insisted and she hesitated, pulling her lips raw with indecision.

'Ay! Young bugger, that hurt! Fancy deciding you're ready now; today of all days when I'm up to my ruddy nose holes in work and wastrels.'

Frowning, Moll glanced around, seeing no one the woman could be addressing – until she followed her gaze. Her mouth fell open.

128

The woman shot a disgruntled look at the liquid that had gushed from beneath her skirts. 'Troublesome swine this 'un shall be by the look of things. Just like its bloody father.' Amusement in the statement matched her hovering smile but this vanished when Moll stepped forward.

''Ere, where did you spring from?' She eyed her evenly. 'You all right, lass?'

Moll nodded. 'I am, aye. Are you?' She indicated the woman's wet clothing. 'I didn't realise . . . Should I fetch help, missis?' To her surprise, the answer was a roar of laughter.

'Didn't realise my condition for all the extra fat, you mean?'

'I . . . Nay, I just . . .'

'Face on thee, young 'un! Don't take on so, I'm only having you on.'

The hint of an Irish twang lay behind the words and despite her brashness, the woman possessed the warmest, most honest eyes Moll had ever seen. She grinned sheepishly. 'Sorry.'

'Don't be! I like my grub, lass, and that's that!' Flashing wide teeth in an easy smile, she cocked her head to the inn door. 'Twit? Pour me a whisky, will you, lovey?' She banged a stew pot against the sooty bricks, shattering the silence that greeted her. 'Twit, d'you hear?'

Moll had to resist covering ears now ringing from the booming voice. 'Twit?' she asked.

'Aye, my 'usband.' The woman dumped the pots by the step, winced and pressed the small of her back. ''Ere, lass, give me the lend of your arm. Daft swine in there . . . Going deaf, he is, I'm sure.'

Moll could well understand why. Hiding a smile, she tucked the podgy arm in the crook of hers and helped the groaning woman inside.

'Through here, lass. Ay, you took your time!' she added when a man barely taller than herself emerged from the vault. 'Fetch us a whisky, lad. Bleedin' babby's on its way.'

The smile he bestowed on his wife shone as brightly as his balding head. 'Now don't you fret, pudding. Owd Twit will see to everything. Let's get thee up them stairs and settled.'

'The kiddies?'

'I'll fetch them down, find summat to keep them occupied, like. Come on, now, come on.' He draped her arm around his neck and, supporting her, herded her towards the stairs. 'You there,' he said almost as an afterthought, addressing Moll, 'give next door's a knock, will thee, inform Mother Blackmore we require her services? There's a good lass.'

'I . . . aye, course.'

The pain-racked woman's 'Eeh, my bleedin' back!' mingled with Twit's soothing assurances that the whisky was on its way followed Moll out.

Looking to the houses either side, she realised he hadn't specified which. She made for the left and on her second knock, the door opened and a craggy face framed by frizzy grey hair poked through. 'Mother Blackmore?'

'That's me.'

'I've been told to collect you. Mrs . . . Mrs . . .' Moll opened and closed her mouth – she didn't know the name!

'Twit the innkeeper's wife? Have her pains begun?'

'Aye,' she affirmed, relieved, then swallowing a giggle: 'That's what she called him: Twit. It's not his proper name, surely?'

The ancient-looking woman shrugged. 'Ain't never

130

heard tell of another. Now, we'd best make haste. Them babbies of hers don't play silly beggars, let me tell you. I'll not be surprised if it arrives afore me.' Pulling the door shut, she took Moll's arm and they hurried off.

They met Twit on his way back upstairs carrying a glass half filled with amber liquid. Mother Blackmore followed, and Moll was left alone in the dim passage. She remained a minute or two, unsure what to do, and was about to slip away when footsteps descended the stairs. 'Mr . . . Twit? I'll be on my way, now.'

'Hold up, lass.' He stood aside and Moll watched, amazed, one, two, three . . . eight, nine, ten . . . eleven children appear in his wake, the youngest, hair the same carroty shade as the rest, including their father's curly clumps over his ears, in the tallest child's clutches. 'Go through thcrc, my dcars, and sit quiet, like. Owd Twit'll be through shortly. Now Benny, mind what that young 'un's about; don't let him pull your sister's hair. Look, he's a chunk wound around his fingers . . . Oh, go on, go on, sort it in there.'

Twit shooed them through a door then bestowed a beaming smile on Moll. 'Did you ever see, in all your born days, a finer stock than mine, lass? The new babby, that'll make twelve kiddies – and norra single loss betwixt! Have you ever heard the like? Proudest fella this side of the Irwell, that makes me. Aye, proud.'

Here was a good man, good couple, a happy family, she thought. The very walls were as though soaked in love. She returned his smile then motioned to the ceiling. 'How is your wife?'

'Gradely, gradely. Not be long, now. Talking of my Beattie, she's asked me to enquire of you: can you cook?'

A frown touched Moll's brow. 'Cook?'

131

'Aye, you know; broths, stews, tattie pie and the like.'

'I can. Does she want me to throw a meal together for youse? I don't mind,' Moll assured him when he shook his head. 'She can't very well be on her feet, anyroad not today at least, and you have to eat.'

'Ay, lass, you're a good 'un, kind-minded to match. But nay, 'tain't that. How would you fancy working here?'

'Oh. Oh, I . . . ? Cooking, like?'

'Aye. For t' customers.'

Excitement flooded through her. Cooking! Fancy her landing such a position. Cooking as a job, like a proper cook in a fancy house! No skivvying with a brush scrubbing floors ever again or ruining her lungs to death in a filthy mill! 'Eeh, I'd like that ever so, sir!'

'That's good, for I don't believe we'll see the last 'un again.' He chuckled and with a pained expression covered his ears, indicating he'd heard well the ruckus earlier, and Moll laughed. 'Beattie will be that pleased, aye. Right, then. Come, kitchen's this way.'

She followed him through a dark-painted door – and stopped dead in her tracks. 'Mother of God . . .'

'Aye.' He nodded slowly. 'I were about to mention that.'

Moll's horrified gaze went around the room slowly, taking in every filthy inch. Piles upon piles of dirty pans and pots teetered by the stone sink, itself filled to the brim with something brown; what, she didn't want to guess. The floor felt sticky beneath her boots, the walls and even the ceiling stained with food splatters in varying shades of decay. And everything, *everything*, held a sheen of old grease; and God above, what was that smell?

Covering her nose with her sleeve, she stepped further

inside. A quick glance at the range showed, unsurprisingly, it befitted the rest of the room with its mound of dead ashes long spilled from the grate, sitting like a fat grey cat on the hearth. The rubbish and crockery-strewn table; the grimy, mould-speckled window . . . The horror of it was too much, she couldn't bear it another second.

''Tain't so bad,' Twit said unconvincingly, having followed her back to the passage. 'A little elbow grease—'

'Elbow grease? A lighted match is what it needs! Lord, the *filth*. How did it get to that state?'

'Last wench what left today. Quite particular, she were, about us going in her kitchen, as she deemed it – now we know why. And we never had reason to, for she'd fetch the meals to the customers' tables herself, and Beattie sees to our needs in our private quarters upstairs.'

'But surely . . . you, your wife, must have noticed . . . ? I mean, the smell alone . . .'

'Aye,' he admitted, 'and Beattie warned her to buck her ideas else she'd be out. The brazen piece said if we were that mithered then to clean it ourselfs, for she were paid to cook not scrub – did you ever hear the like! – and well, busy dawn till night, what with customers and the kiddies . . .' He gave a weak shrug. 'And my Beattie's a delicate soul; tires easy, she does. Brings on one of her funny turns, aye, the thought.'

Moll bit back a retort. That woman upstairs delicate? She'd have laughed at such an utterly unfitting description if she hadn't been so angry. And angry she was, for they clearly believed she'd willingly oblige! She should have known this opportunity was too good to be true. She should have bloody known!

'I'm buggered if I know how the customers ain't come down with every manner of disease, the state of it,' Twit

133

said laughingly, now, but when her face remained stony, the grin melted. He cleared his throat. 'Aye, well. I'll leave you to it.'

'Hold on a minute! You don't expect me to clean that . . . that . . . I don't even have words to describe it!'

'That's up to you, lass.' He pointed ahead. 'That there's the door you need if frightened of a little hard work. If not, mind, which I suspect, healthy strong girl like you . . .' He nodded to the dark door behind her. 'Choice is yours, lass.'

'But Mr Twit—!'

'No mister; just plain owd Twit'll do. Well, I'd best get in to them kiddies afore they cause holy hell.' He threw her a warm smile, nodded once, then left.

As silence settled around her, Moll's shoulders drooped. What choice had she? None, that's what. They needed the brass. Afraid of hard work? Huh! She'd never known anything *but*. Yet God above, that room . . . !

She allowed herself a petulant stamp of the foot. Then dragging up her sleeves, she forced herself back to the kitchen.

After hanging up her shawl, Moll stared around for a moment then, nodding determinedly, headed for the fire. This room required water, boiling at that – she'd scorch the filth from it! Her first task was to light the fire.

She collected fresh water, found a half-clean brush and rags, and after sweeping the ashes and spending the best part of an hour scrubbing away what seemed years' worth of food bits, meat juices and general grime, she changed the water and gave everything a good wiping.

She spotted some blacklead behind a huge teapot atop the wide mantel and afterwards nodded, satisfied with her efforts. A wooden box by the back wall, she discovered, held a fair supply of kindling and coal; in no time, flames were dancing nicely. She then filled with water and dragged on to the heat a mammoth cooking pot and while it boiled, allowed herself a sit-down.

Two days, maybe three, she surmised, looking around. However long it took getting this room in order, she'd do it. Determination had sparked in her, on seeing the fire's pleasing results and she realised she looked forward to the challenge.

She'd just risen to tend to the bubbling pot when the door opened and Twit appeared with his ready smile. 'You're still with us, then? Good lass! I knew you had it in you.'

Moll pulled a wry face. 'How's Beattie faring? Not much noise has reached me from upstairs. The babby . . . ?'

'My Beattie don't make a fuss with the bearing. She were delivered of a lass not half-hour since.' His eyes dimmed slightly. 'Bit sickly-looking, like, but glory be to God . . . She's bright-eyed and her appetite's healthy, anyroad. Seems the plucky sort, you know?'

Sensing his masked worry, Moll smiled reassuringly. 'That's good. Congratulations, sir, and pass on my best wishes to your wife.'

'I will, lass.' His eyes moved to the fire. 'What you knocked up, then?' He sniffed then frowned. 'Some style of broth, is it?'

'That's just water to clean, like.'

'Eh? My customers can't eat that, lass. Ain't you planned up a meal or two? Lord above!'

'I didn't . . . hadn't thought . . . The place needs cleaning and—'

'All right, all right, lass.' Twit scratched his baldness in contemplation. ''Ere's what you'll do. Clear the table, there, for now and get started on some veg. You'll find what you need in, erm . . . well you'll sort summat, I'll be bound, clever lass like you. Do your cleaning betwixt, like, but the grub comes first. Being Saturday, all t' factories and the like shall fall silent shortly. Folk with wages burning holes in their pockets will swarm drinking rooms expecting a decent meal with their ale – mine included. All right? Good lass, good lass. Get started.'

When he left, Moll cleared and scoured the pine table, all the while glancing furtively towards the pantry dreading what further horrors she'd find. What she did discover was, surprisingly, a fairly clean space and well-stocked shelves. Back bacon and a leg of mutton lay on the marble slab and, tucked beneath, a wooden crate overflowing with fresh vegetables.

Some time later, when Twit popped his head back into the kitchen, she turned from where she was busy at the sink and his pleased smile brought one to her lips.

'Eeh. Smells good in here.'

Moll motioned across. 'Customers have the choice of mutton broth or turnip and tattie pie. I've prepared plenty but can allus fry some bacon up if need be. Will that do, sir?'

'I'd say so. And will tha drop the sir, lass, call me Twit like everyone else? 'Ere, d'you know, I've not asked on yours; what d'you go by, then?'

'Moll Chambers.'

'You've worked wonders in here already. I expect you'll welcome that the night.'

She followed his gaze to a palliasse propped against the far wall. 'Oh . . .'

'Just drag it before the fire, later. Blankets are about

somewhere; unless the last un's had them away with her belongings. Shout if you can't find them.'

'But I'll not need them. I've a home and family to get back to.'

'Oh, right. Last 'un slept in on occasion, you see, whenever her fella knocked her about. If you've ever the need of it, it's there, lass.'

'Ta, Twit.'

He returned to his duties and Moll followed suit with a small frown.

His offer had roused in her quiet relief. Because for reasons unknown, she'd the queerest feeling she might, some time, have need to take him up on it.

Chapter 11

TWICE, MOLL HAD been sick. A stinking chicken carcass, which she'd discovered in the sink, caused the first bout but after the waves of nausea subsided, she'd set to again with grim resolution.

'What make of female was that previous employee?' she'd mumbled as she worked. The questions turned to angry curses when she found herself leaning on the table, shaking from further retches that left her throat raw. She'd innocently lifted the teapot lid and, staring curiously at the gloopiness swimming inside, sniffed then poked a finger – into what she realised too late were globules of phlegm in the makeshift spittoon. She'd wring that woman's filthy neck should their paths ever cross, she would really!

The lamplighter had long since done his rounds when Moll headed home and she quickened her pace as rowdy voices carried on the wintry air. Despite her grubbiness and aching body, Twit's praises at what she'd achieved already, and those of the well-fed customers he'd passed on to her, had lifted her mood no end. She was relishing tomorrow's continued clean-up.

Spotting Jilly hovering by the cellar steps, Moll suddenly realised how long she'd been gone. She bit her lip. Mam would be worried sick; had she shared her concerns downstairs and Jilly was keeping lookout for her return?

It was thoughtless being absent this long without sending word of her whereabouts. Would Mam think she'd acted deliberately to hurt her? After all, they'd parted company on bad terms. Guilt stung. She'd make it up to her. She'd apologise for earlier and inform her of her new position – that would surely raise her spirits. She'd prove to Mam they could manage, the four of them, that they needed no one but each other.

'Lass, where have you been till this ungodly hour?'

'I know, I'm sorry. Time ran away with itself. I've a new position, Jilly, as a cook.' Moll couldn't contain a happy smile. 'Mam'll not believe our good fortune. Where is she, in yours?'

The old woman hesitated before shaking her head. 'But why not come down yourself for some tea? Happen you fancy a game of cards? It'll please Alf to see you, and you can tell us all about this new position. Cook, eh? Well! And where's this cooking to be done? Your new premises far?'

Jilly had taken her hand but as she made to lead her to the steps, Moll pulled back. A horrible feeling passed through her and after some seconds, she murmured, 'Summat's afoot. I'm right, ain't I, Jilly?' She closed her eyes. 'Lord help us, Mam's on the bottle again, ain't she?'

'Lass . . . Let me brew you a sup, calm your nerves . . .'

Moll extracted herself from Jilly's hold and her neighbour's shoulders sagged in defeat. 'Goodnight, Jilly,' she said flatly, turning for her own door.

'Aye, lass. All right.' A sad sigh accompanied the words. 'You know where I am. You've only to knock, love.'

Throat thick with crushing emotions, Moll could only nod.

'Ah! She's here, look! We were about to round up a search party, our Moll.'

Her mother's glassy eyes and loose smile as she waved the gin bottle towards her, and Bo's empty chair, Moll took in at a glance. Then her gaze swept to the left and she froze, insides twisting painfully. A roaring fire was a blessed sight to any soul in the land. But not to her, dear God not at this moment, for in their penniless state it meant but one thing . . .

Turning her head slowly, she swallowed hard at the sight of Davy Preston's grinning face.

'I've missed you.'

Moll closed her eyes as the soft mouth moved to hers.

'I can't get you from my thoughts. I dream about you, *ache* for you. Marry me, Moll Chambers.'

She shivered with pure joy. 'Aye, aye. Oh, kiss me.'

The lips duly dipped and her arms went around his neck. The swell of her breasts pressed against his chest and his tongue sought hers. She melted into him, moaning when his hand traced the length of her, lower, lower, and she arched her back to greet it. His touch found what it was seeking and she clung to him, waves of glorious sensation cascading through her . . .

'Go on, girl, that's it. You like that, don't you?'

The gruff words came as though through thick glass, swirled around Moll's brain then were lost in spurts of pleasure as his hot mouth closed around her nipple. Her hands moved to play in his hair and her eyelids fluttered. She blinked down at the dark head. She blinked again, again, again – then dragged in a gasp so sharp, it almost choked her. *Merciful God, no . . . !*

Davy's hand reached her mouth before her scream could. 'I'll tell you what, I had my doubts about you, thought you to be dried up afore you'd ripened, but nay. For all your uppity ways, you'd a fire all asmoulder inside thee, hadn't you? It just needed my dab hands to stoke the flames.'

'Davy, love? Is Moll for wakening? Tell her to shift herself; I'll not see good ham go to ruin.'

He glanced over his shoulder to the door. 'Aye, Ruth, I've roused her. I've done that, all right,' he added in a whisper to Moll. He nodded, winked, then strode from the room whistling.

For a full five minutes, Moll lay shaking as though in the grip of fever. Her chest hurt from her hammering heart, sickness and tears constricted her throat, her flesh burned from his touch. Yet the numbness upon awakening still held her and when she stood, it was as though on another's legs. Dressing, she had to screw her eyes to block out her disgusting, treacherous body. His hands. *His.* And she'd . . .

But you didn't know it was him! her mind screamed. *You were suspended in dream with . . .* Covering her flaming cheeks, she gulped in air. Oh, she was foul. She'd wanted to be touched, opened herself willingly, enjoyed it, *him . . .* How, *how*, would she get through this?

She'd tell Mam! Preston would spew out a denial but she couldn't let this slide, she couldn't. If she kept silent it would seem like she'd wanted him to. In reality, she wanted to scrub herself until the flags ran red.

'Tea there, lass,' said Ruth as Moll entered. 'Though it's likely marble-cold now.'

Davy's easy stare followed her to the table. The smacking of his lips as he sucked bacon grease from his fingers was like knives in her ears and guts. Knowing where

141

they had probed minutes before ... Bile rising, she pressed a hand to her mouth. His leering wink behind her mother's back, proof he was doing it deliberately, and all the while that cocksureness of his dancing behind his eyes, was too much. She stumbled past Ruth to heave up what felt like her soul into the backyard.

'Lass! You all right?' Ruth supported her back to her chair and Moll dropped into it, her breathing ragged.

'What's to do, then? You favour death warmed up. You sickening for summat?'

'Mam.' She struggled to pluck the words from her foggy mind. 'I . . . He . . .'

'As far as I know, there's normally but one reason lasses carry on like that of a morning.'

Their heads jerked round to Davy, who nodded. 'I'll tell you summat else, Ruth. You'd best hope for her sake she's not gorra bastard growing in her belly, for it'd not know its first breath, I tell you. And *she'd* not know many more, neither. I'll have no shameless whores beneath my roof!'

Moll gaped at him in furious disbelief – which gave way to pain in her heart at her mother's expression. 'Nay, Mam—'

'It's not true, is it?'

'That you're even *asking*?' To Moll's chagrin – she didn't want to give Davy the satisfaction – tears spilled down her cheeks. 'You think so little of me?' She dragged her gaze from Ruth's unsure one to direct a look that spat sheer loathing on the man opposite. 'You're filth, you're nowt else! *He's* the reason I were sick, Mam, him,' she almost screamed, 'for he touched me, just then when he came to waken me.'

'Bloody rot!'

Davy leapt up but she stood firm. Her revelation

shocked him; he'd likely believed shame would hold her tongue. 'All that's rotten around here is you, you foul bastard.'

A puce-coloured stain appeared on his jaw, where a muscle pulsated furiously. Moll thought he'd lunge at her but, to her surprise, he laughed.

Folding his arms, he cast Ruth a steady look. His tone matched it. 'If you wakened to some fella or other messing about your person, what would you do? What would *any* respectable lass do, tell me that?'

'I'd . . .' Her mother's ashen face creased. 'Scream blue murder.'

Davy nodded. 'Did you hear a peep from this one? Did she yell the place down, run hell for leather and throw herself on you, tell you I'd been at her? Nay. And shall I tell you why? For she's a bloody liar!'

'Mam, he *did*—!'

'Quiet.'

'But Mam—'

'I said enough!' Ruth scraped a hand across her mouth. The look in her eyes was like a physical force – Moll jolted as though it shoved her. 'As Davy said, you'd have kicked up hell. A new low, this is, my lass.'

'It's true! He had his hand over my mouth—'

'Nay, you'd have struggled. That inner fire of yourn . . . you'd have torn him limb from limb or died trying.'

'I couldn't, Mam! The shock, you see—'

'You've never taken to him – and why? From day one, you've wanted Davy out. And him what's saved us from certain destitution! Never would I believe I'd raise such an ingrate. Well, you've opened my eyes, Moll. If I hear another word against him from your vicious tongue, I'll swing for you! D'you hear me? Well, *do* you?'

If the world and his wife had taken a shot at her, it couldn't have hurt more than this from her mother. Her *mother*. Moll's chin fell to her chest. She closed her eyes. Rejection, disappointment: she was used to it all. But lately, she'd had, for the first time, a semblance of a proper mam, as other kiddies had. She'd liked it. And started to depend on it, aye, believing her mam had changed. She'd felt something blossom, a closeness her mother's selfishness hadn't enabled before. And now Mam had strangled to pulp weeks of slow nurturing, which Moll had grown to cherish, in seconds with a few words.

Aye, Mam had. For despite Davy's actions, his manipulation, he could only do what Mam allowed him. She alone was at fault, really. She was the wickedest of the two by a mile. Whether unwilling or too blind to see what he was doing, she was *letting* him. Oh, she was worse, all right.

'It's time you and that brother of yourn began acting your ages and not the spoilt pieces you have of late,' Ruth said now. 'I'm fed up with the pair of you.' She spread her arms wide. 'If Bo wants to nurse his pride around at that friend's of his, what can I do, I'd like to know? My Davy were all for apologising upon his return the other week; weren't you, love?' She gave him a sad smile when he nodded, then turned her cold stare back to Moll. 'Nay, but the lad wouldn't have it. Snatched up his jacket and had it away on his toes, stubborn swine. Don't youse want me to be happy, is that it? It must be, for I can think of no other reason for this behaviour.'

Moll was too empty for words. She simply stared, silent tears coursing down her face.

'Sissy shows more sense than you pair, lately, and that's saying summat.'

This awoke Moll and for the first time, she glanced to where her sister sat, knees pulled up to her chest, picking the wall's rotten plaster as if in her own world.

'Come here, my lass. Come to Davy.' He held out a hand and Sissy sloped over to his chair.

Moll tasted bile again as Davy lifted the girl into his lap and jiggled her up and down, making her laugh. After this morning . . . seeing those hands on her Sissy made her skin crawl. She made to shout to her sister to come to her but Ruth spoke again.

'See. Likes Davy, the lass does. You would – Bo, too – if you'd but swallow your ruddy pride.'

Moll was silent. Then: 'Never.'

The whisper drew Ruth up to her full height. Her dead eyes looked right through Moll. 'Never, is it?' she murmured. 'Well. You may as well know. Davy and me are to be wed. It's a new father you're getting and grateful you'll be, or you can turn around and get the bleedin' hell from my house.'

Moll was beyond emotion, doubted she'd feel again. Leaving those heart-crushing words in the air, and avoiding Davy's gaze, she crossed to Sissy.

'Where d'you think you're taking her, like? I've said it afore, I sometimes think you forget it's me what gave birth to her. Oh go on, go,' their mother relented with a weary flap of her hand. 'Whilst you're about your work today, you have a good think on what I've said, my lass. I'll see you both later.'

Taking her sister's hand, Moll pulled her gladly from Davy's knee and exited with what she knew was his smug smile at her back.

The sisters walked in silence until the turning to Henry Street. Pointing towards George Leigh Street, where Uriah and his younger brother had dwelled for

145

years with their grandfather following their parents' deaths, Sissy tugged at Moll's hand.

'See Bo? See him, Moll?'

Dragging her mind from the kitchen in Blossom Street to the present, she smiled down. 'He'll be at work, won't he? We might try later.'

'Later, Moll?'

'Aye, lass, mebbe.'

She'd seen Bo most days since Davy's return but still missed him terribly. The house didn't feel right without him. When she'd returned after securing her position at the inn to find Preston there, Bo had already left. And her brother was determined, so long as *he* remained, so he would at Uriah's. It was all such a mess.

Mam wouldn't marry Davy. She'd said that in the heat of the argument to hurt her, Moll was certain. But where would all this end? When? She couldn't just take off like Bo, couldn't leave Sissy with them – with him. How much longer she could bear the situation, however, she didn't know. And what next, after the fresh hell this morning?

She hadn't seen Polly all week and now ached for her warm hug. Since getting her new position, she'd given up hawking tatties. The working hours were much longer than when toiling for Mr Evans; continuing both jobs would have proven a strain, as would finding time to replenish her stock at market. She wouldn't miss standing in all weathers for coppers but did miss her friend's chats and sunny smiles. She also missed Bo's dinner-time visits. And she missed Uriah. He never failed to put a grin on her face with his teasing – something she could do with right now.

Not for the first time, she thanked the Almighty for Jilly. At the old woman's insistence, she and Sissy now

146

spent more time in her cellar than at home. That damp pit was paradise in comparison. Where would it end? she asked herself again.

With a shuddering breath, she pushed back her shoulders and walked on.

Beattie, puffing and red-faced from the short excursion to the door, answered Moll's knock with a surprised exclamation. 'Eeh, hello!' She ushered the girls in. 'And who's this bonny young thing, then?'

'Sissy, my sister. Do you or Twit mind? She'd be no trouble.'

Beattie hitched up the new baby clamped to her mountainous bare breast. 'Course we don't. My brood will keep her entertained.' She studied Sissy before asking, in the forthright way Moll had grown accustomed to, 'She dim-witted, like? I only ask so to warn my lot. They're boisterous beggars at times; poor lass, I don't want her getting hurt.'

Moll nodded. 'She'd like that, Beattie, ta. Few kiddies give her time of day around our way.'

'Cruel blighters. We pass judgement on no one beneath this roof. My lot will see her right. They're used to dealing with simpletons, what with having Twit as a father.' She laughed heartily and Moll couldn't help smiling. The large woman might say it how it was, but meant no harm.

The room Beattie now led the way to held no semblance to that Moll encountered last week; as usual, she experienced a warm glow upon entering. She'd scoured the place to within an inch of its life. Every surface gleamed and once the man whom Twit had promised to get in to whitewash the walls had finished, it would look better still. She'd had her doubts but it now felt like *her* room and she was proud of it.

After lighting the fire and making tea, she joined Sissy and Beattie at the table. 'I don't think I've known the place so quiet. Where's Twit, the children?'

'Well, you've not been here this early afore, have you?'

'Oh. Aye, sorry.'

'Nay, nowt wrong with showing willing. Elder children are out playing, the younger ones upstairs. Twit's having a lie-in, were up all sodding night with this one, bless him.' Beattie smiled affectionately at the pale child now asleep in the crook of her arm. 'You look short of a good kip, an' all, lass,' she added to Moll, eyeing the dark smudges beneath her eyes. She frowned. 'Summat afoot at home?'

'Nay. Well, aye. But it'll work itself out, no doubt.'

'Aye. Offer still stands, mind.' Beattie nodded to the wall.

Following her gaze to the palliasse, Moll bit her lip. Never had something half-rotten and sagging seemed so appealing. But she couldn't leave without Sissy. And Mam wouldn't let her take the girl. 'Ta, Beattie. As I said, matters will sort theirselfs.'

With a nod and a smile, the older woman hauled herself to her feet and held out a hand to Sissy. 'Come on, lass. I'll introduce you to my lot whilst Moll here gets the customers' grub prepared. Our Cathy's around your age and a gentle soul; you'll like her.' She led the hesitant girl out, saying over her shoulder as though reading Moll's thoughts, 'Don't fret, lass, they'll look after her. I'm for resting awhile afore the thirsty mob come banging. If you need owt, shout.'

Minutes later, children's laughter trickled through the ceiling and, donning her apron to prepare red herring at the scrubbed table for frying, Moll smiled. It

warmed her heart to hear. Sissy had seemed with-
drawn since Bo left. They would call by Uriah's before
heading home, she decided. Not only would it make
Sissy happy but she ached to see him, too. Also, it was a
good excuse to stay out longer – anything to postpone
the inevitable.

Lord, if he tries anything with me again . . . Moll's face
hardened. *The swine will know about it.* She nodded
grimly, imagining the fish she was gutting was Davy.

Throughout the busy day, a laughing Sissy burst several
times into the kitchen with Cathy, a small child with bouncing curls and large violet eyes, to give Moll a quick hug
before racing back upstairs to their games. At the shift's
end, Moll went in search of the children and found them
immersed in play with a pile of rag dolls, heads drawn
together, chattering like a pair of excited magpies.

Smiling, she watched from the doorway. Cathy indeed
seemed kind and patient, just what Sissy needed, and
Moll determined to ask Beattie if she could bring her sister again.

As Moll anticipated, Sissy was reluctant to leave her
new friend but the promise of visiting Bo placated her,
so she said goodbye and, minutes later, they were turning into George Leigh Street.

'This one, Moll? This one?' called Sissy skipping in
front, pointing to Uriah's door.

'That's right— Oh.' Moll's stomach dropped. Neither
lamp nor candlelight showed at the window; the house
was in darkness. 'Lass, it looks like they're either out or
they've already retired for the night. I know, I'm sorry,'
she added when Sissy's face fell, sharing the girl's disappointment entirely. 'We'll have to try another day.'

Sissy protested the length of the street and by the

time they reached their own, what with the impending doom of having to return home on top of her own yearning to see her brother, Moll was close to tears. Adding to her torment, she spied her mother and Davy, chatting and laughing, walking towards them holding hands.

'We wondered where you'd got to. Fancy keeping the lass out till this hour.'

Moll bristled at Davy's interference but ignored him, turning instead to Ruth. 'Where you going, Mam?'

As though earlier occurrences had never been, Ruth smiled her usual smile. 'We're away for a few drinks, lass. There's mutton broth warming by the hearth. Go on in; you're ruddy blue with cold the pair of you. See you later. Goodnight, Sissy love.'

'When will you be back?' asked Moll, not wanting to be up on their return.

'We'll not be long, lass.'

Looking directly at Moll, Davy laughed. 'That remains to be seen, eh, Ruth? You can't put a time on a celebration.'

Ruth giggled, eyes shining. 'Aye, aye. Suppose you're right, there.'

In the pit of her lurching stomach, Moll knew, she *knew*. Still, she had to ask: 'Mam? Celebration?'

'Remember, silly, we're to be wed?' She flashed a dazzling smile, took Davy's hand and walked away.

Moll watched until they were out of sight. Even after they had disappeared and the black street blanketed all in oppressive silence, still she stood.

Mam had been calm. She'd been smiling. She'd meant every word.

Moll had thought the earlier announcement but a drink-fuelled untruth, a jibe to hurt her. She and Davy were to be wed. It couldn't be. *It couldn't!*

150

'My lasses. Come in.' Answering Moll's frantic knocking, Jilly held her door wide. When Moll didn't enter, she held up the candle she carried. Studying her face, Jilly's welcoming smile vanished. 'Lass? Oh, what's—?'

'Jilly. Would you . . . ?'

Following Moll's gaze to Sissy, she nodded. 'Aye, I'll mind her. Moll love, what's occurred?'

'Ta, Jilly.'

Before Moll could turn, the old woman caught her arm. 'Hell's teeth, what's happened? Where you bound now?'

'Just a walk. I need to walk.' She sprinted up the cellar steps and down the street.

How long she ran for, Moll didn't know. Each pounding footstep had rung a mantra; left, right, left, right, blocking everything: *Get-ting mar-ried, get-ting mar-ried, get-ting mar-ried* – until she wanted to bash her temples with her bunched fists to kill the torment.

The shop doorway in which she'd slumped gasping, heart and lungs ablaze, she remained in for an age. Her breathing was steady and mind composed when the surprised voice calling her name carried across. She lifted her hand, returning the greeting, and when he reached her, smiled up. 'Hello.'

'Hello.'

Moll shuffled sideways and Uriah took a seat on the step beside her. Neither spoke for a while; they simply sat watching the busy Saturday night go by.

'Cowd, in't it?' he remarked.

'Aye.'

'I reckon there's snow in the air.'

'Aye, mebbe.'

Uriah turned his head to look at her. He nudged her shoulder with his. 'All right, Moll?'

151

Eyes still on the passing traffic and people, she nodded.

'Sure?'

'Aye. I'm all right.'

They lapsed into easy silence again. All around, folk young and old walked and ran, talked, laughed and argued their way about their business. Amber light spilled from windows of small inns and public houses, casting the cobblestones in a misty glow. The clip-clop of horses' hooves as they passed at a steady pace, tired from the day's toil, mingled with a thousand and one other sounds: the purr of conversation, voices throbbing in song and pounding notes from joannas' keys when doors opened; a dog's bark in the distance; a child's cry from a house followed by its mother's soothing humming.

'Mam's to be married.'

Uriah pushed back his cap, scratched his head, pulled it low again. 'Aye?'

For the first time, Moll looked at him. 'I called at yours earlier but it were in darkness.'

'My grandfather and brother were likely abed.'

'I figured as much.'

'Me and Bo went for a jaunt to the Star Hall with some foundry lads.'

She smiled. 'Any sound acts on?'

'The usual. The dancers and singers weren't up to much but the comic man weren't too shoddy. Mind, Bo left early, said he weren't in the mood.'

'Eeh.'

'Aye. I were heading home myself just now.'

Tears had thickened Moll's voice. 'How's he bearing up?'

'As well as can be expected, you know?'

'I should see how he is.'

Uriah shook his head as she made to rise. 'Leave him be the night, eh?'

'I miss him,' she whispered.

'Aye, I know.'

'How could Mam do this? How could she forget Father so soon? Everything's wrong, Uriah. It's all wrong.'

Slowly, his arm went around her and drew her to him and she rested her cheek against his shoulder.

Moll closed her eyes and sighed. His presence was like golden rays breaking through clouds on a grey day and she took strength from it. She could have stayed like this for ever. The emotions his touch would have evoked not long ago had her smiling softly. She'd thought herself in love, thought *him* in love with *her*. She smiled again. How queer that your eyes could open, that you could grow up in so short a time. It wouldn't be difficult for her to imagine this was Bo she sat with.

She snuggled into him and his hold tightened. When her breath fanned his neck, he quivered against her and she giggled.

'Sorry, did that tickle?'

He swallowed once, twice. 'Aye. Yeah.' Suddenly, he jumped up and held out his hands. She placed hers into them and he pulled her to her feet. 'Come on.'

'Where we going?'

'For a walk to Smithfield Market and what's more, sourpuss, you're going to enjoy it.'

'Oh, Uriah, nay. I'm not in the mood.'

'Then you'd best hurry and *get* in the mood, hadn't you? I'm determined to drag at least one smile from you the night if it kills me.'

'But . . . Sissy's with Jilly and—'

'The owd 'un will keep her a bit longer, won't she?

Right then,' he added when Moll shrugged. His face creased in a grin. 'Come on.'

They joked, laughed, chased and pushed each other playfully all the way and when they reached Shudehill and the vast, buzzing marketplace, Moll felt lighter hearted than she had in a long, long while. Gazing at the bull's head above the entrance to the meat stalls, the stone beast surveying all with a welcoming eye, she smiled happily.

The atmosphere inside added to the mood and looking around, her smile grew. Drawn like bees to summer blooms by the promise of knock-down foodstuffs, which stallholders had to get rid of at the week's end, not to mention the free entertainment the market afforded, young and old flocked each week in their thousands.

Tonight was no different. Mostly, housewives clustered around the gaslit stalls, which sold every manner of produce, searching for bargains. The fish and meat stalls especially were teeming; haggling and laughter-pricked banter rang from all quarters. The industrial town's youths, from courting couples to small and large groups, made up a heavy percentage of the heaving swell.

This weekend pursuit broke monotonous routines of work and want for a few glorious hours. Daily strife and struggles were forgotten once the poor stepped into Smithfield Market's warm embrace. The air seduced the senses with a million sounds and smells. Brightly dressed jugglers kept all ages entertained. Fiddlers scratched out lively ditties, rewarded by jigging crowds. Amongst others, sellers of pies, roasted chestnuts and pigs' trotters did a roaring trade. Hungry revellers needed feeding and feed they did, washing down everything with bitter and light ales, which served to add to their merriment.

Mostly, this place and all it stood for smelled of free-dom. And it smelled of fun. It was the perfect opportunity to meet, have a laugh and, if lucky, 'click off'. Little won-der it had such an insatiable pull.

Moll and Uriah swayed leisurely through the throng, pausing to admire enticing goods without much thought or reason. Neither had brass aplenty to fritter; it was simply being here that mattered.

'Ta, lad,' Moll said with feeling, later, as they stood devouring hot chitterlings in a less crowded nook by the market's edge. 'I didn't believe it but you were right. Tonight's just what I needed.'

Uriah smiled, then nodded to a group of young fac-tory hands in high jinks having themselves measured and weighed. 'I reckon I can stretch to a penny – shall we? Or we could try our luck at the amusement stalls?'

Before she could answer, bodies surged by, crushing her against Uriah; laughing, she clung to him to stop herself falling. When they passed, she grinned into his face. 'The rifle range, mebbe?' He simply stared at her, unblinking, and her smile slipped. 'What's wrong?'

'Nowt. Nowt. Come on then.'

'Ah, I see.'

He'd begun leading the way back through the stalls but turned at her words. A frown knotted his brows at her knowing nod. 'What? You see what?' he asked quietly.

'You're scared I'll hit more targets than you, aren't you?' His face relaxed and she giggled. 'Eeh, what you like! All right, I promise to let you win.'

Slowly, his mouth spread in a grin. 'Cheek. I could beat you with both eyes closed.'

'Oh, really?'

'Really!'

Suddenly, ahead, people screamed. Shrieks and yells assaulted the ears, followed by a deafening army of foot-steps. The noise from what was surely a hundred pairs of metal-tipped clogs was incredible. The whoosh of whizzing leather belts, which had the power to smash bones and tear flesh, cracked the air and chaos erupted.

'Moll, over here, quick!'

Struck dumb with horror and confusion, she could only stumble in Uriah's wake as he dragged her, duck-ing and weaving, through the panic-fuelled mass. He pulled her to her knees and hauled her beneath a vegetable-laden cart. She clung to him, gasping, as the stampede raged inches away and had to scream to be heard: 'What the hell's *happening*?'

'It's a scuttle. Stay still and keep your head down.'

'What? Why here?'

Scuttlers were methodical in planning battles, arranged venues and times sometimes weeks before-hand either by word of mouth or via chalked messages. Moreover, they usually took place on crofts – patches of vacant ground – away from eagle-eyed police. This wasn't ordered at all. It was bedlam.

'Why don't youse bugger off with what you're about and leave honest folk in peace!' shouted an elderly shop-per from the crowd, only for several scuttlers to round on her with their fists for her trouble. Their blood was up and nothing would defuse this.

'Two gangs must've run into each other by chance,' Uriah told Moll. ''Ere, I recognise him: Winters. It's the Bengal Tigers.'

'Aye. I recognise *him*, an' all.' She pointed to a figure standing by a cart groaning under the weight of cages packed with chickens. 'He's a member of the Prussia Street lot.' She recoiled as he wielded his belt above his head before smashing the heavy buckle end across an enemy's skull.

'Sammy Simcox.'

'Tha knows him?'

Uriah nodded. 'You may as well know. He's asked Bo to join.'

'*What?*'

'Aye. Seems now both sides mean to have him. According to Bo, Simcox had orders from his cousin to recruit him.'

Her mouth fell open but words failed her. *Horatio.*

She'd neither seen nor heard anything from him since their encounter outside the police station, had convinced herself he'd merely used her to get his family off. She'd told herself he wasn't worthy of her thoughts and, some of the time, managed to keep his memory at bay. Now, her heart banged as his image came to mind. He'd promised to help her. Was *this* his plan to get the Tigers off Bo's back – have his swine cousin cajole him into joining the Prussia gang instead? God above. The damn fool!

Simcox now looked decidedly worried. Winters and two others, alerted by the screams of the boy Simcox had just bludgeoned, had him surrounded, belts ready.

'Let's see what you've got then,' Winters snarled, winding the leather around his arm and hand.

Licking his lips, Simcox glanced about for backup but his members were engaged in battle elsewhere. The Tigers were heavier in number than his gang – he was on his own and he knew it. Then someone caught his attention beyond the cart Moll and Uriah crouched beneath and surprised relief passed over his face. He cupped his hands around his mouth but before he could shout assistance, Winters charged.

157

The brass buckle glinted in the light of a gas jet as it swung. With practised agility, Simcox dodged the onslaught then lunged, grabbing the belt. He wrestled Winters, trying to wrench it from him, and looking beyond the cart again, managed to yell, 'Rat! Rat Green! Over here!'

The Prussia Street gang's leader. Moll craned her neck for a curious glimpse of this lad who Bo, lying, said he hadn't heard of; who, from what she'd gathered, struck loathing and growing anxiety into every Tiger. As he rushed to Simcox, Winters and his associates blanched; judging by the reactions, his reputation was renowned. She soon discovered why. He had his broad back to her but she saw that within seconds the three Tiger members lay in a heap by his feet. Besides them knocking off his cap in the tussle, which had landed near the cart, it looked like he hadn't received a scratch.

Whooping, Simcox snatched Winters' belt from his hand as he lay prone – a trophy for any scuttler – and dashed back into the fray. Moll and Uriah shared simultaneous 'what the hell's wrong with these hooligans?' shakes of the heads.

Rat stood calmly, staring down with folded arms as though surveying his handiwork. Then on a long sigh, he turned and stooped to retrieve his cap.

'My God! *You?*'

At Moll's strangled cry, Rat Green's incredible eyes flicked beneath the cart. Something like shock mixed with regret touched his face but otherwise it remained stony.

'You? You're Rat Green?' She nodded incredulously. 'Ho*ratio* Green . . .'

'Moll—'

'Different. You're different, you said.'

158

A sudden blast of police whistles and the rattle of ricks for summoning assistance, cries of 'Move on there!' intermingled with scuttlers' 'It's the blue bags! Bash 'em! Bash 'em!' shattered the air but still Horatio's steady gaze stayed on Moll.

His brooding eyes and confident silence set her pulse racing. Images trickled through her mind of her dream about him that morning. And remembering Davy's actions, her *re*actions . . . She felt sickened to the core.

Pulling Uriah with her, she crawled out from beneath the cart. Hurt and humiliated tears burned behind her eyes. With what dignity she could muster, she stepped to where Horatio had risen and murmured, 'You disgust me . . . *Rat*. Stay away from me and stay away from my brother.'

Turning on her heel, she strode away.

Chapter 12

ARMS FOLDED, DAVY sat watching Ruth, appreciation clear in his dark eyes.

It was bitter out but cosy in the kitchen. The crackling fire and clock's soft ticking were soothing. Wispy snowflakes fluttered beyond the panes and upstairs, the Luchetti boys' sweet voices carried through in seasonal song. If only Bo was here and Preston wasn't, everything would be perfect, Moll thought longingly, adding another hoop to the paper chain she and Sissy were making.

From her fireside chair, plucking a plump goose for tomorrow's dinner, long skirts tucked around her bare feet, Ruth caught Davy's stare and smiled. 'All right, love?'

'Tha really is a beauty, Ruth.'

'Go on with you!'

His eyes deepened as she laughed. 'By, you are that. Norra man alive wouldn't give every copper coin he possessed for but a minute alone with you.'

Rather than be offended at the insinuation, as was Moll, Ruth heard only the compliment. She preened. 'You reckon?'

'Mam, for God's sake—'

'Ignore her, Ruth,' cut in Davy lightly. 'She's only jealous.'

Her mother frowned. "'Ere, nay. Don't say that. What reason has she to be jealous, bonny lass like her? Mind you, our Moll,' she added, snatching back the moment of motherly loyalty, 'it'd not hurt to smile once in a while. That regular sourpuss of yourn does you no favours. In't that right, Davy?'

He laughed as though vindicated, and Moll almost released an incredulous one of her own. What in God's name had she to smile about lately? Was Mam really so blind?

'Eeh, don't start, eh?' Ruth continued, catching her expression. 'It's Christmas the morrow. We've a healthy fire, a good dinner to look forward to and we've each other. I'd say we've plenty to be thankful for.'

Moll's amazement grew. 'And Bo? Or have you forgot about him? He'll have a reet ol' jolly, I'm sure, in a strange house without his kin around him.' She'd spoken quietly, eyes on the table, but now glanced up with a hollow sigh. 'How could you, Mam? How could you allow *him* to drive Bo away, your own son?'

Her mother rubbed her nose with her knuckles. 'I miss the lad summat awful.'

'He knows where to find us.'

Ruth looked to Davy and nodded. 'Aye, aye.'

'The promise to buck his ideas and an apology would see him back beside his own hearth. Now I can't say fairer.'

Moll gazed in disbelief at her mother, who lowered her head, then at Davy, hands spread wide as though he'd made some grand gesture. The absolute gall of this sod . . . 'Why the hell has *Bo* to apologise?'

'For upsetting your mother – my future wife,' he added slowly, deliberately, and Moll bristled. 'That bombastic pup has broken her heart; flouncing off like a bloody lass, I ask you! He'll change his ways or feel my wrath. And that goes for all of you.'

Don't just sit there picking at that bleedin' bird! Say something, anything! Don't you hear him, Mam? Moll implored in a silent scream. Suddenly, the corner caught her eye. She frowned, puzzled. 'Where's my barrow?'

Ruth, too, looked to the empty space. Her own brow creased. 'I don't know, lass—'

'I smashed it up earlier in the backyard,' announced Davy. He motioned to the flames leaping up the chimney. 'It were fit for nowt bar firewood, anyroad.'

'Oh, Davy, you never did? That were the child's own cart.'

'She ain't hawking no more, is she?'

'Nay, but—'

'Well then.'

Snippets of memory played behind Moll's tear-filled eyes. She saw her brother crouched on the flagstones outside, tongue poking in concentration, the pride on his face building with each cut and knock and hammer. She heard her gentle father praising his son's efforts. And she saw again Mam removing splinters from Bo's hands afterwards then dropping kisses on to the tender flesh. The mam whose attention was back on the goose in her lap.

True, the wheels had been wonky. It was a devil to shift and protruding nails had snagged Moll's already-patched skirts more times than she could recall. But that lump of old wood meant more than she could express because the lad had painstakingly created it just for her, out of love. How could Preston? How *could* he? He was blatantly destroying all she held dear and it didn't seem to matter a jot.

Knowing it was useless speaking out – Mam would

take his side as always – Moll gulped down her tears and crossed to the set of drawers by the door. She brought out a brown-paper-wrapped parcel, donned her shawl and slipped out.

'Moll.' Uriah, answering her knock minutes later, stood aside to let her into the cheerless room.

'Ta, lad.'

He glanced at her then resumed his seat, and Moll suppressed a sigh.

Outpourings of outraged horror had followed the onslaught at Smithfield Market. The damage and loss suffered by traders were shocking but amazingly, only half a dozen townsfolk were injured. The same was true of the perpetrators – despite the degree of violence in the dark pastime, few deaths resulted from scuttling. The aim was to scar the enemy, not murder.

Newspapers had covered the episode extensively. The handful of street Arabs, as the press termed them, unsuccessful in evading arrest, were handed, in the opinion of many, paltry sentences ranging from 'a drag' to 'a nine moon' – three months to nine months. As was commonplace, the unrepentant youths had whooped and laughed in the dock and as they were led to the cells beneath the courtroom they stamped their clogs in defiance, causing a considerable racket.

Upon release from prison, they would be met by crowds of their lads and girls and hailed as heroes; Moll had seen it all before. Their status risen, they would be only too ready to climb higher, whilst those lower in the pecking order eagerly awaited opportunity to emulate these gods.

Walking back that night, Uriah hadn't spoken except to ask Moll how she knew Rat. Lost in her emotions, she'd snapped at him to mind his own business and though regretting her harsh response later, it seemed the damage was done. She'd seen him twice since, when visiting Bo, and each time Uriah had uttered barely a word to her.

Who could blame him? she thought again now, passing his chair to embrace her brother. He'd gone out of his way to cheer her up and she'd repaid him by biting his head off. If not one thing, it was another. She was bone-weary of it.

'All right, Moll?'

She fixed a smile. 'Aye, lad. You?'

Bo nodded. 'How's . . . everyone?'

'Sissy's been like a bucking hare since wakening. I explained she'll find nowt till the morrow, but she's checked that sock a dozen times. I've not even hung it at the end of the bed yet, daft lass.' She chuckled and Bo smiled. 'Mam's . . . Well, she's Mam, you know?'

'Aye.'

Of course he knew. They all did. Mam was always Mam. That was the problem.

Has that Simcox one backed off? she itched to ask him, but knew it would raise questions. Bo hadn't mentioned the market's goings-on. It seemed Uriah hadn't told him they were present. It also meant he'd said nothing about her acquaintance with Horatio and she was grateful. She was guilty of nothing, she knew, but still . . .

Needless to say, she hadn't seen anything of Horatio – she couldn't bring herself to call him Rat. To think she'd trusted that swine, thought about him, *dreamed* of him . . . It made her guts lurch with shame and anger. He was one of those she despised. He was a scuttler. Still, she struggled to believe it. She'd been such a fool.

Half an hour of somewhat strained chit-chat later, Bo walked Moll to the door. No one made mention of him but still, Preston had hung over the meeting, choking the air like a poison. Uriah barely acknowledged her farewell and she suppressed another sigh.

'I don't know how you bear home, our Moll,' murmured Bo. Leaning against the door frame, he swept the street with dull eyes.

'What choice have I? I can't leave Sissy, can I? Especially now,' she added on a whisper without thinking.

'Why? What's he done?' His face slowly paled at her obvious struggle to think up a false explanation. 'Moll, has he *touched* you?'

'Why would you say that?' she almost yelled, shocked he'd guessed.

'Has he?'

Seeing his large fists bunch, she hastily shook her head. 'I meant with their drinking, that's all.' How could she tell him? She couldn't. To her relief, Bo's face relaxed. 'That's all,' she repeated soothingly.

'You think me selfish leaving you with them, him.'

Moll touched his arm. 'I never said that. I understand, I do. I just . . .' She swallowed hard. 'Eeh, but I do miss thee.'

His bottom lip trembled. He caught her in a crushing hug.

'I nearly forgot,' she said, wiping her nose on her hand when they drew apart. She brought the package from beneath her shawl. 'It's not much . . . Happy Christmas, lad.'

He went dull pink. 'Moll, I . . . didn't think, like . . .'

Flapping her hand, she brushed aside his apologies. 'Don't be daft. I don't want you spending your brass on me, anyroad. Go on, open it.'

''Ere, I nearly forgot to mention: I visited Father's grave this morning.'

'Oh?'

'There were fresh flowers.'

Her brow creased. 'Again?'

'Aye. And a message attached—'

'Saying sorry?'

He nodded. 'Did you . . . ?'

'Not me. I planned to go tomorrow. Besides, what have I to say sorry for? Nay, it's like on his birthday. Who could be leaving them, Bo?'

'Mam?' He smiled bitterly when Moll pulled a face. 'Perhaps not.'

'I asked her last time, anyroad. She were just as stumped.'

'Happen it's someone from the foundry?'

'They must have thought reet well of him to remember his birthday.'

'Or an old friend we didn't know of?'

'The note, though. Why are they sorry?'

'Happen it means they're sorry he's passed away?' Bo shrugged. 'I wouldn't worry about it.' As he tore off the last of the paper, his brows rose. 'Ay, our Moll.' He ran the soft woollen, slate-grey muffler that was revealed through his hands. 'Ta ever so.'

'It was new from Howell Brothers on St Mary's Gate; none of your second-hand market tat for you for once, my lad.' It had cost over half a week's wage but she'd been determined to treat him. He deserved it after all he'd been through these past weeks. 'Try it on, then. Oh aye, yes,' she added, nodding, when he wound it around his neck. 'A regular toff, I'm seeing, to be sure.'

Bo pulled a face, smiling, but it slipped when tears pooled in Moll's eyes. He reached for her hand and squeezed. 'Will I see you the morrow?'

'Aye. I'll fetch Sissy, too.'

'Good, good.'

'Bye, lad.'

'Bye, our Moll.'

She turned for work, swallowing pain all the way.

'Go see Bo, Moll? See Bo?'

'Later, lass.'

'Huh. That's the way of things, is it? Can't take the time to visit his own mother of a Christmas Day?'

Moll looked to Ruth, who was seeing to the bubbling pans at the fire. Despite the hour, already a gin slur carried on her words – or perhaps the copious quantity she'd consumed last night still lingered? She and Davy had drunk themselves into a stupor, leaving Moll to put an excited Sissy to bed, tidy up, prepare dinner for the following day and, when the girl eventually dropped off, fill her stocking with the nuts and fruit Moll had bought – Mam had forgotten.

Now, too weary to argue everything that was wrong with her mother's statement, Moll returned her attention to setting the table. Not that she cared how it looked or indeed about the whole, horrid day. But Sissy did, so she must make it as enjoyable for the lass as she could, she reminded herself again. If up to her, she'd have been anywhere in the world but here.

She and Sissy had visited their father's grave this morning. Bo had been right about the flowers – the note, also, was written in the same hand as before. The oddness of it made her head ache. Nonetheless, she'd have passed the day there if possible, had to drag herself back home.

Davy, who had gone for a walk in the crisp air to clear the ale fog from his head, returned as they were placing the last dishes on the clean tablecloth. He was in high spirits and after a sound kiss for Ruth, who giggled like a girl, her son's absence now seemingly unimportant, he set about with gusto sharpening the knife on a strap of leather. 'Sit down, then,' he instructed them cheerfully.

Along with her mother and Sissy, Moll obeyed but when he made to carve the golden bird, she stopped him. 'You can't yet. Jilly and Mr Sax—'

'They'll not be joining us the day.'

She blinked at her mother in confusion. 'They share Christmas dinner with us every year, allus have.'

'Aye, well, not this one,' Ruth snapped, holding up a hand when she made to protest further. Moll did, regardless.

'But, I don't . . . When? Why?'

'I informed them earlier when they returned from church. It's just family this year, I said.'

'Them what can be bothered showing, anyroad,' piped Davy.

Moll's temper rose to the fore. 'It's your doing why Bo's not here. Now you're driving the Saxes from our door? You didn't mind her mince pies, though, did you?' She jerked her head to the tin tray on the dresser, which Jilly had fetched in Moll's absence yesterday. 'Nay, you'll scoff her baking soon enough, you bare-cheeked—!'

'That's enough, Moll. It were my decision, not his.'

Eyes blazing with pure frustration, she swung her head towards her mother. 'You tell *me* enough? Why d'you allow him to *do* this, Mam?'

'You're hurting. I understand.'

She'd spoken with such tenderness, it momentarily threw Moll. 'What?'

'It gets easier, lass.'

168

'What are you talking about?'

Ruth flicked gentle eyes to the chair Davy sat in at the head of the table. 'It's your father you're missing, I know. The first Christmas without him's bound to sting. But lass, he ain't coming back and taking your grief out on Davy won't change matters.'

Moll shook her head slowly. 'You just don't get it, do you?'

'Robert Chambers were a fair husband and father, I grant you. But did you ever see the like with him?' Ruth motioned to the table, groaning under the weight of the goose, potatoes and vegetables. A floury loaf sat in the centre and there was even a plum pudding for afters. She then nodded to the pail by the hearth, filled to the rim with coal. 'We'd have none of this the day, nor each between, but for Davy. He's a sound provider and loves me. I need him, lass,' she finished meekly.

Despite pain from the accusation of her father's inadequacies, she knew quiet relief, too. Mam hadn't said she loved Davy back, just needed him, and that wasn't the same, was it?

Moll turned to Davy. Folding her arms, she frowned. 'What is it you do?' she asked evenly. 'As Mam said, Father's earnings only just kept the rain off our heads – after rent, little else remained. How is it you've brass aplenty to keep yourself, and us, as you do when you hardly shift from these rooms?'

'He lives by his own means,' Ruth answered for him. 'Saved for years, like. A good thing, too, with work so dry of late, for he's able to support hisself till a position presents itself.'

Moll directed her question to Davy, who was looking back calmly. 'Saved from what line of work?'

'This and that.'

169

'This and that?'

'Aye. Labouring and such.'

'Surely a labourer's wage couldn't keep a body for this length of time, however hard you saved?'

He shrugged, but his face had stiffened ever so slightly. 'I'm thrifty.'

Tension-charged silence descended as they stared at one another.

'That's enough talk, eh?' Ruth smiled at them brightly. 'Davy love, get that bird carved afore it shrivels. Moll, pass them plates across. Aye, you help her, Sissy, that's it.'

Suspicion twitched Moll's senses; she wasn't letting Preston off that lightly. However, a glance at Sissy quelled her intention to probe further. The girl, clearly picking up on the ill feeling still holding the table, was chewing her hair as she was wont to when upset, and the fight left Moll. Teasing the lock from Sissy's mouth, she smiled reassuringly.

'See Bo, Moll?'

'Soon, lass. 'Ere first, I'll take you to see Cathy, eh?' She'd asked Beattie last night if her sister could accompany her and she'd kindly consented.

Ruth looked across. 'They want you in today?'

'Only for an hour or two. Tw— Mr Thomas,' Moll amended quickly, 'he said there ain't much call for grub of a Christmas Day as most manage to scrape a dinner of sorts together. I said I'd just do a pan of broth or summat for those what ask.'

Nodding, Ruth turned back to her dinner and Moll hid a relieved sigh. When informing her of her new position, she'd said it was with Mr Thomas and his wife at a tavern several streets from Twit's. She'd surprised herself; the lie slipped from her without thought. Her reluctance to tell the truth, Moll knew, was due to fear of Mam dropping in worse for wear and causing a scene. She couldn't risk that. At work, she was free to be herself, just Moll, an average lass. Her mother and her home life were unknown to all beneath that roof. No one knew the reality and she wanted to keep it that way.

Moll found it impossible to enjoy dinner for worrying if Bo was eating properly – from what he'd hinted, meals at the Crofts' all-male household left a lot to be desired – not to mention how on earth her friends downstairs had managed at such cruel short notice, so she left the table gratefully. She cleaned Sissy up, tidied her hair then secured around her waist the ribbons of the pinafore she'd bought her for Christmas.

To Davy, Moll had given nothing. Therefore, the long-toothed, tortoiseshell hair slides she'd bought her mother sat untouched on the mantel. Ruth had refused them, proclaiming Davy's deliberate exclusion a mean trick she wanted no part in.

'Lass?'

Moll straightened the snowy material over Sissy's skirts and took her hand before answering her mother. 'Aye?'

'Tell Bo . . . I . . . You know.'

For her brother's sake alone, she nodded then guided her sister to the bitter-cold street.

After knocking at the Saxes' and getting no reply, Moll continued to work with a lighter heart. They must have found at the last minute another table to break bread at, she told herself, relieved. She'd call again later, apologise for what had occurred. After everything Jilly had done for them, how could Mam? She seemed a stranger these days.

The second she and Sissy entered the inn, ease

enveloped them. The place oozed togetherness and Moll knew fleeting envy. One day, when married, this was how her home would be, she vowed. Just exactly like this.

'Sissy!'

Cathy, pink-cheeked with pleasure, hurtled towards them and dragged the beaming girl off to play, and with the first genuine smile of the day, Moll headed for the kitchen.

An hour and a half later, Beattie shooed her from the cast-iron cooking pot simmering gently and helped her on with her shawl. 'We've kept you from kith and kin long enough, lass.'

Spiced beer wafted on the words but her bright eyes were focused. This was merely the result of a glass or two to celebrate the day. Here, drink was the exception rather than the rule. Again, envy pricked.

'You sure?'

Dark-leaved holly bunches adorned the passageway and Beattie swore when her dimpled elbow brushed one in the dimness. She rubbed it, grinning. 'Aye, go on. Enjoy what's left of Christ's day. Cathy, fetch Sissy down,' she added on a bawl upstairs. 'Where's that child at? *Cathy!*'

'It's all right,' Moll said over her ringing ears. 'I'll look.'

Shaking her head in amusement, she headed to the children's room. The girls' muffled voices carried beyond the door and as she turned the knob, Cathy's question reached her clearly:

'Shall we play the bad man game again, Sissy?'

'What was that?'

Both girls jumped. They put down their rag dolls, glanced at each other then back to Moll.

'The bad man game? Is that what you said, Cathy?'
She nodded.

'And how d'you play that?' Silence met Moll and she fought to keep her tone light. Sissy mentioned a bad man buying her sweets when Davy took her out that day. Moll had refrained from probing for fear of distressing her. Had she instead confided in her new friend? What was this business about and who was this 'bad man'? 'You can tell me, lass.' Again, silence – Cathy looked to Sissy as though for confirmation and, receiving none, lowered her head. 'Sissy?' Moll persisted. 'What—'

'See Bo? See Bo, Moll?'

She nodded slowly. 'We'll talk on t' way, eh? Say bye to Cathy.'

'Bye, Cathy.' Sissy obeyed then in her innocent way, added, in a loud whisper, 'Not tell, Cathy?'

Looking to Moll, the girl reddened. Then her violet eyes softened and she touched her friend's hand. 'Nay, Sissy. I'll not tell.' To Moll, she murmured, 'Terrible sorry. She made me promise.'

Moll had begun feeling sick with dread. 'I'll remedy it, don't fret,' she told her and led Sissy downstairs.

Passing through the early evening darkness, she went over questions in her mind to put to the girl, choosing each carefully so it wouldn't seem like an interrogation. However, they had got no further than fifty yards when thoughts of Sissy were momentarily banished – Moll recognised the voice before they reached the thin alleyway.

She stopped dead in her tracks. Holding a finger to her lips, she drew her sister to the wall then pressed her back against the bricks. Another voice, deeper than that she loathed, sounded. Heart hammering, she cocked her head to the alley's entrance.

'How long?'

'Soon. Few days – a week at most.'

'You're certain they'll comply without much of a ruckus?'

'They'll do as I bloody well bid. Have no fear of that.'

'Hm. I hope for your sake you're right. Yours, I believe?'

A jingling of coins floated through, then Davy's harsh hiss: 'What the bleedin' hell's this? Where's the rest?'

'You know the rules. You get the remainder on delivery and not afore.'

Moll's heart thumped harder. She *knew* Davy was dealing in something undesirable – how else could he always have ready brass when he barely left the house? Who was this other man? Delivery of what? What the devil was going on?

Davy muttered a curse then clogs struck the cobbles as they walked away. Easing forward, Moll glanced down the alley. She could just make out the retreating men's outlines through the gloom.

'The young 'un: she's ripe?'

This, from the stranger before they disappeared, made Moll's blood run cold. Davy's answer, however, had the power to turn it to ice:

'Aye, is she. Proved it to me herself but a few weeks past.'

A crude quip and leering laughter accompanied their departure, then all was silent.

Moll stood rooted to the spot, breaths escaping in small bursts, mind spinning.

Who . . . ? What . . . ? *What?*

'Davy, Moll?'

It was a moment before her eyes focused on Sissy. 'Aye.' Her voice sounded odd to her own ears.

174

'Not want no sweets, Moll. Moll, Sissy not want none.'

A slow frown creased her brow. 'What, lass?'

'Sissy not want none. Not want none! Sissy not—!'

'All right, now, all right,' Moll soothed her as the voice rose agitatedly.

'Not want none, Moll. Bad man.'

As Moll glanced to the mouth of the alley then back to her sister, sickliness washed through her. 'That fella we heard, then, with Davy? That's the bad man you told us about? The one Cathy spoke of?'

Sissy nodded.

'Why's he bad?'

'Bad man. Bad man.'

Moll settled on her haunches and took Sissy's shoulders gently. 'Why, lass? Tell Moll.' Silence greeted her and she swallowed her impatience. *Christ, Sissy, what's he done?* Breathing deeply, she tried again. 'Has that man . . . hurt you?'

'Aye.'

She slapped a hand to her mouth, trapping a cry, before croaking, 'Lass, you must tell me, what did he—?' The unexpected blow, as Sissy struck out and slapped her full across the face, sent Moll sprawling across the flagstones. She gazed up, stunned, then closed her eyes in relief. 'Is that what the bad man did? Did he strike you like that? Is that *all* he did? He didn't . . . touch you . . . anywhere else, anywhere he shouldn't, like we've talked about?'

'Nay, Moll.'

Thank God. Bastard, bastard . . .

'See Bo?'

'Aye. In a minute.' Moll shuffled to the roadside and patted the ground. 'Come and sit down, lass.' Not caring a fig about her skirts in the gutter's filth, she held Sissy close. 'Why did that man strike you?'

'I didn't tell, Moll? Sissy didn't tell?'

'Did the bad man say you mustn't?'

Sissy shook her head. 'Davy, Moll. Davy said.'

'Davy said you mustn't tell that the bad man struck you?'

'Aye. Bought me sweets. Said they were from the bad man. From the bad man, Moll, to say sorry.'

'For striking you?'

'Aye. But I mustn't tell. Sissy didn't tell?'

'Nay. You didn't tell. Don't fret, lass.' She paused to compose herself – the swell of fury was overwhelming. 'Why did the bad man hit you?'

'I said nay. Bad man said shut it. Shut it, he said, Moll.'

It was akin to fitting a puzzle's missing parts blindfolded, piece by painstaking piece by touch alone, but Moll knew she must take this slowly if she was to discover what the hell was going on. Sissy would become distressed and clam up, otherwise. 'You said nay?' she asked casually. 'To what, lass?'

'Said nay, Moll.'

'Aye. To what?'

'Coming for you, Moll. Coming for you and Mam.'

The dark words spoken in the innocent voice made the hairs on the back of Moll's neck stand. 'The bad man said that to Davy? And you said nay, and he struck you?'

'Aye.'

'Did he say owt else?'

'Stay with Sissy? Moll, stay with Sissy?'

Frightened tears had gathered in her sister's eyes. Moll held her closer. 'I'm going nowhere, lass, you hear?

Don't you fret.' When Sissy relaxed against her, she repeated, 'Did the bad man say owt else?'

'Said me, an' all. Coming for me. "Nay, not Sissy," Davy said.'

'Davy said the bad man couldn't have you?'

The girl nodded. 'Aye. Said Sissy's simple. Said nay, Moll.'

That the devil's own son possessed this shred of decency at least, was quickly lost on Moll. Shock had chased all anger, leaving her numb. She felt nothing.

'The young 'un: she's ripe?'

'Aye, is she. Proved it to me herself but a few weeks past.'

Their words played over in her mind. Preston hadn't set on her for his sexual gratification, she realised. He'd done it for others; sample the goods, so to speak. Perhaps, also, to test her reaction? And what had that been? He must think she'd welcome future encounters, whoever the man. *Dear God above . . .*

'Moll? Moll?'

'Aye?'

'Didn't tell? Sissy didn't tell?'

Her tone was flat. 'Nay, lass.'

'See Bo, now? Moll, see Bo?'

Her body rose of its own accord. She took Sissy's hand, and they resumed their journey.

Bo's face lit up upon answering their knock. 'Eeh, there she is!' He swept Sissy up and spun her around, much to her delight. As he leaned to kiss Moll's cheek, his smile vanished when she sidestepped him to stumble inside. 'Moll?'

She took in the empty room and was thankful. What she must say wasn't for the Crofts' ears – dear God, how she wished it didn't have to be for Bo's, either, but what choice had she?

177

'Moll, what's wrong?'

'Where's Uriah? His grandfather, brother?'

'Gone for a Christmas drink with a relative living up Harpurhey way. You look real awful. You ill or summat?'

'Oh, Bo, I wish it were that . . . Sit down.' She waited until he was facing her, Sissy on his knee. 'I must tell you. I've held things back for fear of upsetting you. I can't with this. I can't, lad. I don't know what to do.'

'Has Davy done summat? Moll, for Christ's sake!' he burst out when she struggled to find the words. 'Please, just tell me.'

'I think he's planning to sell me and Mam.'

'Eh?'

'To a bawdy house or summat. How he supposes to go about it, what he's planning . . . Oh, I don't know! I don't know what the hell's going on, Bo!'

His hand shook as he squeezed her shoulder, voice following suit: 'Calm down, now. It's all right. Tell me what's been happening.'

Once she began, she couldn't stop. She told him everything. Sissy's revelation. Davy's total domination over their home. Him molesting her and Mam not believing it. Mam's own behaviour lately, her drunkenness and volatile moods, her treatment of their neighbours today . . . Though her heart broke time and again as each sordid confession added another line to Bo's face, her shoulders gladly shed the crippling burdens she'd long carried alone.

'I'm sorry, lad, so sorry. I'm the one who looks after you. It's my job to protect you, allus has been. I, I just . . .'

Taking her hand, he curled his fingers through hers and she gripped them.

'I knew it. Yesterday, when I asked if he'd touched you . . .'

178

'I couldn't . . . didn't want you worrying, what with everything else you're going through.'

Guilt creased his face. 'That's it? You sure you've told me everything?'

'Aye— Oh. There is one other thing.' Thankfully, Uriah hadn't mentioned anything and, knowing it would devastate Bo, she'd put it off. However, the time for honesty had come. 'Mam . . . They're to be married.'

His face seemed set in stone. He nodded slowly. Then he moved Sissy off his knee and rose.

'Lad?'

Throwing on his rough jacket, he reached for his cap.

'Lad, where you going?'

He donned his new muffler. Then he inclined his head to the door. 'I need you both to go home, now, Moll.'

'What? Why?'

'There's summat I need to do.'

'What? Bo, please, you're scaring me.'

'Preston said a few days, a week at most. You'll be safe the night.'

'This is why I didn't tell you. D'you see? I shouldn't have come, should've gone to Polly instead—'

'Go home.'

'Whatever you're planning, don't. We'll tell Mam. She'll surely believe this.'

'You reckon?'

The instant answer was a clear no. Nonetheless, Moll nodded.

'Suit yourself. It's a risk I'll not take.'

She clutched his arm as he opened the door. 'For God's sake! What is it you need to do?'

'Summat I should have months ago. Now go. And Moll?'

'What, what?'

'Say nowt. See Sissy does likewise. You understand?'

In the next moment, he was gone, leaving her shaking with cold dread.

Lord, what had she done?

Chapter 13

THE HALF-STRIPPED CARCASS and leftover vegetables, the broth they would make tomorrow ... The good fire, the new ornaments on the mantel above winking in its glow ... The blue glass earrings swinging lightly as Ruth looked from Moll to Sissy in the doorway ... And the man himself. Bare feet warming on the fender, arms folded across his chest, breathing steady in sleep.

'All right, my lasses?'

Moll's eyes continued around the room. Every single thing bought by him had taken on an extra tarnished sheen. The money that had purchased them made, literally, off the backs of unfortunates.

'Sissy, hang your shawl up. Can you manage? Aye, good girl. Moll? You all right?'

Who else? How many more lives had he ruined for profit? How many others had he sold?

'Moll, d'you hear me?'

You sometimes heard whispers of this, in slums such as theirs, where prostitutes and the bullies who ran them were rife. A certain breed of lowlife had no qualms about standing on the necks of the vulnerable to get where they wanted. But it was just talk, concerning folk with unknown faces. It wasn't beneath your roof. Not your own family. Not *you*.

'Lass. Lass!'

Moll's gaze rested on her mother. She was holding Moll's upper arms, frowning, and again, shook her.

'You ill?'

'Nay.'

'Then what?'

Say nowt . . .

'Bo? Is my lad all right?'

'Aye.'

Ruth stared at her sadly in what she thought was shared pain over his absence. 'Sit down. I'll brew a fresh pot.'

The minutes rolled away in silence. Moll kept her eyes rooted to the table, not trusting herself to look at Mam, at him. How she managed to hold her tongue, God alone knew. She glanced to Sissy sipping warm milk, the kitten in her lap. She'd spoken to the girl when walking home, told her not to repeat anything she'd heard at Uriah's, just prayed she wouldn't. What had Bo planned? *Why* did she tell him? There had been murder in his eyes, pure murder, and she was afraid. Afraid for them all.

Just after eight o'clock, a knock came. Moll was out of her seat and darting for the door before anyone else had time to raise their heads.

'Lad! I've been that worried—'

'You've made no mention?'

'Nay.'

'Sissy?'

She shook her head. 'Well? What's going on?' She raised her eyebrows and Bo looked away. 'Oh God. What have you done?'

'I'll explain later. First things first . . .' He stepped past her into the house. 'I'm coming home.'

'You are? But—'

'Bo!' Ruth cried as he opened the kitchen door. 'Oh, my lad.'

Moll watched them embrace. Bo, however, only had eyes for Davy. Staring down at the slumbering form over his mother's shoulder, he wore an expression Moll hadn't seen before, and again fear gripped her.

'You home, now? For good, like?'

'If you'll have me.'

Their mother hugged him again. 'Eeh, but I've missed you.'

'Huh. Come crawling back with his tail betwixt his legs, I see.'

They turned as one towards the fire. Davy rose, stretched, then folded his arms, a smirk at his mouth.

'Now then, love . . .' began Ruth, eyes flicking between them, but Davy silenced her with a look.

'You've got some front, bold 'un. Think you can come swanning back in here, d'you?'

A muscle pulsated at Bo's jaw. However, his voice was even. 'I don't want trouble, Davy. I just want to come home.'

'Ay, my good lad!' Ruth beamed at Davy. 'See. I said all would be well, that the lad would come round. Didn't I say?'

Despite recovering quickly, Davy's countenance momentarily fell. It was clear this had come as a shock. Bo's return wouldn't fit with his scheme. However, that attempt to rile Bo had backfired and all but Mam knew it.

'Let us forget what's passed, eh? Can we, love?'

'After the trouble and upset he's caused?' Davy paused, awaiting an angry response from Bo. Receiving none, he blustered, 'The upstart swine owes me an apology! Aye, he does—!'

'I'm sorry.'

Davy's confused frown matched Moll's. What was Bo up to?

'There, see. What more d'you want from the lad?' Ruth cried.

'We're to be wed, your mam and me,' Davy threw in slyly.

'Moll said.'

'I'll bet. And what says you to that, then?'

'If it's what Mam wants, it's fine by me.'

Davy flushed puce. Eyes never leaving Bo's, he closed the space, halting inches away. 'I'm soon to be your new father and you'll show me the respect the name deserves. Understand, boy?'

'Aye.' Bo answered without hesitation but it was a long moment before Davy could speak again.

'Good. Well. Right.' He shot them all a furious look then stomped to his chair.

Any other time, Moll would have revelled in witnessing Preston bested. But catching her brother's eye, she failed to return his discreet wink. Without knowing why, she had a feeling this night was to change all their lives.

'Well?'

Bo held a finger to his lips until the front door clattered shut behind their mother and Davy. Then he released a slow sigh. 'Did you see the bastard's face, Moll? We've got him rattled good and proper.'

'Will you *tell* me what's going on?'

He leaned forward and rested his elbows on his knees. 'I mean to be rid of him. For good. That's why . . . I'd no choice.'

Moll's hand strayed to her throat. 'What have you done?'

'You'll not like it.'

'Just tell me!'

Bo leapt up and beat the mantel top with his fist, sending the odds and ends rattling in protest. 'I had to do summat.' A nervous quaver lurked in the words. 'All he's done, all he *plans* to . . . And if Mam goes through with this marriage, she'll be shackled to him for life. We all will.' Meeting Moll's fearful gaze, he shook his head. 'I've joined the Bengal Tigers.'

Those five words struck her face like invisible hands.

'Moll, listen to me—'

'You've done *what?*'

'Let me explain. I've got an idea.' Bo resumed his seat facing Moll's and rubbed the young stubble on his chin. 'They've agreed to help us.'

'With what?'

'Ridding our lives of that divil.'

'Oh, Bo . . .' She covered her face with her hands.

'I went to see Winters, told him I'd join in return for their help. He readily agreed. See, I'm not doing it because I want to; the thought sickens me. I *have* to. There's no other way. And once Preston's been dealt with, I'll leave. I'll say to the Tigers, I'll tell them, I've had enough. Everything will be all right, you'll see. We'll have Mam back and she'll be better once free of his grasp. Say summat, Moll. Tell me I've done the right thing.'

Her hands slipped from her face into her lap. An onion-sized lump had lodged in her throat; she couldn't breathe. *What have you done, you stupid, stupid boy?*

'Moll, please—'

'You think it's that simple? You honestly believe they'll let you leave their clutches? For God's sake, wise up! You're theirs, now, don't you get it? All these months,

185

I've struggled to keep them from getting you. The worry, set-tos, just for you to . . . You damn brainless fool!'

'So what d'you suggest? I'm all ears. What's *your* grand plan to get shot of Preston?'

'I . . . don't—'

'He's not going away, Moll,' Bo uttered in a slow, harsh tone. 'What, we do nowt? You fancy a life of prostitution, then? All right. I'll tell Winters I've changed my mind, let Preston sell you and Mam off like livestock.' Nodding, he folded his arms. 'Aye. We'll do that.'

He was right. Lord, that it had come to this. There was no way out, none. How else would they be rid of him? But her Bo a scuttler? Oh, she couldn't bear it!

'I can sort this, Moll. Let me prove it. Let me show you I can be the man you've brought me up to be.'

The sincerity in his words, and their nature, reached at her soul. This was the first time he'd touched upon the truth, that she'd been the constant in his and Sissy's lives, loved and cared for them, nurtured them through the years, *raised* them. To do so was admitting Mam hadn't. This, she appreciated, was hard for him to stomach.

Tears rolled down her cheeks. 'Oh, lad.'

'Then I have your consent? I'll not do it without.'

'They'll just frighten Preston into leaving? They'll not go too far? You've *told* them not to go too far? If they do for him . . . I'll not see you swing—'

'Aye, aye.'

'And you promise' – she grasped his hand – '*promise* me you'll do all you can to leave the Tigers once it's over?'

'I promise.'

The ticking clock filled the silence until, going

against every screaming part of her, she murmured, 'All right.'

They released long breaths then rose as one.

'Winters wants to see me again the night once he's spoken to his best lad. We've to discuss matters. Oh.' He glanced up with a nervous lick of his lips as a knock sounded. 'That'll be him.'

Moll clenched her hands until her nails bit into her palms, forcing herself not to grab him, tell him not to go. God forgive her, he must.

'When Mam and Preston get back, say nowt.'

She nodded.

'See you later.'

She nodded again and he was gone.

Long after Moll had gone to bed, mind exhausted with worry, and lay snuggled against Sissy, she was dimly aware of her mother and Davy's drunken return. Bo, however, didn't come home.

Chapter 14

A HAZE OF tense uncertainty carried them into the new year. More than ever, Moll thanked heaven for her position. Her kitchen was a haven; the minute she stepped in and donned her apron, the worries weighing her fraught mind lightened.

Though she hadn't believed it possible, home had reached a whole other level of unbearable. Davy was intent on making their lives a misery. Sometimes his jibes and peevish acts he performed in front of Ruth, who merely sighed wearily. Mostly, he awaited her absence before making his move.

He'd taken to waking them throughout the night with all manner of bizarre excuses. An apparent trip in the passageway's gloom resulted in ear-splitting thumps against their bedroom door, which had them bolting up, hearts banging, afraid some terrible attack on them and their property was occurring. The Luchettis upstairs, themselves disturbed by this, voiced displeasure, thus giving Davy the excuse to ostracise too 'them greasy scum', as he referred to them, as he'd done with Jilly.

Moll and Bo were exhausted from lack of sleep and mental grief. Fortunately, Sissy could sleep on a battlefield without stirring and this, Moll was certain, Davy knew. The surprising thing was, he didn't direct his reign of hatred towards the girl. With her he was, if not necessarily pleasant, quietly tolerant.

Bo promised matters would come to a head once he and the lads smoothed out the finer details of their plan – what this was, Moll hadn't dared ask. Part of her wanted him to call off the whole business, another hoped they would hurry up and put an end to the torment. One thing, however, was certain: Preston couldn't implement his heinous plan concerning her and her mother while Bo was around.

Wind whipped her shawl and skirts as she left the inn; laughing breathlessly, she hurried for sanctuary. This was an apt description, for tonight she was joining the Wainwrights in celebrating her friend's birthday. Not that Polly wanted fuss; turning twenty-eight was, to her, not worth marking. Her widowed mother thought otherwise, so had sent Polly's young sister, Katie, to Blossom Street yesterday to invite Moll. And Moll was more than glad she did.

'You don't have to say, for I know already,' announced Polly sadly upon answering her knock. 'I look every hour of twenty-eight – aye, and feel it.'

Moll kissed her cheek then clicked her tongue. 'Soft sod. You look no different. Anyroad, twenty-eight's nowt. There's many would give their eye teeth to be your age again.'

'Me for one!' chimed Polly's mother, who was cutting a small loaf into thick slices.

Her daughter poked her tongue at her and motioned to Moll to sit. 'So, you going to give us a sing-song, later, lass?'

'I am not!'

'Oh, go on,' Polly cajoled. 'Besides, it'll give our Katie less chance, then.'

'Ta very much, I'm sure!' the girl cried, and Polly grinned.

'Shurrup, you. I'm only teasing. Well, Moll?'

'Oh, all right. But I warn you, Polly, if the cats hereabouts begin yowling and clawing off their ears, I'm holding you responsible.'

Her friend laughed then leaned in. 'How's things at home, love?'

'Oh, you know,' she answered casually. What she really wanted was to grab Polly's hand and pour out her heart. Bo, however, had insisted she say nothing of their plans to anyone. The fewer who knew, the better – for all concerned.

The next hours were a hive of laughter and song and if Moll tried really hard, she could almost imagine she hadn't a care in the world. She'd needed this; what she'd do without Polly, particularly now Jilly was almost like a stranger to their family, she dreaded to think.

Moll still dropped by the Saxes' and though they greeted her as usual, meetings felt strained. Jilly didn't enquire over Ruth's health as she normally would, in fact made no mention whatsoever. Though Moll asked what had occurred between them over Christmas, Jilly claimed she didn't know. More like she didn't want to say, Moll suspected when, after disclosing that she and Alf had shared Christmas dinner with the Lockes, whom she cooked for, Jilly had quickly changed the subject.

The four of them were doubled over laughing at a joke Polly was relaying from one of her customers when tapping came at the door.

'I'll go,' said Katie, wiping mirth from her eyes. 'Hold on, Polly, till I return. I want to hear the ending.'

'Hurry yourself then, lass. Oh.' Seeing whom Katie

revealed, her laughter died. She nudged Moll and pointed to the door.

Turning, Moll was surprised to see Uriah. Then her eyes travelled down and a concerned frown knotted her brow. 'Lass, what are you doing here?' She looked back to Uriah. 'Lad?'

'Sorry, Moll . . .'

'Why's Sissy with you? Mam said she'd mind her the night—' Realisation came, bringing a mortified blush. 'She asked you to find me, didn't she, to mind the lass? She's out supping the gin palaces dry, in't she?'

'Sorry,' he repeated, glancing at the other occupants. 'I didn't want to embarrass you in front of your friends, it's just, I didn't know what to do, like . . .'

'It's all right,' Moll murmured. 'Ta for fetching her.' She held out her hand and after glancing around shyly, Sissy ran to her. 'D'you know where Mam's gone, Uriah?'

'Nay. I were heading past Blossom Street and she spotted me, shouted me down. She said she'd errands to see to and would I fetch Sissy to you.'

'As I said, ta.' Moll gave him a grateful, albeit hesitant, smile and was pleased when he returned it. This was the first time he'd spoken to her normally, never mind smiled, in weeks.

'Well. I'll be off. Night, all.'

''Ere, come in a while.' Polly beckoned him to the fire. 'You're more than welcome, lad. Warm yourself, I'll pour you some tea.'

'Ta, Polly.'

'No need for thanks amongst friends. Sissy love, you'll have some tea? And some ham and bread? Come with me, give me a hand, eh?'

Uriah perched on the horsehair sofa beside Moll. He made an apologetic face and she shook her head.

'I don't believe Mam. Fancy pulling a trick like this and at this hour – what must they think?' She looked to the Wainwrights, busy by the table with Sissy. 'And you. Eeh, I'm that embarrassed.'

'Don't be. It's not your fault.' His voice dropped. 'How's Bo?'

Something in his tone made her ask, 'You know, don't you?'

'That he's joined the Tigers?' He nodded.

'But he said he'd told you nowt—'

'Nor did he have to. I barely believed my eyes last night seeing him emerge from the Cross Keys with the shower. What's he playing at, Moll?'

'The Cross . . . A pub? Bo *drinking* in a public? Nay, he wouldn't—'

'It were him, all right. He walked right by, an' all, like he'd never before set eyes on me. That hurt, that did. After all I've done for him.'

'Listen, Uriah, I can't talk here. Walk me and Sissy home, later, and I'll explain. You can't breathe a word to a soul, mind. Promise me.'

'Moll?'

'Later. First, you must promise.'

'Course, aye. It'll go no further.'

Soon, the mood relaxed again. Uriah seemed easy in the Wainwrights' kitchen and even Sissy emerged from her shell; it was difficult not to in such pleasant company.

'Go on, Polly, sing the one about the pretty lady with the kid gloves,' begged Katie, following her and Sissy's rendition of an old favourite.

Stifling a yawn with the back of one hand, Polly flapped the other. 'I sang enough earlier. I'll be hoarse come the morrow.'

But Katie was insistent. 'Oh, our Polly. Just one more? Sissy wants to hear it; don't you?' she asked the girl, who nodded.

'All right.' Polly rolled her eyes at a grinning Moll then cleared her throat.

The high, silken voice manipulated each note effortlessly and a stillness touched everything and everyone. Polly's curls shimmered like a crimson halo in the firelight and as she delved deeper into the song, her eyes held a faraway look, as though she sang for someone particular. The lost love she'd mentioned? Moll wondered.

Sissy and Katie, kneeling by her feet, were enraptured. Polly's mother, smiling softly, had her eyes closed and Moll followed suit, shutting out the world to bask in the beautiful strains.

When the song ended, it was as though Polly had cast a spell; no one moved for a long moment.

'Bravo, Polly. Truly lovely, that were.'

At the quaver in Uriah's praises, all eyes turned to him. Moll's surprise matched the others' – more so to see him staring not at Polly but herself. Her puzzlement grew when her mind told her his look seemed suspiciously like the one of sad longing Polly wore while singing.

'Ta, lad, ta,' twittered Polly, on embarrassed laughter.

'We'd best be getting home. Come on, lass,' Moll announced quietly, thoughts in disarray. What did the look mean? she asked herself as she helped Sissy on with her shawl then donned her own. No one else seemed to notice – did she misinterpret it? She stole a glance at Uriah, waiting by the door. His face now held no trace of what she'd seen – what she *thought* she'd seen, she told herself. Daft imaginings she once harboured had momentarily resurfaced, that was all. Relieved, she hid a smile. Lack of sleep, owing to Preston's antics, was undoubtedly the culprit. Lord, she must be more tired than she thought!

After thanking the family for an enjoyable evening, Moll, Uriah close behind, led Sissy out and turned for home. The smell of frost hung in the air and she shivered. The streets were quiet; those with sense were at their firesides, and again she cursed her mother for turning Sissy out, in her need for gin. No doubt lovely and warm Mam was, slumped before some alehouse or other's roaring fire, she'd be bound!

'Preston'll not be best pleased if he finds me at his table,' Uriah stated when Moll beckoned him inside.

'*Our* table. Anyroad, I couldn't give a tinker's cuss for his opinion. Now, you coming in or what?'

The teasing grin he hadn't given her in a while surfaced and, laughing, she ushered him indoors. As she'd suspected, the kitchen was empty. Hours would pass before Mam and Davy rolled in, and Bo's whereabouts was anyone's guess. She'd barely seen him lately. With growing frequency, his evening meal was ruined long before he showed. Some nights, he didn't return at all. He was getting to know the lads and they him – vital, that was, he told her. Trust must be established between them. And of course, there was Preston to discuss; this at great length, it appeared.

After teasing life into the fire's faint embers, Moll tucked Sissy into bed next door and while waiting for water to boil, flitted about the kitchen. Uriah sat patiently and after straightening the rag rug a third time, Moll knew she'd avoided the conversation long enough. Suppressing a sigh, she pulled out a chair.

'So. Bo.'

'Aye.'

'He left mine the other day to return home with barely a word. What's going on, Moll? Why now, after warding them off so long, has he joined their ranks? It don't make sense.'

'He's not done it through choice. He's still the same lad, Uriah, honest. He's not one of them, not really. Davy . . . God above, you wouldn't believe how bad things have got. Bo joining the Tigers . . . it's an arrangement of sorts. They're to help us get rid of him.'

Uriah swore then sighed. 'And once Preston's dealt with . . . ?'

'Bo will leave the gang.'

Splaying his hands on the tabletop, he licked his lips, as though struggling to hold his calm. Worried frustration coated his words. 'Lass, name of Patty Hicks, recently moved off my street. The family had dwelled there longer than ours. They were a good lot. Decent, like. They did a moonlight flit not a month past. No goodbyes, nowt. Why d'you think that were, Moll?'

She blinked, confused. 'They hadn't brass to pay the rent?'

'Nay. Mr and Mrs Hicks discovered Patty was seeing a scuttler. They ordered her to keep away from him; warned the lad off, an' all. Patty agreed but scuttler lasses she'd made friends with, or thought she had, were having none of it. They hounded that poor family, Moll. Day and night they were there, demanding they let Patty out. They smashed windows, even tried setting fire to their door as they slept.

'The crux came when they attacked Mrs Hicks. At her tether's end, she'd threatened them with the police. Six set on her like a pack of wild dogs. The babby she held at the time was dashed to the ground and is lucky to have survived. But for neighbours dragging the

195

scuttlers off, they'd have done for mother and babe, I reckon. The following day, the family were gone.' Leaning forward, Uriah's eyes bore into Moll's. 'Bo will leave, will he?'

Frozen with horror, she could only stare.

'If you believe the Tigers will stand for that, you'll believe owt. They've got him, Moll. They'll not let him go, now. Not for anything.'

'God. Oh, *God.*' With a cry, she buried her face in her hands.

'Mind, I don't believe that's the worst part.'

'What d'you mean?'

'I don't think Bo will *want* to leave. From what I saw outside the Cross Keys, he's fitted in only too well.'

'He's just acting to get them onside—'

'Assaulting innocent folk in the street?'

'What?'

'Knocking off their headwear to become trampled in the gutter? – bonneting, they call it. Linking arms and rushing young and old from the footpath into the busy road? A right lark, eh?'

'Nay. Bo wouldn't do that.'

'I know what I saw, Moll. The status, excitement, call it what you will – he's beginning to enjoy it, and that's the truth.'

'I won't believe that. I won't! Bo's a good lad. He's doing this for us; Mam and me, and Sissy. He's not like them mindless swines. Norra bit.'

Every inch of his face told of his disagreement. However, when great, gulping sobs tore from her, it turned stricken. Nodding quickly, he took her hand. 'You're right. Course you are. I didn't mean to . . . Sorry, Moll.'

'That you'd even consider . . . It's Bo we're talking about!'

'I know. I know.'

His soothing tone calmed her. She looked to their clasped hands then up again in surprise when Uriah pulled away, as though he'd just realised.

'Sorry.'

His cheeks had flushed. He looked like a boy half his age caught doing something he shouldn't. She couldn't contain a smile. 'Eeh, lad. At times, I don't know what I'd do without you.'

'Aye?'

'You're a good friend, Uriah.'

Dropping his gaze, he nodded.

'I've been meaning to say. The night I snapped at you returning from Smithfield Market . . . After you'd gone out of your way to cheer me up, an' all. I'm sorry.'

'Forget it. I have.'

She held up the teapot but he shook his head.

'I've drank enough to sink a sheep.' He smiled when she chuckled, then rose. 'I'd best be going.'

'You'll not breathe a word to another living soul of what's been said the night?'

'I promised, didn't I?'

'Aye. Ta. Goodnight, lad.'

'Night, sourpuss.'

Clicking her tongue, she swatted him to the door. She was still smiling as, after seeing Uriah out and refilling her cup, she sipped her brew. She was glad they were back on comfortable terms. She just hoped his and Bo's friendship wasn't spoiled.

Anxiety churned her guts at what he'd related concerning the Hicks lass. And his assumption that Bo was enjoying . . . No. About that, Uriah was wrong. Likely, thoughts of his main friend finding new acquaintances stung. It was understandable. The two had always been inseparable. All will be well, she told herself firmly. She just prayed this nightmare would soon be over.

The kitten stirred from its hearthside bed and trotted towards her. Bending to stroke it, she frowned when crumpled material beneath the dresser caught her eye. She went to investigate and found it was the muffler she'd bought Bo for Christmas. Holding it against her cheek, she glanced to the clock, wishing he was home. She'd just folded it and laid it over the back of a chair when, as though she'd conjured him up, he entered the room.

'Oh. Moll. I thought you'd be abed by now.'

She couldn't speak. Her gaze travelled the length of him slowly, widening more and more.

His cropped hair he'd attempted to soap over one eye. Above, a cheap billycock hat positioned at the back of his head had replaced his cap. Instead of his rough, fustian trousers, he wore light-coloured bell-bottoms. Finishing the look, a flashy muffler lay around his neck.

She eyed the folded one she'd scrimped to buy. The one he'd discarded as not good enough now it wasn't in fitting with his new uniform. When she glanced up, he had the grace to look shamefaced.

'Sorry about that.' He nodded to her gift. Then holding out his arms, he swivelled around. 'What d'you think?'

Bile attacked her throat. From top to toe, he was a scuttler. Her Bo was one of them. 'What do I *think*?'

'The lads rigged me out. I just need to get some new clogs and a—' He paused abruptly and cleared his throat.

'A belt? Is that what you were about to say?'

'Moll—'

'Mebbe a knife or two to go with it?'

198

Bo thrust his hands into his pockets, frowning, and she went cold.

'Well?'

'Well what?'

'Why not tell me I'm being daft? Why not deny it? Happen you're equipped with one already, is that it?' She grabbed at his pockets but was taken aback when he caught her wrist and thrust her away. Rubbing the bruised skin, she gazed at him in horror. 'That hurt. How dare you handle me like that!'

'Quit the nagging, then!' he shot back, then the anger left his face, the colour with it. 'Eeh, Moll. I didn't mean—'

'Have you been drinking?'

'What? Nay.'

She sniffed the air between them. 'You have, ain't you? Uriah was right. God above! Have you passed your years on this earth with your eyes closed? Drink has been the ruin of this family. We swore to each other as children, swore that when we grew, never a drop would touch our lips. How *could* you?'

'A drop of whisky hardly makes me a drunk, for God's sake. Anyroad, you wanted this, remember.'

Her brows met in astonishment. 'I wanted what?'

'I asked your consent and you gave it. You wanted me to join.'

'I did bloody not, Bo, and you know it! It's like I don't recognise you. What's *happened* to you?'

Slowly, his expression softened. Lifting his hat, he ran a hand through his hair and sighed. When he held out his arms, Moll threw herself into them and clung to him.

'I'm sorry.'

'Oh, lad.'

'It's an act, that's all, just like we planned. The Tigers need to think I'm fitting in, you know?' Feeling her nod, his hold tightened. 'They mustn't suspect otherwise, else we'll never be shot of that bastard, Preston.'

Moll nodded again, wanting desperately to believe him. 'But lad, I must know. You're not . . . you'll never be drawn in, will you, never come round to their way of thinking? Tell me you'll not begin enjoying it, please.'

'God, no. No, Moll.'

'Thank God!'

'Once Preston's dealt with, I'm out.'

'But what if the scuttlers won't let you? Uriah said—'

'Never mind what Uriah said. I'm telling you I'll leave and I will.'

'When? When will it all be over, with Davy?'

'The morrow.'

Moll swallowed hard. 'Aye?'

'Where is he and Mam, anyroad?' Bo asked, looking around.

'Where d'you think?'

'Aye, well. We'd best be to bed. We've a long day ahead the morrow.'

His words were deep with meaning. She whispered, 'What will they do to him, Bo?'

'He'll be gone. That's all what matters. Take yourself through. I'll follow in a minute.'

When did he get so grown up? she wondered as she undressed and slipped beneath the blanket. Gone was the quiet boy with the kind and cautious nature. His expression these days was impassive, almost stony. It was like he'd shut off from emotion, developed a new demeanour, purposeful, almost dominant.

Nonetheless, having him back was a comfort and when he climbed into bed soon afterwards, and she saw his large shape through the gloom, Sissy between them sleeping soundly, calmness filled her. At least she knew, this night at least, where he was and what he was about.

This evoked thought of the Tigers and with a shiver that had nothing to do with the cold room, she bit her lip. What would the new dawn bring? Just what had her family let itself in for?

Chapter 15

'MOLL, WAKE UP.'

'Mm?'

'Mam's gone.'

'What d'you mean, gone?'

'Her bed ain't been slept in. She didn't come home last night.'

Moll lifted the candle in the saucer from the wooden crate that served as a bedside table. Her hands shook as she struck a match and touched the flame to the blackened wick. 'What's the time?'

'Just shy of five. Christ, if Preston's followed through with his plan—'

'Don't say that.'

'But what if he has? What will we do? Where else could she be? She's never stopped out till this hour.'

'Come on.' Taking care in the dim light, she led Bo through.

'Me and the Tigers should have sorted him sooner. We should have got rid of him before this. We—'

'Calm down, lad. We're worrying needlessly, you'll see,' Moll said with more confidence than she felt.

'Look.'

She stared at the bed her father had once slept and died in, now back in the kitchen. Sure enough, the covers were undisturbed. Dread rolled through her but glancing to Bo, she masked it. Pale-faced, he was gnawing his bottom lip. For all his new-found maturity, her brother now was the one who had always looked to her for guidance; naturally, she resumed her role of protector. He needed her to tell him all would be well, what they were to do, and this she did:

'Brew some tea, lad. I'll walk to the end of the street, see if I can spot her. Happen they continued their supping at some friend's dwelling after the publics closed. They're likely on their way home as we speak.'

'Aye?'

Putting on her shawl, Moll nodded and slipped out. At the corner, she glanced both ways along Bengal Street then retraced her steps, continuing past her house to Blossom Street's opposite end. However, Great Ancoats Street leading off yielded similar results: Mam was nowhere in sight.

Bo turned, expectant-faced, when she re-entered. She shook her head.

He dropped into a chair. 'Preston's done it, ain't he? Mam's gone.'

Moll didn't answer. Untying her shawl, she let it fall to the ground and, like Bo, dropped into a seat, numb with the terrible truth.

'The police would be neither use nor ornament.'

Moll nodded agreement. 'Mam's a grown woman, they'll say, free to come and go as she pleases. Proving Preston guilty of wrongdoing would be impossible.'

'Not that they'd be mithered either way, I'll be bound. What's one less drunkard off Ancoats' streets to them?'

'A blessing, likely,' she whispered.

Bo drummed the tabletop then scraped back his chair. 'I can't sit and do nowt.' He shrugged on his jacket and reached for the bowler hat. Then changing his mind, he opted for his cap, pulling it low to conceal his new fringe. 'I'll stick out like a sore thumb otherwise,' he explained needlessly and donned the muffler she'd bought. Moll could imagine what would happen if another gang spotted him.

'Who's that?' Moll murmured when, having walked him to the door, she spied a beshawled figure in the distance. As it drew nearer, she hurried to meet it; the hobbled gait was unmistakable. 'Jilly.'

'Moll?'

'Aye, it's me.'

'Eeh, what are youse two doing out and about at this hour?'

'It's Mam.' Tears welling, Moll motioned to the door. 'Come in, Jilly, will you?'

The old woman glanced through the passage, as though expecting to see someone else. 'Oh, I don't know . . .'

'Davy's not here. Neither of them are. Please, Jilly.'

'Ay, what's to do?' she asked as Moll started crying. 'All right, my loves, all right.' She held up an ancient carpet bag containing the tools of her trade. 'I've been assisting a birth up Piccadilly way. Let me drop this at home and I'll be with youse.'

'Ta, Jilly.'

'So, what's afoot?' their neighbour asked minutes later as they sat with cups of tea. 'More to the point, where's Ruth?'

'We don't know. Mam didn't come home.'

She looked from Bo to Moll then closed her eyes. 'Mother of God . . .'

'Jilly?'

'Ruth's gone and done it, then?'

'Done what?' they asked in unison.

'You mean to say she hasn't told you?' Their confused expressions answer enough, Jilly sighed. 'Christmas Eve, our falling out. When I fetched them mince pies up, she asked me . . . She wanted me to . . . Eeh, I can't bring myself to say.'

'What, Jilly?' whispered Bo.

Moll took a wrinkled hand and chafed it gently. 'We'll not blame thee, honest. Please, we must know. Summat occurred recently and . . . We're worried Davy—'

'Huh! That divil! Aye, he's to blame for all this.'

'All what?'

'The terrible mess your mam's in. He insisted. She asked . . . I couldn't, lass, couldn't. She wanted me to end the child's life.'

'The . . . child?'

'The one she's carrying. Or were afore this night.'

Moll had to gulp several times before she could utter, 'Mam's with child?'

The old woman nodded. 'She'd already tried scalding baths and gin to no avail. I said to her, I'm paid to fetch life into this world, not snuff it out. It's wicked, I said, I'll not do it. I refused, lass, had to. She were upset at first then seeing I'd not be swayed, turned mad with fury. She told me I were dead to her, that my face wasn't welcome in these here rooms again. Then, last evening, I saw her ask the Croft lad to take Sissy to you. "I've sorted it, no thanks to thee," Ruth spat to me when they'd gone, nasty like, you know?'

'Sorted it?' Moll forced herself to ask.

'Someone Davy knows were coming collecting them on a cart. Ruth said she'd not trust just anyone to fix this, that's why she'd come to me, but Davy had told how his mam knew her way around a knitting needle—' Jilly covered her mouth. 'I'm sorry, sorry. I shouldn't talk of such things to youse, young as you are.'

Moll rose jerkily. Her legs felt detached from her as she paced, hands on hips, her mind spinning. Was this why Mam had wanted to marry? Had Davy agreed unaware of the child but upon finding out, forced her to get rid?

'He's took her to Bolton?' ground out Bo.

'I thought it were talk, lad, didn't think she'd actually—'

'He's taken her miles from home to be butchered? His own child . . . At the hands of his own *mam*? What make of foulness are these people?'

'I'm sorry. Eeh, I am, lad . . . Moll . . .' Tears zigzagged the course of Jilly's wrinkles. 'I thought she'd come round. God forgive me for driving the poor lass off but I couldn't end that babby's life. God forgive me!'

Moll held her tightly. 'Shh, now. No fault lies at your door. This is Preston's doing. He's the divil's own spawn. He's been making plans, Jilly, plans to—'

'Moll's right,' threw in Bo, cutting her off with a warning look. 'Don't blame yourself so.' When she'd mopped her tears with her shawl, he took her elbow. 'I'll see you home.'

'You two will be all right? What about Ruth? What's to be done?'

'Don't fret. We'll find Mam. Right, Moll?'

'Aye, yes.'

Jilly, lips quivering, stroked Bo's cheek then Moll's. 'So sorry,' she whispered.

'You should've let me tell her,' said Moll when he returned. 'She might have been able to help.'

'How could Jilly possibly be of use? Nay. It's best no one but us knows what's to come.'

Moll was about to admit that Uriah knew but changed

her mind. It made no difference – Uriah wouldn't tell. He'd promised and she trusted him implicitly. 'So how do we find Mam? They could be anywhere in Bolton. The dangers: what if summat's gone wrong? What if . . .' Moll couldn't say it. *What if she bleeds to death, catches infection, dies . . . ?* 'That she could take off without a word. God in heaven, how could she be so foolish?'

'As soon as it's light, I'll call on t' lads. They'll offer to accompany me to find her, I know it. We'll fetch her back.'

'And Preston?'

Bo's jaw muscles worked furiously. 'He'll not be joining her. I'll make certain of that.'

Their tea grew cold and the minutes ticked away but neither noticed. Each was locked in their own prison of thoughts – one, for Moll, overriding all else: how on earth would they get through this fresh hell and what would follow?

How Moll managed to prepare Sissy's breakfast, clean and help dress her, tidy their rooms then greet Twit and Beattie, all the while with conversation and smiles, she never knew. A solid ball of fear had gripped her guts when Bo left shortly after dawn broke, clad, to her distaste, in full scuttler dress, and she'd carried it since.

She'd rather have stayed home in case, by some miracle, it transpired that this was some hideous mistake and Mam returned, but Bo had insisted she keep her usual routine so as not to draw attention to the fact that anything was amiss. The last thing they needed on top of everything else was the police sniffing about. As well as the disgrace, ending an unborn life could carry a lengthy stretch in gaol.

Despite cruel winds from across the river, a blithe sun

rested high in the sky. Moll had propped the door open while she worked and the bustle of daily life from surrounding streets distracted her tumultuous mind. However, the tightness in her stomach wouldn't leave.

That poor scrap of life. Davy's child, aye, but Mam's also. Their brother or sister, their flesh and blood; her thoughts galloped relentlessly. Mostly, she worried herself sick over Mam. *Please, Lord, we need her. Keep Bo safe, too. Just fetch them home to me,* she'd pray, simply to begin again.

Now, Sissy, hacking at a carrot with a spoon – her way of helping peel the vegetables – glanced to Moll scrubbing burnt-on scrag-end from a pan, and Moll flashed the practised smile. She then trained it across the room as Beattie entered, thick hips swaying, a pile of dirty dishes in each hand.

'Is that the stew finished?' Beattie dumped her load on to the table and wiped her glistening brow.

'It is.'

'Well, they'll have to make do with bread and ham, now, and like it.' As her words died, bursts of laughter filtered through from the drinking area and she shook her head.

'It sounds like you've a rowdy lot in, Beattie.'

'Aye, and it would have to be when Twit's not home. They ain't half putting it away; fair skenning, the lot. Best you stop out of the way the night, lass.'

Occasionally, if business was brisk, Moll took customers' meals through and collected empty dishes to help Twit and Beattie out. Therefore, she said, 'I don't mind if you need a hand. I'm not fazed by those who've had one too many.' *I've had plenty of practice,* she finished to herself.

'Not the night, ta all the same. Stay put here, understand?'

Though miffed by Beattie's insistence, she nodded. 'If you're sure?'

'I am. Now, I'd best get back.'

The door swung shut behind her employer. Shrugging, Moll returned her attention to the pan.

'You think I give a damn? I said fetch her, else I'll drag her through myself!'

The raised voice reached Moll as she was drying the dishes. Frowning, she paused but when nothing followed, thought no more of it and began stacking the pots into the cupboard.

'You'll rue letting Mam go. She could manage better than this with no hands. Tastes like soddin' horse shit, this does!'

This, from the same person as before, was followed by Beattie's demand that he quieten down or leave, and Moll bristled. Ruddy cheek!

'I'm going nowhere till you fetch that useless whore so I can tell her to her face,' the roaring-drunk customer bellowed back, and Moll's anger spilled over.

Mindless of Beattie's instruction, she told Sissy to stay and stormed to the door.

A group of rough-looking youths, around twenty strong, sat watching the proceedings with amusement. The object of their attention turned his hostile gaze to Moll as she marched forward, and she groaned inwardly. *For the love of* . . . She *really* needed this.

'You?' Curling his lip, Sammy Simcox looked her up and down.

From what she'd glimpsed of their house, discovering her predecessor's identity surprised Moll not one bit. 'Did I hear you complaining about my grub?'

'Lass, go on back to the kitchen—'

'Well?' Moll pressed him before Beattie could finish.

'You had fine use of that tongue of yourn a moment since. Spit it out, Simcox.'

He closed the space between them in a swaggering walk. 'You mouthy bitch—'

'Back off, Sammy.'

All turned to the far end of the counter, where a lone male leaned at ease.

'Keep out of this, cuz.'

Simcox's response sent heat through Moll. She looked again at the person she'd realised was Horatio but a cap shadowed his face, showing his mouth and jaw only, just like their first encounter.

'I'm warning you. Don't make me tell you again.'

As Simcox glared back, you could have heard a flea sneeze. The power struggle raged silently until he growled, 'This ain't nowt to do with thee. Mind your own.'

A collective gasp buzzed through the room.

'*What* did you say?'

It was a moment before Simcox answered. 'She can fight her own battles, I'm sure. Mind, it had nowt to do with you last time – didn't stop you defending the whore then, though, an' all, did it? Well, I've grown tired of you telling me what to do. Them days are over. *Horatio.*'

Whatever Sammy's reason for using his cousin's proper name, and with such emphasis, it had the power to strip Horatio of his calm exterior. With a roar, he launched across the counter-top, sending pots of ale flying and people scattering for cover, and threw himself at Sammy.

Unprepared and clearly regretting his folly, the younger lad gritted his teeth as Horatio slammed him against the counter. He held up his hands, though his eyes screamed murder. 'All bloody right! Leave go.'

'One of these days, Sammy, one of these days.'

'All right. Keep your frock on.'

With that last retort from Sammy, Horatio released him with a shove that sent him staggering.

Overcome with indignation at being branded a whore, disgust at the mindless violence these lot thought nothing of displaying at the slightest provocation – not to mention, overriding everything, the queer heat coursing through her at being in Horatio's presence – Moll turned for the kitchen blindly.

'Wait.'

Even had he not spoken, she'd have recognised the touch; her shoulder quivered beneath it. 'Get your hand off me,' she murmured without turning.

'I want to speak with you.'

'I said all I had to last time.' Moll jerked her head towards Sammy. 'Much as it sickens me saying it, he's right about one thing: I don't need you, don't need *any-one*, fighting my battles. As for you,' she added, to Sammy, 'I never stole your mam's position if that's what's got you acting the babby the night.

'I took over after she left – sorry, after she were *dis-missed* for being the slatternous piece she is. The state she left that kitchen . . . If you're used to that beneath your roof, I'm surprised you've reached the age you have!' He simply stared, open-mouthed, and the fight left her. 'Oh, what's the bloody point? Eat the grub or don't. I couldn't care less.'

'I knew the minute that swine walked in he'd start, and that you'd bear the brunt. I gave you strict instructions—'

'Not now,' she told Beattie who, after bellowing at the scuttlers to leave, had followed her to the kitchen. 'Please.' Gripping the mantel, Moll took shuddering breaths.

211

'Ay, what's afoot, lass? I've never seen you like this. Tell Beattie what's to do.'

Her kindness threatened to snap the last thread of strength Moll clung to. 'I'm sorry. Please, give me a moment to calm down . . .'

'Moll.'

Glancing up, mirthless laughter choked in her throat. Horatio filled the doorway. 'Christ's sake. You again? What part of leave me be don't you understand?'

'You heard the lass.' Beattie planted her feet apart, hands on hips. 'Hop it.'

'I want to talk to her.'

'And I want a waist like a bottle-neck but we can't allus have what we desire, lad!'

'It'll only take a minute—'

'God give me strength!' Moll snapped, flinging away from the fire. She looked at Beattie apologetically. 'Would you mind?'

'You sure, lass?'

'Aye.'

'All right. I'll take Sissy upstairs. Shout if you need me.' To Horatio, Beattie added, 'Clock's ticking. Say what you've got to and quick.'

He nodded. When the door closed, he folded his arms. 'I had no idea you worked here.'

'No idea I'd thieved your aunt's job from under her nose, you mean?'

'Ignore Sammy. He's a fool.'

'Aye, and the rest. Had I known this inn was one of your lot's blood houses,' Moll told him bitterly, using the scuttlers' term for their drinking dens, 'I'd have never accepted the position.'

'It ain't. The Prussia lads wouldn't venture this way normally. This here's the fringe of Angel Meadow

212

territory; I don't know what Sammy's playing at. Neither are they "my lot".'

She rolled her eyes. 'Really.'

'Aye, really. I were here alone when they arrived.'

All lies. She sighed wearily. 'What d'you want, Horatio?' The name slipped out without thought. Despite what she knew, 'Rat' didn't come naturally to her tongue.

'I've missed you.'

Just like in her dream . . . Her annoyed frown slipped. Tears just beneath the surface threatened to escape and she swallowed frantically. She wouldn't let him see her cry again.

'Whatever you think you know about me, you're wrong. I weren't lying. I ain't like them. At least I never wanted to be.'

'Don't take me for a fool. I saw you with my own two eyes—'

'Smithfield Market.' He nodded. 'I suppose you'd not believe I were there by myself killing some hours? Sammy spotting me were nowt but coincidence. Had I not gone to his aid, my aunt and uncle would've made my life hell—' He clamped his mouth shut when she shook her head. Moments later, he was striding towards her. 'Look at me,' he demanded.

Moll raised her eyes as he removed his cap. Inky-coloured hair lay in a side-parting, and his forehead was bare. Her gaze fell to his throat and the dark scarf lying loose . . . the cotton shirt and broadcloth suit; down again, settling on his booted feet.

'Do you see me, Moll?'

For the first time, she really did.

'Do I look like one of them to you?'

Slowly, she lifted the bottom of his jacket. The regular buckle of his plain belt winked at her.

'That's why Sammy said your name like that just now,' she murmured almost to herself. '*Horatio*. Not Rat. You've stepped down.'

'The very night we met, I vowed to give it up.'

'Why?'

'You were all I've ever wanted to be. Decent and true. I swore I'd make it happen, become good like you. *For* you.'

'For me?'

He nodded. 'Scuttler scum. That's what you said when Sammy went at you with his belt. I'd not have you see me like that. Not you.'

There was no messing about with him. That Horatio liked her, if she was honest with herself, he'd been open about from the beginning. She'd simply chosen not to see it. She didn't have to second-guess with him as she'd constantly done with Uriah. That one was a man and the other a boy was painfully obvious. Their slight difference in years was more like twenty; in maturity, they were oceans apart.

Yet still . . . She had to ask. 'What are you saying?'

'That I think I love you,' Horatio answered without hesitation. 'Despite my past – and the past it is – I know you could feel the same.'

I think I do already, have from the start, Moll's inner voice responded. But it was madness, wasn't it? How could she think this after what she knew of him? Past or no, it didn't alter all he'd done and who he'd been – everything she despised. Nor did it change the fact that he possessed, and – going by the recent skirmish, always would – an uncontrollably fearsome temper that both scared and sickened her.

'I know what I am,' he said, as though reading her thoughts. 'No amount of sound intentions can smoothen

214

every edge. I'm all you're not. You, you're everything right with the world. You're ... *right*, you know? Yet you've a fire inside; by, you have. I'd want it no other way.'

Then there was his family; Christ, and what a bunch, Moll reminded herself, as the cons of what giving in to this would mean tripped over each other. But he'd said repeatedly he wasn't, didn't *want* to be, like them. Whether naively, this she now believed.

Meeting his stare, she realised she'd barely once seen him smile, doubted those generous lips were capable. Perhaps he'd never had much to smile *about*. Perhaps they weren't so different after all.

'My promise that night to help your brother— Aye, I know,' he added when her brow furrowed. 'I got it wrong. It was a foolish plan. I figured he'd fare better with the Prussia Street lads, that I could keep an eye to him, have his back. I wanted to please you. Trouble is, I went about trying the only way I knew.'

'The Tigers got him in t' end, anyroad.'

'So I hear.'

They gazed at one another. When Horatio reached to cup her cheek, Moll closed her eyes. She sensed his head move in. Then they were kissing, arms around each other, bodies pressed close.

His attentions grew; rather than be shocked or alarmed, Moll matched his fervour. However, when he pushed her against the table and kissed her neck hungrily, and her leg went around him instinctively, she pulled back, panting.

'Stop ... We shouldn't.'

Passion had darkened his eyes to midnight-blue. His mouth, bruised a deeper blush-colour by their kiss, hovered above hers. He licked his lips then, with evident difficulty, forced a nod.

Breaking the embrace took all the strength she had. She entwined her fingers through his. 'You should go.'

Once more, he nodded.

'When will I see you again?'

'Soon. I can't ever let you go, now, Moll.'

The intensity in his quiet words made her ache anew. Neither did she want him to. Never, ever.

'Moll? You there?'

Her head swivelled to the door; she just had time to spring away from Horatio before it opened.

'I— Oh.'

'Uriah! What are you doing here?' Moll fixed hair that had escaped its pins, her face ablaze.

'Bo called on me this morning, asked me to keep an eye to you and Sissy till he returns.' His blank gaze flicked to Horatio then back. 'I thought I'd stop by, walk you home.'

'Aye, lad, all right. Ta.'

'I'll wait out front.'

'Your brother's friend?' asked Horatio when the door clicked shut.

'Aye.' She covered her face with her hands. 'You ought to go.'

'Are you ashamed of me?'

Sighing, Moll let her arms fall. 'I'm ashamed of myself. Had Uriah arrived moments earlier . . . It's not funny,' she insisted when Horatio's eyes creased, though her twitching lips undermined her. 'Mebbe it would be best if . . . Well, I just think . . .' Her words petered out as he put an arm around her waist and drew her against him. 'Horatio—'

'You're not regretting what's occurred the night, are you, Moll?' Slowly, he stroked the tip of his nose up and

216

down her cheek and his warm breath on her neck set her pulse aflame.

'Nay. I mean . . . I don't know. I've much on my mind at present, Mam and Bo and . . .' Mentioning her family shook her awake. A wave of guilt hit her. What was she playing at? She'd never put her own wants first – certainly couldn't start now with all that was going on. She extracted herself from his hold. 'I must go.'

The homeward journey was painfully uncomfortable; Moll could almost smell Uriah's disapproval. Other than Sissy singing snatches of song, no one uttered a word until they reached the corner, where Horatio said, 'I'll take my leave of you here, Moll.'

Despite what her head said, staring up at his handsome face in the darkness, she yearned to hold him, kiss him. She touched his arm in a brief caress. 'Goodnight.'

'I'll be seeing you.' He flashed her a heart-stopping smile and was gone.

Uriah's face was empty as he watched Horatio walk away. He closed his eyes for a moment then continued for Blossom Street, and Moll and Sissy hurried to keep up.

'There were trouble the night with Simcox. Horatio helped calm things down.'

Uriah's stiff nod at her attempt to both explain and break the charged silence brought heat to her cheeks.

'Aye. Simcox, he were roaring drunk and—'

'As you said at Smithfield Market, it's none of my business.'

'Uriah—'

'D'you know, I've just remembered, I've somewhere I need to be.' He inclined his head to their door, visible in the distance. 'You'll be all right from here, I'm sure.'

'But—'

'Bye, Moll.'

'Lad, hold up.'

He didn't. Telling Sissy to wait, Moll caught him up and clasped his arm, forcing him to halt. Anger rose in her. He had no right to treat her offhandedly. After all, whatever she chose to do and with whom was really none of his business.

'I told you, I have to be somewhere.'

'Tripe you do. If this is about Horatio—'

'Horatio? Nay, Moll. He's Rat, in every sense of the word.'

'For God's sake, Uriah—'

'You just don't get it, d'you?'

'Get what? What are you talking ab—?'

'I'm in love with you, yer daft cow!'

They gazed at one another in the moonlight.

'Why didn't you tell me?'

'Moll, surely to Christ you knew . . . ?'

'Mebbe. I thought so once but . . .'

'D'you love him? Rat Green – d'you love him?' he pressed when she looked away.

She swallowed a sad sigh. God help her, she couldn't change the truth nor deny it, least of all to herself. 'I think so.'

His face crumpled. 'Oh, Moll, nay . . .'

'Oh, lad.' She groped for his hand. For a long moment, they clung to each other. 'I'm sorry, so sorry.'

'Aye. Me too.'

Uriah's fingers slipped from hers. He turned and walked away and this time, Moll let him. There was nothing left to say. Whether speaking out sooner would have made a difference, they would never know. He'd left it too late. They both had.

218

Chapter 16

IT WAS MANY hours after Sissy that Moll, curled in the chair by the dead fire, dragged her shivering body to bed.

The past twenty-four hours had played in her mind relentlessly, swirling into a dizzying mass until she wasn't sure any more what had been real and what hadn't. *Did* so much really happen in just a day? It was difficult to believe.

She fell into instant, death-like sleep but it felt like she'd only blinked when Bo's rumbling snores hauled her kicking and screaming back to consciousness. Groaning, she reached across Sissy to prod her brother to turn over – then froze. *Bo wasn't here!* What on earth . . . ?

She blinked wildly in the darkness, and her mouth ran dry. Sure enough, a black bulk was stretched out on his side of the bed. When it shifted suddenly and she caught a waft of stale ale, a scream rose in her – only to fizzle away as the figure coughed. It *was* Bo! The daft young . . . her ruddy heart! But when . . . ? Why wasn't he in . . . ? *Mam.* Springing from the bed, Moll hurried to Bo's side. Eyes now accustomed to the gloom, she saw him clearly – and that he was fully dressed; cap, clogs and all.

'Bo, get up.' She shook his shoulder. He moaned, swatted her hand and turned over. Clicking her tongue, she shoved him harder. 'You've been bloody drinking again, ain't you? Wake up. What are you doing here?'

'Leave off, our Moll,' he slurred, dragging the blanket over his head.

'Where's Mam? Did you find her?'

'Aye.'

'Oh! Thank God.'

'Coming home today.'

'Mam is? Bo, for Christ's sake, wake up!' she snapped as his breathing grew heavy. 'What happened?'

'Huh? What d'you want now?'

'What happened at Bolton? Is Mam well? Is she really coming home?'

'Aye.'

'Then why didn't you stop on with her, see her back to Manchester? What of Preston? Is she still with Preston? Bo? *Bo?*' But it was useless; she'd have got more sense from the cat. She headed to the kitchen knowing that, for herself at least, sleep was now an impossibility.

The winter morning beyond the curtain was still pitch black; therefore, she was surprised the clock showed it was just after six. She'd slept longer than she thought. Her mind buzzed with unanswered questions and she made the fire and brewed tea through habit alone.

Before sitting at the table, she crossed to the nail and plucked down Ruth's apron. Breathing in her scent, she sighed. Lord, but she'd missed her, despite everything. Matters must have gone smoothly, thanks be to God, if she was coming home.

Again, confusion swamped her. Just what had occurred in Bolton? What of Davy? Had Bo, with the

Bengal Tigers' assistance, seen the swine off? Was the nightmare over?

Shooting a disgruntled look at the wall, she shook her head. The state of the lad. That certainly wasn't the workings of a mere drop of whisky, as he'd claimed before. Thick head or no, he'd get a tongue lashing of the highest order when his sodden senses returned.

Thank heaven it was Sunday; he'd never have made it into work. Taking off to Bolton yesterday without a by-your-leave, he'd insisted his gaffer would show him mercy for missing the half-day's work, being the sound bloke he was. Moll doubted it. The course their fortune had run lately, he'd probably get the shove. Life was one worry after another, it was.

The man never far from her thoughts crept through and she heaved a sigh. Was he truthful? Had he changed? Could it work? *Did she want it to?* Last night it was like some glorious spell had been cast on her; she'd been convinced it was right. Now, in the cold light of day . . .

Her sensible side had begun questioning her feelings. Not doubting them, no, no. She loved Horatio. Of that, there was no question. Whether she *should* was what had her wringing her hands with uncertainty.

Their union would pose problems. Both families, for differing reasons, wouldn't approve. Would their love hold under the pressure? Could she follow her heart, be selfish for once? The prospect was alien.

With effort, Moll ignored the ache to see Horatio and forced him from her mind. Right now, there were more pressing matters.

She returned her mother's apron and looked about. She'd clean the room until it shone like a new pin then prepare breakfast, she determined. Everything must be just so for Mam's return and besides, keeping busy would restrain her thoughts. Moll yearned and dreaded seeing her in equal measures. Something like this . . . they could have lost her.

The sole concern of many who rid wombs of unwanted life was brass. Women of all ages put their lives in the hands of these often drunken, backstreet opportunists daily. Unsurprisingly, countless followed from this life the child they were desperate to be free of. Mam was one of the lucky ones but at what price? In what state would she be?

Burying her concerns, Moll nodded purposefully and went to refill the kettle.

As the sun rose unnoticed over the rooftops, she scrubbed their already well-kempt kitchen with gusto. She'd just hung her damp apron by the fire and was pouring a well-earned cup of tea when movement sounded next door. Likely Sissy wakening – as would Bo, soon, thought Moll, smiling grimly. Finally then, she'd get a coherent explanation.

Gulping her tea, she lifted down a heavy, smoke-blackened pan for the herring. The fat had barely warmed when the front door rattled – Mam home already? Moll's heart thumped in anticipation. Reaching the passage, however, she frowned; there was no one there.

Probably the Luchettis leaving, Moll surmised. She then peered into the bedroom. Sissy, sat up in bed rubbing her eyes, greeted her sleepily. But the space beside her was empty. Bo had gone.

With an angry shake of her head, Moll hurried for the front door, hoping to catch a glimpse of him. As she opened it, Jilly, arm raised to knock, almost fell into her arms. They laughed breathlessly.

'I saw the lad leave, reasoned you'd be up.'

Moll let her neighbour in then glanced left to right up Blossom Street but of Bo, there was no sign. She sighed inwardly.

'All right, lass?'

'Aye. Come through. There's a pot not long brewed.'

Looking around, Jilly nodded, smiling. 'You must have been up with the larks. Sparkling, in here, it is.'

'I wanted everything to be nice for Mam. Despite all she's done . . . Eeh, I've missed her.'

'Course you have, love.'

'Bo travelled the ten miles to Bolton, yesterday. What went on, mind, I don't know as yet.'

'Ruth's well, though, aye?'

'So the lad said. She's coming home the day.'

'I suspected she might.'

'You don't reckon it's too soon to travel, Jilly, after . . .' Her words trailed off as Sissy appeared in the doorway. Moll beckoned her over and when she'd clambered on to her knee, added quietly, 'Well, you know?'

'She'll recover quicker in familiar surroundings. She knows her body, lass, wouldn't put it through the journey were she not up to it. Anyroad, you wanting to make everything comfortable for her return, well, I had the same idea.'

'Oh?'

'I were thinking it'd be nice to put a bit of grub on, treat her. Nowt fancy, you know. Some potted sweetmeats and a cut of cheese, mebbe a light mutton pie? 'Ere, I've a fresh batch of almond biscuits downstairs. I know how much she enjoys them.'

'And we've a string of bloaters,' added Moll, warming to the plan, motioning to the high cupboard and the sausages within. 'I could fry them up with some onion

223

in a nice gravy, just how she likes it. Hold on, I'll get the jar.'

'You leave that there. I'm paying for the foodstuffs.'

'But Jilly—'

'I've done all right this week with the tea leaves, had a few wanting readings. I can stretch the brass.' Her expression softened. 'I want to. Happen it'll go some way to putting things right. I don't want ill feeling betwixt us, am that sorry for what's occurred. Ruth needs her friends now like never afore.'

'All right, if you're sure. 'Ere, mentioning tea leaves, Jilly . . .'

'Nay.'

'Aw, go on,' Moll wheedled. 'I know what to do, have watched you enough. I pour the tea and, clearing my mind of thought, sip it quietly.'

'Nay.'

'I swirl the dregs three times and tip them into the saucer. Then, when the leaves in the cup have settled, I pass it to you. Am I right?'

'Aye, but—'

'I need to know what's in store; for us, for Mam.'

'*Nay.* I've told you afore: I'll not read the leaves of someone close. No good can come of it. Many a time I've been tempted with my Alf's – even my own.' She shook her head. 'Whatever awaits will find us whether we're ready or no. What'll be will be.'

Moll stuck her tongue out. 'Aye, all right.'

'Good lass. Right, well. I'll get cracking.' Eyes star-bright with enthusiasm, Jilly bade her goodbye and ambled off.

It was shortly past noon when the front door sounded again and Ruth appeared, pale and drawn, in the doorway.

A good fire bathed the kitchen in a comforting glow. Jilly had left again just before, promising she'd be up later once Ruth was settled. Delicious-smelling dishes she'd helped create were arranged on the clean table-cloth and the warmed teapot sat in the centre. Sissy, neat and scrubbed, stood nearby. Her twin lengths of butter-coloured hair hung over her shoulders, reaching almost to her hips. Eyeing her mother, she fiddled with the plaits' curly ends then released one to plant her thumb in her mouth.

Moll glanced furtively behind her mother and seeing Davy wasn't present, swallowed a thankful smile. She stepped forward. 'Hello, Mam.'

Ruth's eyes were colder than a dead fish's. 'So. Now you know.'

Fighting to keep her gaze from straying to her mother's stomach, she nodded. 'You all right, Mam?'

'Where's the lad?'

'I . . . don't know. He went out earlier—'

'Fetch him.'

'Now? But I don't know where—'

'Aye, now.'

Putting on her shawl, Moll watched with a heavy heart her mother bring out a half-bottle of gin from a stash behind the dresser. After taking a long draught, she lowered herself into a chair, clearly in some discomfort. Clutching the bottle to her breast, she turned from her daughters to stare into the flames.

Moll gave Sissy a weak smile of reassurance, stole a last look at Ruth, then slipped out. Instinctively, she headed for the Cross Keys public house on Jersey Street's corner.

Black shapes bobbed beyond the double-arched windows and recognising Winters' tall figure, she gritted her teeth. He and Bo were never out of each other's pockets; if this one was here, her brother was sure to be.

Conversation halted the moment Moll stepped through the doors. As one, the group of scuttlers hunched over the plain deal table turned scowling faces towards her. She scanned them through narrowed eyes. And when she spotted Bo, her lips met in a hard line. As she stalked forward, her anger reached new levels when the smirking girl on his knee draped her arms around his neck.

How could Bo . . . with *her*?

'Here she is, nose in t' air like there's a bad smell.'

Her retort to Vick's remark died when she caught Bo's face up-close. His left eye was blackened, the cheekbone beneath swollen, and blood had congealed at a gash on his forehead. She hadn't noticed in the bedroom's darkness this morning; was this why he'd slipped away, to conceal his injuries? *Preston* . . . 'Lad, did Davy—?'

'Huh!'

'Then who?'

'What d'you want, Moll?'

Ignoring the brazen piece now kissing his neck, Moll ground out: 'Mam's back.'

Bo took a swig of his ale with a lazy shrug. 'And?'

'She wants you home. Now.'

'I'm busy.'

'Busy at what, like? Lounging with these no-good hooligans? Roaming the streets robbing and bashing folk to a pulp?'

'We don't thieve during battle, thank you,' piped a scuttler mildly. 'Maim and disfigure, aye, but never so far as thieving.' This earned him a round of laughter.

'It's simple, Moll.' Bo eased back in his chair. 'If a blue bag nabs you, violence with robbery carries a hefty

226

sentence with hard labour – never mind a lashing from the cat. Violence *alone* gets you a slap on the wrist. You see? We're not in it for what we can swipe. Well, besides Young, there.' He thrust his chin towards a youth. 'He'd steal the milk from your tea.' This evoked further guffaws. 'Anyroad, as I said, I'm busy so if you don't mind . . .' Bo nodded to the door.

'Aye,' purred Vick, rubbing her breasts against him, and Moll's simmering rage boiled over.

'You, yer shameless article, keep your stinking nose out of this.' Moll shook her head in disgust. 'It weren't long since I saw you offering yourself half-naked to another. Lost your tongue?' she asked when Vick merely glared back. 'Why are you slung across my brother like a dead cat when you're meant to be seeing your main lad? Answer me that, bold 'un.'

Vick laughed. The Tigers grinned, Bo included, and confusion filled Moll.

'I *am* seeing our main lad.' Vick stroked Bo's battered cheek, eyes deepening with admiration as she scanned the cut brow. 'Earned the position, he has, an' all. Ain't that right, Bo-Bo?'

'You . . . ? *You?*' Moll felt light-headed, sick to her stomach, wanted to sob her throat raw. *No! No!*

Bo's grin had gone. He lifted Vick from his lap and when she pouted, slapped her buttock, making her giggle. 'I'd best show my face at home, else I'll never hear the last of it. I'll see youse lot later.'

'I for one will look forward to it, lad.' Winters nodded grimly. 'That bastard, Rat, is in for summat hot. This gets sorted the night.'

Moll blanched. Just in time, she smothered a gasp but before she could think, blurted, 'Rat Green ain't part of the Prussia Street gang. He's given it up.'

227

'And how d'you know that, Miss Prim?' Vick cocked her head.

All eyes were on Moll. She gave what she hoped was a nonchalant shrug. 'I overheard someone mention it. Simcox is main lad, now, so they say.'

'Whether the sod's stepped down or no, he's the bashing of his life coming his way,' snarled Winters, nostrils flaring in hatred. He extracted a clasp knife from his jacket pocket and waved the glistening, six-inch blade in the air. 'If he reckons his setting upon me at Smithfield Market is forgotten, he's another think coming. We'll destroy him and with a grin on our phizogs. His time's up – Simcox with him. I'll do more than thieve *his* belt; I'll smash the shit he has for brains out with it!'

I must warn Horatio. If they should harm him . . . Oh, I wouldn't bear it! Again, doubt about a future together prickled. He couldn't shrug off his past, as he'd claimed. It would never leave him.

'We'll discuss matters later, lads.' Jerking his head at Moll, Bo strode from the pub, leaving her to hurry after him.

'Wait up. Bo—'

'What the *hell* d'you think you're about, coming in there?'

'I—'Ere, that hurts!' she protested when he gripped her and dragged her into a narrow entry.

'Sorry. I'm sorry.' The front and swagger had left him. He took her arm in his large hands and rubbed the spot he'd manhandled. 'All right?' At her nod, he leaned against the soot-blackened bricks and closed his eyes. 'Moll, look. What you've just seen . . . heard . . . I can explain.'

'All still an act, eh?' He didn't answer and she shook

her head. 'What's happening to you? Mother of God, your face. And *her*, Bo? That cow held a knife to me, unless you've forgot.'

'From what I hear, you gave as good as you got.'

'For God's sake—!'

'Aye, I'm sorry. Course Vick were wrong.' He released a heavy sigh. He looked utterly weighed down, the lines on his brow meant for someone twice his years.

'What happened?'

'This?' Bo pointed to his face. 'The Captain decided to teach me a lesson for taking Winters and Young for assistance to Bolton. I didn't ask permission, you see; he thought to make an example of me to the others. The sod set on me like a wild wolf. Captain or no, I weren't having that. The belt or knife would have been sure to follow once he'd exhausted his fists. I nipped it in the bud while I still could.'

'You gave him a beating?'

'One he's not likely to forget, an' all.' He frowned at the disappointment she knew screamed from her eyes then averted his gaze. 'So you see, I've got his title whether I want it or not. I bested him. Vick . . . Well, she's all for the power.' He shrugged. 'Suppose you could say she's my trophy.'

Moll almost dared not ask. 'And d'you?'

'Do I what?'

'Want the title?'

'Course not.'

'Then leave! Leave, lad! Surely you're free to now Preston's taken care of?'

'What?'

She blinked at his puzzled expression. 'Preston's gone, right? Mam returned alone—'

'Oh, Moll.'

After a moment, she whispered, 'What occurred, Bo? Why *did* you return without her?'

'Mam will never leave him. The sooner you accept that, the better. Me and the lads traipsing up there were for nowt.'

'What happened?'

'We found Preston's mam's dwelling easy enough, asked some streetwalkers whether they knew of him. It were no surprise they said aye. Though it's his mam they were more acquainted with.' Bo ran the back of his hand over his mouth. 'They work the streets for her.'

'For Davy's mam?'

'She's a madam, Moll. And that's not all.'

'What?'

'The bloke you overheard Preston with in that ginnel? I've a good idea it were his father.'

'Why? How?'

'They're all in it together. Their place on Moor Lane in the centre of town, where the doxies directed us, were a brothel. Preston's mam runs the show and her husband and son supply the entertainment, so to speak.'

Moll had to lean beside her brother for support. What depraved specimens were these people? 'He were planning to sell us to his own mam?'

'Looks that way. He'd fetched a penniless Irish lass to the house afore I arrived. Desperate-looking, she were, like she'd just stepped off the boat. Preston found her wandering the inns searching for work. His mam – all sickly smiles and assurances, the owd cow were – gave her a meal then took her upstairs. That's the last I saw of the lass.'

'Then surely Mam knows? She'll believe us, now?'

Bo continued in an empty voice. 'Mam were resting by the fire when we arrived. The deed was done – Davy's mam had rid her of the child. Oh, Moll, Mam . . . She were the picture of death. I said I were taking her home. I told her what style of house she were in, what Preston and his parents were about. I begged her to leave that bastard's clutches and come home.' He paused. 'She laughed in my face.'

Moll closed her eyes. *No, no.*

'She said I were mad. She insisted it were a lodging house, that Davy's mam were an angel itself, how she helped folk down on their luck, that I were wicked implying owt else. She ordered me home, said she'd follow the next day. Preston's pig face fell at that – I don't reckon he intended letting her return to Manchester, you know.'

'Thank God she's back safely. You shouldn't have left her, Bo, should have insisted—'

He laughed bitterly. 'I don't know what I were thinking. I pictured us storming in, beating Preston to a mushy pulp and carrying Mam out like some bloody knight in shining armour. But d'you know what I understand, now, our Moll? You can't save someone who don't want to be.'

'Eeh, lad.'

'I said I'd not go, couldn't leave her with them, that what I'd spoken were truth. She turned ugly with rage, told me to get out.'

'Then don't blame yourself. You did all you could.'

'She said she'd remedy this, all right, when she returned.'

Something in his tone made Moll frown. 'What is it?'

'Nowt. It's nowt. You know what Mam's like in drink, the things she spouts.'

Moll sighed in agreement. Aye, only too well. She could be hurtful beyond words when the mood struck.

He'd likely received a mouthful of the vitriol Mam usually reserved for her.

'Come on.' Bo stepped from the entry. 'She'll be wondering where we are.'

Ruth seemingly hadn't moved a muscle. She sat in the exact position Moll had left her; though she'd at least moved her arm occasionally as the bottle was almost empty.

The food Moll and Jilly lovingly prepared was gone. Two bottles had replaced the teapot and Moll realised why her mother had returned home alone. She hadn't left Davy in Bolton. She'd merely got him to leave her at their door while he went to purchase gin. Looking to the fire, where he stood with folded arms, Moll wanted to cry.

'What's happened to you?' Ruth pointed to Bo's injuries.

'Mebbe he stuck that nose of his into some bugger *else's* affairs and received a thumping for his trouble,' Davy growled before Bo could respond.

'Thing is, the foulness spat from his tongue yesterday weren't the workings of his mind. Was it?' Ruth asked harshly, fixing her glare on Moll.

And to think she'd nursed hope her mother would believe her. 'I know what I heard, Mam. What will it take to make you wise up to him? Why would I lie about summat so wicked?'

'Because you hate him. For you do, don't yer? Go on, deny it.'

'I'll deny nowt. I loathe the sod. Aye, I do.'

'And shall I tell you why? I know well enough, my lass. 'Cause he ain't him – the dead man not coming back. That's why!'

White hot fury crashed through Moll's veins. 'How dare—'

'Nay, you hard-faced young mare, how dare *you*.' Ruth rose jerkily. 'How bleedin' dare you invent such filth about that good man there. He plans to *sell* us, aye? Of all the—'

'Mam, I *heard* him. The one he discussed it with – his own father, by all accounts! – handed over brass—'

'Eeh, you're a nasty piece of work! To now drag that kind man away in Bolton into your lies?'

'And Davy's mam; she's in on it, too—'

'Oh, you! What lies! A more selfless couple you'd not find. Shame on you. Have you completely taken leave of your senses, girl?'

'She speaks the truth, Mam.' Bo nodded. 'I saw the way of things in Bolton with my own eyes.'

'Nay, lad. You saw what this one wanted you to. She's poisoned your thinking, is all.'

'It is, it's the truth!' Desperate, Moll fumbled for Ruth's hands but she snatched them back. 'Please, Mam.'

'Enough! By, you're rotten through and through. I see it, now.' Her gin-soaked breath fanned Moll's face. 'I want you out of here.'

'What?'

'You're welcome beneath this roof no more.'

'Nay, Mam . . .' Moll shook her head then swung to face Davy. 'For once in your life, tell the truth.'

'You're a fine one to talk. Huh!'

A frustrated howl ripped from Moll's throat. She pointed to Sissy. 'The lass heard them!' She rushed to her and took her shoulders. 'Tell her. Tell Mam about the bad man. You heard him and Davy, didn't you—?' Her entreaty died when Ruth hauled her from Sissy by the neck of her dress. 'Mam, ask her—'

'Leave that poor lass be and get out.'

'He's warned her not to tell.' Moll rushed at Davy, intent on clawing his face to the bone, but his words stopped her in her tracks:

'Afore you sod off out of it, tell us summat: where did this plotting you apparently overheard take place?'

'You know where. That alley by Pump Street.'

'And for what reason would you have to be up that way?' fired Ruth.

'I passed on my way home from work as I do every night.'

'I *knew* it.'

Moll shook her head in confusion. 'Knew what?'

'The journey from that inn wouldn't take you by there. You couldn't have seen Davy where you claim, no way no how.'

Moll's face fell with terrible remembrance. 'I bent the truth about my place of work. I had my reasons and I'm sorry. The inn where I'm employed *is* on Pump Street. That's the truth, Mam, honest.'

'Truth? You'd not know that were it to swipe you one across the lugholes!'

'Twit and Beattie will back me up if you'd only ask—'

'Stop, stop, stop, stop!'

Turning at the shrill plea, Moll found Sissy gazing back through swimming eyes, hands clamped over her ears. Her heart contracted. 'Oh, lass—'

'No shouting, Moll. Moll? No shouting?'

'You see what you've caused?' Ruth cried. 'Frickening the lass, you are. Out! Out!'

'You heard your mother,' murmured Davy with a definite smirk.

Tears coursed down Moll's face. With what dignity

she could scrape together, she lifted her chin. 'All right, Mam. I'll go.'

'If Moll ain't welcome here, I'm not.'

Whipping around, she pressed a hand to her brother's chest. 'Nay, Bo. Don't leave Mam with him.' She ignored Ruth's snort. 'Stay, please.'

'What style of mother would sling her own on the streets? This ain't right.'

'When's the last time *owt* were right beneath this roof, lad? Don't fret, I'll be fine.' Moll took a deep breath, nodded then looked to Sissy, but Ruth moved in front of the girl.

'Oh no. Don't even think you're for taking Sissy along. You'll not poison her against Davy as you've done with my lad.'

'I'll watch her,' Bo assured Moll when she turned desperate eyes to him.

'You promise?'

'Aye.'

Not rising to Davy's wave, Moll cast a lingering look around and left the house that was no longer home.

'Moll, wait up.' Bo sprinted after her up the street. 'I'm sorry, I am. In Bolton, when Mam vowed she'd do this, I thought it nowt but drink talk . . . Eeh, our Moll. Where will you go?'

Pain of injustice and abandonment was unbearable. 'Twit and Beattie keep a palliasse in the kitchen. They'll put me up, I'm sure.'

'Eeh, our Moll,' repeated Bo helplessly, and she forced a reassuring nod.

'Go on in, lad.'

'I'll visit, fetch Sissy when I can.'

'Aye. Ta. Explain to the lass, eh? She'll be worried, confused. She ain't used to being apart from me.'

'This is the last straw, Moll, I mean it. That divil back there's got to go.'

They stared at one another sadly before going their separate ways. She kept her head high but the moment she turned into Bengal Street, she wilted. Sagging against a wall, she sobbed into her fist.

In all her days, she'd never felt so alone. How could Mam do this? Bo had left for Uriah's, aye, but of his own accord. He'd felt driven to but still, it had been his choice. Mam had actually ordered her out, made her destitute. Her own child! Just what would it take for her to see through Preston?

Moll contemplated retracing her steps to find comfort with Jilly but thought better of it. If Mam should spot her . . . She hadn't strength to bear a second round. Instead, she hurried for the only other soul she trusted to see her side.

'Polly ain't in.'

Swallowing disappointment, Moll squeezed out a smile for her friend's mother. 'D'you know when she'll be back?'

'Your guess is as good as mine. I can't fathom the lass, lately, I can't,' she mumbled as though to herself.

'Is everything all right? Polly, she's well?'

'Well enough.'

A worried frown touched Moll's brow; she'd never known Polly's mother like this. 'Happen I'll call later if it's all right?'

''Ere, our Polly's got herself a fella.'

'She has?' a surprised Moll asked Katie, who had appeared in the doorway.

'Get back inside, you!' Mrs Wainwright pushed her grinning daughter into the house. 'Anyroad . . . I'll tell her you called, Moll. Must go, I've a pan on t' fire.'

Well! A warm glow accompanied Moll to the inn. Polly had kept that quiet! She must definitely return to her friend's later; just who was this man? Despite her own troubles, her mouth retained its smile. If anyone deserved happiness, Polly did. Clearly, she'd once had her heart broken, had harboured feelings for the fool a long time – and a fool he must be to let her go. Maybe now, Polly could put the hurt behind her. Oh, but she was delighted for her!

And what of you? Moll asked herself and she bit her lip. *Was crushing Uriah's hopes for nothing? If you let Horatio slip away, will you one day brand yourself the fool?*

Could she let him go?

The answer came immediately. Smiling softly, she continued on her way.

Chapter 17

MOLL WIGGLED HER toes to the flickering flames. Her hair, dark as a midnight sky, lay loose and she ran a hand through it, her sleepy gaze on the glowing coals.

A smile caressed her lips and she marvelled anew at the change in herself over the days. Bar the yearning for Sissy and Bo, and worry for her mother, Moll had never been happier.

She'd begun to flourish within hours of arriving here on Sunday. Being away from home was good for her and it showed. It was beginning to seem a blessing that she'd been forced from that toxic environment. She was brighter, at ease. Her head felt the lightest it had in many a year.

Never was a voice raised in anger in this family. Though the nature of their business brought steady streams of hard drinkers to their step, and ale and spirits flowed freely, inebriated customers didn't stray into her domain. At the night's end, once the door was bolted and shutters secured at the windows, an easiness embraced the place and Moll would hunker down in this, her haven.

Twice, she'd returned to Polly's house, to be told each time she'd narrowly missed her. Where she'd gone or when she'd be back, Polly's mother could never say. Her obvious displeasure at her daughter's exploits, however, was mounting and Moll struggled to restrain her giggles until she was away from the house.

It had always seemed to Moll that Mrs Wainwright failed to notice Polly's ascent into womanhood. She treated her daughters entirely the same in manner and speech. That fifteen years' difference existed between the two, their mother appeared blind to. Or perhaps fear of losing Polly lay behind her disapproval?

In that sense, imagining how she'd cope when Bo flew the nest, Moll did feel sorry for her. Nonetheless, truth was, Polly was a grown woman. She'd every right to a life, and Moll was pleased she'd finally begun forging one. Spinsterhood didn't suit the vivacious woman. She'd too much love inside just waiting to be given. She deserved this.

Of home, she'd heard nothing. Hugging herself, she closed her eyes. Hopefully, Bo would visit soon with Sissy. Work swallowed his weekdays, she understood, but surely he'd call at the weekend, even just for half an hour? If Twit and Beattie gave permission, she'd take the girl to the library. It seemed an age since they last went and it always proved enjoyable.

Since Sissy's birth, she'd never once been parted from her and longing struck physically. It was like a chunk of her was missing. As with Bo, the girl was more than a sibling. Moll felt like a mother separated from her child. She just prayed Sissy didn't feel the same if going by this pain.

When tapping reached Moll, she struggled opening her eyes. The hour was late; coupled with the fire, her tired mind felt foggy. She listened and when silence greeted her, shrugged and snuggled deeper into the palliasse.

Soft knocking at the kitchen window yanked her from her slumber with a jolt, and now she was on her feet. Her first thought was that something had happened at home; why else would someone be here, at this hour? She hurried to the back door and put her mouth close: 'Who is it? That you, Bo?'

'It's me.'

Her every muscle froze. Her heartbeat drummed through her ears and a queer rush knotted her stomach. With shaky fingers, she teased the lock back. The sight of him, so close she felt heat from his body, snatched her breath. 'Horatio.'

'I had to see you.'

And I you. Lord, how I've missed you.

What she was doing was madness. If Twit or Beattie discovered him, she'd be out – jobless *and* homeless. It would ruin everything. And it mattered not a jot. Nothing did at this moment but that he was here. She couldn't send him away had her very life depended on it. Without another word, for none was needed, she slipped her hand into his and led him inside.

They stood facing one another before the fire. When Horatio's arm went around her waist, Moll melted against him. He lifted the other to gather a handful of her hair and as his fingers played in the tresses, she closed her eyes. Every inch of her cried out for his touch. Of its own accord, her hand moved to stroke his nape and he released his breath slowly.

'I've thought long and hard about us.'

His eyes widened slightly. 'And?'

'God help me, I love you,' she said simply. 'I can't – won't – give you up. Somehow, somehow . . . we'll make this work. Horatio?' she asked, frowning, when his eyes creased. 'What is it? Your feelings for me haven't changed, have they?'

'Changed . . . ?' He blinked rapidly. 'Can you imagine for a single second how it feels for someone like me . . . to hear someone like *you* say . . . and mean it?'

He was verging on tears – surprise had her shaking her head. This tall and powerfully built man, terrifying to most, it was true, was baring his soul to her without a shred of shame. Physically, he was as perfect as any male could wish to be – and that any woman could dream for. Everything was right, not a single thing out of proportion, as though God had taken extra special attention when creating him.

From the high cheekbones to his jaw's angle, straight nose and those exquisite eyes – even his hair and skin-tone, as dark as hers – were just so, accentuating his features and adding another layer to the overall effect. Horatio was, in a word, beautiful. And he'd chosen her, who had never felt pretty, really. Her whose every part seemed slightly too large to be deemed feminine. Here he stood before her, a love of such purity pouring from him that it brought a lump to her throat, when he could have any lass, *any*. Yet it was her and no other he wanted.

Though not understanding why, the notion scared her a little. Inadequacy stung and momentary panic gripped her. It was fear of losing him, she realised. Would it be better to nip this in the bud here? Surely she'd bear the loss easier if she sent him away now than if she lost him later?

'Moll?'

Her lips moved but nothing came.

'Moll, what's wrong?'

'You're by far the most handsome man I've ever laid eyes on,' she managed, almost sadly.

Horatio looked genuinely shocked. 'I am?'

'It's not that, not just your looks. It's how you make me feel inside. How you treat me, the things you say. How can I explain . . . ? What's the word?' She frowned. 'Precious. Aye, that's it. I ain't ever known that from another living soul. I'm . . . I mean, thoughts of you finding someone else . . . that I might lose . . .' She shook her head. 'You think yourself unworthy of me. Truth is, you couldn't be more wrong.'

'Moll, Moll.' He wiped the tears that had spilled down her cheeks then took her face in his hands. His eyes were dark with intensity. 'You're mine alone. You have been since we met. Then, now, always. No one will come between us. Ever. Understand?' he finished almost harshly and she knew for a moment what others must have once under his command. To her, however, his dominance evoked security not fear.

'I do.'

With one hand, he undid the nightdress Beattie had kindly given her, taking his time over each button. Then he eased it from her shoulders and it fell slowly to the floor.

Moll's heart beat so rapidly she couldn't feel it. Completely naked, she squirmed beneath his gaze but he shook his head.

'Don't shrink from me. My God. My God. Just look at you.' He dropped to his knees, encircled her waist with his arms and laid his head against her stomach. 'Never leave me. Promise me.'

She slid to the floor and brushed his lips with a kiss. 'I promise.'

Horatio allowed her to remove his cap and unwind

his muffler. His jacket and waistcoat, he removed himself but when she began unbuttoning his shirt, he drew her hands away. 'Moll . . .'

'What's wrong?'

For several seconds, he stared at her from under hooded lids. Then he reached over his shoulder and pulled the shirt over his head. His breathing had quickened and his face had taken on a look akin to shame mixed with dread.

She ran her eyes over him. Copper pans hanging by the fire winked in the flames' glow, throwing ruby-gold splinters across his smooth torso. Why had he reacted so? He was perfect, perfect – her hands itched to touch him. She glanced up, confused.

'I'm sorry.'

'Sorry for wh—?' Her question died as he turned. Now, it was she who murmured, 'My God. My God.' Though for an entirely different reason. His back was a network of criss-crossed scars. Some were silver with age, some an angry red, some deeper than others. 'What *happened* to you?' she whispered to the back of his head. 'God in heaven . . .'

'Nay,' he cut in. 'I know what you're thinking but nay, this ain't the result of scuttling.'

Thinking of Bo, relief washed through her. Besides the odd mark on his hands, Horatio looked to have escaped his battle years unscathed. 'Then what? Who did this?'

'Let's just say my uncle enjoys the belt's feel against his palm more than any scuttler.'

'Mr Simcox did this? Twit once remarked that your aunt, as I now know she is, sometimes bedded down in this here kitchen out of her fella's road, for he liked knocking her about . . .'

'Don't be fooled. She's every bit as rotten. They're a bad lot, Moll. I told you once afore, remember? That night outside the police station?'

She nodded. 'Why not leave?'

'And go where?'

She didn't have an answer.

'Much as it sickens me saying it, they're all I have.'

He still had his back to her and she traced a tender touch across the shiny welts. Why had he been afraid to show himself to her? Had he believed for a second she'd recoil from this, from him? 'They're not all you have,' she murmured. 'Not any more.'

Horatio turned. His mouth sought hers and in one swift movement, he swept her down on to the palliasse. Wide shoulders rippling in the firelight, he stared down at her. 'You'll never know just how much I love you.'

Gaze soft, she smiled. What they were about to do was inevitable once she'd taken his hand at the back door. She knew then where it would lead. Right now, she'd never wanted anything more. Whatever resulted from their night together, she knew implicitly she wouldn't face it alone. He had her, heart and soul, and she him. Always.

He entered her slowly, eyes never leaving hers, and for a fleeting moment, she realised she wasn't his first. He'd known a woman before; he exuded confidence, knew exactly what he was doing. However, she'd no time to dwell upon this – after initial pain, tides of pleasure stole her senses and she gave herself up without resistance.

Afterwards, neither spoke, they simply held one another tightly. Their breathing had long since steadied and Moll felt sleep closing in when a thought struck. She raised herself on her elbow.

'How did you know I'd be here the night?' She frowned when he broke eye contact to stare into the fire. 'Horatio? How? You couldn't possibly have known what's occurred at home.'

'Your mam told me.'

'What?'

'I called on you at Blossom Street.'

'When?'

'This afternoon.'

Covering her face, she groaned. 'Nay . . . You shouldn't have *done* that.'

'I had to see you. Where's the harm?'

Where was the harm . . . ? Lord, how did it slip her mind? The Tigers' intentions, the threat to him, had been sidelined by Bo's shocking revelations concerning the Prestons. She'd meant to warn him. *She'd forgotten.*

'Moll, what—?'

'Did Bo see you?'

'Your brother?'

'Aye. When you called by my house?'

Horatio shook his head.

'Thank God . . .'

'What's going on?' He was sitting up, now, face serious. 'There's summat you're not telling me.'

'I meant to, need to warn you . . . It's the Bengal Tigers. They mean to harm you – your cousin, an' all. How they spoke . . . I don't believe it an idle threat. They want your blood, Horatio.'

'But I'm done with that. What happens between the Tigers and Prussias has nowt to do with me no more. Sammy's main lad, now. They know that.'

'They want revenge for what occurred at the market.'

Nodding slowly, he sighed. 'Winters.'

'Aye.'

'I thought the Tigers had bigger fish to fry. Your brother ain't mentioned it?' he asked at Moll's puzzled frown.

'Bo tells me nowt where scuttling's concerned. What d'you mean, bigger fish?'

'From what I hear, the Prussia gang ain't no longer high on t' Tigers' list. They're in battle with the Meadow Lads across the water. Some skirmish occurred betwixt the two recently at New Cross, and both sides are eager to prove their mettle.' His voice dropped. 'I reckon the Tigers might've met their match. You'd do well to warn that brother of yourn. The Meadows are a cut-throat lot and no mistake.'

Since Horatio arrived, they had conversed in hushed tones so as not to disturb the family upstairs. Now, Moll's voice was almost a yell. 'Oh, the foolish young . . . Where will it end?'

Suddenly, three short, shrill, male whistles outside cut through the room. A female's distinctive, high-pitched scream followed and by habit, Horatio put his nose in the air. His eyes narrowed.

'A scuttle?'

He nodded. Battle calls for reinforcements were unmistakable.

'The Tigers?'

'I think so.' A muffled screech rang and his mouth tightened. 'Sammy.'

They rose simultaneously and began dressing.

'Stay put. I'll see what's occurring,' muttered Horatio, reaching for his cap. Moll's response had him spinning to face her. He shook his head.

'You stop out of it,' she repeated, expression set. 'That might be my brother out there. He'll listen to me. If what they said about getting revenge on you and Sammy were true . . . if that *were* your cousin you've just heard . . . Please. Stay out their way. Let me sort it. I'll be fine.'

The night Sammy laid into her about her cooking, Horatio had mentioned in this very room he'd been at the market killing some hours. Now scuttling didn't hold him, he'd nothing to occupy him. But he was coping, and doing it well. He was determined not to slip into old ways, and Moll was damned if whatever raged outside would drag him back. The Tigers would be on him in a heartbeat and he'd be unable to resist battling, she just knew. The thrill of the fight was an insatiable pull. No, she'd not risk it.

Leading, she slipped through the back door, pulling it to behind them. The shouts, louder now, were coming from the direction of Oldham Road and flashing Horatio a worried glance, she hurried on.

Like black talons clawing the city, the myriad dark courts and alleyways stretched all around but Moll, her brother at the forefront of her mind, gave barely a thought to her surroundings and possible danger in the shadows. Desperate chancers likely lurked there, but with Horatio by her side, she knew no fear.

Turning from a side street, they emerged into a dimly lit lane where two groups, each some thirty members strong, faced one another in the cobbled road. The odd curtain twitched but no one emerged from dwellings. Folk knew better than to intervene. Fights fizzled out in their own good time and not before; their presence would only exacerbate matters.

All Manchester scuttlers loathed Salford scuttlers, and vice versa. Thus, opposing gangs of the same district would, under pressure, join ranks against the common 'foreign' enemy. The same was true of the law – gangs would momentarily lay aside differences and, banding together, direct their shared hatred towards the police. This also carried with members of the public bold enough to interfere. Every scuttler would make the innocent their target without a shred of mercy.

Damage to property or not, no one would intercede. Better a broken pane than a cracked skull.

It was female scuttlers' job to collect and carry in their aprons for their lads sticks and bricks as extra artillery; these, and curses, now began raining between the Prussia lads and the Tigers. Belts were being wrapped around wrists, fists were bunched, pokers and knives drawn ready. One or two even wielded cutlasses.

Moll scanned the faces desperately and her breath faltered on catching sight of Bo. His twisted face, bared teeth and rage-filled eyes, narrowed into slits as he faced his opponents, were the stuff of nightmares. He was like a different being to the one she knew and loved and suddenly, Uriah's words returned with sickening truth. For all the world, she wanted to deny it but there was no mistaking it – her brother was enjoying every second. *Dear God, dear God . . .*

'Wait here.'

'Are you mad?' Grasping her arm, Horatio hauled her back into the brushmaker's shop's shadows. 'D'you think I'd see you go into that lot's midst?' His mouth hardened. 'I'll sort it.'

'Nay! They'll kill you, yer fool, or die trying. They mustn't see you. Don't you dare let them, d'you hear?'

'But—'

'You vowed you're finished with scuttling and it's stopping that way. If you love me as you purport, you'll do as I beg and stay here.' Before he could respond, she broke from his hold and skittered towards the fray.

'Bastard! Let's see your mettle, now, Simcox.'

Bo rushed at Sammy, landing a heavy punch to his face. The stocky lad stumbled; a second blow brought him to his knees. Bo grinned down and lifted his arm above his head. A belt was wound around his forearm like a flat black snake and as the solid buckle swung for Sammy's head, Moll screeched in horror.

'Stop, Bo! Stop!'

In the split second it took her brother to glance across at her in surprise, Sammy was on his feet. With a scream, he threw himself at Bo and plunged his knife into his shoulder. Bo cried out but Moll's shouts went unheard – sucking in a sharp breath, he gripped Sammy's head in his huge hands and clamped his ear between his teeth. Sammy's animalistic squeals reverberated off the buildings as Bo bit a chunk clean off and spat it into the road.

Other Prussia Street members, admitting defeat by the Tigers' might, had already scarpered, bloodied and bleeding, and now Sammy staggered after them roaring a stream of threats at Bo.

Moll grabbed her brother's arms as he made to pursue him and shook him hard, almost screaming into his face, 'For God's sake, *stop*, lad!'

He looked after Sammy a while longer then brought his blank gaze to her.

'What in hell is wrong with you? You could have killed him. *You* could have been killed, you bloody stupid . . . bloody brainless young . . .' A sob choked Moll's tirade. She shook him again. 'This stops the night!'

He flicked his donkey fringe and stared silently.

'Your shoulder. Let me see.'

Moll reached up but Bo dodged her touch, turned and disappeared into the night. Laughing and patting each other's backs, the Tigers, having chased off the last of their enemies, melted with him. In the now-deserted street, tears dripped down Moll's face. Hands squeezed her shoulders softly from behind and she closed her eyes. 'He's gone, Horatio. I've lost him to them. I don't know who he is any more.'

He drew her close and guided her back to the inn.

'Bo enjoys it. I saw it in his eyes. How could I have let this happen?'

'Don't blame yourself. It drags you in, Moll. The thrill it gives, the excitement . . . It's addictive.' He looked away when she cast him a sidelong look. 'You'd not understand.'

'D'you miss it?' she whispered.

'The truth?'

'Aye.'

His Adam's apple bobbed. 'Sometimes. My love for you overrides any stirring I might get, mind. I'd sooner die than ruin what we have. Never will I be that lad again.' He halted. Looking down at her, he licked his lips several times. 'Moll?'

'Aye?'

'Will you marry me?'

She couldn't speak. Then a smile crept across his face and she laughed brokenly. 'Aye, you daft sod. Course I will!'

Tears misted his eyes but he blinked them back and nodded purposefully. 'Right. All right, then. Married it is.'

'You all right?'

'Aye. Aye.'

She grinned. 'The thought of it . . . bit scary, in't it?'

'Aye,' he agreed, pulling a frightened face, and they laughed.

They reached the inn door and, gazing at him, Moll caressed his cheek. 'Night, lad.'

'Night, my love.'

''Ere. What will happen when you return home?' Her happiness dimmed. 'Sammy . . .'

'He never saw me. My aunt and uncle can't pin a scrap of blame on me for what's occurred the night.'

The scars scoring his back swam in her mind and she looked away. 'If they discovered you stood by whilst he were attacked . . .'

'They'll not,' he answered. Nonetheless, Moll heard the worried tinge.

'You think Sammy's all right? Bo . . . Never would I have believed him capable had I not seen that with my own eyes. *I'll* tear a strip from *him* when I see him. I'll make him leave after this night, I will. I'll bloody knock sense into him with my two hands, you see if I don't. This ends, now.'

'Happen I could have a word, make him see there's more to life than scuttling?'

Her eyes widened with horror. 'Lord, no. Please, let me sort it.'

'Your face. It's gone bone-white. Ah, I see.' Horatio nodded. 'It's just hit you what accepting my proposal means. Your brother shall have to know; that's what you're thinking, ain't it? You're afraid to tell him.'

Terrified was a better description. God in heaven, when Bo discovered she was to wed – wed Rat Green . . . She swallowed hard. How would he react? And Sammy, his family? Just how would they take the news?

Deep within, a trickle of heat spread, swelling to a wave of defiant determination. To hell with their disapproval! This was her and Horatio's lives, their decision, *their* futures they were talking about here. Why should

251

others dictate what they did? If she wanted to marry, *whoever* she wanted to, they either liked it or lumped it, the lot. She was done putting her life on hold, and for what? Where had it got her with Mam? Bloody nowhere, that's where.

Moll looked the man she loved in the eye. 'I'm not afraid a bit. I'll inform my brother next time we meet.' After his behaviour tonight, the lad would have a damn cheek taking her to task over hers.

'Oh, Moll.' Horatio took her in his arms with a long sigh.

She clung to him. 'I love you,' she whispered fiercely, telling herself everything would be all right. It had to be.

Chapter 18

'HELLO, MAM.'

Blinking in the sunlight, Ruth muttered something Moll didn't catch then opened the door fully. Lips puckered, she folded her arms.

'Is Bo home?'

'Nay.'

For all her nerves, Moll's voice was surprisingly calm. She tried a smile and when her mother didn't react, cleared her throat. 'How are you—?'

'Did you want summat?'

'I've missed you, Mam.' And she had.

Ruth's face softened slightly. She looked at her feet.

'Can I come in? Please?'

'I'll have no trouble.'

'Nor am I here to make any.'

After sighing twice, Ruth walked away down the passage. Closing the door quietly, Moll followed.

The sight of Sissy brought a lump to her throat. The girl ran to throw her arms around Moll's neck, and she hugged her tightly.

'Moll! Moll? Love you, Moll.'

'Eeh, and me you.'

Sitting at the table, their mother lifted the teapot lid,

peered inside then replaced it. 'So. What's this visit in aid of?'

'I wanted to see you.' Automatically, Moll crossed to the fire and put the kettle on the heat. 'Ta,' she said, accepting the empty pot from Ruth.

Busying herself with the mugs, she flicked a glance around the space. The room and, if she was honest, its occupants, were unkempt. Sissy and her mother's hair were lank, aprons grubby. Despite the hour, dirty breakfast dishes littered the stained table and a stale odour hung in the air. It appeared no one had lifted a finger in her absence. Surprisingly, however, Mam seemed relatively sober and for that, Moll was grateful. More than anything, she was glad Preston wasn't here.

'Davy will be back shortly so you'd best speak your piece and quick,' Ruth announced, as though she'd plucked the musings from Moll's head. 'There'll be hell to pay if he finds you here. And can you blame the fella after the vitriol you spouted? Treading his parents' good names into the mud as you did? Why, you're lucky you're standing there, my lass, for I'm sure I must need my bumps feeling, letting you across the step. But, you're my daughter and I'll not turn you away from my door, more fool me. No one can say Ruth Chambers don't do right by her kiddies when push comes to shove.'

Moll almost choked on a gasp of utter incredulousness but managed to cover it with a cough. The most incredible thing was that Mam believed what she said; she was nodding to herself, mouth set in conviction. Still, Moll needed this meeting to run as smoothly as possible if she was to get anywhere. Her future rested on it.

'Your employers took you in? You're lodging at the inn?'

Moll nodded.

'All right, is it?'

'Aye.'

'You getting enough to eat, and that?'

'Aye, Mam.'

'That's good.'

Moll poured them tea then lifted her sister into her lap. Discreetly, so as not to antagonise her mother for her inability to look after the girl, she untied Sissy's ribbons and teased her fingers through the tangled tresses before plaiting it neatly.

Watching, Ruth's mouth curved in a gentle smile. Her voice holding a sad note, she murmured, 'You can't come home, Moll.'

'I don't want to.' Moll shook her head quickly at her mother's crestfallen expression. She hadn't intended it to sound like that and gave Ruth's hand a brief squeeze. 'What I mean is . . .' She grinned self-consciously. 'I'm to be married, Mam.'

'Eh?'

'Aye!'

'Wed? Thee? To who? Oh, my lass!'

Enveloped in the familiar, gin-stale embrace, Moll closed her eyes, a surprising happiness running through her. At the end of the day, this was her mam. The only one she'd ever have, and couldn't change. She simply must accept what her mother was willing to give in terms of love. Despite all she'd done and, more painfully, *not* done, were Moll to cut her off as others would, she'd have less than she did now. Wasn't something better than nothing? It was making do with what you had. Life, sometimes, was like that.

'And when were you planning on introducing this lad to your mam?'

'I believe you've already met. He called here for me once and you directed him to the inn, remember?'

'Oh. Aye, aye,' Mam said, though it was evident she didn't. She'd probably been the worse for drink at the time. 'Tell me everything! What's he like, then?'

Animation wreathed Ruth's face and her enthusiasm spread to Moll, who giggled excitedly. 'His name's Horatio Green and he lives with his aunt and uncle on Prussia Street.' She pulled a face. 'They're a reet rotten lot by all accounts but I'll not let that put me off. I . . . love him. Eeh, I do. And he loves me, Mam. A lot, like, you know?'

'You in trouble?' Ruth asked quietly.

Moll's face erupted in a scorching blush, recalling their loving in the inn kitchen, the sensations, his smell, taste . . . She sipped her tea to compose herself. In trouble . . .

The possibility had crossed her mind since. However, she knew instinctively that, should a child result, she wouldn't face it alone. Horatio would love her still and, like her, cherish their creation. 'We love one another, Mam,' she eventually responded. 'That's why we're marrying, nowt more, nowt less.'

'How long you known him? I don't recall you making mention of him afore.'

'We met by chance the day Father passed away. We . . . well, clicked, you know?' She smiled and her mother nodded. 'I know it's fast, madness even. But it's right. We're both certain.'

'Eeh, my own lass wedding! I've been awaiting this day, I have. Robert . . .' Her lips wobbled. She pressed her knuckles against them. 'Your father would be proud.'

'Oh, Mam.'

They clung to each another.

'You've my permission, lass, and gladly.'

With a quiet sigh, Moll's body relaxed. Part of her

had worried Mam would refuse owing to recent events. She wasn't, after all, of age; without her mother's consent, she couldn't marry. How she'd have borne that, she didn't know. The wait until the law deemed her of age to make her own decisions would have been impossible. Twenty-one seemed a lifetime away.

'I mightn't have met the lad but if you say he's all he is, and it's what you want, I'm sure he's sound,' Ruth added. 'I want to meet him, see for myself, mind, and sharpish. How about the night?'

'Aye?'

'I'll cook summat nice, eh? Aye, and we'll get to know him proper, all of us together. What d'you say to that?'

'But . . . Preston . . . ?'

'Just you leave Davy to me. He'll agree when hearing the news. 'Ere, he'll be that pleased to be rid of you, he'll likely offer to do the cooking hisself!'

This, her mother's attempt at humour, hurt but Moll let it go. She wouldn't, however, have her think everything was forgotten – she had to say it: 'What I said about Preston *is* truth, Mam. All of it. But . . .'

'Aye, but?'

'But . . .' Moll took a deep breath. 'I want, nay need, you in my life. And Sissy; I miss her summat awful. I don't want Preston coming betwixt us no more.' She studied Ruth's face but couldn't gauge what her response would be; it was now empty of expression.

'Whoever this lad is, he's good for you, it's plain. You've changed overnight, it seems. For the good,' Mam added quietly, smiling. 'You seem older somehow. And softer, aye. He's smoothed that edge you had to you. Don't lose it altogether, mind, d'you hear, for you'd not be you otherwise.' Affection deepened her eyes. 'You keep a little of that fire, lass, and you'll not go far wrong.'

Nodding, Moll swallowed, wanted to drop her face into her hands and cry. *Why can't you be like this, say these things, all the time?* she wanted to ask. In these moments, Mam made you feel incredibly loved, wanted. If only it was that way always.

'Be sure to inform Horatio the meal will be ready around six. *I'll* be sure to tell our Bo to be here. I'll likely have to strap him to that bloody chair, mind. He failed to come home again last night. Treats this place like a common lodging house, lately, he does. Them new friends of his take up all his time these days.'

'How is he?' Moll asked with what casualness she could muster.

'All right. Mind, he came here bleeding summat awful from his shoulder t' other night. Don't fret,' she added at what she believed was a shocked gasp from Moll. 'I stitched him up and he were none the worse for it. Took a tumble, the clumsy divil did, and fell on a broken bottle in t' road. He were fortunate not to do more damage. Wound were a deep 'un.'

Oh, Mam, Mam. Bo . . . She couldn't tell her. Things had gone too far for that. She'd surely want to know his reason for joining; the truth would bring a raging storm of trouble she doubted they would ever get past. Best Mam remained ignorant as long as possible.

Moll wasn't certain, now, of Bo's intentions concerning Davy. Did he still plan to be shot of him? Was he simply using that to explain his continued scuttling? And what of the Tigers' feud with the Prussia gang – Horatio and Sammy particularly? How in God's name would Bo react tonight when discovering 'Rat' at his table and that she planned to marry him? She had to find her brother, explain. *Why, why, could life never be simple?*

'Moll? Moll?'

Forcing her problems away, she turned to Sissy.

'Getting wed? Getting wed, Moll?'

Moll and her mother shared a smile. 'Aye. 'Ere, how would you like to be a bridesmaid?'

'An angel, she'll look!'

'She will, Mam.' Moll drew the girl close. 'What d'you say, lass?'

'Bridesmaid, Moll? Sissy? Sissy?'

'Aye. I'll ask Polly, an' all— Ay, I've not told Polly, yet! Her face will be a picture.'

'Go on, you go and see your friend,' Ruth said, smiling. 'You don't mind?'

'Nay. Anyroad, we'll see you later, won't we? Don't forget, six o'clock sharp. I can't hardly wait to meet this fella.' She wiggled her eyebrows. 'Handsome, is he?'

Moll's cheeks pinkened. She grinned. 'He is, Mam.'

Chuckling, Ruth led her down the passage. When Moll reached the street and her gaze strayed to the cellar, Ruth nodded. 'Visit Polly and then . . .' She nodded again. 'Aye, inform Jilly.'

Had her animosity towards the old woman faded? wondered Moll with a thankful smile. 'See you later, Mam. Bye, Sissy love.'

The girl took her thumb from her mouth to wave and after a last smile at her mother, Moll turned for Poland Street. She'd lain awake last night worrying about that meeting; it had gone better than she'd dared hope. She just prayed the same was said after speaking with Bo.

Polly's house came into view and excitement quickened Moll's pace. She couldn't wait to relay her news, and afterwards, perhaps Polly would open up about her own romance. Who her friend's mystery man was, Moll itched to know. Who would have believed but weeks ago both she and Polly would be in love? She certainly wouldn't. Yet, it was true! Maybe Polly would marry, too, she thought, excitement mounting.

Lost in daydreams of a double wedding, matching bouquets and Sissy and Katie as bridesmaids, Moll noticed the man behind her too late. With a shove that sent her staggering, Davy laughed twistedly.

'Well, look who it is. I thought we'd seen the back of your ugly phizog.'

Moll lifted her chin. Lord, how she loathed him. 'Leave me be, you rotten swine, yer. God above.' Grimacing, she stepped back from the reek of ale as he swayed closer. 'You drunken mess. You're a disgrace, d'you know that?'

'And you're a bitch. It's telling when your own mam wants nowt to do with you.'

'That's where you're wrong. I've just been to see her and she's invited me for some grub, later, so put that in your pipe and choke on it! We're celebrating.' She nodded. 'I'm to be wed; what d'you say to that?'

'I say God help the blind bugger what's asked you! You'll step foot in that house, mind, over my dead body.'

'That just might be, unless you're careful.'

'What's that meant to mean?'

'Mam's warm to me wedding, to us scraping back a relationship from the ruins you've caused. Somehow, I'll make her see you for what you are, you watch if I don't.'

'Is that right?'

'Get your stinking hands off me,' she cried when he grabbed her arms but further protest died as he slammed her against a nearby house, knocking the breath from her.

'Think you've won, don't you?' he slurred in her ear. 'Nay, bitch! I've a weighty purse coming for that mam of yourn.' He grinned into her horrified face. 'I'll take a loss on you – I'd be lucky scraping a farthing from them where you're concerned. Ruthie on t' other hand . . . Mm.' He licked his lips. 'Many a red-blooded fella will spend over the odds for a taste of her spoils and I'll reap the rewards; not before time. Forked out a tidy sum over the months, I have, keeping her and you brats. Mind, you must speculate to accumulate, eh?'

''Ere, what's your game?'

Davy swivelled around to shoot a scowl at a man across the street. 'You mind your own,' he snarled, and to Moll's dismay, the passer-by threw her an apologetic look and walked away. 'Now,' continued Davy, 'where were we? Oh aye, that nice wet money-pit betwixt your mam's legs—'

'Shut your foul tongue!' Trembling with fury, Moll pressed her face to his laughing one. 'You think you're so smart, don't you? You think you've hoodwinked Mam and got away with it but that's where you're wrong. You've a sharp shock coming your way, Preston. You'll see. You'll be laughing the other side of your face once they've finished with you—'

'What you on about?'

She clamped her mouth shut. No, she shouldn't have *told* him that. He mustn't know . . .

'What you on about?' Davy repeated harshly. 'Once who's finished with me?'

Snatching free of him, she backed away. 'Just you leave us alone, else you'll regret it.' She walked away. With each step, she expected his hand to clamp down on her shoulder but it didn't and when, finally, she forced herself to look, he'd gone.

Gulping relieved sobs, she picked up her skirts and ran to Polly's door. Knocking and getting no reply, she could have screamed. Where was her friend, lately, when she needed her? It was like Polly had forgotten she existed since meeting this new bloke.

Moll moved to the window and, cupping her eyes, peered between the half-open curtains. Fire burned low in the grate, the sagging chairs either side empty. Swivelling her gaze, she squinted harder. White flashes caught her attention but she couldn't make them out. Slowly, slowly, her eyes became accustomed to the dim light and she could only watch, transfixed in shock, the writhing figures on the sofa.

The whiteness – Polly's bare thighs, Moll now realised – stood out against the dark clothing of the man they were wrapped around. Her friend had her head thrown back, eyes closed, face creased in pleasure; cheeks aflame, Moll averted her stare. Her intention to slip away, however, was dashed when she glimpsed a discarded muffler on the floor. Her heart seemed to stop beating before tripping over itself in painful thumps.

Moll cast Polly's lover a last look then scurried for sanctuary.

After slipping undetected into the inn, Moll removed her shawl and made tea to calm herself. However, as she sat staring into space, the brew grew cold and still she was no nearer to understanding what she'd just witnessed.

Polly and Uriah Croft!

Lost in passion, they hadn't heard her knock – what in heaven would have happened had Katie and Mrs Wainwright seen them instead; clearly, they were out and the lovers had taken full advantage. No wonder Polly's mother wasn't pleased. Moll fully understood why, now. The age gap alone; what was her friend playing at? As for him . . .

Moll scraped back her chair. She must see him.

Whatever his intentions towards Polly, they were not of love – how could they be after all he'd declared to Moll herself only weeks before? What was going on? Was he playing her friend to make her jealous? She couldn't stand by and see Polly hurt. The lad had some explaining to do and Moll was determined to hear him.

'Well?' she asked minutes later when Uriah answered his door.

'Moll.' He frowned, surprised. 'All right?'

'I'm lucky I caught you in, eh?'

'As it happens, aye. I've just this minute got home.'

'What's your game, Uriah?'

'Game?'

'You and Polly.' There. She'd said it. She watched his face contort into several expressions. 'You don't love her. I'll not see her hurt.'

He opened the door wide and stepped aside, and she brushed past him into the house. Arms folded, he stood before the chair she'd dropped into. 'Why's it any concern of yours what I get up to?'

'It's not. But Polly's my best friend.'

'What makes you think I don't love her?'

'Do you?' Moll murmured and, when he didn't answer, shook her head. 'Lad, what were you thinking? If Polly finds out . . . It's cruel, that's what. She's besotted, by the look of things. She'd resigned herself to spinsterhood, believed that for her, marriage wasn't to be. What you're doing . . . You've given her false hope. What d'you think this will do when she discovers you're stringing her along?'

'I love you.'

'Lad, lad . . .'

'I thought if I tried moving on with another, I could rid you from my mind. I can't.' He covered his face.

'Polly . . . She's fun, full of life. I never thought she'd take to me this seriously. I don't know what to do.'

Moll's answer was thick with regret. 'You must tell her. The longer you keep this going, the sharper her grief when she does find out.'

'I don't want to hurt her, Moll. I never wanted that. I just want you. Only you.'

He reached for her hand but she pulled back with a sad shake of her head. 'We've talked on this. It can never be, lad. I'm . . . to be married.'

Like soggy wax, he seemed to fold in on himself. Then he sprang up to stare down at her through stony eyes.

'I'm sorry.'

'Both of you, you and that brother of yourn, can go to hell!'

'Uriah! Please—'

'Used me good and proper, the pair of you,' he spat, grey eyes flashing. 'Then, when summat better came along, neither of you wanted to know me, did you?'

Shock numbed Moll. She hadn't thought him capable of such anger. In all the years she'd known him, she'd barely seen him without his ready smile. He possessed a temperament as mild as a late spring morning; everyone thought so. Nothing, as far as she knew, had ever brought him to what she saw now, what *she'd* caused; crushing remorse gripped her.

'Leave. Go on, Moll, afore I say summat I'll regret.'

The last thing she needed was more enemies. And the last person she wanted as one was him. She couldn't bear this.

'Uriah, you must understand, I didn't want it this way. You mean a lot to me. Don't turn your back on me, I couldn't stand it. And Bo, he'll come round. He's caught in the moment with them sods he calls friends, that's all.' She touched his arm tentatively and he lowered his chin. 'You have to tell Polly, lad. Let her down gently, spare her the details if you must, but do it, and soon, for both your sakes.' Her hand tightened on his jacket. 'D'you know summat, it'll be a luck-born lass what snags you one day, Uriah Croft. I hope she realises it, an' all.'

His eyes met hers. Moll smiled softly then slipped from the house.

'You think that's a good idea?'

Having paid a street urchin to deliver a message to Horatio that she needed to see him, they stood on Jersey Street out of sight of his home. After her last experience, thoughts of calling herself made Moll shudder. How she'd overcome this once they went public with their engagement and through the years ahead – the Simcoxes were her intended's family and always would be – she couldn't think about yet.

The afternoon had turned bitter and his next question came through his muffler, pulled up against the cold. 'Can you really see your brother breaking bread with me, of all people?'

She blew into her hands and stamped her feet to drag life into her frozen toes. 'I've searched all their haunts and blood houses, even Winters' lodging house.'

'He couldn't say where Bo was?'

'Winters wasn't in. I don't know where else Bo could be. Whatever brainless grievance the lad believes he has against you and your cousin . . .' She paused to ask, 'How is Sammy?'

'Still licking his wounds. As you might've guessed, he's sworn revenge.'

A sigh escaped her. 'I'm so tired of this! Well, Bo shall

just have to accept how matters stand. I love you and intend marrying you. If only I knew where he was, I could break it to him privately, give him the chance to get his head around it afore the meal.'

'Happen he's at his friend's, the lad what called to walk you home from work the other week. Croft, is it?'

Slight stiffness lurked in Horatio's tone, and Moll felt a blush creep across her face, recalling Uriah's latest declaration. Horatio needn't know, she told herself. Would he be angry or, safe in the knowledge she'd chosen him, scoff at the lad's feelings? She wouldn't risk that. Uriah had suffered enough humiliation and besides, her response had been clear. She loved another, was *marrying* another, and now he knew. It was over as far as she could see.

Nevertheless, guilt stabbed anew with thoughts of their set-to hours before. Uriah was right about one thing: Bo had discarded him like an unwanted plaything in favour of the scuttlers. No, her brother wouldn't be there. She shook her head.

'Then I'm out of suggestions.'

'And me.' *But I can't give up*, she added to herself. *Bo can't walk in tonight and have what I'm about thrust in his face. He doesn't deserve it.*

'You should get yourself home and by the fire. It's cowd enough to freeze the blood in your veins.'

'Nay. I must keep looking. You go. I'll send word, later, let you know what's . . . *Mam*?'

Horatio followed her gaze to Ruth flying up the cobbles towards them. 'Now, Moll, hear what she has to say, first,' he said when she turned concerned eyes to him. 'Happen it's summat and nowt.'

'It's Bo. Summat's happened to him, I know it.' She broke free from him and sprinted to her mother. 'What's happened?'

266

'Oh. Thank God.' Ruth clung to her. 'I've had word from Ancoats Hospital. The lad were taken in last night during the early hours. He's bad, Moll. Bad and . . . my God, if he should . . .'

'What happened?'

'He's been stabbed in the neck.'

'No . . .'

'Police took a deposition from him. They've made an arrest.'

Moll and Horatio exchanged glances. Sammy? Dear God. Was this his revenge for Bo's assault?

'Some varmint from Angel Meadow, name of Quigg,' Ruth added.

'Angel Meadow?' Again, Moll shot Horatio a look and at his brief nod, closed her eyes. *The Meadow Lads.* Horatio had warned something like this would happen. He'd said the Tigers had met their match, that she should warn her brother. This was her fault. Lord in heaven, if Bo . . .

'Who would want to hurt my gentle lad and why, you tell me that? This swine, Quigg, will swing for this, you see if he don't!' Ruth swallowed a sob. 'The house surgeon worked on Bo all night. He lost a lot of blood. They're uncertain whether . . . whether he'll . . .'

'He'll pull through, Mam. He must. Where's Sissy?' she asked suddenly, Davy's twisted face from earlier flitting to mind. Surely Mam hadn't left her with that disgusting . . . ?

'Davy were tired. Aye, too exhausted to mind her awhile, the poor love were.'

Tired! Collapsed skenning drunk, more like.

'I asked on Jilly instead.'

Any other time, Moll would have welcomed the news that the women were on friendly terms again; right now, she had thoughts only for Bo. She grasped her mother's elbow and she and Horatio led her in a run to Mill Street.

An overhanging pall of illness and poverty hit Moll as she threw open the door, intensifying the churning in her guts. Swallowing, she hurried for the desk.

A woman with a pockmarked face and wiry hair peeping from the confines of her stiff cap continued writing in a ledger. 'Yes?' she asked curtly without looking up.

'We're here to see my brother. He were fetched in last night with a stab wound to the neck.'

'Name?'

'Bo.'

Eyes small and black, like raisins in pricked dough, flicked up. Irritation deepened lines already home to her brow. '*Full* name, if you please.'

'Oh. Aye, sister. Robert Chambers.'

With a sniff, she looked them over. 'Indeed. Come this way.'

She knows, Moll thought as they followed her, starched skirts and apron crackling as she passed briskly down a corridor and on past rows of beds. *She knows he's a scuttler.* And why wouldn't she? How many such cases did she witness daily? When warring factions clashed, injuries were inevitable. *As undoubtedly with others, she believes Bo's brought this on himself.* Rude she'd been to begin with but the contempt in voice and expression on discovering who they were here for had been palpable.

Yet *hasn't* he? Moll's mind whispered. Wasn't this his doing entirely? If she'd shared Horatio's warning, would Bo have taken a bit of notice? Likely not. Dreadful as she felt thinking it, perhaps a chink of good could come from this. Happen he'd see what he'd become, that it wasn't worth risking his life. Perhaps now, he'd leave that rabble's clutches.

Without being asked, Horatio held back and Moll smiled gratefully. She took a deep breath then followed her mother to the bed.

Bo, face to the wall, didn't stir. Thick bandages, spotted with blood that had seeped through the soiled gauze, covered his neck and chin. His skin was corpse-grey but his breathing steady; he didn't look in too much pain.

'You may speak with him for a few minutes then I must ask you to leave. Robert must have rest if he's to recover.'

'Thank you, sister,' murmured Ruth in the subservient tone most of the lower class automatically reverted to with those in authority. 'We'll not tire him, 'onest.'

With a curt nod and swish of skirts, the woman returned to her duties.

Ruth, after casting her son a tearful glance, looked to Moll as though for guidance, and it was she who said, 'Lad? Can you hear me?'

Bo's weak response carried like the rustle of winter leaves, dry and delicate, as though it would crumble to dust in his throat. 'Aye.'

'Oh, Bo.' Stooping, Moll pressed her lips to his clammy cheek. Despite her horror that matters had come to this, fierce love overrode everything.

'Mam . . . ?'

'I'm here, son.' Ruth patted the hand lying limp on the bedclothes. Gripping her fingers, his sleeve rode up and Moll glimpsed a dark shadow on the inside of his wrist. She frowned curiously. Horatio had one in the same place, his being dots in the shape of a sword.

Like the missile Simcox wielded at her, scuttlers' belts bore remarkable designs – Bo's, he'd fashioned with images of Prince of Wales feathers, and hearts pierced with arrows – as did their tattoos.

269

Cocking her head for a better view, Moll's mouth hardened to see the letter V, undoubtedly standing for that witch, Vick. He was still seeing her, after everything ... Then another thought struck and her face fell.

Often, belt-wearers fashioned their girls' names into the leather like stamps of ownership. Clearly, scuttlers also branded their skin with their conquests. Horatio bore no initials but the dots ... some twenty in all ... Did he prefer a different method? Did they represent every girl he'd ...? She'd realised, hadn't she, that unlike herself, he'd known another before their night together? Nevertheless, reality stung.

Catching Moll's eye, Bo slipped his hand beneath the bedclothes. With a disgusted sniff, she looked away.

'That this has occurred!' their mother was saying now. 'Eeh, there's great evil in the world. How you feeling?'

'Bad.'

'Well that's to be expected. My poor boy.'

'Will I die?'

Moll exchanged a look with Ruth. 'What's this? Course not.' Her attempt at bright reassurance sounded fake to her own ears. 'You mustn't harbour such thoughts, d'you hear?'

'That's right. It's for your sister, here, you'll next pass through a church door and nowt else!'

At this, Bo slowly turned.

Leaning in, Ruth nodded vigorously. 'You heard right, lad. Moll here's to be married.'

No, not now, like this ... 'Mam, I don't think it's the time or place,' Moll began but her mother's pleading gaze stopped her. Ruth's intentions were clear: she wanted to give him something to look forward to, fight for. Moll hadn't the heart to snatch her hope away. Besides, Bo must find out some time. Whether now or next year, it wouldn't make a difference to his reaction.

'You get yourself well, my lad, you hear?' Ruth murmured, then glanced to the next bed at the sound of hoarse coughing from its patient, head and face swathed in bandages. 'Poor soul.'

Bo followed her gaze and his mouth hardened. Then Ruth turned back and he attempted a smile. 'I need a drink of water, Mam. Would you ask?'

Alone with him, Moll leaned in. 'She's still none the wiser at what you've been about. I think, for her sake, it's best we keep it that way.' Bo stared silently and she sighed. 'The Meadow Lads? What the divil were you thinking, lad? I pray this has opened your eyes to what—'

'Married, eh?'

His brown eyes, darker than usual, held something she couldn't identify. 'Aye.'

Bo motioned for her to come closer. His bottom lip brushed her earlobe as he hissed: 'You treacherous *bitch*.'

Moll drew back slowly.

'My own sister a scuttler's girl? That Rat bastard's girl? I'll finish him afore I see you wed.' He licked spittle from the corner of his mouth. 'I'll finish the pair of youse.'

'Don't you dare speak like that to me,' she choked. 'Horatio's changed – you'd do well to follow his lead. Just who the bloody hell d'you think you are of late? I thought what I witnessed not three moons back were the final straw, but this—'

'I did that for you, yer ungrateful cow.'

'What?'

'Spouting filth about you and that cousin of his, Simcox were. I believed it to be lies – at first, anyroad.'

271

'What are you saying? You bit off someone's ear to uphold my reputation? Lad, who *does* that?' Moll was verging on tears. 'Much as I dislike Sammy, he didn't deserve disfigurement for the remainder of his days.'

'That scum got exactly what he deserved. His cousin, mind, is due a whole 'nother level of hell when I'm out of here. My own sister consorting with the enemy? You make me sick. How could you do this to me?'

'Consort . . . *Enemy*? Listen to yourself! What's become of you?'

The prone figure in the next bed released another weak cough and Bo strained to see him over Moll's shoulder. 'All right, lad?'

'Bo?'

'Aye, it's me. Rest, now. Build your strength. We've scores to settle for this, so just you get yourself well.'

A gurgled chuckle leaked from the bandages. 'Aye. Aye!'

'Who . . . ?' Moll glanced back and forth.

'Winters.'

That was why he hadn't been home earlier when she'd called looking for Bo . . .

'Before setting on me with his blade, Quigg had one of his soldiers throw a paraffin lantern in our path. It hit the cobbles and exploded, splashing all in liquid fire. The rest of us managed to dodge in time but Winters, here, weren't so lucky. He were engulfed and shall carry the scars to prove it. The smell . . . Jesus. It were enough to turn your stomach inside out.'

Moll's horror-filled eyes swivelled once more. Like her brother, this lad was little more than a boy. To carry such marks for the rest of his life! Just what lay beneath those bandages . . . ? She squeezed her eyes to blot out her imaginings. 'You could've been killed, the pair of you! What took you up Salford way and into the Meadow Lads' territory? Surely you must have known the consequences were they to spot you?'

'Course we knew,' offered Winters, and Bo grinned. 'That's part of the fun, in't it?'

Moll was struck dumb. How could any sane person make sense of these scuttlers' thinking? It defied rationality on every level. 'You're mad, the lot of you!'

'I need to get out of here, lively,' Bo said as though not hearing her. 'A blue bag visited this morning with news of Quigg's arrest; I'm damned if I'll miss the court case. I intend laying it on by the shovel-load. Me, with no previous, just an innocent, hard-working, God-fearing lad caught in the mindless fray . . .' He grinned again. 'I'll see the snivelling swine get a seven stretch for this, you see if I don't. Seven years' penal servitude,' he added for her benefit, rolling his eyes, when she shook her head confusedly. *He's* got previous going back sodding years. They'll throw the key away this time.'

'And the Meadow gang will fall without their captain,' wheezed Winters.

'Exactly. We'll round 'em up one by one. Soon, Angel Meadow will be ours. As with Manchester, Salford's streets will ring with the name Bengal Tigers.'

'You're mad,' Moll whispered again. It was all she could lay her tongue to.

'Oh, we're mad, all right.' No trace of Bo's smile remained. 'Me more than most in light of your behaviour, to boot. Nay,' he added, eyes narrowing, when she glanced down the long room. 'Surely to God you'd not be foolish enough to fetch him the day . . . You *did*, didn't you!'

'Bo, please. Calm down—'

'Rat! Rat bleedin' Green, you show yourself!'

'Lad!'

'I know you hear!' Bo rasped over Moll's pleading. 'Coward. I'll slice you into a hundred pieces if I find you've been near my sister again. This ends the day, Prussia scum!'

Moll hovered above her brother, his face wreathed in agony lines. 'Stop, please! You're making yourself ill. Breathe, breathe,' she urged as he moaned and gasped air like a fish stranded on land.

'Swear to me . . . Moll . . .' he managed.

'Lad—'

'Swear you'll stop seeing him. He's . . . the enemy.' He broke off with harsh coughs. 'Swear.'

The air between them thickened like soup. She felt her heart breaking, breaking. This was her brother. Her lifelong ally, protector, charge, her *son* – aye, he felt like a product of her own flesh, and more besides. She could lose this lad of hers in this moment, for as God was her witness, he'd lost his senses as surely as any inmate in the asylum.

His manic look when speaking of his violent exploits and future intentions, the over-zealous talk itself; phrases like consorting with enemies, talk of soldiers and captains and battles – it could well have been a stranger lying here. But to give up the man she'd sworn to marry? Could she do it?

In the blink of an eye, she'd have taken Bo's side in anything every time. Had occasion arisen before this day, it would have been for good cause. But this, now? What he was asking wasn't right. His reasons were unjustified to the point of absurd.

Like a physical force, she was pulled in different directions. Tugging at one elbow was Bo, at the other Horatio, whilst she floundered between, loving both.

'Lad, listen to me. I don't believe you're of sound mind and it scares me. Whatever feud you're convinced exists . . . it's all in your head. Horatio's not who you think. He's changed and he loves me. I love him—'

'I need you to *swear* to me, Moll.'

Silence closed around them. Then: 'I'm sorry,' she heard herself say. 'I can't do that, Bo.'

'Here we are, lad.' Their mother's voice hacked through the tension. 'That's it, sit up. Eeh, that don't trouble thee, does it?'

Biting his lip against the pain, Bo inched further up the pillow. He sipped the water, his hard gaze on Moll all the while, before turning and closing his eyes.

'Ward nurse said we must take our leave of you, now, son. We'll come again soon. You'll be all right?'

'Aye.'

'That's the spirit, my big, strong lad.'

Bo cast Ruth a smile but it was to Moll he said, 'I'll be out of here just as soon as I can, you'll see. I'd not want to miss my sister's wedding, now, would I?'

'That's right,' their mother agreed brightly, blind to both threat and fear passing between her children. 'Eeh, fancy it, lad – our Moll in love!' she teased, chuckling. 'Who'd have thought it?'

'Oh, this union's summat else, all right. I'm certain of another thing, an' all. The wedding shall be one we'll not forget in a long while.' His gaze bore deeper into Moll's. 'You can be sure of that. *Sis.*'

There was nothing to say even had Moll power to. Throat burning with tears, she stumbled after Ruth, her brother and Winters' laughter ringing in her ears.

Chapter 19

THE FOLLOWING HOURS came and went as hours must; clinging to their coat-tails, Moll limped on with them.

Leaving the hospital, she'd found Horatio waiting in the weak sunshine and at the sight of him, her resolve for her mother's sake crumbled and she'd run, sobbing, into his arms. His jaw, pressed to her cheek as he held her close, tightened, but he'd uttered nothing – nor had she needed to; her distress said everything.

Bo would never accept their love. More worryingly, he seemed intent on destroying it. That terrible truth struck sharp. As with Sissy, all his life, she'd put his wants first, strove to ensure her every action was for the good of him, had done her utmost to make him happy. So why now, when she needed just a grain of all she'd given, couldn't he offer it?

Ruth took her tears as a sign of relief at Bo's improvement, had patted her back with coos and smiles. She'd had to bite back the urge to scream the truth. Mam wouldn't have understood. And being Mam, she'd have never taken Moll's word over Bo's. Had Ruth witnessed the bedside conversation, she'd have still tried denying it. If it suited her, the lad could commit no wrong.

'You must be our Moll's intended – Horatio, aye,' her mother had said, touching his arm, when Moll's tears subsided. 'My mind were asunder with worries for Bo to notice you proper on t' journey. It's nice to meet the one what's made my lass, here, smile at long last.'

He'd touched his cap respectfully. 'Nice meeting you, Mrs Chambers. I'll do all I can to make your daughter happy.'

'Eeh, lad.' Ruth had flashed Moll a watery smile of approval. 'It were reet thoughtful of you to hang back in there, but there were no need. You're soon to be family and should have made Bo's acquaintance.'

Horatio hesitated before answering. 'I didn't like to intrude.'

'Well, he's certain to like you, lad.'

Moll had closed her eyes, sadness washing over her, and detected a touch of the same in Horatio's response: 'Time will tell, Mrs Chambers.'

Ruth had drawn her shawl over her head then nodded in the general direction of home. 'Don't forget, the pair of youse. Six and no later.'

'Should we still go ahead, Mam, after everything today?' Moll had asked quietly. She felt drained of emotion and the beginnings of a headache lurked behind her eyes; company was the last thing she'd desired, now. Hiding away in Twit and Beattie's kitchen until this hideous day died the death it deserved appealed much more. 'Happen we should plan summat another evening.'

'Aw, nay. Ay, go on, our Moll, say you'll both come. I've bought foodstuff in ready and all. Will you?'

She'd relented.

'Good. Well, I'll be away home.' However, Ruth got no further than two or three steps before turning back. Tears clouded her eyes. 'Our Bo. He'll be all right, won't he, Moll?'

'Aye, Mam. Course he will.' She'd nodded with conviction and with a small one of her own, her mother had continued on her way.

Now, time just shy of the appointed hour, Moll and Horatio made their way through the dreary evening in silence. She'd given him a watered-down version of her meeting with Bo – she couldn't bring herself to bad-mouth him, even to Horatio – and quiet unease had settled around them.

A squat man with thinning hair and a drinker's nose passed them at the door on his way out. Frowning, Moll headed inside.

Though earlier she'd have welcomed an excuse to postpone, when she and Horatio entered the kitchen she wanted to curl up with shame and disappointment.

She lifted the empty gin bottle lying on its side by her mother's elbow. Sprawled across the tabletop in an odd pose, as though she'd passed out across it while standing, her mother was snoring loudly in a pile of vegetable peelings.

'It's a poor fare you're due the night. Unless you've an appetite for muddy tatties and uncooked rabbit.' From the fireside chair, Davy raised an eyebrow. 'What, you don't fancy it, nay? Thought not. Go on, sling your hooks.'

'Who were that fella I just saw leaving?'

'A friend, why? What the bleedin' hell's it to do with thee?'

Moll's hands bunched into fists. 'Where's Sissy?'

Davy didn't answer. He jerked his head to the table. 'See what you've caused, you and that wastrel brother of yourn? You drive her to distraction and beyond with your antics. She's better off without you. She's better off without the ruddy *pair* of you.'

'Mam don't cope well with worry, that's true enough. Seeing the lad today must have upset her more than I realised. This is her blotting out life the way she knows how.' Voice dropping to a growl, Moll stepped towards him. 'But don't you dare make out it's my fault, or Bo's, or any bugger else's for that matter – though you don't help, plying her with that poison. Aye, Mam's doings are hers alone but you enable her to fulfil them. If anyone's to blame other than she herself then it's you, Preston. Now, I'll ask you again. Where's my sister?'

Throughout, Horatio had uttered nothing. However, when Davy rose, face like thunder, Horatio moved towards him. 'I don't believe we've met.' Through gritted teeth, he threw the icy words into Davy's face. 'What say me and you step outside and get to know each other properly? Or have you only balls big enough to take on lasses half your size?'

Crushing silence crackled between the men. For two pins, Moll would have stepped aside and watched Preston get the beating of his life, gladly. She *would*, had it been anyone bar Horatio doling out the blows. His youth and brawn coupled with his explosive temper would make for disaster. Moreover, were Preston to survive the onslaught, he'd squeal like a stuck pig to the first constable he happened across. Where would that leave the one she loved, their future?

She touched Horatio's arm. 'Nay, lad.'

Davy threw her an almost grateful look. He'd bitten off more than he could chew with this man of hers and knew it. Sweat had sprung on his top lip and, despite his nonchalant stance, his wary eyes told another tale. Looking back to Horatio, he gulped twice and thrust his chin towards the door. 'Get from my home, the pair of youse.'

'*Mam's* home,' snapped Moll and was gratified when he didn't argue.

Horatio's hard gaze was still locked on the older man but when Moll touched his arm again, he breathed deeply and nodded. Addressing Davy for the final time, though calmer, his voice was every bit as deadly. 'Ever, *ever*, use that tone with my girl again and so help me, I'll tear that foul tongue from your head and shove it so far up your arse, you'll be tasting your own innards. Now, I believe Moll asked you a question?'

Scowling, Davy thrust his hands into his pockets. 'Sissy's downstairs with the owd 'un.'

Shooting her comatose mother a last look, Moll led Horatio out. Shutting the door behind them, she closed her eyes. 'I'm so sorry . . . For you to witness the state she was in . . . And *him* . . .'

'Don't be. As you yourself rightly said, she chooses to pour the ruin down her neck. As for him – who the divil is that sod?'

'Davy Preston, Mam's fella. I loathe him, Horatio. The things that brute's done . . . is *planning* to . . . He's the divil's own son, I'm certain.'

'Moll? Look at me. What ain't you telling me?' Horatio asked when she looked away. His voice rose. 'If that blackguard's harmed a single hair—'

'Nay, nay.'

'You're speaking the truth?'

Fear of him doing something foolish had her responding as she had to Bo months before. 'It's their drinking, that's all. It's unpleasant to be around, you know? That's all,' she repeated, taking his hand, and was thankful when his face softened. God above, if he knew only half of what Davy was about, how matters truly lay with Bo because of him, his touching her, his sordid plan for her and her mother . . . The intensity of Horatio's love, she must admit, startled her sometimes.

She brought a smile to her lips. 'I think it's time you met my sister. The Saxes, an' all. Eeh, you'll like them, all right.'

'My lass! Ay, but it's a grand day for us seeing thee. Come in, come in!'

Jilly's face upon opening the door was heartening. Moll embraced her warmly. 'By, it's good to see you.'

Her neighbour's gaze flicked. 'Who's this fine looker you're with?'

'This is Horatio. There's summat I wanted to ask . . . Can we speak inside, like?'

'Here's me, prattling on, while you stand quivering from the frost on my steps! Come on in.'

Chuckling, Moll motioned to Horatio to follow and was pleased to spot him grinning. She just knew he'd take to Jilly on sight. What a stark contrast to the reception minutes before! Not for the first time, she felt an ache in her breast for the home life she'd been cheated of.

'Hello, Sissy.'

'Moll! Moll! Jilly, Moll!'

The craggy face creased as, squealing in delight, the girl pelted into her sister's arms. 'That's right, it's Moll come to see you. Look here, Alf,' she added with a gummy grin to the fire, 'young Moll.'

'I see, wench.' He held out a hand, which Moll gripped. 'It's gradely seeing you, lass.'

To outsiders looking in, it would seem she'd been at sea for years or some such, considering the welcome. Never would they believe she'd seen the Saxes not a week past; as for Sissy, why she'd seen her only this morning! All the same, it was lovely. She giggled happily.

After Ruth and Bo's health were enquired about, and relayed as briefly as Moll could get away with, the table was set with the familiar teapot minus a handle that Jilly treated like an old friend and the well-used jam jars that served as cups. Jilly placed a plate of stale oatcakes alongside and the four sat to a pauper's feast. Alf, knees giving him grief, joined in from his chair.

'Some bloke or t' other were leaving Mam's when I arrived,' Moll stated, removing her shawl. 'Have you noticed this? Is that Preston using the place as a drunkards' den?'

'I've seen one or two come and go, aye,' the old woman admitted.

Anger sparked but she swallowed it. This wasn't the time or place, nor were the Saxes responsible for goings-on upstairs. She'd speak with Mam when she next caught her conscious.

'So . . . How've you been?' asked Jilly casually.

'Keeping well, like?' Alf added.

The couple were itching with curiosity, trying not to gawp at the newcomer, and Moll relented, laughing. 'All right, youse two, I'll put you from your misery. By, you're polite to a ruddy fault!'

'Swine! I've been wondering all sorts about this young chap since opening the door.' Jilly sat forward expectantly.

'This is Horatio Green and we're to be married.'

'You . . . Wed?'

'Aye, we . . . Jilly?' Whatever she'd expected from this second mother, she certainly didn't get it. 'Oh! What's up?'

Tears spilling, the old woman rocked in her chair. However, this was someone overcome not with joyous emotion but anguish.

Alf was as surprised as they were. He tried to rise but his legs gave way and with a small cry, he called to his wife. 'Wench! What's all this?'

Her beloved's distress took effect – with a shuddering breath, Jilly became calm. The disc of moon beyond the strip of window lent her features some of its silver, illuminating pain-filled eyes. 'I'm sorry. I don't know what came over me . . .'

'Jilly, what's wrong? Out of everyone . . . I thought you'd be happy for me.'

'Oh, now. It's over that moon out yonder I am for thee.'

'Then what?'

'Robert, love.'

'Father?'

Wiping her nose on her apron, Jilly nodded. 'Eeh, that he's not here to see the day! A crying shame, it is, and I'm that sorry.'

Moll's chest swelled with overwhelming love for this Titan-hearted woman. 'Please, don't take on so.'

'Why must the Lord take the good of this world and leave the rotten to grow grey? We're not meant to question this, are we? But whether the big Book says it's a sin, sometimes, God's doing is wrong.'

'I don't know why. I've no father to give me away, it's true enough.' She turned a shy smile on Alf. 'Would you do the honours instead, Mr Sax?'

'Oh, lad. A rare honour indeed,' breathed Jilly.

'Me?'

'Aye. If you reckon your knees could manage, mind.'

'Not being blessed with babbies, I never thought . . . I'd be proud to, lass.'

Hugs, kisses and handshakes followed and the next

hours passed in a snug haze of plans. Throughout, Moll couldn't help feeling a tug that Mam wasn't here.

Horatio looked out of his depth when the women discussed Moll filling her bottom drawer and getting the banns read. Grinning, Alf had called him to the fireside, out of the females' way. Snippets of their conversation had reached Moll. Horatio mentioned that a navvy friend had promised to get him work on the Manchester Ship Canal, recently come under construction, and Alf sounded his approval. He, too, had laboured in his younger years and helped build some of Manchester's grander buildings and roads. Soon, they were chatting like old friends.

As Moll predicted, the Saxes' warmth put Horatio at ease, and his politeness in turn quickly won them over. Like her, he seemed to find this dank cellar comforting. She'd vowed to herself that, when they were married, this was how their own home would be.

Later, Horatio had readily agreed when Jilly suggested cards and looking to Sissy, patted his knee. 'How about you come and help me, lass? I reckon they'd not stand a chance against us two.'

To Moll's surprised delight – her sister was normally hesitant around strangers – she clambered into his lap. Catching her eye over Sissy's shoulder, he'd given the softest of winks and her heart skipped for this big tough lad – this beautiful soul who was hers.

Her happiness, however, dimmed somewhat when at one point during the night, he'd rolled his shirt-sleeves to his elbows and Moll's eyes went to the inked sword. She'd peered at it quizzically and, catching her, his cheeks turned dull pink. His reaction said everything. Nevertheless, she'd told herself to stop being foolish; his past was his alone. She hardly had a right to complain of what he'd done and with whom before they met. All in all, the meeting had been a lovely success.

'D'you know, I've not enjoyed myself so much in many a long day,' Jilly announced now, then yawned. 'Eeh, I'm fagged.'

Moll nodded agreement with the rest and rose to give her friend a big hug. 'Thanks for your advice, Jilly. This wedding feels more real, now, I can hardly wait.'

'I think we covered everything.'

'Aye. There's just Polly to ask about being bridesmaid alongside Sissy.'

'Talking of your flame-haired friend, that reminds me.' Jilly slapped a hand to her forehead. 'Sorry, lass, it's this owd age; it slipped my mind entirely. The lass came here in search of you whilst you were gone with Ruth visiting poor Bo. She'd knocked at yours and getting no joy, thought she'd call here on t' off-chance.'

'Did she say what she wanted?' Moll asked quietly. Polly rarely called on her at Blossom Street. This meant only one thing . . . 'Did she seem . . . upset, Jilly?'

'Not at all, lass.'

Moll released a small sigh. Then what? Either Uriah had done as she'd asked and called things off with Polly, who had taken the news better than expected, or he'd gone back on his word and her friend was still in ignorant bliss.

She had to see Polly, find out how matters lay. If she had to sit outside the Wainwrights' house the day through, she'd catch her friend eventually. Her insides twisted with pity for the good-hearted woman she'd come to view over the years as a sister. She'd not see her hurt, not for anything or anyone. *Christ, what were you thinking, Uriah . . . ?*

'Going, Moll? Going now?' asked Sissy, cutting through her thoughts.

'I am, my lass, but I'll come and see you reet soon.' Stooping, Moll wrapped her arms around her and rocked her slowly. By, but she loved this girl; missed her as much. How she wished home could go back to how it was, when they were all together. Before Father died and Davy slithered in. Before Bo got mixed up with those swines . . . She pushed the painful yearnings away before tears threatened. There was no returning to the past, for any of them.

'Sissy can bed down here the night, love,' Jilly assured Moll when she hesitated, as though guessing the situation upstairs entirely. 'You go, and take our warmest congratulations with you. It were a pleasure meeting you, lad,' she added, patting Horatio's arm. 'I know you'll take good care of this lass of mine.'

'And you, Mrs Sax, Mr Sax. Goodnight. Bye, Sissy.' Horatio ruffled the girl's hair then took Moll's elbow. 'I'll walk you to the inn.'

'Ta, love,' she murmured when they reached Twit and Beattie's back door.

He teased a lock of hair from the confines of her shawl and fingered it. 'For what?'

'Being by my side today, through everything. And what a day it's been, eh?'

'The Saxes are good people.'

Moll smiled. 'Aye, they are. Now, go on.' She nudged him in the direction they had come. 'Get yourself home. You must be ready for your bed, I know I am.'

'I'd much rather share yours,' he said gruffly, pressing her closer. She laughed and he grinned. 'I've missed the feel of you more than you can imagine.'

Though tempted to give in to her own growing

desires and sneak him into the kitchen, she shook her head. This was the man she loved and was soon to call husband; she'd never regret their night, it was true. Yet, it had been a foolish act. They were careful not to be caught but she couldn't risk it again. Besides, hoodwinking Twit and Beattie didn't sit easy with her. She liked them enormously. She must respect the kindly pair and their property.

'All right, all right,' Horatio relented. 'There'll be no getting away from me when we're wed, mind. Your flesh will be mine to ravish all night every night.'

'I look forward to it,' she whispered back, blushing. 'Now shoo!'

Horatio's footsteps faded and still Moll stood, arms around herself, a smile at her lips. When eventually she made for inside, she got no further than reaching for the brass knob. Close by, beyond the shadows, the unmistakable scrape of a clog on the flagstones carried. She whipped around but saw nothing and her heart raced.

'Who goes there?'

Silence greeted her shaky query. She was about to bolt for the safety of the kitchen when a waft of cheap hair oil assaulted her nostrils. She stopped dead in her tracks. She recognised that smell only too well of late – he preferred it to the soap the others used to perfect their fringes . . . But it *couldn't* be. He wasn't up to it. Only today, she'd seen with her own two eyes . . .

'Bo?' she called in quiet disbelief. 'Bo, is that you?'

Again, no response, and the noiseless dark closed in further. With a frightened cry, she yanked open the door and fled inside.

Chapter 20

INSTEAD OF CONTINUING down Oldham Road on her return from buying supplies for the inn's kitchen, Moll made for Bengal Street and on towards Jersey Street. Why hadn't she thought of this before? she chided herself, training her eyes over the mound of mill workers ahead. In love, Polly might be, but she still had to eat and keep a roof over her head. To do that, she'd have to drag herself from Uriah for at least a few hours to ply her wares. If there was one place Moll was sure to find her, it was here.

Sure enough, a flash of ginger curls winked amidst the grey-black of flat caps and shawls. Hitching up the large wicker basket laden with vegetables, a leg of beef, eggs, butter, fresh ginger and four large apples that would go into the pies she would bake for today's customers, Moll weaved her way through the hungry throng.

Despite snatching only a few hours' sleep last night, she felt refreshed. The episode in the darkness, she'd since put down to her fraught nerves from the day's events, tiredness and some swine who happened to use the same hair oil playing silly beggars. Bo was in the hospital recovering from a severe injury that had almost claimed his life. Her imaginings were ludicrous in the

cold light of day. Besides, no matter their present grievances, Bo wouldn't scare her like that. Angry he was
but, as she did him, he loved her still. Of that, there
could be no question.

When Polly looked up from her tray and saw Moll,
her eyes widened in surprise.

Smiling, Moll squeezed her arm affectionately.
'Where have you been hiding, then? It seems an age
since I saw you last. I've called by yours a few times but
your mam—'

'Give me a minute to get rid of these last pies. We'll
talk at mine.'

A slight frown touched Moll's brow; what was wrong
with conversing in the street as they did normally?
Nonetheless, she nodded.

'Mam and Katie are out. We'll not be disturbed.'

With this, Moll's next nod was of understanding.
Uriah had done the deed, must have. Polly needed to
unburden herself to someone. Though she tried mask-
ing it, she was upset; it was obvious from her flat tone.
She was right: they certainly couldn't discuss the subject
here. *Oh, Polly love, I am sorry . . .*

Minutes later, Polly led the way to number three.
Inside, she removed her tray and shawl and jerked her
head towards a chair.

Moll obeyed. Placing her basket by her feet, she asked
softly, 'You all right, love?'

'As it happens, nay, I'm not.'

'Oh, Poll . . .'

Sudden tears pooled in her eyes, turning them a
deep emerald. However, her mouth remained a thin
line.

'Polly, I don't know what to say . . .'

'It's a prime fool I feel and no mistake.'

289

Moll's heart contracted for her. 'Nay, love. You've done nowt to warrant it. If anyone's a fool, it's Uriah Croft.'

Polly closed the space between them. Bending forward, she flattened her palms on the table. 'Oh no, Moll. It's me, all right. I'm the fool to fancy as long as I did that you were a friend.' She pressed her face closer. 'You don't know the meaning of the word!'

Moll could only blink. 'What on earth are you talking about?'

'There's no secrets bewixt Uriah and me – he's told me everything. Did you really think flaunting your scuttler in front of him would make him jealous, entice him away from me? You had your chance and blew it. He's mine. So the sooner you get into that skull of yourn he ain't interested, the better for you.'

She felt sick with shock. 'Is that what he told you? That *I'm* in love with *him*? Polly, listen to me—'

'Nay, *you* listen.' Never had Moll seen her friend like this – molten fire sparked from her eyes. 'Uriah's tired of your declarations so save them for some bugger else. You missed out long ago to tell him how you felt. He's moved on. Do yourself a favour and do the same.'

An angry storm of injustice had built in Moll throughout Polly's speech – now, it boiled over and she was powerless to prevent it. 'My *God*. The snidy, lying young . . . He's deceiving you, Polly!'

'Nay, he ain't. The night of my birthday, after he'd walked you and Sissy home, he returned and announced he were fond of me.'

'The selfsame night I told him I weren't interested! He's the one in love with me. He's turned this whole thing round to suit his own ends. Open your eyes, lass. You must believe me.'

'You bleedin' Chambers women. You're all the same.'

'What?'

'First your mam – I'll not have her daughter snatch away another man I love.'

'*What?*'

'That's right.' Polly jutted her chin. 'I'd have made Robert Chambers happier than that mam of yourn could have dreamed if only he'd given me half the chance.'

'You . . . ? *Father?*' Moll scraped back her chair. Clinging to the table for support, she rose slowly. 'Are you telling me you had an affair with my father?'

A little of the anger left Polly's face. She shook her head.

'Then what *are* you saying?'

'I loved him,' she answered simply. 'I loved that dear, pure-hearted man with every piece of my heart.'

'But . . . when did you . . . for how long?'

'Ten years, mebbe longer.'

Moll dropped back into her chair.

'I were a slip of a lass when I fell for him, it's true. But as a fully-grown woman, I loved him still and more. He weren't like other men from these parts. He had summat, a softness, a way of making you feel special. That's what he made me feel, aye. He'd make a beeline for me every afternoon, none of the other hawkers. We'd talk as he ate, you know?' Her eyes misted with remembrance. 'I hung off his every word and he listened to *me*. *Really* listened. Where I found the courage, I'll never know, but I told him my feelings, had to. It were sending me daft keeping silent.'

Moll's voice was barely above a whisper. 'How did he react?'

'As I'd expected, deep down. Oh, but how I loved that

291

man – and he liked me, he did. Alas, being the good, moral soul he was . . .' A shuddering sigh escaped her. 'He said he were sorry. He said he'd vowed to love your mam for better or worse, in sickness and health, that we could never be. She dragged him through hell, didn't deserve him, his loyalty, love. A flutter of her pretty little eyelashes had him forgiving her ill-doings in a heart-beat,' Polly finished with a shake of her head.

The pies she used to insist Moll take to tempt his appetite when he fell ill . . . Her genuine concern . . . Her barely contained dislike for Mam and her ways . . . It was all now terribly clear.

And what of our friendship? The sudden thought hit Moll. *Did Polly merely use me all these years to retain some form of connection with Father?* She had to ask.

'All this time . . . Have you only pretended to like me because of whose daughter I was?'

Polly's face showed genuine hurt. 'That you could even think that! Nay, and that's the truth. So, now you've heard it, *now* d'you see? I'll not lose Uriah. At my age, this might be my last chance. I'll not allow another man I love to slip from me as easy. I mean it, Moll. You just stay away from him.'

No trace of Moll's anger remained. She felt but deep and heavy sadness, now, for this woman. 'Like Father wasn't right for you, neither is Uriah. I know you don't want to believe it and I hate myself for doing this; you're my best friend and I'd not hurt you for the world. But you must hear it. Uriah doesn't love you. He told me as much.'

'That's a lie. You just want him for yourself.'

Moll went to stand before her friend, hands on hips. 'Now you listen to what I'm about to tell you, Polly Wain-wright, and listen well. I'm in love with a man called

Horatio Green. I'm going to *marry* Horatio Green. That's right,' she continued, nodding, when Polly's gaze swivelled to hers. 'I love him with everything I am. I want *him*, for the rest of my days, and no one else.'

'You say now you don't want Uriah, so why can't I have him? What, Moll, I'm too old? Why do you care, anyroad?'

'Christ's sake.' She flung away with a growl. 'Haven't you heard a word I've said? Uriah's *lying* to you, lass. He *is*. D'you know, I'll wring his bloody neck when I next set eyes on him!'

Polly's hand strayed to her midriff. 'Say what you will. I'll believe what I like.'

'Nay. Are you . . . ? Oh, Polly!'

'I'd like you to leave, now. I think it's best if we don't see each other for a while.'

'Love, please—'

'Now, Moll.' Polly bit her bottom lip as it wobbled. 'Go on.'

One thing was certain, now, thought Moll as she dragged her feet back to the inn, eyes stinging with unshed tears. The mystery of the flowers on Father's grave was cleared up. Polly had denied all knowledge of the blooms when Moll first mentioned it. But of course, she would, wouldn't she? Yet why the need to keep telling him she was sorry? Sorry for what could have been in another lifetime but never in this? Aye, that was likely it. Oh, but it was tragic, really.

She could barely comprehend it. Her friend, in love with her father? *Pregnant* with Uriah's child? Whatever Polly said about keeping her distance, Moll wasn't going anywhere.

Whether or not her friend realised it, Polly needed her like never before. By, she did.

Chapter 21

'HOW ABOUT NOW, Moll? Is it time now?'

Nudging aside a plate of ham sandwiches and another piled with dainty lemon tarts and scones, Moll placed a large orange jelly on the bright-clothed table. 'Soon, Cathy lass.'

In her best frock and apron, shiny ringlets framing a face pink with anticipation, the girl nodded. Nevertheless: 'Now, Moll?' she asked again not a minute later.

Wiping her hands, Moll couldn't help laughing. She'd worked all morning preparing the party tea to celebrate the child's birthday. Twit and Beattie, generous to a fault and more where their children were concerned, had spoiled Cathy with an armful of cheap playthings. Her siblings had invented games for the young guests after the feast. And Cathy? Though she'd rewarded them with shy smiles and soft thanks, all she really wanted today was to see Sissy.

Twit, surveying the kitchen walls and his friend's efforts – Beattie had threatened to take the stew pot to her husband's head if he didn't get them whitewashed, as he'd promised for an age, in time for the party – turned to admonish his daughter gently. 'Here, now, lass. Enough of that, enough of that. Moll's said soon, and soon it shall be.'

Abashed, Cathy lowered her eyes. 'Aye, Father. Sorry, Moll.'

Moll exchanged smiles with Twit. 'I'll finish up here then we're all set,' she told him, crossing to the crockery-filled sink.

'Will it be time to collect Sissy once that lot's washed?' blurted Cathy then shot her father an apologetic look.

'It will, lass.'

'I'll do them, then, shall I?' The girl was already pulling up her sleeves. 'It's no hardship, honest,' she added in a tone that suggested she was doing Moll a favour and there was no ulterior motive behind her offer whatsoever. 'Aye, you've done enough for one day.'

The adults burst out laughing, much to Cathy's confusion, and Moll bent to kiss her plump cheek. 'You young imp, yer. All right! I'll go and fetch Sissy.'

'Don't forget, send word to that fellow of yourn,' called Twit as she untied her apron and donned her shawl. 'There's enough grub the day to feed a clemmed army. He's more than welcome.'

'I'll do that now. Ta, Twit,' said Moll with feeling.

She'd been nervous telling the couple of her marriage plans. They had been good to her and she was sorry to be leaving them in the lurch – Horatio insisted it was the man's job to bring in the bread and Moll respected this. However, she needn't have worried. Though they expressed regret and were certain they would never find another cook as fine as her, they congratulated her warmly.

Moll waited in the entry nearby Prussia Street some twenty minutes until a child happened along. However, the young lad scarpered with her penny before she could relay her message; cursing the robbing swine, she peeked towards Horatio's.

Skulking around like this was ridiculous – she'd soon be part of the mob lot beyond that door. She had to face them some time, didn't she?

Lost in thought, she jumped when she heard movement at the entry's opposite end but when she glanced around, no one was there. And her puzzled frown melted when, again, the sickly smell of cheap hair oil wafted towards her.

It felt like someone was hitting her heart like a drum; she peered for an age towards the opening but no, all remained still. *Am I going mad?* she asked of the damp-covered bricks then laughed softly. *Talking to walls, Moll? Oh no, you're perfectly sane!* She mentally shook herself. Worry, that's all it was, and her vivid imagination making something from nothing. And that she missed her brother terribly was no doubt playing a part.

Tomorrow marked a week since that dreadful visit and each hour, minute, since had increased the weight on her shoulders and mind. Moll had called on her mother the previous day to deliver Cathy's invite for Sissy and after assuring Ruth, who was full of apologies for how the meal had turned out, that it mattered not, that she understood her reasons over what had happened to Bo, she'd tentatively asked how her brother fared.

Her mother said he grew stronger daily, then explained she'd been informed the Meadows lad, Quigg, had stood trial that morning at the imposing, neo-Gothic structure of the Manchester Assize Courts. In light of his previous brushes with the law and the severity of Bo's injuries – Quigg could very well have been facing a murder charge – they seemed to have made an example of the young Protestant. He'd been convicted of unlawful wounding and sentenced to five years on the *Akbar*, a reformatory ship for youthful offenders, moored on the River Mersey at Birkenhead.

Bo wasn't well enough to attend the hearing but Ruth had been delighted with the verdict. 'Serves the young rebel right!' she'd proclaimed.

Though she hadn't voiced it, Moll wasn't so certain. Surely the Meadow Lads wouldn't take this blow lying down? If she knew anything about scuttlers, they would already be plotting revenge. Just what did that mean for Bo?

Now, yet again, worried tears for him came but she forced them back. There was no getting through to him so what, at all, could she do?

With effort, she brought her mind back to the task in hand. Aye, she must face this Simcox lot. Now, she supposed, was as good a time as any.

Squaring her shoulders, she crossed the cobbled road. 'Sammy.' Moll nodded a stiff greeting upon his answering her knock. 'I'm here to see Horatio. Can you fetch him for me, please?'

The lad folded his arms. 'You've gorra nerve showing your face here.'

'I don't have time for this. Just fetch him, will you?'

'Look at this, look.' Sammy jabbed his thumb towards his mangled ear. Knobs of crusty black scabs lined the jagged top where the part was missing – it looked like a bat's crumpled wing.

'You gave as good as you got,' she said quietly.

'What, that scratch to his shoulder?'

'Scratch my eye. You stabbed him!'

'Pity I didn't do as good a job as the Meadow Lads, eh?'

She refused to be provoked. 'Whatever gripe lies betwixt you and my brother is no business of mine. Now, can you tell your cousin I'm here?'

'Nay, I can't.'

'For Christ's sake, Sammy. Give over and just fetch him—'

'I *can't* because he's not here.'

'Oh right. Sorry. When will he be back?'

A slow grin spread across his face. 'Now that, I *can* tell you.' Leaning in, he motioned for her to come closer. 'Never!' he whispered into her ear.

Moll's head snapped back. 'What's that meant to mean?'

'He's gone.'

'What are you talking about, gone? Gone where?'

Sammy shrugged. 'All he said was he'd made a mistake asking you for your hand and that he had to get away from you. Packed up his things t' other night and had it away on his toes, he did. I doubt you'll set eyes on him again.'

She couldn't breathe. *It's not true. He loves me . . .* 'I don't believe you. Horatio wouldn't do that.'

'Believe what you will. He would and he has.' Sammy nodded. Then, slowly, his mouth widened and he laughed hysterically. 'Your face! Had you there good and proper, didn't I?'

It took a moment to realise he'd played her. Relief swamped her. Then tears sprang to her eyes and her whole body shook with rage. 'You evil-minded sod, yer! How could you *do* that?'

'Christ, it were only a bit of kidment.' Sammy laughed harder. 'You and him are made for each other; he's too serious for his own good, an' all. The sooner he weds you and gets the hell out of here, the better.' He turned and went inside the house.

Forcing down the urge to thump the smirk from his face, Moll followed. Like before, a dishevelled group of humanity, some sleeping, some talking quietly, littered the front room floor, looking as though they hadn't stirred since her last visit. Lodgers, she surmised, glancing around. Though why any sane being would actually pay to stay in this hovel beggared belief. Covering her nose with her shawl to block out the stagnant air, she made for the door Sammy was disappearing through.

'Moll.'

'Ho*ratio*?'

His eyes creased in despair. He dropped his gaze. 'You should have sent a message. Lord . . . You shouldn't *be* here.'

Moll took in the scene slowly, heart breaking further with each second, each excruciating expression that flitted over her love's face. His degradation crushed her chest like a physical thing.

Sammy jerked his head with a snort. 'Not so big and tough in that rig-out, is he?'

Moll heard again the youth's words from the inn when Horatio went for him: *'Keep your frock on.'* Doing her utmost to stop her gaze swivelling back to Horatio's attire, she fell to her knees before him. 'Love. What have they *done* to you? Tell me, who's responsible for this?'

Horatio dropped the scrubbing brush to cover his burning face with his hand.

'Pick that up and finish that floor or so help me, you'll regret it.'

At the growled order, Moll's head snapped around. It was then she noticed the man sprawled in the chair by the fire, a thick belt in his hand. 'Mr Simcox.'

Horatio's uncle spread his arms. 'The one and only. As for him, the waif will learn some respect one way or t' other, I'll see to that.'

She'd known Horatio's home life was bad, but *this*? It was like she'd slipped into some twisted nightmare. Never, ever, would she have guessed the extent of it. Tears spilling, she shook her head. 'That you can speak of that! You disrespect him like this yet believe you're deserving of *his* respect? Just look at him!'

'Nowt wrong with a dose of good owd fashioned humiliation to break an unruly spirit. Beatings ain't enough these days. But laddo here's not so bold when he's sporting one of my Annie's frocks, that's for sure.' Mr Simcox turned his narrowed gaze back to Horatio. 'Well? Is the bonny lass going to do as I bid and clean this floor, or must I be forced to let owd Lucifer here do the talking?' He let the dark leather he held drop to swing through the air.

'Leave that damn brush and go and get that dress off. Do it.' Moll's words trembled with bubbling rage. 'I'm taking you from this hell pit right now and you'll not return.'

'He goes nowhere till I say. Nigh on fifteen year we've keep that waif in grub and clothing, put a roof over his worthless head. He owes us.'

'He owes you nowt,' Moll spat, stepping forward. 'So help me, if you try stopping us—' She broke off, frowning, and with the others, glanced to the open window at the terrible screeches that had started up outside.

As one, Sammy and his father moved to the door, the elder still clutching his belt, his son snatching up the poker on the way. They vanished without a word.

'What's afoot? What on earth's that awful din?'

Horatio didn't answer. Shoulders slumped, arms hanging loosely by his sides, he stared at Moll through pain-ravaged eyes.

He looked utterly broken; a sob caught in her throat.

What must he feel, standing here like this, knowing she was now aware of the goings-on beneath this roof? His suffering, all of it, lay exposed to her and it was killing him. She threw herself at him and held him so close, closer than she'd ever held anyone, to the point she could barely breathe. He shook against her and she wept with him.

'Moll, I tried, tried my best to hide it from you, the way of things . . .'

'My love, my love. You shouldn't have. You thought I'd view you differently? Oh, my love! You mustn't ever feel you have to hide things from me.'

'I'm pathetic.'

'Nay! Don't *ever* utter those words again! I won't listen to it. These people are divils, they're *divils*, but you, you're my angel and I'll make this right. You're to get changed right now, collect your belongings and come with me.' Holding his face, she nodded emphatically. 'Do it, lad. Hurry.'

He did as she bid, returning moments later as the Horatio she knew. As it always did, the sight of him stole her breath and she marvelled that this man should have chosen someone so plain to make his wife.

'Who *is* that?' she asked him of the demonic screams, which had risen further still in pitch. 'God above, it's enough to summon the dead from their graves.'

'That would be my aunt.' He motioned for Moll to follow. 'Let's get out of here.'

Amused neighbours had gathered to watch the drunken spectacle playing out in the centre of the road. Like prime pugilists, two women were battling with fists and savage kicks.

'That all you've got, yer stinking whore? I'll break your face afore I'm through with you!'

301

Annie Simcox, Moll realised if the mouth on this fat, mean-eyed woman was anything to go by, released a beast-like screech and hurled herself at her opponent. Adults and children alike cheered and whooped, their morbid enthusiasm adding to the chaos, while the woman whom Annie now rained blows on crouched in a ball on the ground.

Horatio's embarrassment was tangible, which tore at Moll. She understood his shame completely. Mind, even Mam's behaviour wasn't on this level. 'Come on,' she told him but he shook his head.

'I'm slinking nowhere. She'll hear me out first.'

'All right, come away, you.' Chuckling, Mr Simcox lifted his wife bodily from her bloodied challenger and plonked her, kicking and cursing, on the flagstones by their door.

The bested woman picked herself up and staggered away, and the crowd shuffled back to their hearths.

'I ain't finished with you, missis!' squalled Horatio's aunt at her opponent's retreating back.

'It's finished for today, you are, for it's that kitchen you're headed next, woman. I'm fair clemmed; I want my dinner.'

Without a scrap of shame, Annie lifted her filthy skirts to her knees, squatted and opened her bladder on to the cobblestones. Squinting up at her husband through her drunken haze, she hiccuped twice. 'Cow heels and tatties do you?' she asked cordially, as though they were conversing around the kitchen table and the fight moments before never took place.

'Aye. Shift yourself then.'

The beginnings of a black eye were showing – Annie prodded the tender spot. 'Eeh, my bleedin' peeper.'

'Be a beauty, that will, come the morrow,' agreed her husband.

'Vicious bitch. Just you wait till I . . .' For the first time, Annie spotted her nephew hovering nearby. 'And what the bugger are you standing there gawping at, yer gormless swine?'

'Aunt Annie, I'm leaving.'

'Oh, are you, now?'

Horatio's arm tightened around Moll's waist. He nodded.

'Ah, I see it. This here's the fresh meat you're dipping your wick in, is it?'

Moll and Horatio shared an appalled glance but before either could respond, Sammy nodded, snarling.

'And you'll never guess who she is, Mam. She's only the smug bitch what swiped your position at the inn from under your nose.'

Annie's nostrils flared. 'Is that right?'

'Aye. It were her own cow-son brother what chewed my ear away, an' all!'

Hands bunching, Annie swayed towards Moll but Horatio stepped in between. 'Shift,' his aunt grunted.

He stood his ground. 'You leave Moll be. She's to blame for none of this.'

'Like hell she ain't,' butted in Mr Simcox, grabbing Horatio's collar. 'You'd have never thought to leave off your own bat. This young slut's turned you. Showing us your back? Your own kin, I ask you!'

'It's me he's shown his back to – and every single mark you've left imprinted there,' Moll ground out. 'Thrashing him ain't enough, though, is it? God above, what I've witnessed in yon kitchen the day . . . You're nowt but a brute and the rest of your no-good lot ain't much

303

better. If this good man here never claps eyes on you shower again, it'll be too soon. I'm his family, now. Me. I'll love him as he deserves. I'll love him as none of you ever could.'

Annie Simcox could only gawp in astonishment. Her husband, on the other hand, sprang to life. Thrusting Horatio into the road, he rounded on Moll with bared teeth and drew back his meaty arm. But his intended backhander never reached her – Horatio leapt, halting his uncle's assault with an iron-like grip.

'Don't you even think about it, yer bastard,' Horatio hissed, eyes spitting steel. 'I'll snuff you out in a heartbeat afore you lay a finger on my girl.'

To say Mr Simcox was surprised was putting it mildly. He gazed at his nephew's hold upon his arm. 'You've gone and done it now, lad,' he murmured. 'I'll say this: you'd best finish what you've begun, here, for your only road out of this now is you knocking me down first. Mind, you'd need summat betwixt your legs for that, wouldn't you? Them you've got dangling there never did mean much, did they?' Leaning in, his mouth contorted in a mirthless grin. 'My *Annie* has bigger bleedin' balls than thee!'

Horatio stared at the man who had tortured, terrorised and beaten him almost his entire life. Each cruel act, every thrashing, mean word and humiliation that chipped at his being from a small boy showed in his face. With a howl that seemed to come from his soul, he threw back his powerful shoulder and delivered a bone-crushing blow of such force to his uncle's face, the older man was unconscious before he hit the ground.

For a long moment, everyone stared at the prone figure, open-mouthed. Sammy recovered soonest. Yanking off his belt, he turned murderous eyes to his cousin.

'Bastard!' the youth screamed, swinging the buckle, but seconds later, he too visited darkness – Horatio threw his fist again, sending Sammy sprawling across his father's back.

'See what you've done! They're out cold, the pair. You'll pay in blood for this, you stray dog swine!'

Moll had taken Horatio's elbow and was drawing him away. At Annie's screeched threat, she rushed at her, grabbed her shoulders and shook her hard, sending the few teeth Annie possessed rattling in her head. 'He's given them not nearly as much as they deserve. I've a good mind to send *you* asleep with them! If any of you come near Horatio again, I'll have the law on you, d'you hear me?' Moll thrust her aside and taking Horatio's elbow once more, guided him from hell.

More than ever before, Moll now understood how scuttlers were sucked into their dark world. The twisted unity must give those from fractured homes a sense of belonging. The security of being part of something had them forming close bonds with one another – their gang came to be their all. They relied on each other, clung to their new 'family' which, for most, was the nearest they had ever got to one.

She felt she knew the man she loved better after today. More importantly, she understood. Thank God she hadn't turned her back on him, had seen through to the real him.

'What's to become of me, now?'

Horatio had spoken almost to himself. Moll drew him to a halt. 'That, I can answer. You'll be happy, my love, that's what. How does that sound?'

The ghost of a smile touched his mouth. 'Gradely.'

'They'll harm you no more, wouldn't dare try, now. It's over, lad.'

They hugged each other then continued for Blossom Street arm-in-arm.

'The Saxes are kind souls and fond of you, to boot. They'll put you up till we figure summat else out, I'm sure,' Moll assured him as they approached the cellar steps.

'Are you certain that's a good idea? Me dwelling just feet from your brother? I don't want to fight him, Moll. For you, I'll not do that. But if he were to go at me . . . Words are cheap when the blade smiles in your direction. I'll not risk it.'

A shiver for both men ran the length of her spine but she swallowed her misgivings. 'It's all I can think of for now. Besides, Bo's still recovering at the hospital. It may be weeks afore he's well to come home.'

'I can't stay holed in there for ever. It'll only be a matter of time afore he discovers the truth.'

'Just you leave Bo to me. Somewhere inside that turned head of his is the brother I know and love. He'll come round, you'll see.' And she prayed hourly she was right.

'Well, if you're sure, and the Saxes don't mind . . . Ta, Moll. Truly.'

He reached to stroke her cheek and Moll snatched a glance at his wrist. She caught his hand and turned it over. The tattooed dots and all they symbolised were gone. Fresh ink stood against old. Some dots, he'd incorporated into the sword. The rest, he'd joined into swirling arcs to create the letter M.

Their eyes met. Though neither spoke, Moll knew they both felt it – a deeper connection was formed. Their lips found each other in a tender kiss.

'I love you, my Moll.'

'And I you. Come on. Our Sissy will be having ruddy kittens by now over this party at the inn.'

306

After a brief explanation to Jilly, who welcomed Horatio over the threshold with sympathetic sounds, Moll told him to take his time getting settled and if he felt up to it, to join her and Sissy at the party later. Then she retraced her steps to her mother's door.

'Sissy, you ready, lass?' she called down the passage and grinned when, just as she'd anticipated, her sister raced from the kitchen to meet her. Moll picked her up and twirled her around. 'Eeh, but you look bonny! I see you've donned your new apron. Good girl.'

Sissy nodded proudly. 'Aye, Moll. Keep it clean, Moll?'

'That's right. Mind you keep your hair tidy today, an' all, eh? It does look bonny. Did you sit like a good lass while Mam plaited it all nice like that?' Moll was heading for the kitchen but the girl's response stopped her in her tracks. She turned slowly. 'What were that, Sissy?'

Again, she pointed to her hair. 'Vick, Moll. Vick.'

Moll's gaze swivelled to the kitchen door. *She* was here, in this house? That meant but one thing . . .

'Bo. You're home.' Moll pushed the door wider but remained in the doorway.

Seated in the fireside chair stitching a pile of material – mending Bo's trousers by the look of it when she paused to measure the legs' width – Vick didn't even look up. Gang members' uniforms followed a strict code; their 'bells' or 'narrow-go-wides' had to measure just so: twenty-one inches around the foot and fourteen around the knee. Moll had heard this, just one of many rules scuttlers lived by, from her brother often enough.

Unlike his girl, Bo slowly laid down the penny dreadful he'd been reading to look at Moll.

'Where's Mam?'

He lifted a shoulder. 'Out.'

Her feet itched to run to him and she ached to throw

her arms around him but she forced herself back. He'd spoken calmly enough. Their time apart looked to have taken away the edge of his animosity for her but still, she was wary. His level of anger that day, the venom he'd spat . . . She motioned to the bandage peeping under his muffler. 'How you fettling, lad?'

'Better.'

'Aye?'

He nodded. 'I discharged myself not an hour since. They've signed me as an out-patient at the dispensary instead. I'd have finished up in the asylum if I'd had to stare at them four walls any longer.'

'And Winters?'

At this, Vick glanced her way but didn't speak.

A shadow passed over Bo's face. He lowered his eyes to his clasped hands. 'He died from his injuries this morning.'

Moll's hand strayed to her mouth. When all was said and done, Winters, for all his faults, had been but a boy. Such an utter waste of life. 'I'm sorry to hear that, lad.'

Silence filled the space between them.

'It's good seeing thee,' she said with feeling, and again he nodded. 'Well, I'll just get Sissy's shawl and we'll be away. My employers' daughter,' Moll explained, crossing to the nail in the wall, 'it's her birthday, you see, and . . .' Her speech died as she passed Vick. Peering down at the hard-faced girl, Moll sniffed the air and shook her head. 'You . . . ?'

'Me what? What you going on about?'

Vick's lazy tone brought angry heat to Moll's face. 'I thought I were going mad but nay, it's been *you* all along.' Again, she leaned in and sniffed. 'You're wearing Bo's hair oil.'

'And what?' Vick smoothed her fringe over her eye.

'It keeps my hair in place better than soap – not that it's any of your concern.'

'You young bitch. You've been following me, ain't you?' At Vick's smirk, Moll turned to Bo, now standing in the centre of the room, arms folded. 'This is your doing. You asked her to keep tabs on me while you were in the hospital.'

'And what a tale she reported back,' he murmured.

Moll felt like crying. His voice held that hardness again – his anger concerning her and Horatio hadn't abated at all. The last thing she needed today was another row. She asked quietly, 'And what's that supposed to mean?'

'Two words: Rat Green.'

Moll had to force her gaze from straying to the floor and the very man holed up with the Saxes beneath. 'What about him?'

'I told you—'

'And I told you. I can't do what you're asking. I love you, Bo, Lord knows I do, but this time, *this* time . . .' She grasped his hands. 'I can't put you first, for you're wrong, lad. This feud exists only in your head. Horatio's changed, he has. Please. Stop all this. *Please.*'

'That's your final word on the matter, is it?'

She nodded. 'I'm sorry.'

'First, we plan to avenge Winters' death. We'll sniff out the Meadow scum what threw that lantern and make him pay.' He winked to Vick, who grinned. 'All-out war's coming their way and no mistake.'

'Bo, nay . . . Haven't you learned anything from recent events?'

'Then it's Rat and Simcox's turn. So, *sis.*' He spat the term mockingly. 'You enjoy what time you have left together, for lover boy's days are numbered.'

Through a haze of tears, Moll's eyes followed him across the room. He resumed his seat and flipped open his reading matter. However, as she watched him, his expression and posture, right down to the cocksure tilt of his head, sent a sudden rush of fury through her and she marched over. She spoke calmly but firmly, as she had when they were children.

'Right, you listen to me and listen good. I'll not stand for this any longer. You're to leave the Tigers today. This business with Preston? We'll find another way to be shot of him.' Not that that problem had much worried Bo, lately. He looked to have adopted an 'I tried and failed to save Mam – what's the point if she's not willing to help herself?' attitude. It seemed so long as Davy stayed out of Bo's road, his presence meant nothing to him, now.

'I'm reading, unless you hadn't noticed, so if that's all . . . ?'

'I haven't finished yet,' Moll snapped. His attitude infuriated her but she breathed deeply and continued. 'Once you've told the Tigers you're stepping down, you're to meet me back here and you're going to sit and speak with Horatio, air your grievances, man to man. You'll hear him out, and him you, and afterwards, we'll put all this bloody foolish nonsense behind us and get on with our lives.'

Bo looked her straight in the eye, threw back his head and laughed, and Moll's resolve crumbled. Who *was* this person, at all? This wasn't her brother any more; never, never.

'Just what will it take to get *through* to you?' she cried. 'Do as I bid, please, before it's too late.'

'What are you talking about, too late?' he spluttered, wiping tears of mirth from his eyes.

'Bo, you've already been stabbed – twice. You're willing to take a chance at third time lucky, are you? D'you really want to end up like Winters, cold in the bone yard afore you're twenty? I'll turn informer afore I see that happen.'

This last gambit had the desired effect. All trace of laughter melted from Bo's face. Eyes narrowing, he shook his head slowly. 'You wouldn't.'

'If telling the police what you're planning on the Meadow Lads keeps you safe . . . Then believe me, Bo, I will.'

His breathing heavy, his eyes blazed. 'I'm warning you. Keep that nose of yourn from my affairs.'

'I can't do that. I'm terrified for you, don't you see? I want you *alive*, lad. I want you with me. I want you at my wedding, to see your nephews and nieces born, watch them grow. I want to be there for you, to care for you, always. I want this whole, monstrous nightmare to end.' She dashed away tears with the back of her hand. 'What I've witnessed today, I can understand it for some . . . but you don't need the security you think the Bengal Tigers provide, for you have me. I want us to be like we were. I miss you, lad, summat terrible. You and Horatio need to talk. You *need* to leave that stinking bloody gang! The worry of it, I'm not sleeping, barely eating—'

'I mean it, Moll. Back off.'

'Bo—'

'Enough! You never could get it into your head, could you, yer sad sow?' Thrusting his face into hers, he bellowed at the top of his lungs: 'You're not my mam, Moll – and thank the Lord for it! D'you know summat else? I'd sooner slit my two wrists than it were so.'

She bent forward as though winded. After a blade-sharp silence, her speech came on tortured breath.

'Aye. True. You're not born of my body. I didn't feed your veins with my lifeblood, nor nurture you with my milk. But I loved and protected you as though you were my own, from as far back as I can remember – still do. You and Sissy are my all. My everything.'

He'd hurt her in the worst possible way and he knew it. His eyes creased with contrition. 'Look, Moll, I didn't mean—'

'Yes you did. Every word. Well, d'you know what, lad? I've had a bellyful of *you*. I wash my hands of you. You, to me, no longer exist. That suit you?' Moll turned on her heel and stalked to the door. 'Come on, Sissy. We've a party to attend.'

'Moll. You don't mean that. Moll, I'm—'

His last word was lost on her, swallowed by the slamming door.

Chapter 22

'IT'S A GOOD job you've made of today and I thank you for it. I'm surprised our Cathy's face ain't cracked in two with all the grinning; I've never seen her so animated.' A sudden frown touched Beattie's brow. 'You all right, lass? You favour you've the weight of the world and his wife on your mind.'

Moll scraped together what she hoped was an adequate smile. 'Aye. A bit tired, mebbe, but that's all.' And she was tired. Utterly exhausted by it all.

After patting her arm, the large woman swayed off to replenish the sandwich tray and Moll closed her eyes. Never had she known so strong an urge to be alone. She'd give anything to shut out the world, curl into a ball, bury her head in her arms and sob her throat ragged. Then she caught a glimpse of Sissy, head thrown back laughing at something Cathy was saying, and she smiled softly. Well, not shut out everyone. Horatio aside, Sissy was her main focus, now. Her *only* focus . . . Bo was lost to her. Not by his doing, as she'd worried might happen these last weeks, but hers. She'd vowed to cut him from her life. And it hurt like nothing she'd known before. *My lad, my lad.*

'Your brother's back. I've just seen him leaving your mam's house with that Tiger girl of his as I were on my

313

way here. Don't worry, I crouched on the cellar steps out of sight; he didn't spot me.'

Imprisoned in her own thoughts, Moll hadn't noticed Horatio enter the kitchen. She scrambled for his arm and clung to it.

'Did you hear me, lass? Your brother—'

'I have no brother.'

Though Horatio frowned, he said nothing to this.

'Moll, play! Play, Moll, play?' Alight with merriment, Sissy waved an old sock they were using as a blindfold in their games.

'Want me to ask her if I'll do instead, if you're not up to it?' asked Horatio gently.

Moll shook her head. For once in her turbulent young life, her sister was happy and she'd make sure that, for a few short hours at least, she'd remain so. 'We'll both go. Here, lass,' she added to Sissy, 'Horatio wants to be the blind man first!'

The cheering children clambered to him. Laughing, he gathered them up, which sent them all tumbling to the ground in fits of giggles. Smiling, Moll tucked Bo into a safe recess in her mind and joined in the fun.

When they donned their outside garments some time afterwards, she was feeling a little brighter. Not even thoughts of having to leave her sister and Horatio at Blossom Street later and return here alone could dampen her spirits. The children, particularly Sissy, had lifted her mood no end. As for Horatio, Moll had never seen him so at ease.

'I can't wait to be a father,' he confessed as they strolled down Oldham Road through the late afternoon sun, proving what she'd suspected when watching him play. 'Our children won't catch a breath, I'll smother them in so much love,' he vowed with feeling. ''Ere, that's your mam coming with that fella of hers,' he said suddenly, pointing ahead.

Besides their unsteady gaits, even from far away Moll saw their drunken state – their slack-jawed smiles and ribald laughter had her toes curling in her boots.

'Moll! Sissy, lass! 'Ere, and is that you, Horatio, lad?' Ruth called, raising one arm to wave and the other to push her wonky hat from her eyes.

Moll opened her mouth but her response never reached her mother – a thunderous clap of footsteps grasped the air by the throat, stealing all sound. A foaming grey wave of similarly dressed youths, sparks flying as their brass-tipped clogs struck the cobbles, charged around the corner like an angry swarm of bees.

The lads' war cry bounced from brick to brick, building to building, stealing the colour from Moll's face: 'The Meadow! The Meadow!'

Her arm went instinctively around Sissy; Horatio's protective hold fastened around Moll.

'Bo said the Tigers were planning all-out war on *them* – what are the Meadow Lads doing in Ancoats?'

Horatio's voice was grim. 'They likely got wind of the Tigers' intentions and reasoned a surprise ambush would stand in their favour.'

By now, Ruth and Davy had reached them and they all watched the armed mass of yelling youths descend on the Locomotive Inn, known locally as Jack Rook. A notorious haunt for young pugilists, it seemed an unlikely target. Then the doors burst open and roaring like crazed bulls, out charged the Bengal Tigers, deadly belts in hand. It astounded Moll how scuttlers got their information; they could pinpoint enemies precisely when the need arose, sometimes marching miles to seek them out.

'Can you see your brother?'

'There's too many, I don't know . . .'

'Can you see him?' Horatio repeated. 'Look harder, Moll.'

His urgency brought her head around. 'Horatio?'

'I can't be sure . . .'

'What?' she shouted over the cacophony of noise.

'I promised Mrs Sax I'd not tell.'

'Jilly?'

'She insisted that sometimes, they get it wrong, but . . .'

'Get what wrong?'

'The tea leaves. I cajoled her into reading mine, earlier. After everything today, the uncertainty of what I'm to do . . .'

'Aye, go on,' Moll pressed.

'I needed to know what my future held. Mrs Sax informed me of a few things that put my mind at ease, then she . . . She blurted that the one whose heart I've claimed will face great sorrow. It was like she couldn't stop herself; the words fell afore she could bite them back.'

'Jilly . . . she never would read my leaves. I asked and asked but . . . Now I see why. What else did she say? Please, I must know.'

'She said you'll bear the passing of a loved one but that another shall ensure the soul lost to you lives on.'

Moll swallowed hard. 'A loved one? Like . . . a parent?' she asked through trembling lips, gaze flicking to her mother.

Horatio, however, cast his to the two gangs now in full battle. Lads, some no older than Sissy, were bludgeoning and being bludgeoned at every turn; their cries were terrible to hear. 'Or a sibling?'

316

Liquid ice burst through her, making her gasp. Her desperate eyes scanned the chaos. She spotted Vick and another girl in the bar, pelting stools and bottles through the smashed window at the medley outside, and her heart leapt. 'I think Bo's still inside. There may yet be time.'

Having moved to the roadside for a better view, Ruth shook her head at Davy. 'What a to-do!'

Swaying on the spot, he nodded agreement. Then, eyes narrowing, he pointed with his chin to the pub door. ''Ere, that bombastic bugger of yourn's in t' thick of it, Ruthie! The swine – I'll tear his head from his neck for him!'

Thrusting her sister aside and rushing forward, Moll followed Davy's gaze. Sure enough, there was Bo, a demonic grin on his face and a clasp knife in each hand. As she made to tear across the cobbles, she almost collided with a girl who appeared from nowhere. She could only watch as the child ran smiling and waving towards the fray.

'Bo! Bo! It's me, Bo!'

To Moll the world seemed to tilt, appearing as though through steamy glass. That sunny voice . . . The flash of snowy apron and honey-coloured hair . . . *No!* The thunder of hooves and growl of four iron-rimmed wheels approaching at speed . . . *No! No!*

'Sissy!' she screamed. 'Look out!'

The girl halted and looked back over her shoulder. Her beautiful smile meant for Moll remained, frozen in time, as the hansom cab veered into her, catapulting her through the air like a rag doll. She landed on the hard stones with a sickening crunch and was still.

'No!'

In the seconds it had taken, no one moved, horror

317

rooting them to the spot. Now they scrambled, yelling and screeching, into the road as though one body.

Moll reached her first. Skidding to her knees, she cradled Sissy's head. 'Lass! Oh, my lass!'

'Moll?'

The girl's eyelids fluttered like butterfly wings and a hopeful cry tore from Moll. 'Sissy? Thank God, thank God!'

Shutters had been hastily secured at windows at the start of the gangs' onslaught – now, alerted by these new cries, faces appeared from tentatively opened doors. Within moments, a crowd had gathered around the broken girl whilst others rushed to assist the hansom driver in harnessing his beast.

'Moll?' Sissy breathed again, fingers searching the air.

Moll grasped them, caressed them with her cheek, kissed them again and again. 'I'm here, my lass. Don't fret, now, you're going to be all right.' She looked to a knot of women nearby. 'Don't just stand there gawping! Summon the ambulance, for God's sake!' They stared as though they hadn't heard. One turned her face with a sob, another buried hers in her apron, but no one moved away. 'D'you hear me?' Moll screamed. 'What's wrong with you? Fetch help, quick!'

'Moll. Moll, love . . . please . . .'

She blinked up at Horatio's broken plea. 'Fetch help!'

'Oh, Moll . . .'

Why won't anyone listen? These strangers, Horatio . . . Mam. Mam will listen. 'The ambulance, Mam, the ambulance!' she rasped as she looked around wildly. She spotted Ruth lying in a dead faint. Davy sat slumped by the roadside, his head in his hands. 'For God's sake. Won't someone please help my sister?'

'The ambulance has been summoned . . . It's too late,

lass,' murmured a woman, her eyes wet. 'It'll be of no use to the poor child.'

'But . . . Sissy's all right, look. She spoke to me. She's *looking* at me; see!' The woman shook her head. Frowning, Moll gazed down.

'Apron . . .'

'What, lass? What's that?'

Sissy mouthed the word again.

'Apron?' Moll asked. 'Apron . . . ?'

'All . . . mucky. Mustn't . . . mucky it, Moll?'

'Oh, love. Sshh, now. Don't fret over that!'

'Sorry. Mucky . . . Sorry . . .'

By now, men and women alike were openly weeping. Moll glanced again at the one who spoke before. 'Please . . .'

'Her head, lass. It's too late.'

Craning her neck, she looked to where the woman indicated. From the front, Sissy didn't have a mark on her. *But God above, the back . . . !* Warm liquid poured from her concave skull, swelling the crimson pool on the cobblestones to a river. 'No, no, no, *no* . . .'

'Talk to the child, lass. Help her pass from this life to the next peacefully. Cherish these last precious moments with her.'

Blinded by tears, Moll could barely make out her sister's features. 'How I love thee! I love thee! Don't *leave* me, Sissy!'

'Love you, Moll.'

'Oh lass, lass!'

'Moll? Love you . . . Moll.' Sissy's last words fell gently on a final breath.

Dipping its head in grief, the sun slipped behind the clouds. Muffled sobs enveloped the two girls. Moll closed her eyes and uttered no sound.

The lone squall of a passing bird touched the roof-tops. It was then, from somewhere deep inside her brain, she noticed the stillness. Battle sounds no longer polluted the air. The world had lost its voice.

The searing of her smashed heart lessened, slowly, slowly. For another feeling, quite new to her, popped and sparked inside, choking emotion in its path. It swelled to touch every inch, leaving stone coldness. She opened her eyes. Then she laid her sister on the ground and rose.

She saw him straight away. His eyes, hollow puddles in his bone-white face, met hers across the street. His body was slumped, breath coming in short gasps. Standing tall, Moll's, like all aspects of her, remained steady, flat.

'You . . .' Her voice contained no sound. Then, pointing in Bo's direction, she threw the word again in a dry rasp, '*You!*'

Devastation screamed from his gaze. It fell on Sissy before crawling back to Moll. He turned and fled.

When he'd gone from view, Moll turned, too. But she didn't dash from the scene as Bo had. She walked sedately, straight. The subdued crowd's pity-filled eyes followed her but she saw no one. She moved past Davy, still sitting numb by the roadside, past her wailing mother, now roused and crawling across the cobbles towards her broken daughter. On, without a backward glance. When a hand touched her shoulder, she didn't break her pace.

'My love . . . Oh, Moll.' Horatio's voice barely brushed the outskirts of her mind.

'Leave me be,' she murmured with a dry-eyed calmness.

'You can't be alone at a time like this. Moll, please—'

'Leave me be,' she repeated. With some reluctance,

he did. Emptiness her only companion, she continued on her way.

The horse-drawn ambulance rattled past her as she approached the corner. She paused for the briefest moment. Then the nothingness settled within her once more and on she walked.

Her blood-soaked garments and dead expression drew stares and gasps and enquiries about her health all the way. Moll uttered nothing, and felt even less.

Jilly, on her way out, halted on the cellar steps. Her eyes widened further as they followed the length of Moll's body. 'I prayed they were wrong. The leaves – I prayed . . . Dear God, may He forgive me.' Her voice broke. 'Oh, lass, what . . . ? *Who . . . ?*'

Moll's hand stilled on her mother's door.

'Poor Ruth . . . ? The *lad*?' Jilly added, shaking her head wildly. Slowly, her every feature dropped. Her mouth formed an O. She gripped the iron rail beside her. 'Nay. Nay, it's not true. I won't believe it. Not her. Not the lass. I won't believe it!'

Wordlessly, Moll lifted the latch and went inside, closing the door on Jilly's howls.

She saw it from the bedroom doorway. For a long time, she stared at it, standing stark against the dark counterpane. When eventually she moved, it was on jerky limbs. Again, she looked upon the golden strand for an age, then took an end between her thumb and forefinger and lifted it from its bed.

Closing her eyes, Moll threaded Sissy's hair through her fingers. Life left her legs. She crumbled like dry earth.

Chapter 23

'I CALLED ON the Colemans again this afternoon.'

'Who?'

'The Colemans: Moll's employers.'

'Oh. Aye.'

'They said she's not to fret about the inn but to concentrate on getting herself well. They insisted she's to take however much time she needs.'

'That's good of them.'

'Aye.'

There followed a pause. In the adjoining room, eyes trained on the wall, body curled beneath the thin blanket, Moll sighed softly. She'd only caught part of their conversation but it was all she'd needed to grasp the topic. They were talking about her again but it mattered not. Nothing did or would again because Sissy was dead. And Moll was dead because Sissy was dead. And nothing and no one mattered any more, not now Sissy was dead.

'Mam?'

'Aye?'

'When d'you reckon our Moll will snap free of this darkness?' Fear lingered in Bo's dull tone. 'It's been over a fortnight since our Sissy . . . And I'm frightened for her, Mam, our Moll. I keep on praying life will return to normal somehow, normal as it ever can be for any of us, but I don't think it will. And I don't know what to do for her, for you. And me? I'm struggling to stay strong and I don't know how to do it any more and . . . and . . .'

Ruth and Bo's muffled sobs seeped through the thin plaster and swirled wispy fingers around Moll's heart but still, the fog snare held her and she clung to it like a drowning man to driftwood. Their voices sounded again but, as she knew it would, the numbness began pulling her back to the desolate wasteland she'd grown accustomed to and, once more, she felt nothing. Not a thing. Sissy was dead.

Now and then, she'd noticed that the sky visible through the curtains had turned from light to dark, dark to light. That days passed, she was dimly aware but wasn't part of. She'd hear her mother's fraught wails in the middle of the night, catch snippets of voices and the footfalls of people who called during the early days to pay their respect. Had Polly been one of them? Moll wasn't sure, now. She thought she'd heard her voice from the kitchen at some point but memory was cloudy. Visitors had dwindled but a steady procession passed through this room still, regular as clockwork.

Someone, occasionally her mother or Jilly, most often Bo, would lift her up in the bed with soothing words, stroke a brush through her hair, run a damp cloth over her face and hands. Soup or broth – anything that meant she didn't have to exercise effort – would be spooned into her mouth and she'd swallow, nourishing by instinct alone the tortured soul she no longer cared for.

The women would talk to her, plead and cry and hug her limp form, beg her to come back to them, for she might be there in the house at Blossom Street, but mentally may as well be marooned on another realm. And

Bo spoke to her, too. Each night, he'd lie beside her in this bed they'd shared, all three, since they were children, and say her name in the darkness, once, twice, a dozen times, until his quiet weeping carried him to a fitful sleep.

One night in particular – when, Moll couldn't recall – he'd snuggled into her back, put his arm around her and held her tightly. He'd been crying for some time and dry sobs punctured his words.

'I'm sorry. I'm sorry, I'm sorry, a thousand times and more. Sissy's dead because of me, I know this, as you do. Your face that day when you looked across the road at me . . . I wanted to die, too. She wanted to say hello, just say hello, and now she's *dead* because of me. It's the end, Moll, I swear. I'm no longer in the Bengal Tigers. God, how I've treated you . . . I'm a scuttler no more and never shall be again and that's the truth.'

Moll had stared straight ahead. His words had no more impact than a dull tapping on the window of her emptiness; he might as well have been speaking another language for all the feeling they evoked.

'You hate me, I know. For the remainder of my days, I'll do everything in my power to make it up to you. I loved Sissy more than I can express and if I could, I'd take her place in a heartbeat. But I can't, Moll, I can't, and I don't know what to do. How do I make this right? Please say you believe me. Please say you'll forgive me, one day. Don't shut me out, Moll. *Speak* to me, please! Hold me, tell me all will be well, like you used to. I'm sorry, Moll, I'm sorry.'

Bo's body had convulsed with fresh sobs for some time until, eventually, he'd fallen quiet and sleep had steadied his breathing. It was a long time before she was afforded the same release.

Of Davy, Moll had neither seen nor heard a thing. The same was true of Horatio. But Sissy was dead so it didn't matter and never would. Perhaps if she lay here long enough, she'd be dead, too, and she and her sister would be together, as they should be. Sissy would be pleased to see her, and Moll would promise never to leave her again. And she wouldn't. She'd look after her for ever, as she'd always done.

'Moll? Come on, take a sup.'

Strong arms under her hunkers brought her up to sit on the side of the bed. As usual, she offered no resistance. The strength it would have required was beyond her capabilities. The rim of a cup touched her lips. Staring ahead at nothing, she sipped the lukewarm tea.

'I visited your employers today,' Bo repeated now. 'They said you're to take all the time you need.'

Moll turned her head and lay back down.

'Happen we could go for a short walk later, eh? D'you feel up to that? Or mebbe you could come and sit in the kitchen? Just for an hour or so?' He waited for a response and, receiving none, ran a hand through his hair. 'You haven't surfaced from this room, from that bed, since . . . You can't lock yourself away for ever. You're making yourself ill, ill in the head, and it has to stop. We need you. Please, Moll, *please* will you just look at me? Moll?'

Squatting beside her, he tilted his head and put his face close to hers. Still, she looked beyond him, stare unfocused, and he closed his eyes in despair. 'All right. All right, Moll. I'll do it. I'll likely receive a bashing for my troubles, but if it makes you well again . . . I'm willing to try owt.' Bo dropped a kiss on her cheek. Then he rose and left the room.

She wondered fleetingly where he'd gone. Then

Sissy's bonny smile returned to her thoughts and her eyelids grew weighty. She was slumbering within seconds.

'Through here, is it?'

'Aye.'

The deep voices from the passage reached Moll through the gloom of the candlelit room. One in particular stood out and a stirring of life fluttered in her chest. She blinked, surprised. She'd barely known any semblance of emotion for weeks.

'Listen, Bo, I appreciate this. It can't have been an easy decision asking me to come.'

'It weren't. Mam mentioned you were lodging with the Saxes, but . . . I were unsure what your reaction would be upon seeing me. But I had to try. Had to for Moll.'

'The Tigers? You've left, then?'

'Aye. I stepped straight down, after Sissy . . . you know.'

'I've no problem with you, Bo, never have.'

'I see that now. It's the way of things; they . . . get out of hand, like. Well, you'll know, eh?'

'I do, aye. I know summat else, an' all. Scuttling? It's a fool's game. The day I quit were the day my life began, for the better.'

'Aye?'

Horatio's voice softened with understanding. 'Once in, the shackles take a while to shake off. You'll see, lad. Give it time, you'll see.'

'Aye. Well, you'd best go in to her. We've tried everything but I don't believe it's us she wants at this moment.' Bo paused before continuing quietly, 'If anyone can snap her out of this, I think you can. At least I hope so. You'll do your best?'

'I will.'

Footsteps crossed the passage, the scrape of the latch being lifted sounded and the front door closed. All was still, and again a stirring inside Moll brought a frown to her brow. Had they left? For where?

'Moll? It's me.'

The sudden voice from what she'd assumed was the empty passage made her lift her head. The bedroom door opened and there Horatio was. She peered across as though seeing him for the first time. She loved this man, knew this without question, but it was as though what little feeling had penetrated was diluted – her body seemed incapable of passing further through the black grief.

'Your mam and Bo have gone for a walk to give us time alone. Oh, my love. I ain't half missed you.'

The familiar death-like fatigue wrapped its cloak around her and her head drooped to meet the pillow once more. In a few strides, he was beside her. He ran his fingers in a tender touch through her hair and she closed her eyes.

'Moll. My poor Moll. I didn't want to impose on your family's grief. Out of respect for your mother – brother, too, aye – I thought it only right to wait until you sent for me. Jilly's kept me informed of how you are, but dear God, I hadn't realised you'd been taken so bad.' He dropped a kiss on to her temple. 'The ache to see you . . . Lord above, it's killed me inside.'

For the first time since Sissy left them, Moll's mouth moved and scratchy words emerged but didn't sound right. Was that really her voice?

'What did you say, my love?'

She tried again. 'Or a . . . sibling. A sibling, you said. You were right. Only you predicted the wrong one.'

Horatio reached for her hand. 'Oh, Moll . . .'

'Sissy . . . Sissy's dead.'

'I'm sorry, so sorry.'

'She's dead because of me.'

He jerked back. 'Nay, lass!'

'I failed to protect her. I should have been watching her, should have stopped her running into the road. I need to see her, say sorry. I want to die.'

'Moll! Nay—'

'I want to die. I want to die, want to die!'

With a gruff sob, Horatio scooped up her thrashing body and held her, tightly, tightly, rocking her until her screams subsided. When, exhausted, she flopped against him, quiet now, the release having shrunk the crushing, solid block in her chest, he lifted her chin with his forefinger.

'Listen to what I'm about to say and believe it, for it's the truth. Not you, nor I, nor anyone could've altered what occurred.'

'But the hansom cab, mebbe I could've—'

'That growler, through no fault of yours nor the driver's, neither, was upon her afore we could blink. No one could've reached Sissy in time. No one's to blame for her death. You say you want to die and I understand, I do, but ask yourself this: would Sissy want that? Would she want to see you like this? You must pull yourself through the midnight of your grief. Do it kicking and screaming – bloody *claw* your way, inch by inch, if that's what it takes – but do it. *Do* it, Moll. For yourself, for us. Do it for Sissy.'

The tears that pooled, now, soothed her arid eyes like balm. Finally letting them spill, she breathed a sigh of blessed relief.

'You're the reason my heart gives its every beat.

Without you . . . I'll not lose you, Moll. Promise me you'll fight your way through this.'

She cried until her tears dried out. Then she nodded against his chest. Again, tightness in her breast lessened and in her mind's eye, Sissy's angel smile deepened. A shadow of a smile touched Moll's lips in response. 'I promise,' she whispered.

With Horatio lying beside her, stroking her hair, Moll had settled down to snooze. When he woke her some time later, she felt as though she'd passed a full night's sleep, so refreshed did she feel, though in reality, it could only have been a few hours.

She smiled softly. 'You stayed with me all this time? There were no need.'

'I did. And there was every need. Come on, let's get you out of this stuffy room for a while.' He lifted her in his arms, smiling when she rested her head on his shoulder, then planted a quick kiss on her head and carried her to the door.

'Horatio?' Moll glanced up at him then to the tin bath, steam rising from it gently, where it was set before the fire. 'Did you . . . ?'

'You've barely moved in weeks. Your muscles will benefit from a hot soak, coax some life back into them.'

She was overcome with gratitude. His thoughtfulness made her want to weep.

Like a deciduous tree being stripped by the wind of its winter leaves, Moll stood unresisting, arms outstretched, while he undressed her. Again, he lifted her up, stooped and lowered her into the water. The warmth rose around her like a blanket. Hugging her knees, she closed her eyes and sighed.

Without a word, Horatio washed and rinsed her hair.

329

With his caring touch he then ran a cloth over every inch of her, feeding her pale skin with life's hue once more. Afterwards, he dried her body and helped her back into her clothes. He then lugged out and emptied the bath and returned to her, still standing in the centre of the kitchen, collecting a brush from the dresser drawer on the way. Taking her hand, he led her to the fireside chair. Flames crackled softly and sitting her on the rag rug before them, he took a seat behind her and slowly drew the brush through her damp locks.

After a while, she leaned back between his legs and snuggled into him. His arms went around her and here they stayed for a time, neither speaking, the glowing coals casting dancing shadows across them in the fading light.

'Thank you,' Moll murmured sleepily.

'Thank *you*, lass. Thank you for being strong, coming back to me.'

'I love you, Horatio Green, with all that I am.'

He turned her about. Moll raised herself on her knees and their mouths met in a feathery kiss.

They were finishing a light meal – prepared by Horatio, much to Moll's surprise – of boiled eggs and milky tea when the front door opening sounded and Ruth and Bo entered.

Catching sight of her daughter, Ruth's eyes immediately filled with thankful tears. 'Moll . . . Oh, lass. Thank the Lord! Ta to thee, lad,' she added to Horatio, putting her arms around them both.

Moll's misty gaze settled on Bo in the doorway. He stood chewing his thumb, chin buried in his neck, staring at his feet. Moll's eyes took in the dove-grey muffler around his neck, which she hadn't seen him wear in a while.

330

The lad who had snapped at her and brushed aside her pleas for months past, the lad who spat threats to her in Ancoats Hospital, the lad who had roared into her face his thankfulness that she wasn't his mother – not one of these remained. Neither did the lad she'd pointed across the road to when Sissy lay broken between them. These effigies had dissolved, leaving only the boy. She saw him as she always had. Her brother. Her life.

She took a step towards him. Then she held out a hand. 'Bo.'

'I'm so sorry, Moll. So sorry.'

'Come here to me, lad.'

He flew across and fell on his knees before her. His arms went around her waist, his shoulders heaved and a harsh cry ripped from him. 'You asked time and again what would it take to make me realise. Why didn't I listen to you? Why did it have to be this to make me see sense? Why Sissy? I *miss* her.'

Murmuring words of comfort, Moll stroked her brother's hair. 'It's just you and me, now, lad. Just you and me. God willing, we'll get through this, somehow.' And she meant it.

Chapter 24

RUTH PLACED THE teapot on the table and pushed Moll's filled cup towards her. 'You were ill. Don't berate yourself for that, for no one else does. Drink your brew, now, there's a good lass.'

Beyond the window, the approaching spring winked far in the distance. Daylight hours crept by a little longer each day; the heavy nights would soon be behind them. Yet wintry fingers still cast their bitter touch on streets and rooftops and Moll secured her shawl around herself tightly in readiness against it.

'I'd accompany you were I able,' Ruth continued as Moll sipped her tea. 'You understand, don't you? I can't face it, I can't.'

She reached across to touch her mother's hand. 'I only wish I'd been there for you when Sissy was laid to rest. I missed it and I'll never forgive myself. Hopefully, visiting her grave today will make me feel a bit better.' She drained her cup then rose. 'I'll be off, then.'

'Give Sissy . . . Give her my love, won't you?'

'I will, Mam,' she assured her softly. 'You'll be all right? Bo should be back shortly to sit with you till I return.' Davy, who was lounging by the fire, she didn't count. He was about as much support as a crutch made of jelly.

Ruth nodded and after tidying her hair in the mirror, Moll left the house. She took her time on her journey. It was true she'd regained most of her strength during the past days; still, she tired easily. It would take her a while to get back to her usual self; she realised this and accepted it. There was no rush, after all.

Physically, yes, she'd soon return to normal. Her mental state was another matter, but this, also, she understood. She'd never be the same, she knew, and accepted this, too. When Sissy died, so did something within her and just as her sister could never return to her, neither would the part of herself that Moll had lost. What exactly was gone, she didn't know, but felt it all the same. But she'd manage. She must. Death touched everyone's life at some time or another. It was how you chose to deal with it that set you apart. She just prayed that the constant ache that dwelled deep within her breast would leave her over time. Of this, she wasn't so sure.

She was glad she had supportive folk around her, for without them, she doubted she'd have ever risen from that bed. Her and Bo's relationship was on the mend; even Mam was trying, as hard as Moll this time, to fix their shaky relationship. Jilly, of course, was as wonderful as she'd ever been, and kind and understanding Beattie and Twit were angels from heaven, it was true. As for Horatio . . .

Moll smiled softly to herself. He made life worth living. As he'd done with her mother and Jilly, he'd slowly brought Bo around. That the men would ever be the best of friends was debatable but considering how matters stood a few short weeks ago, it was enough. Aye, for now, it was.

The only fly in the ointment was Preston, but when

was there anything new there? His drunken sniping and sulky moods, in fact his mere existence, she largely ignored.

Through the churchyard and on towards Sissy's resting place, Moll managed to hold it together. However, at the sight of the fresh soil, one of little Cathy's rag dolls sitting forlornly on top, a flood of images battered her mind. Sissy's voice, laughter, her innocently cheeky ways, the feel of her arms around her neck, the last words she'd spoken – 'Love you, Moll . . .' – clear with a love as bright and true as Moll's would always be for her . . .

'Oh, lass. Oh, Sissy, Sissy.'

As she'd known she would, Moll dropped to her knees at the graveside and sobbed. And later, after kissing her fingertips and pressing them to the earth, she wandered with a calmer heart between the rows of grey stones towards her father's mossy bed. This place, she knew, would always bring her comfort, now. As with her mother, some found visiting lost loves too difficult, but not Moll. A quiet acceptance, some sense of peace, wrapped around her and the pain, for a while at least, was at bay.

'Hello, Father.' The moment the greeting left her lips, Moll spotted what she'd believed she wouldn't again following her heated conversation with Polly. She fingered the wilted blooms with a frown. Again, attached to the stems, a single word was scrawled upon a scrap of paper: *Sorry*.

The petals were browning and curled around the edges – death had destroyed these roses a number of weeks past at least, it was clear. Had Polly placed them after their last meeting? The dates certainly matched. Why, though, if what her friend had said about her love for Uriah Croft was true, did she still feel compelled to come? It didn't make sense.

A sudden breeze whipped across, swirled around her skirts and continued on its lonely journey. Moll watched the disturbed leaves blowing about her father's grave settle. And something that had been unearthed from beneath the foliage suddenly caught her eye. It was a fawn-coloured tassel from the border of a shawl. However, it wasn't the nature of the object that made her rise slowly, shaking her head. It was the truth of whose garment this had once been attached to that filled her with a queer sense of anxiety.

Her eyes flicked to the flowers and note once more, and the feeling intensified. Polly always wore a shawl of faded red with tassels to match. The only soul Moll knew who wore one in this particular shade ... But why? Why would *she* ... ? What on earth was going on?

Picking up her skirts, Moll turned towards the church gates and ran for home.

'By, but it does my heart proud to see you out and about, lass. Aye, it does that. Eeh, come here and give owd Jilly a hug.'

Having slowed her pace upon spotting the old woman chatting with Mrs Coombes outside her door, Moll now halted beside them. Gazing at the one who had always been more of a second mother than just a friend and neighbour, the frown that had accompanied her home deepened.

'Lass?' Letting her outstretched arms fall back to her sides, Jilly's brow creased in return. 'What's to do? What's happened?'

Moll's eyes travelled to the brown woollen shawl around Jilly's shoulders. They scanned the edges and the fawn-coloured tassels swinging there – then stopped suddenly. Sure enough, there it was: a gap where one was missing.

'Moll? Love?' Shooting Mrs Coombes a worried look, Jilly took Moll's elbow. 'Come on, let's get you in to your mam. You've tried to gallop afore you could trot. You're not yet well—'

'What are you sorry for, Jilly?'

The old woman blinked; once, twice. 'Eh, lass?'

Moll held out her bunched fist. When she turned it over and opened it, Jilly stared at what was revealed in her palm. 'What are you sorry for, Jilly?' she asked again.

'I don't know what . . . what you mean.'

'I found this just now.'

Jilly swallowed. 'Oh?'

'And there were roses again with the selfsame note as afore. This – this is from your shawl.' Moll held the tassel up. 'You've been at Father's grave. It's *you* what's been leaving them flowers, ain't it? Why? *What* are you sorry for?'

With a sharp intake of breath, Jilly crumbled. Covering her face with her hands, she rasped through her fingers, 'I never thought he'd . . . never thought death was so close. I'd have never left Robert had I known . . . You must believe me.'

Moll shook her head. 'Jilly, what do you mean?'

'The flowers, lass; at Christmas, on his birthday. The ones I took to him after you told me you were to be wed . . . They were times he should've been here to share with you, his family. But he couldn't, could he? And I had to tell him I was heartsore sorry for that. I let him down, you see, your father. I let you all down.'

'I don't . . . What are you saying?'

'I left to check how my Alf was faring. I were away no longer than a handful of minutes. When I returned, he was gone.'

Colour rushed to Moll's face then drained away at lightning speed, leaving her light-headed. She ran a shaky hand across her mouth. 'Are you saying you weren't with him at the end as you stated you'd been?'

Biting her lip, Jilly nodded, sending tears coursing down her face to splash on the cobbles.

Moll had told her mother that Ruth was the last word on her father's lips. She'd assumed it to be. Jilly's reluctance that day when asked if he'd uttered anything at the end . . . She hadn't hesitated to answer, as Moll had believed, to spare her mother's feelings. Jilly had struggled to think up a response because she didn't know. *Oh, Mam . . .*

'You've kept this to yourself all this time? Why didn't you tell us the truth?'

'I thought you'd never forgive me; God in heaven, *I* won't ever. I did it to save you the hurt but the guilt, it'll not leave me. Every one of those sorrys you saw on them notes, I meant and more, more than I could express in a hundred lifetimes besides. Lass, don't hate me. Lass, please. I couldn't bear it!'

Moll's response was released with a whimper. She closed her eyes in despair. 'Oh, Jilly. Father died *alone.*'

Mrs Coombes had been looking from one to the other in puzzlement. Now, she shook her head and smiled, much to their bewilderment. 'No need to fret so! Nay, for the pair of you will feel the better for what I'm to tell you.' Nodding, her smile broadened. 'Robert Chambers didn't shuffle from this mortal coil without a kind word in his ear or hand to hold, I'm sure of that much.'

'What?' Moll and Jilly asked in unison, the elder adding, 'Edna Coombes, what's this you're saying?'

'I'm saying that Robert Chambers didn't die alone.'

Moll shook her head. 'But Jilly here's just admitted she left Father to tend to Mr Sax.'

'Aye. And the moment she disappeared down her cellar steps, another entered yon house.'

'*What?*'

'Aye. I seen it with my own two eyes from my very window, there,' Edna confirmed, jerking her thumb.

'Who did you see enter?'

The answer Moll received saw her whole life changed for ever. Seconds later, she was flying across the cobbles towards home.

Chapter 25

'BLOODY BOMBASTIC WHELP, you're nowt else.'

Bo's weary tone reached Moll as she neared the kitchen door. 'Oh give it a rest, will you? You're drunk.'

'Aye! Aye! Skennin' I am, it's true, and ask yourself why. No sane man could cope a night beneath this rotten roof sober. I'll tell you that for nowt!'

Shaking from head to toe with such an all-consuming rage that it scared her, Moll pushed open the door.

'Well, Preston. I could draw you a map to the street if you'd only say the word.' Bo paused in eating his meal to stare at the man standing over him. 'And good riddance to bad rubbish.'

Ruth's sigh whispered around the room. 'Bo, enough. Davy, you sit yourself down in that chair, now, love. A sup of tea do you? Aye, I'll pour you one. Sit down, sit down.'

Davy glared at Bo's bowed head as he resumed his meal then, with a frustrated growl, flung around and stomped to the chair by the fire. 'Young whelp. Needs taking down a peg, aye. Bloody wastrel,' he muttered to himself, then, 'Aye, it's *you* this house needs to see the back of!' he shot, stabbing a finger. 'I for one don't go in for rubbing shoulders with murderers!'

The whole room seemed to hold its breath. Ruth

turned to look at Davy slowly and Bo, face now blood-less white, lowered his fork. It was then Moll stepped into the kitchen.

'Oh, and here's t' other one, bloody Lady Muck,' Davy crowed. 'Taking to your bed as you did without a by-your-leave, having your mam here waiting on you hand and bloody foot like some unpaid chambermaid.'

'What did you say about the lad?'

Squinting up at Ruth, who had come to stand in front of him, Davy frowned. 'Eh?'

'The lad, Davy. What did you say?'

'Oh aye, aye. Well it's the truth! No bugger's putting words to the fact but we all know it.' He pointed again towards Bo. 'He, that one there, killed young Sissy as sure as if he'd taken a bloody knife to her throat. Deny it, whelp!'

Scraping back his chair, Bo leapt to his feet. He shook his head wildly. 'Nay! I didn't, I . . . I never meant—'

'That's neither here nor there, is it? The fact remains: that lass is still gone, ain't she? Because of you and your hooligan ways. *You* killed her as sure as eggs is eggs, didn't you? Didn't you!'

'Nay! Nay, please, I—'

'Murderer!' Davy yelled, staggering to his feet. 'You're a bloody murderer! It's the noose about your neck you need the feel of, that's what! Murderer, murderer—!'

'Aye, what? Like you?'

At Moll's words, heavy silence once more gripped the small room. All three stopped to stare at her with puzzled frowns and stepping forward, she spoke again. 'If anyone's a murderer, it's you, Davy Preston. I'd stake my life on it.'

'She's turned in the head, this one.'

'Oh no.' Looking him straight in the eye, Moll spoke

with an icy calmness. 'My mind's as clear as crystal, now, you can be sure.'

'Who's Davy meant to have murdered, like?' Ruth asked mildly. 'Lass, are you sure you're feeling all right? I think visiting Sissy's grave has taken its toll on your strength.'

Tears scorched behind Moll's eyes. She swallowed hard. 'Father. He killed Father.'

Ruth laughed incredulously. Even Bo pulled a face, scratching his head in confusion. The man in question, however, did neither. Nor did he bluff and bluster and call Moll a liar. He simply stared at her through huge eyes. An odd stillness filled her. She'd gone out on a limb accusing him of what she suspected but his reaction said it all. She *knew* he'd only have entered this house with her father here with devilment in mind.

'I knew it. You wanted rid of him to get your hands on Mam. You knew we'd all be out at work that day. You lay in wait, didn't you? Seeing Jilly leave, you took your chance.'

Taking the very air by surprise, Davy shrugged. 'That mess of a man were on his last legs, anyroad. I just helped him on his way. That pillow did him more good than harm; aye, it brought him peace. His suffering were lessened by my actions.' Nodding, he spread his arms wide. 'If owt, you should be thanking me.'

'Wha— Nay, nay, you ... *Bastard!*' With a furious scream, Bo made to lunge at the older man but Moll held him back.

'Wait, lad. Wait,' she told him. 'He'll get his soon enough, but he's going to tell it all afore then.' She turned to where her mother stood frozen to the spot gazing at Davy, her mouth hanging loose, hands gripping the hair at her temples. 'Mam, ask him. For once, the taste of honesty sits on his palate. Ask him about his parents' brothel, what he had planned—'

'*Had* planned?' cut in Davy with a grin, eyes spewing venom. 'Have, don't you mean, bitch? *Have* planned.'

'It's true? What the lass has said all along is true?' Ruth almost choked on her own speech.

'Aye, well, you may as well hear it, now. I'm done wasting any more days on this whole bloody business. We'll be away in Bolton by nightfall so you may as well be prepared.'

'I'm going nowhere with you! Nowhere!'

Davy's smile vanished. 'Oh, but that's where you're wrong, Ruthie. You're coming with me if I have to drag you there kicking and screaming blue bleedin' murder. You owe me. I've kept you and your brood for bloody months without so much as a thank-you in between. Now, it's time you paid up. I'll see you clear your debt, all right, I'll see to that!'

Again, Bo made to throw himself at Davy but the older man's next words stopped them all in their tracks:

'The odd bob or two I've made off the back of you so far, Ruthie, ain't even scratched the surface, let me tell you. Oh no, missis.'

Ruth staggered. Gripping the back of the fireside chair for support, she gazed at Davy, eyes screaming devastation. 'You don't . . . don't mean . . . ?' At his nod, she let out a cry. 'But you said . . .'

'Aye, I did. But here's summat you don't know. Them occasions you've awakened from a gin sleep with the sting betwixt your thighs and I told you it were my doing, that I'd taken my conjugal rights, as I'm entitled . . . ? Guess what? I lied. And you were none the wiser. You see, it's not so bad, eh? Whether it's my prick you open up your legs to greet or that of another, it's all the same to you with the drink inside yer.'

Ruth, and even Bo, struck dumb by the revelations, could only gaze in sheer horror. Moll, on the other hand, wasn't afforded the same numbing shock. Images darted through her mind then slotted into place; darted and slotted. She doubled forward as though winded.

The man she'd seen leaving this house the day Mam invited them for dinner ... her queer, half-standing position, sprawled across the tabletop ... Jilly's confirmation afterwards that it hadn't been a one-off, that she'd seen men coming and going, too ... Moll had thought them to be but drunken acquaintances. *Preston, he'd ... And those men had ... with her mam ...*

'Get packing, Ruthie,' Davy was saying now. 'We've a train to catch. Aye, there's nowt to keep you here, now, since Sissy went – and that were weeks ago. I've given you ample time to grieve, I'd say. Now it's time we got a shift on. The sooner my mam gets you settled in at Moor Lane, the quicker I'm back in the brass.' He smiled almost warmly. 'You'll not find it a trial so long as the bottle's been at your lips. And I'll keep you in supply of that, lass, have no fear.'

On unsteady legs, Ruth took several steps towards him. 'You had men in my home?'

'Oh aye.' Davy nodded casually. 'I sneaked them in at all hours.'

'You let them have their way with me, when I was out of it, to line your pockets?'

'Aye, that's right.'

Ruth's voice dropped further. 'And the worst of it, you murdered my husband to have him out of the way so you could begin your activities sooner? You *murdered* my poor Robert?'

'As I said, he were dying anyroad—'

'You shoved a pillow over his face! You removed him from this earth when he'd time still to spare. And all for brass? You took away the love of my life . . . for *brass*?' Suddenly, Ruth's mouth opened wide, her eyes followed suit and she swayed dangerously. 'The child.'

'Child? What child?'

'*My* child. The child you had your mother rip from my womb. That's why you cared not a fig for it, ain't it? Those fellas . . . The child weren't yours, was it?'

'That's summat we'd never have known. Fetching up another bloke's brat? Huh, not me! I weren't taking the bloody chance.'

The hatred pouring from her mother's eyes filled Moll with a host of emotions: pity, anger, sadness – but mostly, overwhelming relief. Finally, *finally*, Mam had seen Preston for what he was. She'd realised. At last, they would be shot of him, this time for good . . .

With a deafening scream, Ruth ran at Davy with bunched fists, taking him completely by surprise. Before she reached him, he staggered sideways just once – that was all it took. Sissy's kitten let out a yowl as he trod on its tail, making him jump and sending him stumbling headlong towards the fire. His temple made contact with the corner of the mantel with a dull thud. Making no sound, he slithered to the floor.

Moll had been waiting with bated breath for her mother to find her voice in the darkness of her shock and order Davy to leave. What had transpired instead shocked her to her essence. She could do nothing but stare at the man lying prone on the flags.

'Dear God. Is he . . . ?' asked a voice from behind them.

They all whipped around to find Horatio in the doorway.

'I heard a commotion from the cellar, thought I'd check if everything was all right . . .' He held out his arms to Moll. She rushed into them and buried her head in his chest. 'What happened?'

Bo, having crossed to Davy to check for a pulse, let the limp arm fall to the ground. 'Mam's finally woken up the night, lad. That's what's happened.' As Horatio had done with Moll, he beckoned a dry-eyed Ruth to him and, after casting Davy a last, lingering look, she walked into her son's arms.

'So,' said Horatio, moving to close the door. 'What's to be done?'

Ruth glanced around. 'Done?'

'Aye, with the body. The sooner we get shot of it, the better for us.'

Us . . . Blinking back tears, Moll shook her head. 'This ain't your problem, love. I'll not see you dragged into our mess.'

Horatio took her hand in his. He looked at each of them in turn. 'You three are my family, now. And families are meant to be there for one another.'

Knowing he was thinking of the Simcoxes and all their failings towards him in that respect, Moll shook her head again sadly. 'Horatio, think about what you're saying. This is serious. That's a dead body lying there.'

Without hesitation, he nodded. 'And if you don't mind me saying, I can't pretend surprise. From what I saw of him that time, he had it coming.'

'I'm the one what done it. I killed him,' said Ruth. 'You three, you should all just go, go now, save yourselfs.

It's me what deserves to be punished, not youse. I must go to the police.'

'Nay,' said all three simultaneously.

'I'll tell them everything, that his death were an accident.'

'The law is rarely friend to the common man,' Horatio stated. 'And if they knew harsh words passed betwixt youse afore his death . . . We can't trust they'll see the truth.'

'But . . . I must. There's no other way.'

'There's allus a way.' Bo kissed the top of Ruth's head then paced the room, eyes creased in thought. Finally, he halted. 'I've got it. We'll wait till darkness falls then we'll dump Preston in the Rochdale Canal. Moll, where's that old handcart I made you to ply your tatties from? We'll transport him in that.'

Moll couldn't believe what she was hearing. Was this actually happening? Dumping dead bodies into the drink? It was like something from a penny dreadful. Nay, this was a bad dream, aye. She'd waken in a minute and all would be well again. It would, surely.

'Moll? Did you hear me? The barrow?'

'Preston fed the thing to the fire ages back. But Bo, never mind that. We can't—'

'Aye, lad.' Horatio nodded slowly. 'That just might work. The police hereabouts, I know their beats by heart.'

At this, Bo nodded understanding. 'Scuttlers do well to learn a constable's movements,' he murmured to Moll. 'Knowing their whereabouts night and day means the difference between a cell and freedom.'

'Bo, nay,' she told him. 'We can't—'

'PC Sweeny normally foots the locality at around one-fifteen,' Horatio cut in, screwing up one eye as he

346

attempted to recall the patrols. 'He's relieved by about two o'clock by PC Gray. From, say . . . two-twenty, it's a clear run for some ten, mebbe fifteen minutes and then—'

'Stop! Just bloody stop, youse two, will yer? God above! No one is dumping anyone in the canal. It's madness. Besides, it'd never work.'

'It might.'

'You want to take that chance, do you, Bo? What if you're spotted? It ain't just the police what trawl these streets of a night. There's folk coming and going at all hours. Anyroad, even if you did manage it, what if he washes up somewhere in a few days' or weeks' time? If he's dragged out and someone identifies him, we're done for. How would we explain away his absence?'

'We'll think of summat. 'Erc, happen we could fill his pockets with rocks to weigh him down, keep him in his watery grave?'

Moll shook her head. 'It's too risky. Besides, don't you think his parents will grow suspicious after a while when he fails to show his face in Bolton? They're bound to come looking. I overheard Preston that night in the alleyway with his father, remember? He might know where we dwell and turn up one day on the doorstep.' Again, she shook her head. 'Nay. There's only one thing for it.'

Bo's eyes widened. 'I ain't chopping him up, Moll!'

'*What?* Christ's sake, Bo, course not!' Moll clicked her tongue. 'Chopping him up indeed – the way your mind works at times!'

He exchanged a look with Horatio and both lads stifled a laugh.

Moll turned to Ruth sitting dazed in a chair. 'Mam, have you gin in?'

347

'What?'

'Gin, Mam. Is there any in the house?'

Frowning, she shrugged. 'If there is, it'll be in the cupboard, there.'

To Moll's relief, she found two bottles. She removed the cork from one and placed it on the table in front of Ruth.

'Lass?'

If someone had told her before this night that she'd be stood here encouraging her mother to drink, she'd have laughed in their face. Then again, she reminded herself wryly, it had been a bit of a queer day all round. She inclined her head. 'Get supping, Mam.'

'Moll?' asked Horatio in confusion.

'It's the only way.' Taking a seat beside Ruth, Moll motioned to the lads to join them. 'Sit down and I'll explain what we're to do.'

Chapter 26

'I KNOW YOU'RE in there, Bo-Bo!'

Letting the scrap of curtain fall, Moll turned to face her brother. 'Vick? Bloody Vick, Bo? You swore to me you'd left all that behind you.'

Running a hand through his hair, he sighed. 'I have, Moll. And that's the problem: she can't accept it.'

'She's been back afore today?'

He glanced away guiltily. 'She called around once or twice when you took to your bed but I told her where to go. I thought she'd got the message.'

'Clearly not, eh?'

The girl's drunken, maudlin voice swept through the passage again and Bo raised his eyes to the ceiling. 'I can't leave her out there raising hell in the street like that. I'll have to face her, tell her to leave.'

Moll placed a hand on his arm. 'I'll tell her.'

'Nay. Vick's my problem—'

'And I'm going to sort it once and for all.' She sighed and Bo did likewise. 'Just as things are looking up, eh, lad? Why must summat always spring up to bite us on the backside when we're doing all right?' Mouth set, she crossed to the front door and yanked it open.

'I don't want you!' Stumbling sideways off the step at Moll's unexpected appearance, Vick jutted her chin

349

towards the door. 'I don't want you,' she whined again. 'I want to see my Bo-Bo and I'll not leave this house till I do, so there!'

'Well that's just tough, in't it, for he don't want to see you. God, the state of you. Get away home, you drunken fool, and don't darken this door again.'

'Where is he?' Vick leaned across Moll's shoulder to squint through the passage. 'I know you hear me! Face me, you bleedin' coward! How could you leave me like this after all we were to one another? I love you. You said you loved *me*, you rotten, stinkin'—!' She broke off on a loud wail. 'Bo-Bo! *Bo-Bo!*'

'You don't love me, Vick, and never did.'

'Go back inside, lad,' Moll told her brother, who had appeared behind her. 'I'll deal with this.' Eyes narrowing, she began rolling up her sleeves, intent on hauling this hard-faced mare out of their lives once and for all – and not before time.

'It's all right, Moll. Go on in. It'll not take long.'

Reluctantly, she went to stand in the passage. Nonetheless, she remained poised. If that vicious piece lifted a hand to her brother or, horror of horrors, touched at his big heart with her forced tears and began wheedling him around, she'd be on her so fast, Vick wouldn't know what day it was. Why couldn't they just leave him alone? He'd broken free, was rebuilding his life, was done with the Tigers. What would it take to make them see that?

Vick's cries had risen in pitch, the racket having drawn several people to their doors.

'Give over bawling,' Bo hissed. 'Folk are looking.'

Dragging a sleeve across her nose, Vick scowled about her. 'And what are you nosey buggers gawking at? Mind your bloody own, else I'll be back with an apron full of enough rocks to see there's norra single window in this street intact!'

'Leave the neighbours be, for Christ's sake. Look, just get gone, will you?'

'How can you talk so? I love you, I do! You're my Bo-Bo.'

Bo's response was weary. 'I'm your nowt. Why can't you get it into that head of yourn? It were the status you wanted me for, nowt else; same as you have with every other captain what's led the Tigers. I've told you, I'm done with scuttling. It's finished with, over. Now, go home.'

'You're not done. I know you. You'd not abandon us. We need you to lead us into battle against the Meadow mob. They're growing bolder by the day, d'you know that? They're saying you've turned soft. They're *laughing* at you, Bo!'

There came a moment of silence and Moll's heart dipped. She held her breath. *Don't break, lad. She's toying with your ego, that's all. Rise above it, please.*

'We understood you needed time, losing little Susie, like.'

'You bloody stupid . . . Her name was Sissy. *Sissy*, Vick!'

'But it's been weeks, now,' she continued, unfazed. 'It's time you remembered where your loyalties lie. Young, he's running things in your absence but it's you we need. The lads are growing restless. They'll not put up with this much longer.'

Again, there followed silence. Then Bo ground out words through gritted teeth. 'You listen to me. Open them lugholes and bloody *hear*. I couldn't care a damn about the Bengal Tigers. I'm done with the Bengal Tigers. To hell with the Bengal Tigers! And the same goes for you, an' all.'

'Huh. Is that right?'

'Aye, yes, that's right!'

Vick laughed harshly. 'You'll regret this. You just see if you don't.'

'It's you shower what will have summat to regret if any one of you show your face again at this house!' Bo threw after her before slamming the door.

Moll led the way back to the kitchen. Neither spoke as she collected cups and brewed tea. After placing the teapot on the table, she put her hand on his in a brief but tender touch. 'I'm proud of thee.'

Bo broke his frown to raise an eyebrow.

'It's true. Let's just hope that's the end of it.'

'Aye.' He glanced to the wall leading to the bedroom. 'The row seems not to have disturbed Mam, anyroad.'

'Thanks be to God.'

'Have I to check on her, Moll? She's barely surfaced from that bed for days.'

Moll bit her lip in deliberation then shook her head. 'Sleep's helping hold her cravings at bay. Leave her a while longer. You can take her some tea through soon.'

The ticking clock on the mantel and the cat's gentle purrs from the rag rug were the only sounds as they lapsed into silence.

'She's doing well, though, Mam, ain't she, Moll?' Bo murmured after a time.

The gin she'd insisted Ruth drink the other night had been the last to pass her lips. Moreover, the turnaround had been her mother's decision. 'Aye. It'll not be much longer now till that poison's free from her system.'

'You're starting back at the inn the morrow, ain't you?'

'Aye but don't fret; Jilly's promised to keep Mam company whilst we're at work.' Moll smiled to herself. She was looking forward to returning. It would help keep her mind busy. Besides, now Preston was gone, the family would need the brass; perhaps she'd even manage to put aside a little each week towards her and Horatio's wedding. And she'd missed Beattie and Twit. They had been ever so good to her.

'You reckon Mam meant what she said to Preston? About Father, I mean.'

'That he were the love of her life?' Moll sighed thoughtfully. 'I think she did. I know she treated him terribly over the years but she loved him, aye. So far as Mam's capable of loving anybody, anyroad.'

'I can feel it in here, can you?' Bo said after a pause. 'The very air, it's sort of . . . settled.'

Moll knew exactly what he meant. She glanced around the neat space. Soon, she was certain, it would be as though Davy Preston had never existed. Already, he seemed but a distant memory.

Their mother had played out the following events that fateful night surprisingly well. She'd listened to Moll's plan carefully, asked questions, offered suggestions. When, finally, each was certain they had covered every possible eventuality, Ruth had reached for the bottle with a determined nod.

Staggering back into the kitchen some time later with two grim-faced constables in tow, it was clear she'd followed Moll's instructions to the letter. Lamenting the evils of alcohol, tears of grief and regret flowing expertly, she'd led them to her 'beloved's' body where they undertook the preliminary inspection.

'You had both been drinking excessively all day, you say?'

Screwing up her face, Ruth had nodded. 'Aye, constable.'

'No altercation took place prior to the accident, no disagreement between the two of you?'

'Nay, nay. We rarely argued and certainly not this night.'

'The deceased was making for this chair, here, when he took the tumble, is that correct?'

She'd nodded.

'And what was the cat's position?'

At this, she'd blinked confusedly. 'I don't rightly recall, constable. It had one leg up in the air grooming itself, I think.'

The officer had shot a glance to his colleague, who quickly lowered his eyes, then cleared his throat. 'No, no. I mean where was the cat at the time of the incident? Was its position directly in the path of the deceased?'

'Oh. Oh, aye. Just there.' Ruth had pointed. 'He noticed too late. That's when he stumbled and hit his head on the mantel's corner, there.'

'Indeed.'

'Glory be to God, he didn't linger. He were gone in t' blink of an eye. Oh, why, constable? We were due to wed, were looking forward to growing grey together. Why must the Lord take only the good?'

'Take comfort that the deceased didn't suffer,' he told her, not unkindly. He'd then turned to Moll and Bo. 'According to your mother, you were in the next room when the incident occurred, miss?'

Moll had nodded. 'That's right. In the bedroom, constable, taking a nap.'

'And you, sir, were in the cellar beneath our feet where dwells a Mr and Mrs Sax?'

'Aye. I'd called in to see my friend what lodges with them, constable.'

'Hm. Well, I think we have all we need. We may need

to question you further, you understand?' he'd added, snapping his notebook shut. However, his expression hinted that was unlikely. Ruth's stellar performance and the fact that there were no visible marks on the body left little reason to disbelieve their version of events. Besides, the death of a drunkard slum dweller was nothing new. Such incidents were a daily occurrence in these quarters. 'Someone will be around directly to see to the removal of the body. In the meantime, see that your mother gets some rest.'

And that had been that. Within hours, Preston was gone and the family were looking to the future.

As far as everyone else knew, the story they told the police was fact. Preston had suffered a terrible accident. Afraid Jilly would only reproach herself further if she knew the truth of things – her absence from Robert's bedside had, after all, made possible Preston's opportunity to commit his terrible deed – she, too, had been given the same tale. If she suspected otherwise, she never voiced it.

Moll had, however, reassured the old woman she was guilty of no wrongdoing. After all, Ruth had gone in search of gin that day, leaving their neighbour to care for two invalids alone. Jilly couldn't avoid needing to check on sick Alf. No one could have foreseen the outcome.

Now, fresh knocks at the front door pulled Moll back to the present. She and Bo exchanged a weary look.

'God above. Will Vick never get the message?'

'She will this time, for I'll be the one what delivers it. I've had a bloody bellyful of this.'

'Hello, Moll.'

Having wrenched open the door, the tirade died on Moll's lips. 'Polly? Polly, it is you!'

Her friend gave a small smile. 'Aye. It's me.'

'Come on in, lass.'

'Aye?' Polly's face showed uncertainty.

'Course. Come inside.'

Lowering her shawl to her shoulders, Polly followed her through. Spotting Bo at the table, she nodded. 'Hello, lad.'

'All right, there, Polly? I'll fetch you a cup.'

'Don't trouble yourself; I can't stop long.'

Moll sat and motioned for the older woman to do likewise. 'It's good to see you.'

Polly's eyes flicked up then back to the table. 'How you bearing up since . . . you know? I called when I heard but you weren't fit to see me.'

'I weren't fit to see anyone. It near broke me losing . . . losing her.' Moll blinked back tears. 'Ta, mind, all the same. It were good of you to come.'

'I couldn't believe it when I found out . . . I am sorry. Truly.'

Moll nodded. Uncomfortable silence fell and regret filled her. Polly was one of her oldest friends so why this strained atmosphere? She didn't *want* it this way. She missed Polly, a lot. Why must things change? Why couldn't everything just go back to how it was?

'I came to tell you we're moving away.'

'Moving?'

'Not far, mind, just to Uriah's uncle's in Harpurhey.' Polly's face clouded. 'Mam slat me out when she discovered . . . And Uriah's grandfather won't have me there. We're to lodge with Uriah's uncle till we find a dwelling place of our own. I just . . . I thought you should know.'

'You . . . *Uriah*?' Bo looked from one to the other. 'The two of you . . . ?'

Polly lifted her chin defensively. 'That's right. We're to be married in three weeks' time. I thought Moll would have told you we were seeing each other.'

'Nay. I had no idea!'

'I didn't think it my place to tell anyone your business, Polly,' Moll murmured. 'Married, eh? Well, I'm pleased for you both. I am, honest,' she added at Polly's unconvinced nod. She reached for her hand and squeezed. To Moll's relief, after a hesitation, Polly tightened her fingers around hers. 'Be happy, love. You deserve it.'

'Ta, Moll. Ta.'

She itched to know how matters really stood – Polly didn't exactly look to be fizzing with joy, it must be said. How had Uriah reacted upon hearing they were to have a child? she wondered. Whatever his feelings, he'd asked Polly to marry him. He was doing the right thing, now, at least.

'How is Uriah?' asked Bo quietly. His eyes deepened with raw guilt. 'I miss him. I do, aye. I . . . I treated him badly, I know, and I hate myself for that. He were good to me, always. I've wanted to call on him, apologise . . . I couldn't pluck up the nerve.'

'He's . . . aye, all right.'

'He must hate me.'

'Can you blame him?' Anger in Polly's response brought Bo and Moll's heads up in shock. 'Well, you've played him for a fool, ain't you? The pair of youse, for that matter. He's hurt, course he is. What he's for doing—' She clamped her mouth shut, cheeks reddening. 'Look, I shouldn't have come. I'll see myself out.'

'Polly?' Suspicion narrowed Moll's eyes. Sickly dread ran through her and as her friend made to rise, she clutched her arm. 'Polly? What's going on? What ain't you telling us?'

'Nowt, there's nowt.'

'There is, I can feel it. What—?'

'Uriah knows you killed your mam's fella.'

Moll jerked back as though she'd been slapped. She glanced to Bo, who had turned a shocking shade of grey. 'He . . . *what*?'

Polly's animosity was fading rapidly. She bit her lip. 'He reckons you'd made plans to be rid of him once afore. He said he heard it from your very lips, Moll.'

No, no . . . She closed her eyes in horror. Bo had said they should keep it to themselves. He'd said the fewer people who knew he and the Tigers were to get shot of Davy, the better. But she'd told Uriah, hadn't she? She'd felt she must, had needed him to understand why his friend joined the scuttlers' ranks. She'd confided in him without a second thought. She'd trusted him implicitly. She'd been such a fool.

'Folk say Preston's death were an accident but Uriah's certain it's a lie.'

Bo wiped a hand across his mouth. 'You said summat a moment ago, Polly, summat about what Uriah's for doing. What did you mean?'

She shook her head. 'I don't . . . can't . . .'

'What's he planning to do? *Polly*?'

'Uriah don't know I'm here. He told me to go straight on to his uncle's, said he'd follow shortly. He . . . made me swear . . .'

'You must tell us. Polly, please!'

'I can't. I mustn't!'

Moll sucked in deep breaths to steady her thumping heart. 'Whatever Uriah thinks occurred here with Preston, he's wrong. We wanted rid of him, it's true. But his death, it really were an accident. Mam, she went for him and he stumbled and fell.'

'Went for him?'

'Aye but she never got chance to reach him.'

'Ruth seemed blind to his behaviour. What occurred?'

'We discovered . . .' Moll bit her lip to stem fresh tears. 'He murdered Father, murdered him in his own bed. He smothered him, Polly, to have him out of the way.'

'Wha – *What*? Nay. Nay, not Robert . . . Oh! Oh, my poor . . .' Screwing up her face, Polly slapped a hand to her mouth.

'Preston deserved all he got and more,' said Bo. 'But though I wish to God we had, we didn't kill him. So you see, whatever Uriah thinks he knows, whatever he's planning—'

'He went in search of a detective, name of Mr Jerome, to tell him his suspicions.'

'Jerome Caminada?' Bo's face paled further. 'I know of him.'

'You do?' Moll asked.

'He's loathed by the criminal class the length and breadth of this city. Like a dog with a bone, he is, when he's on a case and come hell or high water, he nearly allus gets his man. Or woman.'

Moll swallowed hard. 'Where would we find him, Polly? Did Uriah say where he planned to speak to him?'

Tears streaming, the older woman shook her head. 'What has Uriah *done*? Oh, don't hate him. He ain't bad, not really. He's upset with youse, that's all. That's all.'

'We could never hate him. He's been like a brother to us since we were kiddies.'

Bo nodded agreement. 'We must find him, explain. Mr Jerome's in the habit of meeting informers in the back pews of the Hidden Gem.'

'St Mary's?'

'Aye.' Already, he was making for the door. 'There might still be time.'

Moll snatched up her shawl. 'I'm coming with you, lad.'

'Moll, Bo. I'm sorry, I am. Find Uriah. Tell him what you've told me. He'll see sense, I'm sure.'

Outside, Moll held back. She and Polly stood staring at one another for a long moment. As of one mind, they embraced tightly.

'Goodbye, lass. Goodbye.'

'Goodbye, Polly. You look after yourself, you hear?'

'You too, lass.' After giving Moll a last hug, Polly drew up her shawl and scurried away.

'Should we knock at Jilly's, inform Horatio?' asked Bo.

With reluctance, Moll shook her head. Given Uriah's animosity towards her future husband for claiming her heart, Horatio's presence would only antagonise him further. 'We'd do better speaking with Uriah alone.' Closing her eyes, she heaved a sigh. 'Oh, lad. When will these nightmares pass, at all?'

Bo turned for Mulberry Street. 'It's just one thing after a bloody 'nother.'

Nodding agreement, she hurried after him.

The bells' doleful ringing was declaring the end of the Sunday service as Moll and Bo reached the church cushioned between Albert Square and Deansgate in the city's centre. Slowing their pace, they scanned the faces of the flock spilling through the doors.

'Moll. There he is.'

Following her brother's gaze past numerous smoke-stained warehouses, her heart gave a flutter. Uriah stood in the distance on the opposite side of the road. Leaning against a wall, hands in his pockets, head hanging low, he looked in a world of his own.

'You reckon he decided he couldn't go through with it?' suggested Bo hopefully.

Moll touched his sleeve as he made to cross the street. 'The lad might grow defensive if we both confront him. You wait here. Let me speak to him.'

When she reached Uriah, she had to say his name twice before he became conscious of her presence. His eyes widened and a red hue spread from his muffler-clad neck to meet his cheeks.

'Can we talk, lad?'

'Slowly, his frown melted into a scowl of realisation. 'Polly.'

'She told us what you've a mind to do.'

'Aye, well, as you can see, I'm more pathetic than you already believe. This is as far as I managed to tread afore losing my nerve so don't fret, you're still in t' clear.'

'Oh, lad. That it's come to this. I'd have never thought it possible. You, me and Bo; we were such sound friends. That you could turn against us like this—'

'It were the two of youse what did that – to me, remember?'

'Uriah Croft, I didn't turn against you. Us . . . it just weren't meant to be. And Bo, he knows he treated you bad. He feels terrible, honest, he does, lad. He'd like nowt more than to make it up to you.'

A little of the anger left his face. 'Aye?'

'Aye, yes. He misses you. Deep down, you miss him, an' all. I know it.'

With a heavy sigh, he covered his face with his hands. 'God above, look at me. What have I become? This ain't me. This ain't me,' he repeated, as though he'd just realised the truth in the statement. 'I couldn't give two hoots about Davy Preston either way. What were I thinking?'

'That you wanted to hurt us and I understand, I do. But it don't have to be this way. Can't we try and get back what we used to have? Can't we, lad?'

'You really mean it? You could forgive me this today?'

'There's wrong been done on both sides,' a voice behind them answered for Moll. 'You're not the only one who's made mistakes.'

Uriah turned. He and Bo thrust their hands into their pockets and, casting each other small glances, stubbed the ground with the toe of their boots, bashful around one another as a couple of eight-year-olds. Moll watched on with a soft smile.

'Sorry, lad,' Bo mumbled.

Nodding, Uriah shrugged. ''S'all right. I'm sorry, an' all.'

'Aye. No bother.'

'You knocked that scuttling lark on t' head, then, aye?'

'Aye, lad.'

'That's good.' Uriah was quiet for a moment, then, 'Listen, Bo, about Sissy . . .' He glanced to Moll then back again. 'Sorry.'

'Ta. Ta, lad.'

'She were a gradely lass.'

Bo blinked rapidly. 'She were, aye. So . . . You and Polly . . .'

Uriah grinned self-consciously. 'Aye.'

'That's a bolt from the blue beyond, eh?'

'She's norra bad lass.'

Sounding agreement, Bo slapped his friend's shoulder. 'Oh aye. Polly's grand. You've done well, there, lad.'

'Aye,' Uriah agreed with feeling, much to Moll's pleasure. 'I reckon so. I think, in fact, she deserves better than me.'

Moll shook her head. 'Nay. You're a good lad, perfect for a good woman.'

'Our Moll's right enough there. Listen, lad. Once you and Polly have had time to get yourselfs settled at your uncle's, would you fancy . . . well, mebbe meeting for a sup one night?'

The slow smile that neither brother nor sister had seen for too long spread across Uriah's face. 'Aye. Aye, I'd like that. Well, I'd best be making tracks to Harpurhey. Polly will be fretting over me else.'

'See you soon, eh, lad?' Bo held out a hand and, without hesitation, Uriah shook it warmly.

Moll lifted her shawl over her head as she and Bo prepared to take their leave. Feeling a hand on her arm, she glanced up.

'Moll, wait.'

Uriah's gaze in those seconds said everything – his regret at the bad feeling between them; for twisting the truth about her to Polly; and his desire, now, to put things right. Mostly, it portrayed acceptance of how things must be, and hers creased in response.

'See you, sourpuss.'

Moll smiled tenderly. 'Ta-ra, lad.'

A cloak of happy relief enveloped brother and sister as they journeyed back home. Preston was gone, Mam was on the mend and their friendship with Polly and Uriah was restored. Moll and Horatio's upcoming wedding was a cause to be joyful about, and Bo looked forward to it more than anyone – a fact Moll hadn't thought possible not long ago. Yes, it seemed finally, everything would be well. The Chambers' run of bad fortune had passed.

'It's over, ain't it, lad?' she murmured, linking her

arm through Bo's. 'For once, I reckon things are going to go our way.'

'Moll.'

Studying his face, her smile waned. 'Lad? You've gone as white as tripe.'

'Moll . . .'

'What? What's wrong?'

He'd been looking at the ground as he spoke but now, glanced ahead to the end of Blossom Street. 'Moll, listen to me—'

'Oh for the love of . . .' she ground out, spotting the four youths making towards them. They could have been of one body; their rolling walk and stiff faces matched entirely. It was as though they had decided beforehand that their distinctive clothing wasn't enough . . . 'I knew it, *knew* a happy beginning for us was too good to be true.'

'I want you to turn and walk away. It's clear they want bother. I'll not see you caught up in it. For me, please, leave. Do it, Moll.'

'There he is, lads!' Vick informed the three stocky males in her company. 'And take a look at the phizog on him, an' all. Anyone would think he weren't pleased to see us.'

The tallest of the group lifted the knife he held and pointed the tip at Moll and Bo. 'If it ain't just the fella we've come to see,' he snarled, his free hand straying to his belt. ''Ere, *Captain*. We want a word or two in your ear.'

'I'm going nowhere,' Moll said determinedly when again Bo tried beseeching her to make her escape. 'I'm not leaving you to their mercy.'

'But—'

'Listen to me.' For his sake, she forced her voice

364

steady; not an easy task when she noticed each of the lads now held a menacing looking clasp knife in his fist. The tallest had removed his belt, was wrapping the leather around his wrist. 'When they reach us, you must brazen it out. Just for a moment or two; can you do that? Keep them distracted whatever way you can while I slip away and alert Horatio.'

Even as Moll uttered this, every fibre of her screamed at her not to. These Tigers were already baying for her love's blood – should he appear, they would think all their lucky days had arrived at once. Besides, she'd made him promise he'd never battle again. She'd been adamant, and he'd sworn he wouldn't let her down. He was trying to change and she'd aided him willingly. And now here she'd be, begging him to confront this mob? Actually *encouraging* him to fight, after all she'd said?

It was a senseless notion. She'd be actively putting him in danger; he could be injured, killed . . . But God above, what choice had she? Her brother wouldn't stand a chance against this. She couldn't let him face it alone, for without doubt, he wouldn't come through in one piece.

Going against all she believed in, she took a deep breath. 'Horatio will know what to do. He's a strong fighter. You can't front this alone, you can't.'

Sweat had sprung at Bo's temples. He nodded. 'All right. I'll not be able to hold them for long, though, Moll.'

By now, a mere few yards stood between them and the Tigers. They halted and the gang did likewise. Four pairs of eyes, glinting dark with menace, fixed on Bo. Meanwhile, Moll trained hers on the opening of the Saxes' cellar a short distance away.

'Look, Young. I want no bother.' Bo addressed the

365

taller lad at the front. 'I'm done with scuttling and that's that. What you've a mind to do here won't change that.'

The youth's face twisted in furious disgust. 'I can't believe I'm hearing this from you. Turning your back on us like this? You're *meant* to be our leader.'

'Well now *you* can be captain instead. What d'you say, Young? I'll step down, proper, like, here and now, and you can take my position. You can't deny it – leading the Bengal Tigers is what you've allus wanted. Now's your chance. What d'you say?'

'I say we gut you like a fish.' Young nodded and his friends jeered agreement; none louder than Vick. 'You spineless bastard, you're nowt else. Nay, you're with us whether as captain or no. It took us long enough to get you; we ain't letting you slip from us now. You're going nowhere, no bloody how.'

They loomed in on Bo and though it killed her to leave him, Moll knew this was her chance. In moments, they would be on the lad and she'd be too late. Slowly, slowly, she inched past them. Then, heart pounding, she picked up her skirts and sprinted for the cellar.

Vick called after her but Moll didn't look back. She was midway down the steps when suddenly, the cellar door swung wide and there he was. 'Horatio . . .'

'I were just on my way to see you.'

'Help him. *Help* him, please!'

Horatio's face dropped. Taking the steps two at a time, he was at her side in a heartbeat. 'Who? What's happ—?'

'The Tigers, they've come for Bo. They're out for his blood. You have to help him.' Without pause, Horatio made to dart for the street but Moll grabbed his jacket. 'Be careful. Please, please. You must promise me.'

Taking her face in his hands, he kissed her fiercely. 'I love you.'

Before Moll had time to catch her breath, he was gone from her. Gulping down panicked tears, she raced after him.

As she'd feared, Horatio's appearance fed the Tigers' anger to a whole other level. He rushed to Bo's side and, spitting incredulous curses and threats, they spread out to form a ring around the pair.

Young turned murderous eyes back to Bo. 'You stand shoulder to shoulder with him, of all people? Why you slippery, double-dealing bleeder, yer!' he almost screamed. 'We'll paint these flagstones crimson with your blood for this – then it's your turn, Rat swine!'

Unarmed and outnumbered, Bo and Horatio faced their opponents with grim acceptance. Yet despite their disadvantage, the powerfully built males made a for-midable duo. These former leaders of two of the worst gangs Manchester's streets had ever seen had joined forces and Moll knew it wouldn't end well for either side. Even victory would come at a price.

The first swish of a belt barely stroked the silence when Bo was on his knees. The heavy buckle had smashed into the side of his head before he had chance to duck and blood quickly saturated his face, moment-arily blinding him. One hand clawing the air above him in an attempt to shield himself from further onslaught, he scrubbed desperately at his eyes with his sleeve and staggered back up.

Two of the Tigers had closed in on Horatio. They struck out with their knives in frenzied sweeps but with expert precision, he weaved from reach. Like an enraged bull, he lowered his head and charged, arms outstretched, carrying them both off their feet.

The three landed in a writhing mass of muscle on the ground and as they grappled to overpower the enemy, Bo, who had lunged at belt-wielding Young, pummelled him, not ceasing until he lay prone at his feet. Bo then rushed to assist Horatio. Lifting one scuttler by the throat, he tossed him headlong into the gutter.

Desperate to summon assistance, Vick had moved to the edge of the road. Hands cupped around her mouth, head swinging left to right, she released a series of high-pitched yelps before disappearing around the corner. Moll, frozen with terror, could only gaze at the pandemonium in dumb silence.

With two lying bleeding and unconscious, Bo and Horatio closed in on the remaining scuttler. If the lone combatant was afraid, he didn't show it. With a roar, he charged at them, knife drawn.

Whether Horatio was caught off guard or missed his footing, no one could say. He stumbled and taking advantage of his momentary vulnerability, the scuttler seized his chance. He threw himself on top of Horatio and drew back his arm.

Gasping, Bo rushed to disarm him – only to crumple to the cobbles when the lad took a lightning speed swipe at him, slashing through Bo's trousers and tearing a deep wound in his thigh. With a grin, the scuttler swung his attention back to the man beneath him.

The silver tip was an inch from Horatio's chest when he grabbed the wrist. In the ensuing wrestle, Horatio managed to twist the knife from his grasp. However, as he made to throw it into the road out of harm's reach, the scuttler, believing his own weapon was being turned on himself, cried out in blind panic. In a desperate move to regain control, he brought his knee up between Horatio's legs.

It proved a deadly error. With an agonised groan, Horatio lurched, toppling the lad, and in a silent scream, the scuttler fell forward with all his weight on to his own blade.

Having limped to their side, Bo gazed in stunned disbelief at the knife's handle protruding from the dead youth's chest. The blade had entered his body to the hilt, slicing through his heart and extinguishing him instantly.

'God, no! *Horatio!* God, please, *no, no!*' Howling, Moll ran to them and skidded to her hands and knees. Shock had paralysed her man and still he lay on his back, face as void of colour as the dead one on top of him. 'Speak to me! You bloody well *speak*, Horatio Green! You can't leave me; don't you dare, don't you dare! Oh God, I can't lose you! Not you!' Moll turned eyes utterly wild with terror on to her brother. 'He'll get ten, fifteen years for this! He might *hang*, Bo. What will I do? What will I do? Tell me!'

Bo tried soothing her hysterics but she wouldn't listen, *couldn't*, for Horatio's life was finished as surely as if that blade had plunged into his own chest. Soon, he'd be gone from her and she'd wither and die because, without him, there was nothing for her.

Alerted by the ruckus, people began emerging cautiously from their homes and Bo snapped to life. He'd offered no answer to Moll's desperate questioning, only gazed at her in sorrow, eyes wet with sorry tears. Now, wisdom smoothed the worry lines etched into his brow and he nodded calmly.

'Bo, what—?'

'Hush. It's all right, lass,' he told her as she made to halt his reach. 'You must trust me. I know what I'm doing,' he murmured, placing his hand on Horatio's still clasping the knife.

369

Quickly, not in panic but with a swift efficiency that belied the enormity of the decision he was about to make, Bo uncurled the frozen fingers. He then closed his own hand around the cold metal.

Terrible realisation almost snapped Moll's head from her shoulders in a wild shake of denial. 'Nay. Nay, you . . . you can't . . . !'

'Listen to me and do exactly as I say.' Bo spoke with a sureness that matched his demeanour. 'See Mrs Coombes over there? You see her, Moll?'

She flicked her eyes up and nodded. 'Aye, she's making to cross the cobbles towards us.'

'You must run to her. Do it now and beg her help. Tell her I stabbed this lad in self-defence, that it was either him or us. Say it nice and loud, loud enough for everyone to hear. Can you remember all that? Can you do it?'

'I'll not . . . not let you do this, Bo—!'

'These scuttlers, the bane of every constable in the city's working life, came to my own door armed and out for blood. Anyone in this street will attest to that, for more than one curtain twitched upon their arrival. Horatio came to my aid and this one turned his knife on him. In the struggle, I tried to disarm the scuttler and he fell on his own blade. No witness can say different, for I'd reached the lads' sides by that point, blocking all view,' he added in a whisper.

'I'll not be part of this. I'll not let you be taken from me!'

Checking Mrs Coombes' progress, Bo continued quickly, though still in the quiet, steady tone. 'I've no previous convictions. Think about it – circumstances all point in my favour. I'll receive a year, mebbe. Two at a push. I can handle that, Moll. For you, for your happiness, I can do it. With Horatio's past form, he'll fare

370

much worse. They'll throw the key away, d'you under-stand, and I'll not see that happen. You need him here. You're meant to be. I see it now.' Bo pushed her gently. 'Go, do as I told you. Remember, Moll, nice and loud.'

Still, doubt held her frozen. Then Bo looked her full in the face and as clearly as if given a voice, his eyes spoke to her: *Let me do this for you. Let me put things right, for I've wronged you, Moll, time and again and still, you're here at my side. Let this be for you, and let it be for Sissy, and afterwards, we can wipe the slate and it will be our time, ours to live and know peace. The Tigers are finished with us now. We'll be a family once more and nothing will come in the way of that again. For once, I'm looking out for you. Let me put you first as you've done all your life for me. Please. Please.*

Slowly, Moll found herself rising to her feet. 'I love you,' she mouthed to her brother and he repeated the words back. Moments later, she was flying across the road to fall, sobbing out Bo's guilt, into Mrs Coombes' arms.

Chapter 27

ITS DEEP VOICE spanning the abutting buildings, the Town Hall clock had announced the seventh hour shortly before. Across town, in the shifting shadows of its great walls, tower and turrets, the forbidding edifice of Strangeways Prison seemed to bow to the high clock face in acknowledgement.

Moll drew the baby in her arms closer to her. Her gaze, trained on the huge, studded doors, creased in quiet anticipation and the yearning, now like an old friend, flared as though in final salute. Shortly, she'd have no need of it and it would be gone, dipping its head in graceful acceptance of the emotion that would be her new companion – the precious gift of peace.

A scraping of metal floated through the gatehouse and a narrow section of the right-hand door swung like an arm setting free its captor. Then there he was. Taller and wider in shoulder by several inches than when he'd entered, he lowered his head to pass through again, for the final time.

The door clanged shut at his back and for half a minute, he simply stood, eyes closed, face directed at the grey-white sky.

Moll moved forward but didn't speak. Not for anything would she interrupt this moment of his. Like dry soil in the rain, his senses absorbed all he'd once known, seeming to breathe back life into him. With a hint of a smile, he released a steady sigh.

When he opened his eyes to find her standing there, he took in her face carefully, as though re-acquainting himself with every contour, and she did likewise through a blur of tears. At Bo's insistence, no visits had taken place during his incarceration. The agony of goodbyes, he'd admitted, would have broken him. He'd chosen to get through his sentence his way. Despite their missing him, the pain like a physical thing inside, always with them, they had respected his decision.

'Moll.'

'Oh, lad.'

Bo's mouth widened in a shaky grin. Crossing the cobbled ground, he opened his arms and she ran into them with a broken laugh and a mended heart.

'It's over, Moll.'

She nodded against his chest. 'Thanks to thee. I'll never forget this, Bo. Neither of us will.'

'In a heartbeat, I'd pass back through those doors and do the last eight months all over again.'

'Eeh, Bo.'

'I regret nowt, Moll.'

'Horatio and Mam, they're waiting for you at Blossom Street. It's selfish of me, I know, but I begged them to let me come alone, had to have this moment with you to myself.'

Nodding, he held her closer. 'I wouldn't want it any other way.'

When at last they drew apart, Moll lifted the baby up and watched through fresh tears as Bo gazed at the new life in wonder. 'Here's your uncle,' she whispered to the sleeping infant. 'Say hello, Sissy.'

As he took his niece in his arms, tears ran down Bo's cheeks unchecked. 'I'll tell you summat, little lady, you've hit the jackpot bagging yourself our Moll for your mam.' His lips met her brow in the whisper of a kiss. 'I can see *our* Sissy in her, Moll,' he murmured, and she nodded.

Another shall ensure that the soul lost to you lives on.

As it did often, the last piece of Jilly's prophecy envisioned in the leaves flitted through Moll's mind, its truth making her smile. This precious child would indeed do just that. Through her, the one they were fortunate enough to know for such a brief time would be with them always.

'Mam's well?' Bo asked as they emerged arm-in-arm into Southall Street. 'She's not . . . ? Hasn't . . . ?'

'Not a drop,' Moll assured him. 'She vanquished that demon with the other one that night and glory be to God, hasn't looked back. She's a whole different being since taking over my position at the inn. Beattie and Twit became firm friends the moment she met them; and the children, 'specially little Cathy, helped bring back the smile to her lips.' *As had a certain customer with kind eyes and a gentle smile very much like Father's,* Moll added to herself with warm approval.

Bo breathed happily then, casting his tiny niece another besotted look, said, 'I'll bet Uriah and Polly's son is coming on, now, eh?'

'Oh, he's a strapping young fella, and talk about handsome! Eeh, he'll break some hearts when he's grown, he will.'

'Well that's hardly surprising, is it? Takes after his namesake, don't he?' Bo winked as Moll chuckled. 'I feel honoured that Uriah chose to name him after me,' he added proudly. 'Polly really didn't mind?'

'Nay, lad,' Moll assured him, hiding a soft smile. 'She were only too willing to agree they call him Robert.'

'So, Mrs Green,' Bo said when they rounded the corner of Blossom Street, 'how's your new home coming along?'

Moll couldn't help but laugh. 'All right. Mind, I do miss the Luchettis. They kept them rooms like a palace; me and Horatio barely had to do a thing when we moved in. And we're close to Mam – the Saxes, too. Aw, aggrieved the owd loves were when their cellar was finally closed but they've settled into their new dwellings around the corner well enough. Jilly still marvels over their normal-sized window – cleans it half a dozen times daily, she does! 'Erc, best of all, though?' Moll told him with a teasing wink, 'there's not much distance for you to tread when this one needs minding.'

Throwing back his head, he laughed. 'Not far.'

Those words from Bo, her and Horatio's words, the ones she'd played over and over in her mind during the early days of their meeting and, even now, did still, sent a rush of warmth through her veins. Because the one waiting for them a few doors ahead was here still and forever would be, thanks to this one walking beside her. The love she held for these men of hers took her breath away.

Linking her arm through her brother's, Moll released a contented sigh. 'Aye, not far, lad. Not far.'

As good as Dilly Court
or your money back

We hope you enjoyed this book as much as we did.
If, however, you don't agree with us that it is as good
as Dilly Court and would like a refund, then please send
your copy of the book with your original receipt, and your
contact details including your full address, together with
the reasons why you don't think it is as good
as Dilly Court to the following address:

Emma Hornby Money-Back Offer
Marketing Department
Transworld Publishers
Penguin Random House UK
61–63 Uxbridge Road
London
W5 5SA

We will then send you a full refund plus your postage costs. Please note you have 60 days
from the date of purchase to make your claim and only one claim is permitted per person.
We will only use your details in compliance with the Data Protection Act and in
accordance with our privacy policy. The promoter is Transworld Publishers,
Penguin Random House UK, 61–63 Uxbridge Road, London W5 5SA.
No retailer is responsible in any way for any refunds under this money back-offer.